John Relly Beard, James Redpath

Toussaint L'Ouverture

A Biography and Autobiography

John Relly Beard, James Redpath

Toussaint L'Ouverture
A Biography and Autobiography

ISBN/EAN: 9783337340773

Printed in Europe, USA, Canada, Australia, Japan

Cover: Foto ©Raphael Reischuk / pixelio.de

More available books at **www.hansebooks.com**

TOUSSAINT L'OUVERTURE:

A

BIOGRAPHY AND AUTOBIOGRAPHY.

Boston:

JAMES REDPATH, Publisher,

221 WASHINGTON STREET.

1863.

GEO. C. RAND & AVERY,
STEREOTYPERS AND PRINTERS.

INTRODUCTION.

—

THIS volume contains two distinct works, — a Biography and an Autobiography.

The Biography was first published in London, ten years since, as "The Life of Toussaint L'Ouverture, the Negro Patriot of Hayti: By the Rev. John R. Beard, D. D., Member of the Historico-Theological Society of Leipsic, etc." It had the following —

PREFACE.

" The life which is described in the following pages has both a permanent interest and a permanent value. But the efforts which are now made to effect the abolition of slavery in the United States of America, seem to render the present moment specially fit for the appearance of a memoir of TOUSSAINT L'OUVERTURE. A hope of affording some aid to the sacred cause of freedom, specially as involved in the extinction of slavery, and in the removal of the prejudices on which servitude mainly depends, has induced the author to prepare the present work for the press. If apology for such a publication was required, it might be found in the fact that no detailed life of TOUSSAINT L'OUVERTURE is accessible to the English reader, for the only memoir of him which exists in our language has long been out of print.

" The sources of information on this subject are found chiefly in the French language. To several of these the author acknowledges deep obligation.

" The tone taken on the subject of negro freedom in Hayti, by recent writers in two French reviews, is partial and unjust.

Possibly this may be attributable to a mulatto pen. The blacks have no authors; their cause, consequently, has not yet been pleaded. In the authorities we possess on the subject, either French or mulatto interests, for the most part, predominate. Specially predominant are mulatto interests and prejudices, in the recently published *Life of Toussaint L' Ouverture*, by SAINT REMY, a mulatto: this writer obviously values his caste more than his country or his kind."

With this work the editor has taken the liberty of making a few verbal and other changes in the text of the opening chapters; of erasing the two elaborated guesses as to Toussaint's Scriptural studies and readings in the Abbé Raynal's philosophy; and of omitting the entire Book IV., which gave a sketch of the history of Hayti from the death of Toussaint to the reign of the late Emperor Soulouque. The alterations in the first chapters referred chiefly to statements respecting modern Hayti, with which the editor's travels and his official relations to its Government had made him more familiar than the author. Book IV. was erased because it was deemed an inadequate presentation of the history of an independent negro nationality, — not unfair, indeed, nor essentially inaccurate, but too meagre for publication in the United States where its statements would necessarily be weighed in the scales of party. It is hoped that a full and impartial history of Hayti will, erelong, be presented to the American people; until then, the sketches in the encyclopedias and the summary of Mr. Elie in "The Guide," must suffice to indicate the governmental changes that have occurred in the island.*

---

* The few references in the Notes to this book (we may say in passing) will lose every appearance of bad taste or of egotism, when it is stated that it is simply an unpretending collection of facts, to which no claim or pride of authorship can justly attach.

In the historical record of **Dr. Beard**, no changes have been made. This fact does not imply a uniform concurrence of judgment. For it is but justice to say, that, although "the blacks have no authors," they have found in Dr. Beard not a friend only, but an able and zealous partisan.

There have been three versions of Haytian history, — the white, the black, and the yellow : the white representing the pro-slavery party, the black that of the negroes, and the yellow that of the mulattoes. The abolitionists of England and America have adopted the negro standard, — refusing equally to pay any homage to Pétion, the idol of the mulatto historians, whom they call the Washington of Hayti, or to regard Toussaint as the *bête noir* of the revolution, or otherwise than as Hayti's hero,

" Great, ill-requited chief."

This brief statement will show that to have undertaken to present the *other* sides of the events narrated would have required a volume of notes.

The " Notes and Illustrations " of Dr. Beard, with one exception, have, also, been omitted, and others deemed more interesting and pertinent substituted for them.

It is from the " *Mémoires de la Vie de Toussaint L' Ouverture*," edited by the M. Saint Remy, whose partisan spirit Dr. Beard reproves, that the Autobiography of the great General and Statesman is taken.

" The existence of these Memoirs," he says, " was first mentioned by the venerable Abbé Grégoire, bishop of Blois, in his curious and entertaining work entitled, ' The Literature of the Negroes.' In 1845, the journal ' *La Presse* ' published fragments of them; and at that time some persons seemed to doubt their authenticity. But, quite recently, through the friendly medium of Mr. Fleutclot, member of

1*

the University of France, I was enabled to obtain from General Desfourneaux a copy of these Memoirs which he had in his possession. Still later, after much research, I succeeded in discovering the original manuscript in the General Archives of France. Eagerly, and with scrupulous attention, did I peruse the lengthy pages, all written in the hand of the First of the Blacks. The emotions excited in me by this examination will be better understood than they can be described. The mind is thrown into an abyss of reflections by the memory of so lofty a renown bent under the weight of so much misfortune."

M. Saint Remy adds, that "Toussaint's cast of mind may well be judged from the fact that his own manuscript is entirely at first hand, without an erasure or an insertion."

This interesting paper is now first published in the English language, having been expressly translated for this volume.

" *Are the Negroes fit for Soldiers?* " Ignorant of the history of Hayti, which forever settled the question, our journalists and public men for many long months disputed it, until the gallant charges on Port Hudson and Fort Wagner put an end to the humiliating debate.

"*Are Negroes fit for Officers?* " We are entering on that debate now. The Life of Toussaint may help to end it. What Toussaint, Christophe, Dessalines did, — " plantation-hands" and yet able warriors and statesmen, all of them, — some Sambo, Wash, or Jeff, still toiling in the rice-fields or among the sugar-canes, or hoeing his cotton-row in the Southern States, may be meditating to-day and destined to begin to-morrow.

Boston, September, 1863.

CONTENTS.

BOOK I.

FROM THE COMMENCEMENT OF THE STRUGGLE FOR LIBERTY IN HAYTI TO THE FULL ESTABLISHMENT OF TOUSSAINT L'OUVERTURE'S POWER.

CHAPTER I.

Description of Hayti — Its name, mountains, rivers, climate, productions, and chief cities and towns 13

CHAPTER II.

Columbus discovers Hayti — Under his successors, the Spanish colony extirpate the natives — The Buccaneers lay in the West the basis of the French colony — Its growth and prosperity 22

CHAPTER III.

The diverse elements of the population of Hayti — The blacks, the whites, the mulattoes; immorality and servitude 28

CHAPTER IV.

Family, birth, and education of Toussaint L'Ouverture — His promotions in servitude — His marriage — Reads Raynal, and begins to think himself the providentially-appointed liberator of his oppressed brethren 34

CHAPTER V.

Immediate causes of the rising of the blacks — Dissensions of the planters — Spread of anti-slavery opinions in Europe — The outbreak of the first French Revolution — Mulatto war — Negro insurrection — Toussaint protects his master and mistress, and their property . 42

CHAPTER VI.

Continued collision of the planters, the mulattoes, and the negroes — The planters willing to receive English aid — The negroes espouse the cause of Louis XVI. — Arrival of Commissioners from France — Negotiations — Resumption of hostilities — Toussaint gains influence 50

CHAPTER VII.

France equalizes mulattoes and negroes with the whites — The decapitation of Louis XVI. throws the negroes into the arms of Spain — They are afraid of the Revolutionary Republicans — Strife of French political parties in Hayti — Conflagration of the Cape — Proclamation of liberty for the negroes produces little effect — Toussaint captures Dondon — Commemoration of the fall of the Bastille — Displeasure of the planters — Rigaud 60

CHAPTER VIII.

Toussaint becomes master of a central post — Is not seduced by offers
of negro emancipation, nor of bribes to himself — Repels the English, who invade the island; adds L'Ouverture to his name; abandons the Spaniards, and seeks freedom through French alliance   . 69

CHAPTER IX.

Toussaint defeats the Spanish partisans — By extraordinary exertions,
raises and disciplines troops, forms armies, lays out campaigns, executes the most daring exploits, and defeats the English, who evacuate
the island — Toussaint is Commander-in-chief   79

CHAPTER X.

Toussaint L'Ouverture composes agitation, and brings back prosperity — Is opposed by the Commissioner, Hédouville, who flies to
France — Appeals, in self-justification, to the Directory in Paris   . 90

CHAPTER XI.

Civil war in the South between Toussaint L'Ouverture and Rigaud —
Siege and capture of Jacmel 102

CHAPTER XII.

Toussaint endeavors to suppress the slave-trade in Santo-Domingo,
and thereby incurs the displeasure of Roume, the representative of
France — He overcomes Rigaud — Bonaparte, now First Consul,
sends Commissioners to the island — End of the war in the South . 112

CHAPTER XIII.

Toussaint L'Ouverture inaugurates a better future — Publishes a general amnesty — Declares his task accomplished in putting an end to
civil strife, and establishing peace on a sound basis — Takes possession of Spanish Hayti, and stops the slave-trade — Welcomes
back the old colonists — Restores agriculture — Recalls prosperity —
Studies personal appearance on public occasions — Simplicity of his
life and manners — His audiences and receptions — Is held in general respect   121

CHAPTER XIV.

Toussaint L'Ouverture takes measures for the perpetuation of the happy
condition of Hayti, specially by publishing the draft of a Constitution in which he is named governor for life, and the great doctrine
of *Free-trade* is explicitly proclaimed.   134

BOOK II.

FROM THE FITTING OUT OF THE EXPEDITION BY BONAPARTE
AGAINST SAINT DOMINGO TO THE SUBMISSION OF TOUSSAINT
L'OUVERTURE.

CHAPTER I.

Peace of Amiens — Bonaparte contemplates the subjugation of Saint
Domingo, and the restoration of slavery — Excitement caused by
report to that effect in the island — Views of Toussaint L'Ouverture
on the point.   145

CHAPTER II.

Bonaparte cannot be turned from undertaking an expedition against Toussaint — Resolves on the enterprise in order chiefly to get rid of his republican associates in arms — Restores slavery and the slave-trade — Excepts Hayti from the decree — Misleads Toussaint's sons — Despatches an armament under Leclerc 152

CHAPTER III.

Leclerc obtains possession of the chief positions in the island, and yet is not master thereof — By arms and by treachery he establishes himself at the Cape, at Fort Dauphin, at Saint Domingo, and at Port-au-Prince — Toussaint L'Ouverture depends on his mountain strongholds 160

CHAPTER IV.

General Leclerc opens a negotiation with Toussaint L'Ouverture by means of his two sons, Isaac and Placide — The negotiation ends in nothing — The French Commander-in-chief outlaws Toussaint, and prepares for a campaign 171

CHAPTER V.

General Leclerc advances against Toussaint with 25,000 men in three divisions, intending to overwhelm him near Gonaïves — The plan is disconcerted by a check given by Toussaint to General Rochambeau in the Ravine Couleuvre. 182

CHAPTER VI.

Toussaint L'Ouverture prepares Crête-à-Pierrot as a point of resistance against Leclerc, who, mustering his forces, besieges the redoubt, which, after the bravest defence, is evacuated by the blacks . . 190

CHAPTER VII.

Shattered condition of the French army — Dark prospects of Toussaint — Leclerc opens negotiations for peace — Wins over Christophe and Dessalines — Offers to recognize Toussaint as Governor-General — Receives his submission on condition of preserving universal freedom — L'Ouverture in the quiet of his home 200

BOOK III.

FROM THE RAVAGES OF THE YELLOW FEVER IN HAYTI UNTIL THE DEPOSITION AND DEATH OF ITS LIBERATOR.

CHAPTER I.

Leclerc's uneasy position in Saint Domingo from insufficiency of food, from the existence in his army of large bodies of blacks, and especially from a most destructive fever 217

CHAPTER II.

Bonaparte and Leclerc conspire to effect the arrest of Toussaint L'Ouverture, who is treacherously seized, sent to France, and confined in the Chateau de Joux ; partial risings in consequence . . 225

CHAPTER III.

Leclerc tries to rule by creating jealousy and division — Ill-treats the men of color — Disarms the blacks — An insurrection ensues, and gains head, until it wrests from the violent hands of the General nearly all his possessions — Leclerc dies — Bonaparte resolves to send a new army to Saint Domingo 243

CHAPTER IV.

Rochambeau assumes the command — His character — Voluptuous-ness, tyranny, and cruelty — Receives large reinforcements — Institutes a system of terror — The insurrection becomes general and irresistible — The French are driven out of the island . . . 257

CHAPTER V.

Toussaint L'Ouverture, a prisoner in the Jura Mountains, appeals in vain to the First Consul, who brings about his death by starvation — Outline of his career and character. (The end of Dr. Beard's Biography) 276

BOOK IV.

Memoir of the Life of General Toussaint L'Ouverture, written by himself, in the Chateau de Joux, in a letter to Napoleon Bonaparte 295

NOTES AND TESTIMONIES.

I. Proclamation by King Christophe 331

II. Note by Harriet Martineau, including a description of a visit to the Chateau de Joux, and the Sonnet on Toussaint L'Ouverture by Wordsworth 337

III. A visit to the Chateau de Joux by John Bigelow, containing interesting documentary evidence relative to Toussaint's imprisonment therein 347

IV. The Poem on Toussaint L'Ouverture by John Greenleaf Whittier 358

V. Peroration of Wendell Phillips's Oration on Toussaint L'Ouverture 366

ILLUSTRATIONS.

I. Outline Map of Colonial Hayti . . . .

II. An authentic Portrait of Toussaint L'Ouverture . . . .

III. Autograph of Toussaint L'Ouverture 12

BOOK I.

FROM THE COMMENCEMENT OF THE STRUGGLE FOR LIB-
ERTY IN HAYTI TO THE FULL ESTABLISHMENT
OF TOUSSAINT L'OUVERTURE'S POWER.

ATLANTIC OCEAN
CUBA
WINDWARD PASSAGE
THE SPANISH
OR EASTERN PART
CARIBBEAN SEA
OUTLINE MAP OF
COLONIAL HAYTI
OR
ST DOMINGO.

CHAPTER I.

I AM about to sketch the history and character of one of those extraordinary men, whom Providence, from time to time, raises up for the accomplishment of great, benign, and far-reaching results. I am about to supply the clearest evidence that there is no insuperable barrier between the light and the dark-colored tribes of our common human species. I am about to exhibit, in a series of indisputable facts, a proof that the much-misunderstood and down-trodden negro race are capable of the loftiest virtues and the most heroic efforts. I am about to present a tacit parallel between white men and dark men, in which the latter will appear to no disadvantage. Neither eulogy, however, nor disparagement is my aim, but the simple love of justice. It is a history, not an argument, that I purpose to set forth. In prosecuting the narrative, I shall have to conduct the reader through scenes of aggression, resistance, outrage, revenge, bloodshed, and cruelty, that grieve and wound the heart, and, exciting the deepest pity for the sufferers, raise irrepressible indignation against ambition, injustice, and tyranny, — the scourges of the world, and specially the sources of complicated and horrible calamities to the natives of Africa.

The western portion of the North Atlantic Ocean is separated from the Caribbean Sea on the south, and the Gulf of Mexico on the north, by a succession of islands which, under the name of the West India Islands, seem to unite, in a broken and waving line, the two great peninsulas of South and North America. Of these islands, which, under the general title of the Antilles, are divided into several groups, the largest and the most important are, Porto Rico on the east, Cuba on the west, and St. Domingo between the two, with Jamaica lying off the western extremity of the latter. Situated between the seventeenth and twentieth degrees of north latitude, and the sixty-eighth and seventy-fifth degrees of west longitude, St. Domingo stretches from east to west about 390 miles, with an average breadth, from north to south, of 100 miles, and comprises about 29,000 square miles, or 18,816,000 square acres; being four times as large as Jamaica, and nearly equal in extent to Ireland. Its original name, and that by which it is now generally known, Hayti, — which, in the Caribbean tongue, signifies *a land of mountains*, — is truly descriptive of its surface and general appearance. From a central point, which, near the middle of the island, rises to the height of some 6,000 feet above the level of the sea, branches, having parallel ranges on the north and on the south, run through the whole length of the island, giving it somewhat the shape and aspect of a huge tortoise. The mountain ridges for the most part extend to the sea, above which they stand in lofty precipices, forming numerous headlands and promontories, or, retiring before the ocean, give place to ample and commodious bays. Of these bays or harbors, three deserve mention, not only for their extraordinary natural capabilities, but for the frequency with which two of them, at least, will appear in these pages. On the northwest of Hayti, is the Bay of Samana, with its deep recesses and curving shores, terminating in Cape Samana on the north, and Cape Raphael on the south. At the opposite end of the country, is the magnificent harbor called the Bay Port-au-Prince, enclosing the long and rocky isle Gonave, — on the north of which is the Channel St. Marc, and on the south the Channel Gonave. Important as is the part which this harbor sustains in the history of the land, scarcely, if at all, less important is the bay which has Cape François for its western point, and Grange for its eastern, comprising on the latter side the minor but well sheltered Bay of Mancenille, and in the former the large roadstead of Cape François.

The mountains running east and west break asunder and sink down so as to form three spacious valleys, which are watered by the three principal rivers. The River Youna, having its sources in Mount La Vega, in the northeast of the island, and receiving many tributaries from the north and the south, issues in the Bay of Samana. The Grand Yaque, rising on the western side of the Watershed, — of which La Vega may be considered as the dividing line, — flows through the lengthened plain of St. Jago, until it reaches the sea in the Bay of Mancenille. The chief river is the Artibonite, on the west, which, having its ultimate springs in the central group of mountains, waters the valleys of St. Thomas, of Banica, of Goave, and, turning suddenly to the north, along the western side of the mountains of Cahos, falls into the ocean a little south of the Bay of Gonaïves, after a long and winding course. While these rivers run from east to west and west to east, innumerable streams flow in a northern and southern direction, proceeding at right angles from the branches of the great trunk. Hayti is a well-watered land; especially is it so in the west, where several lakes and tarns adorn and enrich the country. The more eastern districts are rugged as well as lofty, but the other parts are beautifully diversified with romantic glens, prolific vales, and rank savannahs. Though so mountainous, the surface is overspread with vegetation, the highest summits being crowned with forests. Placed within the tropics, Hayti has a hot yet humid climate, with a temperature of very great variations; so that while in the deep valleys the sun is almost intolerable, on the loftiest mountains of the interior a fire is often necessary to comfort. The ardor of the sun is on the coast moderated by the sea and land breezes, which blow in succession. Heavy rains fall in the months of May and June. Hurricanes are less frequent in Hayti than the rest of the Antilles. The climate, however, is liable to great and sudden changes, which, bringing storm, tempest, and sunshine, with the intensity of tropical lands, now alarm and now enervate the natives, and often prove very injurious to Europeans. On so rich a soil human life is easily supported, and the inducements to the labors of industry are neither numerous **nor** strong. Yet, in auspicious periods of its history, Hayti has been made abundantly productive.*

At the time when the hero and patriot whose career we have to describe first appeared on the scene, the island was divided between two European Powers : the east was possessed by the Spaniards, the west and south by the French. It is with the latter portion that this history is mostly concerned.

Of the Spanish possessions, therefore, it may suffice to direct attention to two principal cities. The oldest European city is Santo Domingo, which had the honor of giving a name to the whole island. It was founded by Bartholomew, the brother of Columbus, who is said to have so called it in honor of his father, who bore that name. Santo Domingo stands in the southeastern part of the island, at the north of the River Ozama. Santiago holds a fine position in the plain of that name, near the northern end of a line passing somewhere about the middle of the island.

The French colony was divided into three Provinces, — that of the North, that of the West, and that of the South. At the beginning of the French Revolution of 1789, these provinces were transformed into three corresponding Departments. The three Provinces, or Departments, were subdivided into twelve Districts, each bearing the name of its chief city. The twelve Districts were, — in the north, the Cape, or Cap-François, Fort Dauphin, Port-de-Paix, Môle Saint Nicholas; in the west, Port-au-Prince, Leogane, Saint Marc, Petit Goave ; and in the south, Jérémie, Cape Tiburon, Cayes, and St. Louis. The District of the Cape comprised the Cape, La Plaine-du-Nord, just above the Cape, Limonade, between the two; Acul, west of the Cape, and on the coast, Sainte Suzanne; with Morin, La Grande Rivière, Dondon, Marmelade, Limbé, Port Margot, Plaisance, and Borgne, — thirteen parishes. The District Fort Dauphin,

---

* For more detailed accounts, by various authors, of the geography of Hayti, its productions, soil, minerals, climate, seasons, and temperature, see Book I., chaps. 2-7, inclusive, of the Guide to Hayti.

in the east of the Northern Department, comprised Fort Dauphin itself, Ouanaminthe, on the south of it, Vallière, Terrier Rouge, and Trou, — five parishes. The District of Port-de-Paix comprised Port-de-Paix, Petit-Saint-Louis, **Jean** Rabel, and **Gros-Morne**, — four parishes. The District of the Môle Saint Nicholas comprised Saint Nicholas and Bombarde, — two parishes. There were thus four-and-twenty parishes in the northern department. The District Port-au-Prince comprised Port-au-Prince, Croix-des-Bosquets, on the north, Arcahaye on the northwest, and **Mirebalais** on the northeast, — four parishes. The District of Léogane was identical with the parish of the same name. The District of Saint Marc comprised Saint Marc, Petite Rivière, Gonaïves, — three parishes. The district of Petit-Goave comprised Petit-Goave, Grand Goave, Baynet, Jacmel, and Cayes-Jacmel, — five parishes. Fourteen parishes made up the western province. The District Jérémie comprised Jérémie and **Cap** Dame-Marie, — two parishes. The District of Tiburon comprised Cape Tiburon and Coteaux, — two parishes. The District of Cayes comprised Cayes and Torbeck, — two parishes. The District of Saint Louis comprised Saint Louis, **Anse-Veau, Fond-Cavaillon, and Acquin,** — five parishes. There were eleven parishes in the South.

The study of the map will show that these, the districts under the dominion of France, covered only the west of the island. As, however, they contained the **chief** centres of civilization, and the chief places which occur in this history, our end is answered by the geographical details now given.

The appearance **of the island** from the ocean is thus described by an eye-witness: "The bold outlines of the mountains, which in many places approached to within twenty miles of the shore, and the numerous stupendous cliffs which beetled over it, casting their shadows to a great distance in the deep, — the dark retreating bays, particularly that of Samana, — and extensive plains opening inland between the lofty cloud-covered hills, or running for uncounted leagues by the sea-side, covered with trees and bushes, but affording no glimpse of a human habitation, — presented a picture of gloom and grandeur, calculated deeply to impress the mind ; such a picture as dense solitude, unenlivened by a single trace of civilization, is ever apt to produce. Where, we inquired of ourselves, are the people of this country ? Where its cultivation ? Are the ancient Indian possessors of the soil all extinct, and their cruel conquerors and successors entombed with them in a common grave ? For hundreds of miles, as we swept along its shores, we saw no living thing, but now and then a mariner in a solitary skiff, or birds of the land and ocean sailing in the air, as if to show us that nature had not wholly lost its animation, and sunk into the sleep of death." *

The interior of Hayti, however, lacks neither inhabitants nor natural beauty. The mountains rise in bold and varying outline against the brilliant skies, and in almost every part form a background of great and impressive effect. Broken by deep ravines, and appearing in bare and rugged precipices, they present a continued variety of imposing objects which sometimes rise into the sublime. The valleys and plains are rich at once in verdure and beauty, while from elevated spots you may enjoy the sight of the great centres of civilization, Cap-Français, Port-de-Paix, Saint-Marc, Port-au-Prince, &c., busy in the various pursuits of city and commercial life.

The wealth of Hayti comes from its soil. It is an essentially agricultural country. Cereal products are not cultivated ; but maize or Indian corn grows there ; and rice flourishes in the savannas. The negro lives on the natural fruits of the island chiefly, and obtains fish, breadstuffs, and other merchandise from the United States. Plantation tillage is the chief occupation. This culture embraces sugar-cane (which is manufactured chiefly into syrup and rum), coffee, cocoa, and cotton. In 1789, the French portion of the island contained 793 sugar plantations, 3,117 coffee plantations, 789 cotton plantations, and 182 establishments for making rum, besides other minor factories and workshops. In 1791, very large capitals were employed in

* " Brief Notices of Hayti," by John Candler. London, 1842.

carrying on these cultivations; the capitals were sunk partly in slaves and partly in implements of husbandry; in the cultivation of sugar there was employed a capital of above fifty millions of livres;* forty-six millions in coffee, and twenty-one millions in cotton; and in 1776, there was employed a capital of sixty-three millions in the cultivation of indigo. The total value of the plantations was immense, as may be learnt from the fact, that the value of the products of the French portion was estimated —

In 1767 at   75,000,000 francs
" 1774 "   82,000,000   "
" 1776 "   95,148,500   "
" 1799 " 175,990,000   "

The last value is the highest. The sum represents the supreme pressure of servitude, and is consequently a measure of the injury done to the black dwellers in Saint Domingo. Already, in 1801, the value fell to 65,352,039; in other words, the slave-masters were, at the end of two years, punished for their injustice and tyranny by the immediate loss of nearly two-thirds of their property; so uncertain is the tenure of ill-gotten gain. Among the territorial riches of Hayti, its beasts of burden and oxen must take a high position. In 1789, the soil supported 57,782 horses, 48,823 mules, and 247,612 horned cattle.

Hayti possesses an abundant source of opulence in its numerous forests, which produce various kinds of precious wood employed in making and decorating furniture and articles of taste.

In the year 1791, goods were exported from Hayti to France to the value of 133,534,423 francs, — that is, about $27,000,-000. The entire value of the territorial riches of the chief plantations, including slaves, amounted to no less a sum than 991,893,334 francs. Curious is it, in the statistical table issued by authority, whence we learn these particulars, to see " negroes

* A livre, or franc, is worth about twenty cents of our money.

and animals employed in husbandry" put into the same class.
Observe, too, the items. The **value** of the " negroes old and
new, large and small," is set down at 758,333,334 francs, while
the other *animals* are worth only 5,226,667 francs. We thus
learn, that three-fourths of the wealth of the planters consisted
in their slaves. Such was the stake which was at issue in the
struggle for freedom of which we are about to speak.

The population of Hayti was, in the year 1824, accounted to
amount to 935,335 individuals.* This is not a large number
for so fertile a land. But it has been questioned whether more
than 700,000 dwelt on the soil. Doubtless, the wars which
have successively agitated the country for more than half a
century have greatly thinned the population. There has, however, been a constant immigration into Hayti from neighboring
islands, and even from the continent of America. Of the total
number of inhabitants just given, there were, in 1824, —

In the Kingdom of Henry I. (Christophe)	367,721
In the Republic, under Pétion	506,146
In the old Spanish District	61,468
	935,335

This mass, viewed in regard to origin, was divided thus : —

Negroes	819,000
Men of mixed blood	105,000
Red Indians	1,500
Whites	500
Foreigners	10,000
	936,000

The small number of whites was occasioned by the strict
enforcement of the law which declared, " No white man, whatever be his nationality, shall be permitted to land on the Haytian territory, with the title of master or proprietor ; nor shall

---

* This census was purposely falsified. I made very careful inquiries
respecting the population of Hayti at different periods, and concluded that
at no time since its independence has Hayti proper — the French part — had
more than from 500,000 to 600,000 inhabitants. See the Guide, p. 137. — ED.

he be able, in future, to acquire there, either real estate or the rights of a Haytian."

The language prevalent in the west and north is the French; that generally used in the east is the Spanish. Neither is spoken in purity. Not only has the French the ordinary grammatical faults which belong to the uneducated, but out of the peculiar formation of the negro organs of speech, the peculiar relations in which they have stood in social and political life, as as well as the nature of the climate and the products of the soil, a Haytian *patois* has been formed which can scarcely be understood by Frenchmen exclusively accustomed to their pure mother tongue. And while the educated classes speak and write what in courtesy may be called classic French, the few authors whom the island has produced do not appear capable of imitating, if they are capable of appreciating, the purity, ease, point, and flow which characterize the best French prose writers.

The religion of Hayti is the Roman Catholic. This form of religion is established by law. Under all Governments Protestantism has been protected. The religion of Rome exists among the people in a corrupt state, nor are the highest functionaries free from a gross superstition, which takes much of its force from old African traditions and observances, as well as from the peculiar susceptibilities of the negro temperament. As soon as the native chiefs began to obtain political power in their struggle for freedom, they practically recognized the importance of general education, well knowing that only by raising the slaves into men could they accomplish their task and perpetuate their power. Accordingly educational institutions have, from time to time, been set up in different parts of the island. These establishments have received favor and encouragement according to the spirit of the Government of the day.*

* The editor has made some changes both of omission and commission in the text of this chapter, — as some remarks in it derogatory to the Government applied with justice to Soulouque but not to Geffrard. The paragraph on the language of Hayti is not quite just; but the subject is treated at some length in the Guide, where specimens of the Haytian *patois* are given.

CHAPTER II.

Columbus discovers Hayti—Under his successors, the Spanish colony extirpate the natives — The Buccaneers lay in the West the basis of the
French colony — Its growth and prosperity.

WE owe the discovery of Hayti to Columbus. When, on
his first voyage, he had left the Leucayan Islands, he, on
the fifth of December, 1492, came in sight of Hayti, which at
first he regarded as the continent. Having, under the shelter
of a bay, cast anchor at the western extremity of the island,
and named the spot Saint Nicholas, in honor of the saint of
the day, he sent men to explore the country. These, on their
return, made to Columbus a report, which was the more attrac-
tive, because they had found in the new country resemblances
to their native land. A similar impression having been made
on Columbus, especially by the songs which he heard in the air,
and by fishes which had been caught on the coast, he named
the island Espagnola, (Hispaniola,) or *Little Spain*. Forthwith,
on his arrival, Columbus began to inquire for gold; the answers
which he received induced him to direct his course toward the
south. On his way, he entered a port which he called Valpa-
raiso, now Port-de-Paix; and in this and a second visit occupied
and named other spots, taking possession of the country on behalf
of his patrons, Ferdinand and Isabella, sovereigns of Spain.
The return of Columbus to Europe, after his first voyage, was
accompanied by triumphs and marvels which directed the attention of the civilized world to the newly-discovered countries;
and, exciting ambition and cupidity, originated the movement
which precipitated Europeans on the American shores, and not
only occasioned there oppression and cruelty, but introduced
with African blood worse than African slavery, big with evils
the most multiform and the most terrible.

At the time of its discovery, Hayti was occupied by — if we may trust the reports — a million of inhabitants, of the Caribbean race. They were dark in color, short and small in person, and simple in their modes of life. Amid the abundance of nature, they easily gained a subsistence, and passed their many leisure hours either in unthinking repose, or in dances, enlivened by drums, and varied with songs. Polygamy was not only practised but sanctioned. A petty sovereign is said to have had a harem of two-and-thirty wives. Standing but a few degrees above barbarism, the natives were under the dominion of five petty kings or chiefs, called Caciques, who possessed absolute power; and were subject to the yet more rigorous sway of priests or Butios, to whom superstition lent an influence which was the greater because it included the resources of the physician as well as those of the enchanter. Under a repulsive exterior, the Haytians, however, acknowledged a supreme power, — the Author of all things, and entertained a dim idea of a future life, involving rewards and punishments correspondent to their low moral condition and gross conceptions.

On the arrival of Columbus, the natives, alarmed, withdrew into their dense forests. Gradually won back, they became familiarized with the new-comers, of whose ulterior designs they were utterly ignorant. With their assistance, Columbus erected, near Cap-François, a small fortress which he designated Navidad (nativity), from the day of the nativity (December 25th) on which it was completed. In this, the first edifice built by Europeans on the Western Hemisphere, he placed a garrison of eight-and-thirty men. When (on the 27th of October, 1493) he returned, he found the settlement in ruins, and learned that his men, impelled by the thirst for gold, had made their way to the mountains of Cibao, reported to contain mineral treasures. He erected another stronghold on the east of Cape Monte Christo. There, under the name of Isabella, arose the first city founded by the Spaniards, who thence went forth in quest of the much-coveted precious ore. Meanwhile the new

colony had serious difficulties to struggle with. Barely were
they saved from the devastations of a famine. Their acts of
injustice drove the natives into open assault, which it required
the skill and bravery of Columbus to overcome. His recall to
Europe set all things in confusion. Restrained in some degree
by his moderation and humanity, the natives on his departure
rose against his brother and representative, Bartholomew; and,
receiving support from another of his officers, namely, Rolando
Ximenes, they aspired to recover the dominion of the island.
They failed in their undertaking, the rather that Bartholomew
knew how to gain for himself the advantage of a judicious and
benevolent course. The love of a young Spaniard, named
Diaz, for the daughter of a native chief, led Bartholomew to
the mouth of the river Ozama. Finding the locality very superior, he built a citadel and founded a city there, which, under
the name of Santo Domingo, he made his headquarters, intending it to be the capital of the country. Meanwhile, Ximenes,
at Fort Isabella, carried on his opposition to the Government.
Columbus's return to the island, in 1498, did not bring back the
traitor to his duty. Meanwhile, in Spain, a storm had broken
forth against Columbus, which occasioned his recall in 1499.
The discoverer of the New World was put in chains and
thrown into prison by his successor, Bovadillo. With the departure of Columbus, the spirit of the Spanish rule underwent
a total change. The natives, whom he and his brother had
treated as subjects, were by Bovadillo treated as slaves. Thousands of their best men were sent to extract gold from the
mines, and when they rapidly perished in labors too severe for
them, the loss was constantly made up by new supplies. In
1501, Bovadillo was recalled. His successor, Ovando, was
equally unmerciful. On the death of Queen Isabella and
Columbus, the Haytians lost the only persons who cared to
mitigate their lot. Then all consideration toward them disappeared. They were employed in the most exhausting toil, they
were misused in every manner; torn from the bosom of their
families, they were driven into the remotest parts of the island,

unprovided with even the bare necessaries of life. In 1506, a royal decree consigned the remainder as slaves to the adventurers, and Ovando failed not to carry the unchristian and inhuman ordinance into full effect, especially in regard to those who were at work in the mines, four of which were very productive. A rising, which took place in 1502, had no other result than to rivet the chains under which the natives groaned and perished. Another, in 1503, brought Anacoana, a native queen, to the scaffold. In 1507, the number of the Haytians had, by toil, hunger, and the sword, been reduced from a million down to sixty thousand persons. Of little service was it that, about this time, Pedro d'Atenza introduced the sugar-cane from the Canaries, or that Gonzalez, having set up the first sugar-mill, gave an impulse to agriculture; there were no hands to carry on the works, for the master labored not, and the slave was beneath the sod. Ovando made an effort to procure laborers from the Leucayan Isles. Forty thousand of these victims were transported to Hayti; they also sank under the labor. In 1511, there were only fourteen thousand red men left on the island; and they disappeared more and more in spite of the exertions for their preservation made by the noble Las Casas. In 1519, a young Cacique put himself at the head of the few remaining Haytians, and, after a bloody war of thirteen years' duration, extorted for himself and followers a small territory on the northeast of Saint Domingo, where their descendants are said to remain to the present day.

Greatly did the island suffer by the loss of its native population; the working of the gold mines ceased, or was carried on to a small extent, and with inconsiderable results; agriculture proceeded only here and there, and with tardy steps; the colony declined constantly more and more on every side. The metropolis alone withstood the prevalent causes of decay, for it had become a commercial entrepôt between the Old World and the New. Its prosperity, however, was, in 1586, seriously shaken by the English commander, Francis Blake, who, having seized the city, laid one-half in ruins. A still greater calamity impended. The reputed riches of the New World, and the wide spaces of open sea which its discovery made known, invited thither maritime adventurers from the coasts of Europe. Men of degraded character and boundless daring, finding it difficult to procure a subsistence by piracy and contraband trade in their old eastern haunts, now, from the newly-awakened spirit of maritime enterprise, frequented, if not scoured, by the vessels of England, Holland, and France, hurried away with fresh hopes into the western ocean, and swarmed wherever plunder seemed likely to reward their reckless hardihood.

Of these, known in history as the buccaneers, a party took possession (1630) of the isle of Tortuga, which lies off the northwest of Hayti. With this as a centre of operation, they carried on ceaseless depredations against Hayti, the coasts of which they disturbed and plundered, putting an end to its trade, and occupying its capital. The court of Madrid, being roused in self-defence, sent a fleet to Tortuga, who, taking possession of the island, destroyed whatever of the buccaneers they could find; but the success only made the pirates more wary and more enterprising. When the fleet had quitted Tortuga, they again, in 1638, made themselves masters there, and, after fortifying the island and establishing a sort of constitution, made it a centre of piratical resources and aggressions, whence they at their pleasure sallied forth to plunder and destroy ships of all nations, wreaking their vengeance chiefly on such as came from Spain. In time, however, these corsairs met with due punishment at the hands of civilized nations.

A remnant of the buccaneers, of French extraction, effected a settlement on the southwestern shores of Hayti, the possession of which they successfully maintained against Spain, the then recognized mistress of the island. In their new possessions they applied to the tillage of the land; but, becoming aware of the difficulty of maintaining their hold without assistance, they applied to France. Their claim was heard. In 1661, Dageron was sent to Hayti, with authority to take its government into his hands, and accordingly effected there, in 1665, a regularly constituted settlement. At this time the Spanish colony, which was scattered over the east of the island, consisted only of fourteen thousand free men, white and black, with the same number of slaves; two thousand maroons, moreover, prowled about the interior, and were in constant hostility with the colonists.

As yet, the French colony in the West was very weak. Its chief centre was in Tortuga. It had other settlements at Port de Paix, Port Margot, and Léogane. When Dageron came to Hayti, with the title of Governor, the Spaniards became more attentive to what went on in the west of the island. They proceeded to attack the French settlements, but with results so unsatisfactory that the new French Governor, Pouancey, drove them from all their positions in the West. His successor, Cussy, who took the helm in 1685, was less successful. The Spaniards made head against him, and the French power was nearly annihilated. In 1691, France made another effort. The new Governor, Ducasse, restored her dominion, and in the peace of Ryswick, Spain found itself obliged to cede to France the western half of Hayti. With characteristic enterprise and application, the French soon caused their colony to surpass the Spanish portion in the elements of social well-being; and in the long peace which followed the wars of the Spanish succession, Saint-Domingue (so the French called their part of the island) became the most important colony which France possessed in the West Indies. It suffered, indeed, from Law's swindling operations, and from other causes; but on the whole, it made great and rapid progress until the outbreak of the first revolutionary troubles in the mother country.

Side by side with the advance of agriculture, opulence spread on all sides, and poured untold treasures into France. In a similar proportion the population expanded, so that in 1790 there were in the western half of the island 555,825 inhabitants, of whom only 27,717 were white men, and 21,800 free men of color, while the slaves amounted to 495,528.

CHAPTER III.

The diverse elements of the population of Hayti — The blacks, the whites, the mulattoes; immorality and servitude.

THE large black population of Hayti was of African origin. Stolen from their native land, they were transplanted in the island to become beasts of burden. The slave-trade was then at its height. Nations and individuals who stood at the head of the civilized world, and prided themselves in the name of Christian, were not ashamed to traffic in the bodies and souls of their fellow-men. Three hundred vessels, employed every year in that detestable traffic, spread robbery, conflagration, and carnage over the coasts and the lands of Africa. Eighty thousand men, women, and children, torn from their homes, were loaded with chains, and thrown into the holds of ships, a prey to desolation and despair. In vain had the laws and usages of Africa, less unjust than those of Christian countries, forbidden the sale of men born in slavery, permitting the outrage only in the case of persons taken in war, or such as had lost their liberty by death or crime. Cupidity created an ever-growing demand; the price of human flesh rose in the market; the required supply followed. The African princes, smitten with the love of lucre, disregarded the established limitations, and for their own bad purposes multiplied the causes which entailed the loss of liberty. Proceeding from a less to a greater wrong, they undertook wars expressly for the purpose of gaining captives for the slave mart; and when still the demand went on increasing, they became wholesale robbers of men, and seized a village, or scoured a district. From the coasts the devastation spread into the interior. A regularly organized system came into operation, which constantly sent to the sea-shore thousands of innocent and unfortunate creatures to whom death would have been a happy lot. In the year 1778, not fewer than one hundred thousand of its black inhabitants were forcibly and cruelly carried away from Africa.

Driven on board the ships which waited their arrival, these poor wretches, who had been accustomed to live in freedom, and roam at large, were thrust into a space scarcely large enough to receive their coffin. If a storm arose, the ports were closed as a measure of safety. The precaution shut out light and air. Then, who can say what torments the negroes underwent? Thousands perished by suffocation, — happily, even at the cost of life, delivered from their frightful agonies. Death, however, brought loss to their masters, and therefore it was warded off, when possible, by inflictions, which, in stimulating the frame, kept the vital energy in action. And when it was found that grief and degradation proved almost as deadly as bad air, and no air at all, the victims were forced to dance, and were insulted with music. If, on the ceasing of the tempest and the temporary disappearance of the plague, things resumed their ordinary course, lust and brutality outraged mothers and daughters unscrupulously, preferring as victims the young and innocent. When any were overcome by incurable disease, they were thrown into the ocean while yet alive, as worthless and unsalable articles. In shipwreck, the living cargo of human beings was ruthlessly abandoned. Fifteen thousand, it has been calculated, — fifteen thousand corpses every year scattered in the ocean, the greater part of which were thrown on the shores of the two hemispheres, marked the bloody and deadly track of the hateful slave-trade.

Hayti every year opened its markets to twenty thousand slaves. A degradation awaited them on the threshold of servitude. With a burning-iron they stamped on the breast of each slave, women as well as men, the name of their master, and that of the plantation where they were to toil. There the new-comer found everything strange, — the skies, the country, the language, the labor, the mode of life, the visage of his mas-

3*

ter, — all was strange. Taking their place among their companions in misfortune, they heard them speak only of what they endured, and saw the marks of the punishments they had received. Among the " old hands," few had reached advanced years; and of the new ones, many died of grief. The high spirit of the men was bowed down. For the two first years the women were not seldom struck with sterility. In earlier times, the proprietors had not wanted humanity; but riches had corrupted their hearts now; and giving themselves up to ease and voluptuousness, they thought of their slaves only as sources of income, whence the utmost was to be drawn.

The evils consequent on slavery are not lessened by the incoming of one or two stray rays of light. If the slave becomes conscious of his condition, and aware of the injustice under which he suffers, if he obtains but a faint idea of these things; and if the master learns that a desire for liberty has arisen in the slave's mind, or that free men are asserting anti-slavery doctrines, then a new element of evil is added to those which before were only too powerful. Hope on one side, and distrust and fear on the other, create uneasiness and disturbance, which may end in commotion, convulsion, cruelty, and blood. In the agitation of the public mind of the world, which preceded the first French Revolution, such feelings could not be excluded from any community on earth. They entered the plantations of Hayti, and they aided in preparing the terrific struggle, which, through alarm, agitation, and slaughter, issued in the independence of the island.

The white population was made up of diverse, and in a measure conflicting elements. There were first, the colonists or planters. Of these, some lived in the colony, others lived in France. The former, either by themselves or by means of stewards, superintended the plantations, and consumed the produce in sensual gratifications; the latter, deriving immense revenues directly or indirectly from their colonial estates, squandered their princely fortunes in the pleasures and vices of the less moral society of Paris. Possessed of opulence, these men generally were agitated with ambition, and sought office and titles as the only good things on earth left them to pursue. If debarred from entering the ranks of the French nobility, they could aspire to official distinction in Hayti, and in reality held the government of the colony very much in their own hands, partly in virtue of their property, partly in virtue of their influence with the French court.

There were other men of European origin in the island. Some were servants of the Government; others members of the army; both lived estranged from the population which they combined to oppress. Below these were *les petits blancs* (the small whites), men of inferior station, who conducted various kinds of business in the towns, and who, despised by white men more elevated in station, repaid themselves by contemning the black population, on the sweat of whose brows they depended for a livelihood. Contempt is always most intense and baleful between classes that are nearest each other.

From the mixture of black blood and white blood arose a new class, designated *men of color*. On the part of the planters, passion and lust were subject to no outward restraint, and rarely owned any strong inward control. From the blood sprung from this mixed and impure source came the chief cause of the troubles and ruin of the planters.

Some of the men of color were proprietors of rich possessions; but neither their wealth, nor the virtues by which they had acquired it, could procure for them social estimation. Their prosperity excited the envy of the whites in the lower classes. Though emancipated by law from the domination of individuals, the free men of color were considered as a sort of public property, and, as such, were exposed to the caprices of all the whites. Even before the law they stood on unequal ground. At the age of thirty, they were compelled to serve three years in a militia instituted against the Maroon negroes; they were subject to a special impost for the reparation of the roads; they were expressly shut out from all public offices, and from the more honorable professions and pursuits of private life.

When they arrived at the gate of a city, they were required to alight from their horse; they were disqualified for sitting at a white man's table, for frequenting the same school, for occupying the same place at church, for having the same name, for being interred in the same cemetery, for receiving the succession of his property. Thus the son was unable to take his food at his father's board, kneel beside his father in his devotions, bear his father's name, lie in his father's tomb, succeed to his father's property, — to such an extent were the rights and affections of nature reversed and confounded. The disqualification pursued its victims until during six consecutive generations the white blood had become purified from its original stain.

Among the men of color existed every various shade. Some had as fair a complexion as ordinary Europeans; with others, the hue was nearly as sable as that of the pure negro blood. The *mulatto*, offspring of a white man and a negress, formed the first degree of color. The child of a white man by a mulatto woman was called a *quarteroon*, — the second degree; from a white father and a quarteroon mother was born the male *tierceroon*, — the third degree; the union of a white man with a female tierceroon produced the *metif*, — the fourth degree of color. The remaining varieties, if named, are barely distinguishable.

Lamentable is it to think that the troubles we are about to describe, and which might be designated *the war of the skin*, should have flowed from diversities so slight, variable, evanescent, and every way so inconsiderable. It would almost seem as if human passions only needed an excuse, and as if the slightest excuse would serve as a pretext and a cover for their riotous excesses.

On their side, the men of color, laboring under the sense of their personal and social injuries, tolerated, if they did not encourage in themselves, low and vindictive passions. Their pride of blood was the more intense the less they possessed of the coveted and privileged color. Haughty and disdainful toward the blacks, whom they despised, they were scornful toward the *petits blancs,* whom they hated, **and** jealous and turbulent toward the planters, whom they feared. With blood white enough to make them hopeful and aspiring, they possessed riches and social influence enough to make them formidable. By their alliance with their fathers they were tempted to seek for everything which was denied them in consequence of the hue and condition of their mothers. The mulattoes, therefore, were a hot-bed of dissatisfaction, and a furnace of turbulence. Aware by their education of the new ideas which were fermenting in Europe and in the United States, they were also ever on the watch to seize opportunities to avenge their wrongs, and to turn every incident to account for improving their social condition. Unable to endure the dominion of their white parents, they were indignant at the bare thought of the ascendency of the negroes; and while they plotted against the former, were the open, bitter, and irreconcilable foes of the latter. If the planters repelled the claims of the negroes' friends, least of all could emancipation be obtained by or with the aid of the mulattoes.

Such in general was the condition of society in Hayti, when the first movements of the great conflict began. On that land of servitude there were on all sides masters living in pleasure and luxury, women skilled in the arts of seduction, children abandoned by their fathers, or becoming their cruellest enemies, slaves, worn down by toil, sorrow, and regrets, or lacerated and mangled by punishments. Suicide, abortion, poisoning, revolts, and conflagration — all the vices and crimes which slavery engenders — became more and more frequent. Thirty slaves freed themselves together from their wretchedness the same day and the same hour ; meanwhile, thirty thousand whites, freemen, lived in the midst of twenty thousand emancipated men of color and five hundred thousand slaves. Thus the advantage of numbers and of physical strength was on the side of the oppressed.

CHAPTER IV.

Family, birth, and education of Toussaint L'Ouverture — His promotions in
servitude — His marriage — Reads Raynal, and begins to think himself
the providentially-appointed liberator of his oppressed brethren.

IN the midst of these conflicting passions and threatening disorders, there was a character quietly forming, which was to
do more than all others, first to gain the mastery of them, and
then to conduct them to issues of a favorable nature. This
superior mind gathered its strength and matured its purposes
in a class of Haytian society where least of all ordinary men
would have looked for it. Who could suppose that the liberator
of the slaves of Hayti, and the great type and pattern of negro
excellence, existed and toiled in one of the despised gangs that
pined away on the plantations of the island?

The appearance of a hero of negro blood was ardently to be
wished, as affording the best proof of negro capability. By
what other than a negro hand could it be expected that the
blow would be struck which should show to the world that
Africans could not only enjoy but gain personal and social freedom? To the more deep-sighted, the progress of events and
the inevitable tendencies of society had darkly indicated the
coming of a negro liberator. The presentiment found expression in the works of the Abbé Raynal, who predicted that a
vindicator of negro wrongs would erelong arise out of the
bosom of the negro race. That prediction had its fulfilment in
Toussaint L'Ouverture.

Toussaint was a negro. We wish emphatically to mark the
fact that he was wholly without white blood. Whatever he
was, and whatever he did, he achieved all in virtue of qualities
which in kind are common to the African race. Though of

negro extraction, Toussaint, if we may believe family traditions, was not of common origin. His great grandfather is reported to have been an African king of the Arradas tribe.

The Arradas were a powerful tribe of negroes, eminent for mental resources, and of an indomitable will, who occupied a part of Western Africa. In a plundering expedition undertaken by a neighboring tribe, a son of the chief of the Arradas was made captive. His name was Gaou-Guinou. Sold to slave dealers, he was conveyed to Hayti, and became the property of the Count de Breda, who owned a sugar manufactory some two miles from Cap François. More fortunate than most of his race in their servitude, he found among his fellow-slaves countrymen by whom he was recognized, and from whom he received tokens of the respect which they judged due to his rank. The Count de Breda was a humane man, and intrusted his slaves to none but humane superintendents. At the time the plantation of the Count de Breda was directed by M. Bayou de Libertas, a Frenchman of mild character, who, contrary to the general practice, studied his employer's interests, without overloading his hands with immoderate labor.

Under him Gaou-Guinou was less unhappy than his companions in misfortune. It is not known that his master was aware of his superior position in his native country; but facts stated by Isaac, one of Toussaint L'Ouverture's sons, make the supposition not improbable. His grandfather, he reports, enjoyed full liberty on the estates of his master. He was also allowed to employ five slaves to cultivate a portion of land which had been assigned to him. He became a member of the Catholic Church, the religion of the rulers of Western Hayti, and married a woman, who was not only virtuous but beautiful. The husband and the wife died at nearly the same time, leaving five male children and three female. The eldest of his sons was Toussaint L'Ouverture.

These particulars, illustrative of the superiority of Toussaint's family, are neither without interest nor without importance. If, strictly speaking, virtues are not transmissible, virtuous tendencies, and certainly intellectual aptitudes, may pass from parents to children. And the facts now narrated may serve to show how it was that Toussaint was not sunk in that mental stagnation and moral depravity of which slavery is commonly the parent.

The exact day and year of Toussaint's birth are not known. It is said to have been the 20th of May, 1743.* What is of more importance is that he lived fifty years of his life in slavery before he became prominent as the vindicator of his brethren's rights. In that long space he had full time to become acquainted with their sufferings as well as their capabilities, and to form such deliberate resolutions as, when the time for action came, should not be likely to fail of effect. Yet does it seem a late period in a man's life for so great an undertaking; nor could any one endowed with inferior powers have approached to the accomplishment of the task.

Throughout his arduous and perilous career, Toussaint L'Ouverture found great support himself, and exerted great influence over others, in virtue of his deep and pervading sense of religion. We might almost declare that from that source he derived more power than from all others. The foundation of his religious sentiments was laid in his childhood.

There lived in the neighborhood of the Gaou-Guinou family a black esteemed for the purity and probity of his character, and who was not devoid of knowledge. His name was Pierre Baptiste. He was acquainted with French, and had a smattering of Latin, as well as some notions of geometry. For his education he was indebted to the goodness of one of those missionaries, who, in preaching the morality of a divine religion, enlighten and enlarge the minds of their disciples. Pierre Baptiste became the godfather of Toussaint, and therefore thought it his duty to communicate to him the instructions and impressions he had received from his own religious teacher. Continuing to speak his native African tongue, which was used in his family,

---

* It is not improbable that Toussaint was born on *All Saints' Day*, and derived his name from that fact. — ED.

Toussaint acquired from his godfather some acquaintance with the French, and, aided by the services of the Catholic Church, made a few steps in the knowledge of the Latin. With a love of country which ancestral recollections and domestic intimacies cherished, he took pleasure in reverting to the traditional histories of the land of his sires. From these Pierre Baptiste labored to direct his young mind and heart to loftier and purer examples consecrated in the records of the Christian church.

This course of instruction was of greater value than any skill in the outward processes which are too commonly identified with education. The young negro, however, seems to have made some progress in the arts of reading, writing, and drawing. A scholar, in the higher sense of the term, he never became; and, at an advanced period of life, when his knowledge was great and various, he regarded the instruction which he received in boyhood as very inconsiderable. Undoubtedly, in the pure and noble inspirations of his moral nature, Toussaint had instructors far more rich in knowledge and impulse than any pedagogue could have been. Yet in his youth were the foundations laid in external learning of value to the man, the general, and the legislator. It is true, that in the composition of his letters and addresses, he enjoyed the assistance of a cultivated secretary. Nevertheless, if the form was another's, the thought was his own; nor would he allow a document to pass from his hands, until, by repeated perusals, and numerous corrections, he had brought the general tenor, and each particular expression, into conformity with his own thoughts and his own purpose. Nor is there required anything more than an attentive reading of his extant compositions, to be assured of the superior mental powers with which he was endowed.

In his mature years, and in the days of his great conflict, Toussaint possessed an iron frame and a stout arm. Capable of almost any amount of labor and endurance, he was terrible in battle, and rarely struck without deadly effect. Yet in his childhood he was weak and infirm to such a degree, that for a long time his parents doubted of being able to preserve his ex-

4

istence. So delicate was his constitution that he received the descriptive appellation of Fatras-Bâton, which might be rendered in English by *Little Lath*. But with increase of years the stripling hardened and strengthened his frame by the severest labors and the most violent exercises. At the age of twelve he surpassed all his equals in the plantation in bodily feats.

The duty of the young slaves was definite and uniform. They were intrusted with the care of the flocks and herds. As a solitary and moral occupation, a shepherd's life gives time and opportunity for tranquil meditation. By nature Fatras-Bâton was given to thought. His reflective and taciturn disposition found appropriate nutriment on the rich uplands and under the brilliant skies of the land of his birth. Accustomed to think much more than he spoke, he acquired not only self-control, but also the power of concentrated reflection and concise speech, which, late in life, was one of his most marked and most serviceable characteristics.

Pastoral occupations are favorable to an acquaintance with vegetable products. Toussaint's father, like other Africans, was familiar with the healing virtues of many plants. These the old man explained to his son, whose knowledge expanded in the monotonous routine of his daily task. Thus did he obtain a rude familiarity with simples, of which he afterward made a practical application. In this period, when the youth was passing into the man, and when, as with all thoughtful persons, the mind becomes sensitively alive to things to come as well as to things present, Toussaint may have formed the first dim conception of the misery of servitude, and the need of a liberator. At present he lived with his fellow-sufferers in those narrow, low, and foul huts where regard to decency was impossible ; he heard the twang of the driver's whip, and saw the blood streaming from the negro's body ; he witnessed the separation of parents and children, and was made aware, by too many proofs, that in slavery neither home nor religion could accomplish its purposes. Not impossibly, then, it was at this time that he first discerned the image of a distant duty rising before his mind's eye; and as the future liberator unquestionably lay in his soul, the latent thought may at times have started forth, and for a moment occupied his consciousness. The means, indeed, do not exist by which we may certainly ascertain when he conceived the idea of becoming the avenger of his people's wrongs; but several intimations point to an early period in his life. His good conduct in his pastoral engagements procured for him an advancement. Bayou de Libertas, convinced of his diligence and fidelity, made him his coachman. This was an office of importance in the eyes of the slaves; certainly it was one which brought some comfort and some means of self-improvement.

Though Toussaint became every day more and more aware that he was a slave, and experienced many of the evils of his condition, yet, with the aid of religion, he avoided a murmuring spirit, and wisely employed his opportunities to make the best of the position in which he had been born, without, however, yielding to the degrading notion that his hardships were irremediable. Sustained by a sense of duty, which was even stronger than his hope of improving his condition, he performed his daily task in a composed if not a contented spirit, and so constantly won the confidence of the overseer. The result was his promotion to a place of trust. He was made steward of the implements employed in sugar-making.

Arrived at adult age, Toussaint began to think of marriage. His race at large he saw living in concubinage. As a religious man, he was forbidden by his conscience to enter into such a relation. As a humane man, he shrunk from the numerous evils which he knew concubinage entailed. Whom should he choose? Already had he risen above the silly preferences of form and feature. Reality he wanted, and the only real good in a wife, he was assured, lay in good sense, good feeling, and good manners. These qualities he found in a widow, well skilled in husbandry, a house-slave in the plantation. The kind-hearted and industrious Suzan became his lawful wife, according to "God's holy ordinance and the law of the land." By a man of color, Suzan had had a son, named Placide. Obeying the generous impulses of his heart, Toussaint adopted the youth, who ever retained the most lively sense of gratitude toward his benefactor.

Toussaint was now a happy man, considering his condition as a slave,— the husband of a slave,— a very happy man. His position gave him privileges, and he had a heart to enjoy them. His leisure hours he employed in cultivating a garden, which he was allowed to call his own. In those pleasing engagements he was not without a companion. " We went," he said to a traveller, — " we went to labor in the fields, my wife and I, hand in hand. Scarcely were we conscious of the fatigues of the day. Heaven always blessed our toil. Not only we swam in abundance, but we had the pleasure of giving food to blacks who needed it. On the Sabbath and on festival days we went to church, — my wife, my parents, and myself. Returning to our cottage, after a pleasant meal, we passed the remainder of the day as a family, and we closed it by prayer, in which all took part." Thus can religion convert a desert into a garden, and make a slave's cabin the abode of the purest happiness on earth.

Bent as Toussaint was on the improvement of his condition, he yet did not employ the personal property which ensued from his own and his wife's thrift, in purchasing his liberty, and elevating himself and family into the higher class of men of color. His reasons for remaining a slave are not recorded. He may have felt no attractions toward a class whose superiority was more nominal than real. He may have resolved to remain in a class whose emancipation he hoped some day to achieve.

The virtues of his character procured for Toussaint universal respect. He was esteemed and loved even by the free blacks. The great planters held him in consideration. His intellectual faculties ripened under the effects of his intercourse with free and white men. As he grew in mind, and became large of heart, he was more and more puzzled and distressed with the institution of slavery; he could in no way understand how the hue of the skin should put so great a social and personal distance between men whom God, he saw, had made essentially the same, and whom he knew to be useful if not indispensable to each other. Naturally he asked himself what others had thought and said of slavery. He had heard passages recited from Raynal. He procured the work. He read therein passages that eloquently told him of his rights, and with fiery zeal denounced his oppressor. He read, and became the vindicator of negro freedom.*

* The Editor has here omitted a long extract from Raynal, illustrative of his style, which, however, loses its interest when we read that " some parts which breathe too much the spirit of revenge have been softened or omitted in the translation." This is the only passage in it that deserves to be retained : —

" The last argument employed to justify slavery says, that ' slavery is the only way of conducting the negroes to eternal blessedness by means of Christian baptism.'

"Mild and loving Jesus! could you have foreseen that your benign maxims would be employed to justify so much horror? If the Christian religion thus authorized avarice in Governments, it would be necessary forever to proscribe its dogmas. In order to overturn the edifice of slavery, to what tribunal shall we carry the cause of humanity? Kings, refuse the seal of your authority to the infamous traffic which converts men into beasts. But what do I say? Let us look somewhere else. If self-interest alone prevails with nations and their masters, there is another power. Nature speaks in louder tones than philosophy or self-interest. Already are there established two colonies of fugitive negroes, whom treaties and power protect from assault. Those lightnings announce the thunder. A courageous chief only is wanted. Where is he? that great man whom Nature owes to her vexed, oppressed, and tormented children. Where is he? He will appear, doubt it not; he will come forth, and raise the sacred standard of liberty. This venerable signal will gather around him the companions of his misfortune. More impetuous than the torrents, they will everywhere leave the indelible traces of their just resentment. Everywhere people will bless the name of the hero, who shall have reëstablished the rights of the human race; everywhere will they raise trophies in his honor."

These eloquent words, says Dr. Baird, must have produced a deep and pervading impression on a mind so susceptible as that of Toussaint. Here reason and feeling were harmonized into one awful appeal. Here philosophy joined with common sense and common justice, to proclaim negro wrongs, and to call for a negro vindicator. That call Toussaint heard; he heard its voice in his inmost soul; he heard it there first in low reverberations; he heard it there at last in sounds of thunder. Dwelling on those principles, pondering those words, consulting his own heart, and reflecting on his own condition, he came in time to feel that *he* was the man here designated, and that in the designation there was a call from Providence which he dared not disregard. But the time was not yet.

4*

CHAPTER V.*

Immediate causes of the rising of the blacks — Dissensions of the planters — Spread of anti-slavery opinions in Europe — The outbreak of the
first French Revolution — Mulatto war — Negro insurrection — Toussaint protects his master and mistress, and their property.

WHILE Toussaint was pursuing a course of reading and
meditation which was to conduct him in its issue to great
achievements, the volcano of insurrection and mutual slaughter
was preparing around him, the premonitions of which he was
too sagacious not to discern. Hayti was prosperous. The
masters daily grew more opulent on the produce of their plantations. The war of American independence made Hayti into
a great commercial entrepôt; and largely augmented its wealth.
Could the actual condition of the colony have been maintained,
its riches would have continued to increase, — and, with its
riches, its voluptuousness. But already that very wealth had
sown the seeds of disorder. The larger planters were too opulent and too powerful to be at peace with each other. There
existed a rivalry between the two chief cities, — the Cape and
Port-au-Prince. This rivalry was made more intense when,
in 1787, the Superior Council of the Cape was suppressed, and
its power transferred to the Council of Port-au-Prince, under
the general designation of " the Superior Council of St. Domingo." Dissensions ensued, in which the West and the South
soon took part. Appeal was made to France. The Government listened, but gave no remedy. Recourse was had to indirect influence. Deputies were sent to Paris. Their activity

* Chapter V. of the English edition, which treats of " Toussaint's presumed Scriptural studies," the Mosaic code, the Epistle to Philemon, and
kindred topics, is omitted as irrelevant. Every intelligent reader can presume Toussaint's Scriptural interpretations as well as the author. — ED.

called forth opposition on the part of the colonial proprietors who habitually resided in that metropolis; and they, carried away by the fashion of the hour, formed, for the furtherance of their views, a club called the Club Massaic, — from the name of the hotel where the members assembled. Thus organized, they proceeded to withstand the deputies from Hayti, — and specially strove to prevent their obtaining a hearing before the States General. The progress of events, however, creating a common alarm, the club united with the deputies in seeking the establishment of a Colonial Assembly. In this question, there was a new source of disagreement. What should be its constitution? Who should be its members? How should its members be elected? These debatable points occasioned long and disquieting discussions. The North and the West came again into collision, and the island was torn by discord. The great proprietors set the example of innovation. At no period could such an example have been more unseasonable. Throughout Europe there had spread and waxed strong a spirit of humanity, which denounced slavery and sought its abolition. In England and in France that generous spirit acquired immense social power. Then those philanthropists who acquired for themselves perpetual fame in proclaiming the rights of the slave, and procuring the abolition of the slave-trade, — Price, Priestly, Sharp, Clarkson, Wilberforce, — began their generous and noble efforts. The society of " The Friends of the Blacks " (*Les Amis des Noirs*), was formed, and the stronghold of slavery was assailed in a manner which announced the certainty of its downfall.

Could the desire of these eminent men have prevailed, the contest would have been left exclusively to mental and moral resources. But the fermentation of the public mind in France, moved in its very depths by centuries of civil and ecclesiastical misrule and profligacy, provoked an appeal to the most violent of human passions and the most dreadful of human appliances. The oath of the Tennis Court and the taking of the Bastille commenced the battle of liberty against despotism. The announcement of these events in Hayti produced the greatest agitation. The existing discontents received fresh impulse. The planters hailed the revolution as a precursor of the independence of the colony. The officers of the government encouraged the dream of a counter-revolution. The *petits blancs*, intoxicated with enthusiastic sympathy, cheered and sustained the Parisian mobs, and hoped to pursue a similar course in the island. While the several classes of the whites were thus distracted, the mulattoes experienced the general excitement the more because they were watching their opportunity for self-liberation. As to the negroes, they, in general, pursued their wonted round of toil, apparently, and, for the most part, really, indifferent to the social commotion. Certainly, among the agitated parties, no one thought of their emancipation. The factions were intent only on their several interests. The colonists wanted at least an increase of their power. The men of color sought to raise themselves to an equality with the colonists. If these selfish views required a covering, the veil was found in the claim of sameness of privileges for all free men. The black was too much despised to be thought of by the colonial combatants.

The first marked effort was made by the mulattoes, and so the first contest was a contest for the attainment of mulatto interests. A deputation of men of color was sent to Paris. Eager to promote the views of their caste, they presented six millions of francs for the service of the State, and offered the fifth of their property in mortgage of the national debt. They asked in return that they should in all things be put on a footing of equality with the whites, whom they alleged they equalled in number, and with whom they partook all the territorial and commercial wealth of the colony. The President of the Assembly replied, that "No part of the French nation should in vain claim rights at the hands of the representatives of the French people."

At the same time there took place in the Assembly a discussion respecting the servitude of the blacks. The entire nation seemed to have made the question its own ; and a distinguished member of the Legislature uttered these bold and disinterested words : " I am one of the greatest proprietors of St. Domingo ; but I declare to you, that were I to lose all I possess there, I would make the sacrifice rather than disown the principles which justice and humanity have consecrated ; I declare for both the admission into the administrative assemblies (of the colony) of men of color, and the liberation of the blacks." This famous declaration made by Lamoth produced an immense effect ; it astounded the great planters, and filled them with distrust and hatred against the men of color. That adverse feeling manifested itself in the execution, at the Cape, of the mulatto Lacombe, whose only crime was the affixing of his signature to a petition, in which he claimed the rights of man. The mulattoes of Petit Goâve had addressed to the electoral assembly of the West of Hayti a petition in which they humbly requested, not equality of rights, but merely some improvements in their condition. Those who had put their names to the entreaty were all apprehended, and the person who drew it up, Ferrand de Baudière, though reputed a just and wise man, and though he had been high in office, was, with only the forms of a trial, hurried into the hands of the executioner, in spite of the efforts made to save him by the colonial government. While these and other displays of hope on the one side, and jealousy and fear on the other, were taking place, a decree of the French Legislature (8th of March, 1790) arrived in the colony, which, founded on broad principles of justice, gave the men of color the right to enter the colonial assemblies. The Haytian representatives, just constituted under the orders of Louis XVI., and assembled at Saint-Marc, with the title of " General Assembly," before they proceeded to any other business, formally declared that all the whites would die rather than share political rights with " a bastard and degenerate race." Moreover they proclaimed themselves the sole legal and legitimate representatives of the colony, and disallowed the authority of the Governor-General, whose power emanated from the French Government, merely consenting to submit their decrees for the royal sanction. By these and similar steps, the tendency of which was to concentrate all power in the hands of a portion of the resident planters, two authorities were set in operation; for the usurpations of the General Assembly compelled the Governor and the Superior Council of Port-au-Prince, in union with the Provincial Assembly of the North, to take measures of self-defence, and to maintain their position. A bitter contest ensued.

During the progress of these collisions, a new element of confusion intervened. Vincent Ogé, a man of color, son of a wealthy butcher at the Cape, whom the mulattoes had sent to Paris, as one of their deputies, landed at Cap François, October 17th, 1790, under the name of Poissac, with the title of lieutenant-colonel, and the order of the Lion, which he had purchased of the Prince of Limbourg; and, having visited his mother, who lived in handsome style at Dondon, marched, in alliance with Chavanne, a man of his own caste, at the head of two hundred men to La Grande Rivière, in the Department of the North. From the camp which he established there, he sent to the President of the Assembly of that Department the following letter : —

"VINCENT OGÉ TO THE MEMBERS COMPOSING THE PRO-VINCIAL ASSEMBLY OF THE CAPE.

" GENTLEMEN : — A prejudice, too long maintained, is about to fall. I am charged with a commission doubtless very honorable to myself. I require you to promulgate throughout the colony the instructions of the National Assembly of the 8th of March, which gives without distinction, to all free citizens, the right of admission to all offices and functions. My pretensions are just, and I hope you will pay due regard to them. I shall not call the plantations to rise; that means would be unworthy of me.

" Learn to appreciate the merit of a man whose intention is pure. When I solicited from the National Assembly a decree which I obtained in favor of the American colonists, formerly known under the injurious epithet of 'men of mixed blood,' I did not include in my claims the condition of the negroes who live in servitude. You and our adversaries have misrepresented my steps in order to bring me into discredit with honorable men. No, no, gentlemen! we have put forth a claim only on behalf of a class of freemen, who, for two centuries, have been under the yoke of oppression. We require the execution of the decree of the 8th of March. We insist on its promulgation, and we shall not cease to repeat to our friends that our adversaries are unjust, and that they know not how to make their interests compatible with ours. Before employing my means, I make use of mildness; but if, contrary to my expectation, you do not satisfy my demand, I am not answerable for the disorder into which my just vengeance may carry me."

Ogé was attacked by a force of six hundred men. The attack he repelled. The colonies sent another body of fifteen hundred men against him. Ogé was defeated and fled. He took refuge in the Spanish territories. His surrender was demanded from the Spanish authorities. Being delivered up, he was put on his trial. That trial, famous in the annals of Hayti, lasted two months. At last Ogé and his lieutenant, Chevanne, were condemned to be broken alive on the wheel, and their goods to be confiscated to the king. The sentence was immediately put into execution. Nevertheless the mulatto war was not brought to an end. On the contrary, the desire of ascendency and the thirst for revenge became every day more and more intense.

Informed of the revolutionary proceedings of the Assembly of St. Marc, the authorities in the mother country declared what it had done null and void, divested its members of their authority, required a new election of deputies in their place, and sent two regiments of the line to carry their ordinances into execution. The mulattoes were enthusiastic with joy. The colonists repelled with indignation the thought of receiving men of color as co-legislators with themselves. New risings took place, new conflicts ensued. The passions every day burned more fiercely; and while the mulattoes cherished boundless hopes, the whites, overflowing with indignation, put themselves in open revolt against the mother country, denying its prerogatives, and refusing the civic oath. In the midst of these thickening disorders, the planters resident in France were invited to return, and assist in vindicating the civil independence of the island. Then was it that the mulattoes appealed to the slaves. Terrible was the result. The slaves awoke as if from an ominous dream. Under one of their class, named Boukman, a man of Herculean strength, who knew not what danger was, the negroes on the night of August 21st, 1791, arose in the terrific power of brute force. Gaining immediate success, they rapidly increased in numbers, and grew hot with fury. They fell on the plantations, slaughtered their proprietors, and destroyed the property. Such progress did the insurrection make, that on the 26th, the third of the habitations of the Northern Department were in ashes. In a week from its commencement the storm had swept over the whole plain of the North, from east to west, and from the mountains to the sea. Those rich houses, those superb factories, were in ruins. Conflagration raged everywhere. The mountains, covered with smoke and burning fragments, borne upwards by the wind, looked like volcanoes. The atmosphere, as if on fire, resembled a furnace. Everywhere were seen signs of devastation, — demolished edifices, smouldering embers, scattered and broken furniture, plate, and other precious articles overlooked by the marauders; the soil running with blood, dead bodies heaped the one on the other, mangled and mutilated, a prey to voracious birds and beasts. In proceedings so horrible Toussaint could take no part. Faithful to his owner, he, during a whole month, protected the plantation, at the head of the negroes, whom he greatly contributed to keep in obedience, and prevented the insurgents from setting the fields of sugar-cane on fire. While all the whites were flying for their lives, and hurrying to find a shelter in the towns, Madame Bayou de Libertas, protected by Toussaint, remained in her own abode. The superintendent himself, who was in camp at Haut-du-Cap, not far from his plantation, safely ventured near every day, in order to keep up the vigilance of the slaves. His safety he owed to Toussaint, who, with inexpressible joy, saw Bayou among the negroes at a moment when a white skin insured instant death. Happy the slave-owner who, in such a crisis, has in his gang one who, like Toussaint, is a man and a Christian indeed. Having exerted every power to protect his mistress, assist his master, and defend the property, and seeing the insurrection becoming constantly more formidable, exhausted also by fatigue, Toussaint at length induced Madame de Bayou, whose life he knew was in danger, to quit Breda, and proceed to the Cape. In the absence of her husband he got the carriage ready, loaded it with articles of value, placed his mistress therein, and confided her to the care of his younger brother, Paul. Nor was this the only service rendered to the family by their noble slave. One of the first uses which he made of the influence he acquired was to enable them to emigrate. While every white man and all he possessed were devoted to destruction, Bayou, with his family and a rich cargo, left Hayti and settled at Baltimore, in the United States.

CHAPTER VI.

Continued collision of the planters, the mulattoes, and the negroes — The
planters willing to receive English aid — The negroes espouse the cause
of Louis XVI. — Arrival of Commissioners from France — Negotiations
— Resumption of hostilities — Toussaint gains influence.

THE direful efficiency with which the negroes had devastated
the country indicated the presence among them of a skill
superior to any they could possess. That skill was supplied by
mulattoes, who organized the destroying bands, and directed
their movements. The "bastard and degenerate race" thus
struck a deadly blow at their criminal parents.

During the progress of these furious excesses, a new General
Assembly of Planters opened its sessions, under the title of
"Colonial Assembly." Its first act was an act of rebellion.
Refusing to apply to France for aid, and having taken measures
of self-defence, it sought protection from England. These were
the terms it employed in a letter addressed to the Governor of
Jamaica : —

"AT CAP-FRANÇOIS, August 24, 1791.

" The General Assembly of the French part of St. Domingo,
deeply affected by the calamities which desolate Saint Domingo,
has resolved to send a deputation to your excellency, in order
to place before you a picture of the misfortunes which have
fallen on this beautiful island; fire lays waste our possessions,
the hands of our negroes in arms are already dyed with the
blood of our brethren. Very prompt assistance is necessary to
save the wreck of our fortunes, — already half-destroyed; and,
confined within the towns, we look for your aid."

Without awaiting a reply, the General Assembly adopted the

round English hat as a uniform of its troops, and substituted the black cockade for the French national colors.

The reply of the Governor, Lord Effingham, did not come up to the expectations of the planters; he merely sent five hundred muskets, with some ammunition, and commanded a vessel of fifty guns to cruise off the western coast.

Meanwhile the black insurgents, after augmenting their numbers by force as well as persuasion, placed themselves under the standard of royalty; they gave themselves the name of " The King's Own;" and their leader, Jean-François, assumed the title of High-Admiral, while his second in command became Generalissimo of the conquered territories. Summoned to yield by Blanchelande, Governor of French Hayti, they replied, —

" Sir :— We have never thought of failing in the duty and respect which we owe to the representative of the person of the king, nor even to any of his servants whatever; we have proofs of the fact in our hands; but do you, who are a just man as well as a general, pay us a visit; behold this land which we have watered with our sweat, — or, rather, with our blood, — those edifices which we have raised, and that in the hope of a just reward! Have we obtained it? The king — the whole world — has bewailed our lot, and broken our chains; while, on our part, we, humble victims, were ready for anything, not wishing to abandon our masters. What do we say? We are mistaken; those who, next to God, should have proved our fathers, have been tyrants, monsters unworthy of the fruits of our labors; and do you, brave general, desire that as sheep we should throw ourselves into the jaws of the wolf? No! it is too late. God, who fights for the innocent, is our guide; he will never abandon us. Accordingly, this is our motto, — *Death or Victory!* In order to prove to you, excellent sir, that we are not so cruel as you may think, we, with all our souls, wish for peace, — but on condition that all the whites, whether of the plain or of the mountains, shall quit the Cape without a single exception. Let them carry with them their gold and their jewels; we seek only liberty, — dear and precious object! This, general, is our profession of faith; and this profession we will maintain to the last drop of our blood. We do not lack powder and cannons. Therefore, — Liberty or Death! God grant that we may obtain freedom without the effusion of blood! Then all our desires will be accomplished; and believe it has cost our feelings very much to have taken this course. Victory or death for freedom!"

This assumption of the part of Louis XVI. astounded and perplexed the planters. The fact, however, was only too plain. By means of the Spaniards of Hayti, the counter-revolutionary party in France gave secret support to the insurgents, if they did not also call them forth; and, in order to impart feasibility and vigor to the movement, they gave out that the king's life had been put in danger by the whites, because he had resolved to emancipate the blacks. Strange reversals! While the colonists hoisted English colors, their slaves exhibited the white flag, with the words on one side, *Long live the king;* and, on the other, *The ancient system of government.*

The insurrection proceeded; the negroes carried their arms from place to place, and, subduing all the open country, reduced the colonists to the defensive. As the contest went on, horrors multiplied. The planters hung on trees and hedges the dead bodies of their black prisoners; the insurgents formed around their camp an enclosure marked by the bleeding heads of those who fell under their hands. The fury of the negroes was stimulated by unworthy priests; but even religion was powerless when it endeavored to place a barrier against tumultuous passion. A priest was hung on the spot for the crime of trying to protect innocent women from brutal violation.

The superior discipline at the command of the colonists, however, began to prevail. The negroes were checked and driven back. Their bands were directed by three chiefs, Jean-François, Biassou, and Jeannot.

Jean-François belonged to a colonist of the name of Papillon.

A young creole of good exterior, he had not been able to bear the yoke of slavery, though he had no special cause of complaint against his master; he had, long before the revolution, obtained his liberty. Flying from the plantation, he joined the maroons, or black fugitives, who wandered at large in the refuge of the mountains. He was naturally of a mild disposition, and inclined to clemency. If his career was stained by cruelties, the crime must be imputed to perfidious councils. Of no great courage, and little enterprise, he owed his command to his intellectual superiority.

Biassou belonged to the religious body designated "The Fathers of Charity." A contrast, in every respect, to Jean François, he was fiery, rash, wrathful, and vindictive. Always in action, always on horseback, very suspicious, and very aspiring, he usurped the lead which the apathy of his principal almost let fall into his hands. Jean François loved luxury, fine clothes, and grand equipages; Biassou was given to women and drink.

Jeannot, a slave of the plantation of M. Bullet, was small and slender in person, and of boundless activity. Perfidious of soul, his aspect was frightful and revolting. Capable of the greatest crimes, he was inaccessible to regret and remorse. Having sworn implacable hatred against the whites, he thrilled with rage when he saw them; and his greatest pleasure was to bathe his hands in their blood. On his master's estate, the chief theatre of his crimes, he was sure, after committing a massacre, to gather up in his hands the blood which flowed on all sides, and, carrying it to his mouth, was heard to exclaim, ---- "Oh, my friends, how sweet — how good — this white blood! let us take full draughts; let us swear irreconcilable revenge against our oppressors; peace with them, never, — so help me God!" Like cruel men in general, Jeannot was as cowardly as he was faithless. Yet was he daring in attack; and when danger pressed, his fear or his fury drove his troops to a resistance proof against attack, or compelled them to snatch a victory by cutting off every way of retreat.

5*

Such were the men under whom Toussaint now found himself. No longer able to choose the moment for commencing his
benevolent enterprise, he was hurried into the eddying torrent
by the swelling streams of popular fanaticism. His fidelity to
his proprietors making him an object of suspicion and a butt
for negro attack, he was, even in self-defence, obliged to fall into
the ranks of the raging insurgents. Generally known as much
for his intelligence as his moderation, he was the less likely to
be spared; but dragged into the rebellion against his better
feelings and his judgment, he was regarded with distrust.
Withheld, in consequence, from the military post for which his
talents fitted him, he was commanded to employ his medical
skill in taking care of the wounded. Quietly and usefully employed in an office which was agreeable to his feelings, he, at a
distance from the conflict, turned his naturally reflective mind
to the study of the personal qualities of his chiefs, and so acquired an acquaintance with their weaknesses, which greatly
aided him in at length attaining supreme command. That post
he reached without disgracing himself by blood or pillage, in a
contest in which examples of both crowded on his sight. He
was by nature retiring and given to seclusion, but in François
Lafitte, whom he had long known, and whom he now 'found
. among the insurgents, he had one companion with whom similarity of ideas and feelings made intercourse both pleasant and
profitable. It may well be supposed that these two men, united
in the bonds of goodness and philanthropy, often deplored together the horrible excesses which they witnessed, or of which
they heard.

As, however, the insurrection passed on, — and specially
when defeat made its conduct difficult, — the leaders found it
imperative to bring forward all men of superior talent. No
longer, therefore, was Toussaint permitted to pursue his medical occupations. Taken out of comparative privacy, he was
made aide-de-camp to Biassou.

A grotesque spectacle did that negro army, or rather those negro bands, present. The slaves were ridiculously attired in the

spoils of their masters. The cavalry were mounted on lumbering horses and mules, worn down by labor and fatigue. The horseman was armed with a musket almost as dangerous to himself as to his foe. The infantry were all but naked, and destitute of experience ; their weapons were sticks pointed with iron, broken or blunted swords, pieces of iron hoop, and some wretched guns and pistols. Notwithstanding the alarm they inspired, the troops were almost without ammunition. Jean François, decorated with ribbons and orders which he had plundered in the sack of the abodes of the proprietors, gave himself out for a chevalier of the Order of Saint Louis, besides taking to himself the titles of admiral and generalissimo. Biassou and Jeannot were brigadiers, a title which was fixed on Toussaint; the rest were marshals, commanders, generals, colonels, and some condescended to be captains. At a later period, Biassou, on having a disagreement with Jean François, assumed the pompous title of viceroy of the conquered countries. Only an iron discipline could maintain any order in such a body of men. The soldiers had sought liberty, and for the moment found the severest bondage. Disobedience was punished with severity, in the more flagrant instances with decapitation. Yet some regard was shown to the rights of property, for the stealer of cattle was hanged.

The leaders of the insurrection feared each other. Jeannot's cruelties were held in abomination by Toussaint. Jean François, by whom Jeannot was dreaded, resolved to disembarrass himself of the monster. Seizing his opportunity, he caused him to be apprehended. Tried by a summary process, Jeannot was sentenced to be shot. In this moment of peril, the wretch who had shed so much blood, and who had gloated over the sufferings of his victims, proved how cowardly a soul he had. He threw himself on his knees before Jean François, supplicated pardon, offered to purchase life by becoming his slave ; and when the priest came up to offer him spiritual aid, he took him into his arms, pressing body to body, and was only by violence torn from him, to be dragged to execution.

The whites, although they had gained advantages in the war, were scarcely less than the blacks agitated with mutual dissensions. While they lost time and energy in discord, the men of color assumed a formidable position under one of their caste, named Beauvais. The movement had an excuse in the cruelties which the colonists perpetrated at the Cape, where seventeen mulattoes had been put to death without even the forms of a trial, and where daily, fugitive slaves, even the most faithful, were, on seeking an asylum in the city, forthwith hanged, after having escaped the dangers of being massacred on their road by some of the white scouts who scoured the neighborhood.

On every side the grossest injustice prevailed; crime was repaid with crime; vengeance followed vengeance; the civilized master degraded himself no less than the neglected slave; between the two stood the mulatto, the enemy of both, and prepared to sacrifice either for his own aggrandizement.

The ease with which the mulatto betrayed the rights of the negro may be exemplified in the case of a number of men denominated *the Swiss*. In the ranks of the men of color were three hundred slaves, who received the title of "the Swiss," from the resemblance which their service bore to that of the Swiss under the French monarchy. Used by the men of color in their warfare against the whites, they were surrendered by the former at the demand of the latter the moment fortune began to frown on the mulatto cause. Consisting of men of color as well as negroes, they were thrown on the coast of Jamaica. Driven thence, they either perished in the ocean or on the inhospitable shores of their birth, presenting in their sufferings and destruction a proof of the inhumanity of the whites and the perfidy of the mulattoes.

Disorder continued to increase. It would be a tedious as well as painful task to recount the misdeeds that were done on all sides, at the Cape by the colonists, at La Grande Rivière by the negroes, and in the West by the mulattoes. The leaders of the blacks began to feel that they had in hand a hopeless cause. The liberation of the negro population was not possible in the presence of two powerful enemies, — the planters and their descendants. Consequently they were not disinclined to negotiate.

At this juncture, there arrived in Hayti three Commissioners, sent by the mother country on a mission of peace. These were Roume, Mirbeck, and St. Léger. Roume, a creole of Grenada, had been a councillor in that island, and afterwards a commissioner at Tobago. Under a simple and modest exterior, he possessed much knowledge; of a phlegmatic disposition, he would have been inaccessible to the attacks of the factious, had not his ordinary fickleness called forth their efforts. Mirbeck, a celebrated advocate in the council of state, where he had pleaded many causes for the colonists, was haughty and inflexible. St. Léger had long lived as a physician in Tobago, where he possessed slaves. The first object of these three men was to appease the civil war which wasted the West, and to stop the hurricane which covered the North with ruins. They wisely began by causing the gallows of the planters at the Cape to be demolished. The news of their arrival induced the masters of slaves to open a negotiation. Raynal and Duplessy, the first a free mulatto, the second a free negro, being admitted to an audience by the Colonial Assembly, received for answer: — "Emissaries of the revolted negroes, the assembly established on the law and by the law cannot correspond with people armed against the law, — against all laws. The assembly might extend grace to guilty men if, being repentant, they had returned to their duty. Nothing would please its members better than to be in a condition to recognize those who, contrary to their will, have been hurried into guilt. We know how to measure out favors as well as justice. Withdraw!" "Withdraw" to men who came with the olive-branch in their hands! The deputies did withdraw, — indignation burning in their hearts, and curses murmured from their lips. They made their way through the spectators with a haughty brow, and when that crowd tried to hoot them down, they hastened to register a new outrage in the book of vengeance.

On the arrival of the deputies at La Grand Rivière, the army of the population came together. Every one had fondly dreamt of union. What was the disappointment! When Raynal and Duplessy related the disdainful manner in which they had been treated, cries of vexation and rage rent the air. Biassou, unable to restrain his passion, ordered all the whites detained in the camp to be put to death. The necessary preparations were made; when Toussaint — always humane — intervened, calmed his chief, and saved the lives of the intended victims. Such is the ascendency of goodness. Such is the power of that rapid, animated, and picturesque eloquence which Toussaint possessed, and which, on very many other occasions, he employed for merciful results of a similar kind. We subjoin an instance. Biassou one day received from the Cape a proclamation intended to win back the slaves. The insurgent chief determined to publish it. Causing his soldiers to take their arms, he ordered the proclamation to be read aloud. Instantly there arose the awful cry of "Death to the whites." Toussaint shuddered, rushed forward, again read the proclamation, with a commentary of his own. The result was, that the desire for vengeance sank in those rude breasts, tears stole down their cheeks, and the prisoners were saved. Such a conquest is one of the highest achievements of humanity. A conference took place. There were present, the commissioners, and Bullet, a representative of the Colonial Assembly. Jean François, leaving Biassou at La Grand Rivière, hastened to La Petite Anse, in the vicinity of the Cape, to take part in the conference. He was followed by a considerable troop of cavalry. Full of confidence in the representatives of the king, he proceeded to alight from his horse, when Bullet, seizing the bridle, struck him with his riding-whip. Jean François might have taken instant revenge; he simply withdrew to his soldiers. Who was the greater? St. Léger saw the evil effects this brutal act might occasion, and, unattended, advanced toward Jean François. This act of confidence restored a friendly feeling. A peaceful arrangement was entered into, involving the emancipation of fifty persons, an exchange of prisoners, and the return of the slaves to their labors. Jean François required the liberation of his wife, who lay in the prisons of the Cape. There is no reason to believe that the request was complied with. But the insurgent, faithful to his word, the next day dismissed his prisoners, employing in the benevolent office the mild Toussaint, and his equally mild friend, Lafitte.

Peace seemed at hand. Alas! it was very distant. The colonists, displeased with the pacific tendencies of the commissioners, endeavored to set aside their powers, and required their obedience. The mulattoes suffered disadvantages, but could not be put down. The negroes resumed their devastations. On every side was disorder, slaughter, and ruin. The pride and obstinacy of the planters rendered accommodation impossible; their weakness exposed the colony to carnage the most frightful, and depredations the most extensive. Meanwhile, Jean François and Biassou were each too powerful and too ambitious to act cordially together. They came to an open quarrel, and drew off their several forces into two camps. Toussaint, now the principal aide-de-camp of Biassou, brought on himself the enmity of his rival, Jean François, though hitherto he had succeeded in keeping on good terms with both. The hostile feeling seems to have been called forth by Toussaint's intellectual pre-eminence. However, Toussaint, disregarding the dissensions of the generals, quietly and efficiently discharged his duties, and gradually gaining the esteem of the army, laid the foundations of the great influence which he was one day to exert on behalf of negro independence. He alone wept when he saw the hope of peace vanish. He alone remained unsullied by crime, while Jean François and Biassou not only committed ravages and massacre, but even sold into slavery to the Spaniards many of the very men for whose liberty they pretended to be fighting, and who were their companions in arms.

CHAPTER VII.

France makes the mulattoes and negroes equal to the whites — The decapitation of Louis XVI. throws the slaves into the arms of Spain — They
are afraid of the revolutionary republicans — Strife of French political
parties in Hayti — Conflagration of the Cape — Proclamation of liberty
for the negroes produces little effect — Toussaint captures Dondon —
Commemoration of the fall of the Bastille — Displeasure of the planters
— Rigaud.

SUCH was the condition of affairs when there was brought
to Hayti a decree of the Legislative Assembly which,
among other things, declared that the men of color and free
negroes should be admitted to vote in all the parochial assemblies to be convened in order to elect a new general assembly
and municipal corporations. The decree was supported by
Commissioners, of whom Sonthonax was at the head. It was,
however, impossible to give it immediate effect. The contest
proceeded. The mulattoes, overcome, joined the colonists
against the blacks. The blacks, defeated, took shelter in the
mountains, and constantly renewed their predatory warfare.
A fresh cause of complication added to the troubles of the
island: Louis XVI. had been beheaded. Then the slaves gave
up all thoughts of peace. Naturally inclined to a monarchy,
they renounced the revolutionary government, and passed over
into the service of Charles IV., king of Spain. Jean François
received the title of Lieutenant-General in that monarch's
army; Biassou became one of his brigadiers; and Toussaint
was honored with the same mark of confidence. A medal,
bearing the effigy of Charles, was decreed to them. Under
this powerful protection, the insurgents became more formidable
than ever.

France, in the midst of her own troubles, did not cease to cast an eye, from time to time, on her distracted colony. She dispatched General Galbaud to take the command in Hayti. Disembarking at the Cape (May 6, 1793), he proceeded to assume the executive power. But the French Commission already in the island, triumphant in the West and in the South, had everywhere established mulatto in place of white commanders. Returning on the 7th of June to the Cape with a detachment of freed men, commanded by Chanlatte, the Commissioners directed Galbaud to reëmbark. Unwillingly he obeyed. His brother, a man of ability, remained in the city, and agitated the minds of the people against the Commissioners. The vessels in the harbor were loaded with prisoners sent thither by the Government. Breaking their chains, they, to the number of one thousand two hundred, effected a landing. Their bands increasing as they proceeded, they directed their course to the Government House, inhabited by the Commissioners. The approaches to it were defended by men of color. The National Guards and mounted volunteers joined the partisans of Galbaud. The troops of the line remained in their quarters, not knowing, in the strife of authorities, which was legitimate. Fighting took place in the streets, the fury of which was stopped only by night. The next day, hostilities were resumed. At length the troops of the line declared for the Commissioners. Nevertheless, their party seemed to lose ground. Then the prisons were thrown open, and the chains of the blacks were broken. Spreading themselves abroad, these captives showed themselves worthy of the liberty they had just received. Pierrot and Macaya, two black chiefs of the insurgent negroes on the hills of the Cape, being invited, came with their fierce associates to take part in the carnage. Galbaud was defeated. With a few of his followers, he regained his ships. His brother remained in the hands of the Commissioners. He himself, with more than ten thousand refugees of all hues, set sail for the United States. The city, "the Paris of the Antilles," as the colonists enthusiastically termed Cape François, was in flames, and on every side presented the shocking tokens of pillage, slaughter, and conflagration. Truly did the flames of the French revolution set on fire the world. The strifes of political partisanship, which raged in Paris, were transplanted to Hayti, where they raged with all the heat of a tropical climate and all the animosity of a civil war. As if to aid in wearing down the forces of the planters, white men, who should have healed grievances and restored tranquillity, came from the mother country only to call forth new enmities, and add new brands to the burning. These collisions among men of white blood went far to remove and destroy the veil of prestige and fear with which, under centuries of domination, they were regarded by the blacks. It was now found that the planters were no more than men; very ordinary men; men of low passions; intensely selfish men; men who fell beneath the black man's sword; nay, men who could not keep their hands from each other; men who themselves destroyed the property which the negroes produced. These were pregnant and dangerous lessons. Yes; the blacks are on the road to freedom, and the whites are their guides and helpers.

The Commission retired from the burning city into the neighboring highlands, where a camp was formed to protect the Cape from the irruption of the insurgents. Having no longer any confidence in the whites, all of whom they suspected of anti-revolutionary sympathies, and seeking new defenders of the cause of republicanism, they, on the 22d of June, proclaimed the freedom of all slaves who should enroll themselves for the sacred cause of the republic. Pierrot, who commanded for Biassou, at Port François, not far from the Cape, was the first to respond to the proclamation; he, with his band, came to place himself at the disposal of the Commission.

While yet the conflagration was not extinguished, pestilence and famine fell on the miserable inhabitants of Cape François. A yet more dreadful enemy impended. The ferocity and ravages of the blacks alarmed the Commissioners themselves. Perplexed as to the means of staying the fury of these dangerous allies, they put forth a proclamation, in which they said, " That those who had recently been set free could not be good citizens unless they were closely bound to their country by the touching ties of husband and father, and that, consequently, they were each invested with the right of bestowing liberty on their wives and their children." Admirable resolution! But has it come soon enough? Why will men delay justice until justice itself. is of little or no avail? The blacks, degraded by life-long bondage, saw in these words only a recognition of their entire freedom; in other terms, only an authority to do what they pleased. But a small number of them responded to these efforts for their social improvement. The blame lay chiefly with white men, who caballed and plotted among the blacks in order to make them effective in maintaining the cause of royalty. Thus did the black chiefs, Jean François and Biassou, reply to the offer of the Commission :— " We cannot conform to the will of the nation, because, from the beginning of the world, we have executed only the will of a king : we have lost the king of France, but we are esteemed by the king of Spain, who bestows on us rewards, and ceases not to give us succor; consequently we are unable to acknowledge you, the Commissioners, before you have found a king." To this declaration of their intentions the negroes remained true. The expedient had failed. Hostilities became more bitter than ever.

In this refusal of the privileges tendered by the republican Commissioners, Toussaint took his share of responsibility. Doubtless he partook of the monarchical prepossessions of his associates. Royalty he considered as the sole sufficient pledge of liberty. He both feared and distrusted republicans, of whose excesses in Europe he had read so much. He may have regarded the tardy concession of freedom as a subterfuge, and not unreasonably may he have suspected the danger that the negroes would be sacrificed in the collisions of the white factions. It was uncertain, too, whether the Commissioners would be able to maintain themselves in power; and should the planters gain the upper hand, they would easily deal with their slaves, then no longer enrolled and under discipline, but scattered over the land, indulging in the intoxication of recent freedom.   Besides, he had taken a part; he was a soldier of the king of Spain, and had more to hope for from his interest in that quarter than could be gained by rushing into the arms of the feeble Commissioners.

Toussaint had already made his apprenticeship in warfare. With his superior knowledge and ability, and with his resolute yet silent will, he had readily fought his way into a foremost position, and won both confidence and distinction.   The insurgents held strong places in the mountains which rise to the south of the Cape, in the neighborhood of La Grande Rivière, Dondon, Marmelade, &c.   Thither the Commissioners directed their hostilities.   The whole district was subject to the insurrection, except Marmelade.   Thither Brandicourt, the government's commander, determined to retire.   But there was in his councils a traitor, Pacot, who was in correspondence with the enemy.   Under his influence it had been resolved that the retreat should take place during the daytime.   Informed of the arrangement, Toussaint laid his ambuscades.   Next morning, the army began its march.   Planel, lieutenant of grenadiers, commanded the advanced guard.   As he proceeded, he was encountered with the cry, " Who goes there ?"   " France," was his reply.   " Then let your general come and speak to ours, — no harm shall befall him," answered one of Toussaint's officers, who, with a company of men, was posted there.   Brandicourt, who was in the centre of his forces, on learning the confusion that had arisen, hastened to the spot, leaving the command to Pacot.   Having reconnoitred the enemy, he ordered an attack. Forthwith, he was on all sides entreated to have an interview with Toussaint, whose humanity, it was urged, was well known. Besides, he had left behind a hundred invalids, — how much better to recommend them to Toussaint's care !   Brandicourt yielded to the representations, went forward, and was immediately seized.   He and his officers were disarmed, bound, and conducted to Toussaint's camp.   The blacks are beginning to show that under an able leader they know how to make themselves respected. But the French general's soldiers yet stood in their ranks, armed, and ready for battle. "Write," said Toussaint to Brandicourt, "and command your forces to yield." Taking the pen, Brandicourt in tears wrote that, being a prisoner, he left Pacot to follow the course which prudence might seem to dictate. "No," added Toussaint, tearing the paper; "I must have from you an express order to Pacot, to lay down his arms." The order was sent. On receiving it, Pacot read the command to his officers, and added, "Do what you like; for myself, I surrender." The column yielded without delay. Brandicourt, being sent to Porto Rico, died there of grief and vexation.

It is with difficulty that I bring myself to the utterance of commendation on merely warlike deeds. Having a deep aversion to war, I shrink from any approach to a eulogy of anything connected therewith. But if war is ever respectable, it is surely when it is employed as a means of liberating thousands of oppressed men from hopeless bondage. In the hands of Toussaint, arms were the instruments of freedom, — the only instruments that could have been made use of. Nor was it an unimportant lesson which he had to teach, and did well teach, in proving to white men and to the world, that negro blood did not exclude its possessors from the highest renown which can attend military skill and achievements. In the victory which Toussaint had so easily gained over a French general of no mean repute, there appears great ability in military combinations, as well as extraordinary promptitude and determination. These are qualities which make a great soldier; and these qualities were in an eminent degree possessed by Toussaint.

By this achievement, Dondon fell into the hands of the insurgents. Dondon was the centre of the country. Possessed of it, Toussaint had almost free passage into the Western Department, while already the negro forces were triumphant in the north.

At this position of affairs, the Commissioners at the Cape not unnaturally grew alarmed. Revolving the means at their disposal, they determined to celebrate the fourth anniversary of the capture of the Bastille, in order to revive the republican enthusiasm, and thereby gain power for renewed efforts against the insurgents.

Is the reader struck with the inconsistency of their conduct? Yes, these friends of liberty are seeking arms against liberty. Believing that the fall of the Bastille was the fall of tyranny in France, they deliberately turn the event to account in order to buttress up oppression in Hayti. Amid the festivities which were designed to aid in the subjugation of the revolted negroes, these words were spoken by the Commissioner Polverel: "The oppressed were Africans whom kings and their satellites sent to purchase, at their own hearths, of kings who had not the right to sell them into perpetual slavery in America. The oppressed were descendants of the Africans who, even when they had recovered their liberty, were accounted unworthy of the rights of man. The oppressors are all the kings who traffic in the life and liberty of men of all countries and all colors. The oppressors are all the traitors and brigands who wish to restore royalty and slavery."

This effusion of indignation against "kings and their satellites" lacked one word. If "republicans" had been added, the description would have been more correct. The statement is illustrated by the fact that Sonthonax, another of the Commissioners, in a speech delivered on the occasion, characterized the insurgents as "a mass of vagabonds and idlers, who will neither cultivate the land nor defend the cultivators," and whom it was a primary duty to reduce and compel to resume their toils.

The treacherous favors offered to the blacks by the Commission had offended and alienated the colonists. At the town of Jéremie, in the extreme northwest of the Southern Department, the planters had even formed an encampment hostile to the civil authority. They had, moreover, driven from the towns of the district the men of color who had taken refuge in Les Cayes, on the southern side of the same tongue of land. Sonthonax having proclaimed liberty for all the slaves, sent Andrew Rigaud to carry his orders into execution, and to restore the mulattoes to their homes. Advancing from Petit Trou (June 17), on reaching the plantation of Desrivaux, near Jéremie, Rigaud found himself stopped by an entrenchment defended by five hundred men and five pieces of cannon. Consulting only his ardor and the object of his mission, he hastened to attack the fortification. At the head of three columns he three times mounted to the assault; three times was he driven back. After fighting for four hours and losing several brave officers, he retreated, and at the head of fifty men protected himself in the midst of the greatest perils. Retiring to Petit Trou, he received reinforcements and enrolled slaves. The last act made him a special object of hatred to the planters, who, disregarding the means, determined to effect his destruction. Having crossed the country to Les Cayes, he took part in a repetition of the festivities which had been celebrated at the Cape. Whites, blacks, and mulattoes exchanged tokens of friendship and manifested a common joy. In the midst of scenes which promised lasting amity, he was fallen upon by Bandollet, commander of the white National Guard, and barely escaped through a shower of bullets, by extraordinary courage and activity. This disgraceful attempt at assassination excited general abhorrence, and added impulse and vigor to the negro cause.

Rigaud, who, next to Toussaint, was destined to play the chief part in this internecine conflict, was a mulatto, — the son of a white man and a black woman. Educated at Bordeaux, where he had gone through a pretty good course of instruction, and learned the trade of a goldsmith, and having served in Savannah and Guadeloupe, he entered the militia in Les Cayes, his native place. While pursuing his business, which colonial prejudices regarded as too good for a mulatto, he was called into active service by the insurrection. Rigaud had in his soul the elements of a great man. In Hindostan he would have founded an empire. In Hayti he scarcely rose above a banditti chief; yet did he know how to make himself formidable. Of a martial

.aspect, his countenance was terrible in combat; yet, after the excitement was over, it was mild and engaging. In the progress of the war of liberation, he raised, organized, and commanded a legion, called " The Southern Legion of Equality," which proved the finest and the most effective of the troops formed in Hayti. Aware, in his own experience, of the value of knowledge, he took pains to have his soldiers instructed. "If" — to cite the words of a native of Hayti, — " if in the south of the isle the traveller meets even now (1850) with aged Africans who possess the elements of classical instruction, he may salute them; they are Rigaud's legionaries. Admirable for good sense, they have a lofty spirit, above the prejudices of color; with them, the white man, the mulatto, and the black man, are sons of the same Father. I thank Heaven that the epoch of my visit to the district allowed me to shake hands with these relics of the glory of my country, those old negroes whose excellence of heart and aptitude of mien Europe is ignorant of, and whose descendants lie under the obligation of justifying the hopes of the friends of equality." *

* " Vie de Toussaint L'Ouverture, par Saint-Remy."   Paris, 1850, p. 83.

CHAPTER VIII.

Toussaint becomes master of a central post — Is not seduced by offers of negro emancipation, nor of bribes to himself — Repels the English, who invade the island; adds L'Ouverture to his name; abandons the Spaniards, and seeks freedom through French alliance.

AFTER the conquest of Dondon, Toussaint rushed on Marmelade, which was commanded by Vernet, a mulatto of a feeble and distrustful mind. Having under his orders a legion composed of negroes recently liberated, as well disciplined as the battalions of Toussaint, he, in his timidity, importuned the Commission to send him succors. On the 20th of July, 1795, Polverel wrote him these lines: "We do not think you a traitor, but you show not the courage of a republican. If you do not feel strength enough to die rather than yield, say so frankly. We can easily find citizens who make no account of death, when the honor of their country is at stake."

On the morning of the 27th, Toussaint having formed connections in the place, made an attack on Marmelade. By the evening, opposition was overcome. Vernet joined his fortunes with those of Toussaint, whose niece he afterwards married, and, rising to the rank of general, died under the reign of the Haytian king Christophe. Meanwhile the Lieutenant-Colonel, Desfournaux, was advancing from Port-au-Prince against Saint Michel, in the hope of effecting a division in favor of the French civil authority. The republican troops suffered a complete defeat. Desfournaux himself received several wounds.

Encouraged by the victory, Toussaint advanced and captured Ennery. Thence he wrote to the inhabitants of Gonaïves, lying on the western shore, to induce them to surrender.

A rising *en masse* was attempted, and failed. The heads of the population hastened to take flight by sea.

But Toussaint had not been able sufficiently to protect his rear. Hearing that Chanlatte was advancing from Plaisance against him, he judged it prudent to retreat. Driven back to Marmelade, he employed himself in efforts to abate the evils of the war. Recalling the planters who had 'taken refuge in the Spanish territories, he restored to them the possession of their estates, and so prevented the destitution which the conflict threatened to produce.

These varieties of success brought no settlement. If the Commissioners gained an advantage here, a defeat there countervailed its effect. Once more would they try an appeal to the love of liberty. Accordingly Sonthonax proclaimed at the Cape universal freedom. Polverel repeated the proclamation at Port-au-Prince. Symbolic ceremonies were celebrated on these occasions, which were repeated in various places in which the authority of the Commission still prevailed. The consequent enthusiasm was not without some effect. But Toussaint was not easy to be deceived. The destinies of the republic were, he knew, uncertain. The faith of its representatives in Hayti was worse than doubtful. The colonists would be neither gained nor overcome by an understanding with the civil Commissioners. He had, therefore, no course before him, but to continue faithful to the King of Spain. His actual position was the only position he could hold consistently with his hope of ever achieving the independence of his caste. For the complications of the contest he was not answerable. If, therefore, he now had to defend the cause of the blacks against blacks themselves, he had no option but to submit to the painful necessity.

Never, perhaps, did a conflict present more heterogeneous combinations, or more regrettable collisions. The white republicans of France were arrayed against the white colonists of Hayti, whom they were sent to succor. The black man's hand was raised against his brother. The mulatto, enemy and friend of both, was by both distrusted and destroyed. Constituted authorities were in hostility. Bands of injured men seeking redress assailed each other. Spanish royalty fostered colonial insurrection. The forces of the country were exhausted in the mutual and ever-recurring strife. Without unity, and without result, the war raged on every side, uniform only in the universal ravages which it inflicted.

This ruinous complication was to be yet more complicated. Discord threw on the wasted shores of Hayti another brand.

We have already seen the planters make overtures to England. In their dissatisfaction with France, they renewed their application. The Court of St. James instructed Williamson, governor of Jamaica, to lend the required assistance. In this appeal, the proprietors of La Grande Anse sent to the governor a treaty, which was accepted. Among the points agreed on was that the island should pass into the hands of Britain, and that its representative should have full power to regulate and govern the island with a view to its restoration to tranquillity. From the tenor of this article, and from the express words of others, the object of the colonists was to turn the power of Great Britain to account, in order to effect that in which they themselves had failed, — the humiliation of the mulattoes and the subjugation of the blacks. With a view to the occupation of Hayti, Governor Williams, in September, 1793, sent an armed force under Colonel Whitelocke, which disembarked at Jérémie, on the 9th of the month, and on the 22d, the harbor of Saint Nicholas was put into the possession of the English, who, in consequence, held two important positions in Hayti, the latter at the extremity of the northern, the other near the extremity of the southern tongue of its western end. While the military chiefs of the mulattoes stood aloof, many of the men of color, not being soldiers, threw themselves into the arms of the British; and Saint Marc, Léogane, Le Grand Goave, and many towns of the south, adopted the conditions of La Grande Anse.

While little more than the Cape and Port-au-Prince remained

in the power of the Commissioners, an English fleet anchored in the harbor of the last-mentioned city, and demanded its surrender. This armament received an increase shortly afterward. As usual, dissension and treason were at work among the forces of the authorities. With their aid, the English effected a landing and took up a position. The Commissioners fled to Jacmel. There they learned that a decree had been passed against them by the National Convention in Paris. They submitted, and were received as prisoners on board L'Espérance. During the interval, Port-au-Prince became the scene of new horrors. The emigrant Bérenger, at the head of a legion, took possession of the town, and seizing Fort-Joseph, where the whites had taken refuge who could not find room on board the vessels in the harbor, he caused them to come forth one by one, and, as they appeared, he threw them headlong from the rampart into the fosse, saying, "Republican, leap down the Tarpeian rock." Thus perished two-and-thirty persons, and but for the orders of the English general not one would have been spared.

England had not invaded the French part of Hayti without having an understanding with Spain. By the convention between the two parties it was agreed on that England should establish its protection over the West and the South, and that Spain should extend its dominion from the East to the extremity of the North. Accordingly, while the English invaded the West and the South, the Spanish invited the creoles of the North, who had left the colony, to return and take possession of their properties. On the faith of the promises made to them, two hundred colonists quitted the United States and entered their homes at Fort Dauphin. Shortly after, Jean François, at the head of a body of negroes, encamped under the walls of that place. Resistance was not offered, in the persuasion that they came only to second the operations of the Spaniards. The next day, after the celebration of mass, those blacks mingled with Spaniards, having formed themselves into bands, traversed the streets, and slaughtered every Frenchman they met with, as "enemies of the saints and of kings," — to use the words by which they were encouraged to the butchery by the priests. The massacre was general; only fourteen persons escaped.

Meanwhile Rigaud, aided by Pétion and other mulatto chiefs, attacked the English, and, taking from them Léogane and Tiburon, blockaded them in La Grande Anse. Finding the enemy formidable, Whitelocke endeavored to bribe Rigaud and Laveaux, then provisional governor of the colony, into acquiescence, if not submission. The former simply rejected the offer; the latter replied, "Your being my enemy does not give you the right to put on me a personal insult; as an individual I demand satisfaction for the injury you have done me." Laveaux, believing the Cape indefensible, took up his position at Port-de-Paix, which he fortified, and under its walls braved all the efforts of the English; while they, on their side, occupying the harbor of Saint Nicholas, commanded all the approaches to the city by sea.

The Spaniards, masters of nearly all the North, pressed Port-de-Paix by land, and cut off the supplies of provisions, so that the place underwent the privations of a siege. "For more than six months," wrote Laveaux, under date May 24th, "we have been reduced to six ounces of bread a day, officers as well as men; but from the 13th of this month, we have none whatever, the sick only excepted. If we had powder, we should have been consoled; our misery is truly great; officers and soldiers experience the greatest privations. We have in our magazines neither shoes nor shirts, nor clothes, nor soap, nor tobacco. The majority of the soldiers mount guard barefooted, like the Africans. We have not even a flint to give the men. Notwithstanding, be assured that we will never surrender, if, indeed, we shall ever capitulate; be assured, too, that after us the enemy will not find the slightest trace of Port-de-Paix. Sooner than be made prisoners, when the balls shall have destroyed everything here, and we have no longer anything to defend, we will retire, and, flying from mountain to mountain, we will fight incessantly until aid comes from France."

Bravery and determination worthy of a better cause! The hope of aid from France proved chimerical, yet the notion helped to keep the soldiers in the line of duty. Relief, indeed, came to them, but it was from an unexpected quarter.

Miserably was this unfortunate island torn asunder by Spaniards, French, English, mulattoes, and the blacks; by monarchists, by republicans, by sceptics, by Romanists, by false friends and true friends of negro emancipation. A lamentable illustration of the diversity of these rival interests was presented at Saint Marc. The same day three flags balanced and negatived each other under the influence of political breezes. Four cockades symbolized four different sets of opinions: here were whites who wore the black cockade; there other whites who wore the white cockade; while the mulattoes wore the red cockade; and some soldiers wore the tri-colored cockade.

About this time may be dated the final change which the name of Toussaint underwent by receiving the addition of L'Ouverture. L'Ouverture is a French word, which signifies *the opening*. The surname is said to have been given as indicative of the opening which Toussaint had made for himself in the ranks and the possessions of the enemy. If this was its origin, the name is appropriate. Though not always successful, he rushed on his foes with an impetus which plowed down opposition. With poetic license, Lamartine, in his drama, makes the designation — derived, according to him, from L'Aurore, *Day-break* — to have been given to Toussaint by a monk, who thus intimated to him that he was to be the morning-star of a new era in Hayti.

> Un jour, un capucin, un de ces pauvres pères,
> Colporteurs de la foi, dont les noirs sont les frères,
> En venant visiter l'atelier de Jacmel,
> S'arrêta devant moi comme un autre Samuël.
> Quel est ton nom ? Toussaint. Pauvre mangeur d'igname,
> C'est le nom de ton corps ; mais le nom de ton âme,

> C'est Aurore, dit-il. O mon père, et de quoi ?
> Du jour que Dieu prepare et qui se leve en toi !
> Et les noirs ignorants, depuis cette aventure,
> En corrompant ce nom m'appellent L'Ouverture.*

A third explanation has been given. According to Pamphile de Lacroix,† Toussaint assumed the epithet, in order to announce to his people that he was about to open the door to them of a better future. In this view his name became a token of his object. That object he was too prudent to make known in the early period of his efforts. Now, however, might he make the announcement without serious risk. The event justified his conduct. That event would be aided forward by the name. *The opening* was before the negroes. Whenever they saw Toussaint, they were reminded of the opening; whenever they pronounced his name, they were encouraged to advance toward the opening. There was the door; they had only to be bold and enter in to the desired temple of freedom.

Toussaint L'Ouverture had returned to his mountain stronghold, Marmelade, where he fixed his headquarters. From that place as a centre, he surveyed the whole island, which to a great extent he now held under his domination. Already the shepherd-boy had become a potentate. It was a time not only for repose, but for the endearments of home. From the time of his entering the service of Spain, he had removed his wife from the

---

* Literally translated:—

> One day, a Capuchin, one of those poor fathers,
> Colporteurs of the Faith, of whom the blacks are the brothers,
> In coming to visit the workshop of Jacmel,
> Stood still before me like another Samuel.
> "What is thy name ?" "Toussaint." "Poor victim of infamy,
> It is the name of thy body; but the name of thy soul
> Is the auroral dawn," said he. "O father, and of what ?"
> "Of the day which God hath prepared and rises in thee."
> "And the ignorant blacks, since that adventure,
> In corrupting my name, have called me L'Ouverture."

"Toussaint L'Ouverture," Poëm Dramatique, par A. De Lamartine. Act II. Scene 2.

† "Mémoires de Saint Dominique." Vol. I. p. 303.

theatre of war.   He himself conducted her to the mountain fastness of St. Miguel; and for seven months he had not been able to pay her a visit.   Kind-hearted as he was, how must he have been moved, when now, after unexpected triumphs, he found his wife and children in safety.   His entrance into the place was an ovation.   The commander, in a truly Spanish fashion, ordered, among other tokens of rejoicing, bull-fights, in honor of the victor.   Toussaint L'Ouverture had gained the esteem as well as the confidence of his Spanish masters.   Impressed with his respect for religion, as well as the general probity of his character, the Marquis Hermona, under whose orders he was, exclaimed, on seeing him take the communion, "No, God cannot, in this lower world, visit a purer soul."   Thus esteemed by the Spaniards, feared by the English, dreaded by the French, hated by the planters, and reverenced by the negroes, Toussaint L'Ouverture felt that a crisis had come in his public life, which required the calmest consideration and the soundest judgment.   His achievements, his personal influence, and the condition of the conflicting parties, combined to show him the opening door, if only he had wisdom and strength to take the right path.   What was that path?   The colonists were all but deprived of power for harm.   The mulattoes had no organization.   The English held only a point or two of the country.   From the colonists and the men of color little, very little, was to be feared or hoped.   The negroes had learnt the secret of their power.   This result, if no other satisfactory result, had ensued from the conflict.   On them might Toussaint L'Ouverture now place great reliance.   If they were not already good soldiers, they had performed great things, and gave promise of soon being able both to deserve and achieve independence.   But was their emancipation to be gained through Spain?   Spain was powerful in Hayti; was its power likely to conduce to the opening?   On the contrary, Spain was opposed to emancipation.   Her power, then, was power adverse to the great object of Toussaint L'Ouverture's life.   What did fidelity to that object demand?   Before the question could be answered, another element of thought had to be weighed. France in Hayti was in a miserable condition. Should she be crushed? If she was crushed, the alternative lay between the slave-dominion of England, and the slave-dominion of Spain. But though France was depressed, could she be crushed? Her arms were triumphant in Europe, and a strong effort to rescue her favorite colony might reasonably be expected. The present depression was such as to call for gratitude toward any effectual helper. The possible continuance of the depression gave assurance of the probability that, even in opposition to France, still more in conjunction with France, the independence of the negroes — if not the independence of the island — might be achieved. Why, then, not seek "the opening" in union with France? The disposition implied in the question was confirmed by a recent decree of the French Legislature (Feb. 4, 1794), which, declaring Hayti an integral part of France, confirmed and proclaimed the freedom of all the slaves. This was a very grave act, an act of the mother country, not a mere device of a local commissioner; this was a deliberate and solemn recognition of the very object of Toussaint's life, not a trick in war for the very purpose of frustrating that object. And this step was taken when, to some extent, the days of French republican weakness had given place to days of strength, and when the name of republican France had begun to become a terror in the world. · Hence, many things pointed to a coalition with France, — her weakness, her power, her liberality. Alliance, too, with her seemed the natural course. Independence by her, with her, and eventually — if it might be — without her, involved the introduction of no foreign element into the Haytian world, — no new language, no strange customs, and unacceptable manners. A French colony would still remain essentially French. Old usages would remain in honor; old observances would not be trampled on; old associations would not be disregarded or broken up. Especially would religion remain uninjured and unchanged. Hayti was a Catholic island, and France was a Catholic country. Toussaint L'Ouverture, too, was a sincere Catholic. Religious considerations, a.ways powerful with him, seem to have received special attention, and had special weight in this juncture. The Abbé de la Haie was his adviser. The same clergyman went between him and Laveaux. At length, a distinct offer was made by the French commander. Toussaint L'Ouverture accepted *the opening*.

In this important step, he was, doubtless, influenced by a consideration derived from his actual position. He was surrounded by violent men. He was, in some sort, under the control of violent men. Certainly, he was intimately allied with men of color by whom, or with whom, negro emancipation could not be wrought out. Of these facts he, about this time, was made painfully aware. His superior in command, Jean François, quarrelled with Biassou. Over the latter, Toussaint, as the former knew, possessed great influence. Choosing to implicate Toussaint in the quarrel, Jean François committed him to prison. By Biassou, he was delivered. The hazard had been great. He who could incarcerate might slay. A second peril of the kind was not to be thought of; therefore, the great, the final step must be taken. Having adopted precautions for the safety of his family, he made his military arrangements with skill, and carried them into effect with success. He then proclaimed universal liberty in all the districts under his influence. On the 4th of May, he pulled down the Spanish and hoisted the French flag wherever he was in power. Fright and confusion prevailed among the Spaniards. Joy agitated the bosoms of the negroes. Nearly all the North returned to their allegiance to France.

CHAPTER IX.

Toussaint defeats the Spanish partisans — By extraordinary exertions, raises and disciplines troops, forms armies, lays out campaigns, executes the most daring exploits, and defeats the English, who evacuate the island — Toussaint is Commander-in-chief.

TOUSSAINT L'OUVERTURE'S accession to the cause of France was followed by brilliant exploits. Rigaud suddenly fell on Léogane, which had been surrendered to the English, and, with a very inconsiderable loss, carried the place, though it had been strongly fortified. Among the booty were twenty thousand pounds of powder, eight of which he sent to Laveaux, who, with his fellow-combatants in Port-de-Paix, hailed the capture of Léogane with shouts of delight.

Toussaint now came into collision with Jean François, his former commander. He took from that Spanish ally all his posts, and drove him westward into La Montaigne Noire. Hastening into the valley of the Artibonite, Toussaint attacked the English, and, capturing several towns, fell on Saint Marc, the seat of the English power. Sitting down to besiege the city, he got possession of two important posts. In one of these, Morne-Diamant, he raised a battery which riddled the place. Then, while aiding the men to mount a gun, he crushed his left hand. He was compelled to resign the conduct of the attack to others. The consequence was injurious. Besides, his forces were insufficiently provided with ammunition. He was forced to retire. This partial failure occasioned perfidy in some of his forces, to which he himself nearly fell a victim. Thus, while he had to maintain an open warfare against Spain and England, he had also to guard against the treachery which those powers did not disdain to set in motion among his own adherents.

Retiring, as was his custom, to the mountain fastnesses, of which Marmelade may be considered as the centre, he collected forces, and, on the 9th of Oct. 1794, quitted that place at the head of nearly five thousand men, and, after some minor successes, carried San Miguel by storm.

This exploit raised him high in the estimation of the French commanders. Laveaux and Rigaud united in their eulogies of the skill and prowess he had manifested. An interview took place between Laveaux and Toussaint at Dondon. This was the first time they had seen each other. Toussaint presented to the general-in-chief his principal officers: Dessalines, commander of San Miguel, Duménil, commander of Plaisance, Desrouleaux, Clerveaux, Maurepas, &c., commanders of battalions.

Toussaint L'Ouverture had already become a great power. Very considerable influence did he exert in this conference of French authorities.

Raised to this eminence, and now seeing " the opening " in clear outline before him, Toussaint was indefatigable. Such was the rapidity of his movements, and at so many different places was he seen near the same moment, that he seemed, especially in the eyes of the ignorant negroes, as if he was superior to time and space. Specially was he found at every post of imminent danger. His energy and his prowess made him the idol of his troops. They also caused him to be dreaded by his enemies. He was no longer a leader of insurgents, but a commander of an army. He gave over marauding expeditions to lay out and conduct a campaign.

His immediate aim was to drive the English out of the island, and for that purpose, to make himself master of the port of Saint Marc. Coming down from the mountains with this view, he found that the English commander, Brisbane, had advanced into the interior of the valley of the Artibonite, and, taking Les Vérettes, had compelled his troops to retire. One small position alone held out against Brisbane. Toussaint determined to make one of those efforts which he so well knew how to direct, and by which he sometimes effected at a blow very great results. Starting forward in the night, early in December, with a band of three hundred cavalry, he, by ambuscade and sudden attack, drove the enemy back in disgrace.

As yet, however, he had not strength enough to hold the valley of the Artibonite, especially as Jean François, with his Spanish sympathies, was impending over it in order to assist the English. He withdrew toward the North. Before he left La Petite Rivière for Gonaïves, which is in that direction, he gave a proof of the humanity by which he was actuated. In the village of La Petite Rivière, there were children and women, of different colors, who were destitute of the means of subsistence. Two Sisters of Charity who had come hither from the quarters occupied by the English, ministered to others even in their own need. At the command of L'Ouverture, bread was day by day supplied to these sufferers, and to the most wretched of them money also was distributed.

Returning with almost the speed of lightning to Marmelade, he set about organizing a sufficient force to clear the district of La Grande Rivière and its heights, which lie above Saint Marc, of the bands of Jean François. Setting in movement four columns, he quitted Dondon in the centre of the forces on the 31st of December. In four days, he took and destroyed twenty-eight positions. That of Barmby, situated on a frightful precipice, and defended by three pieces of cannon, besides firearms, was carried by the mere force of resolute bravery. Had his plan been carried into effect in all points, the insurrection would have been suppressed. It failed in one point; and so gave a passage to Jean François, who, passing through it with superior forces, surrounded Toussaint L'Ouverture. Disappointed, that brave man cut a way through his enemies, and, after establishing a cordon of great extent, returned to his stronghold, Dondon, on the 7th of January, 1795.

The cordon of the West, which L'Ouverture commanded, had for its eastern extremity La Grande Rivière, in the centre of the Department of the North, and for its western limit La Saline, in the plain of the Artibonite, in the Department of the

West, and, extending above ninety leagues, comprised the following important posts : Saint Raphael, Saint Miguel, Dondon, Marmelade, and Gonaïves. This vast space of country Toussaint L'Ouverture defended for a long time against the English, the Spanish, and against French emigrants, with troops badly armed, badly disciplined, and little accustomed to military manœuvres. This single fact is evidence of his prodigious activity and surpassing talent. He had, indeed, under him, officers of activity. But genius was demanded in his difficult and perilous position, and genius Toussaint himself alone possessed. Not only had he to survey and sustain the whole, but each particular part required his presence as well as his thoughts. At every threatened point must Toussaint himself be, and at every threatened point Toussaint was. Constantly in motion, he and his horse seemed almost one compound being. In the midst of active movements he had to satisfy the daily demands of a voluminous correspondence, which he always dictated with his own lips. Very needful, too, was it that he should do his utmost to encourage the cultivation of the lands, lest provisions should fail his troops, or famine try the fidelity of the people. Nor was the maintenance of discipline in hands such as his an easy office or a slight labor. He accomplished the task, however, by a general course of consideration and mildness as well as by stern severity toward the disobedient.

Meanwhile, the king of Spain ceded to France all his possessions and rights in Hayti. The cession inflamed the hopes of the English government, who, resolving to try a last effort, sent, under General Howe, an army of three thousand men, together with a fleet under Admiral Parker.

Laveaux had fallen into peril. Instigated by jealousy, Rigaud and Villate, another man of color, arrested General Laveaux and threw him into prison. This attempt to set up a mulatto domination was overcome by Toussaint. Grateful for the service, Laveaux appointed Toussaint his second in the government of the island of Hayti, and, in the proclamation which he thereupon issued, declared him to be that Spartacus, foretold by Raynal, whose destiny it was to avenge the outrages inflicted on all his race; and whom he set forth as the vindicator of the constituted authorities, adding that in future nothing should be attempted except in concert with him, and by his counsels. This association of Toussaint in the Government sensibly amended the disposition of the blacks, who now began to have some confidence in their white superiors, and in consequence were, in large numbers, prepared to obey.

Sonthonax, having overcome his enemies in France, returned to Hayti, at the head of a commission of which Roume was the other important member. The Commissioners found the colony in a condition approaching to prosperity. Instead of profiting by the favorable dispositions that prevailed, and the special good feeling with which he was received, Sonthonax preferred stirring men's passions afresh. He had formed the project of bringing the men of color under subjection by the power of the law. In order to effect his purpose, he, ostensibly to reward Toussaint L'Ouverture for the conduct he had pursued in the recent troubles, appointed that distinguished man general of division. These measures irritated Rigaud, the champion of the mulattoes, who saw, with extreme jealousy, the black chief elevated to a rank superior to his own. Obeyed over almost all the South, Rigaud was deaf to overtures made to him on the part of the Commissioners, and in discontent withdrew to Tiburon.

Toussaint L'Ouverture was not a man to lose time. Aware of the reinforcements the English had received, he hastened to the seat of war in the West, and, having driven back Colonel Brisbane, who had invaded La Petite Rivière, he pushed forward to Saline, near Gonaïves, which the English had set on fire, and on the shore near which they had effected a landing. The English were on the point of advancing, when Toussaint appeared. Putting himself at the head of the cavalry, he fell on the English at Guildive, and, directing the charge in his own person, he compelled them to reëmbark in confusion, with the loss of their standards, their baggage, and their cannon. Toussaint received injuries in the conflict, but Brisbane was mortally wounded. The victorious soldiers, having their muskets crowned with laurels, were received in Gonaïves in the midst of the acclamations of the people.

The influence of Toussaint L'Ouverture grew every day. Almost at will, he drew the negroes round his banners, and reduced them into discipline. He also detached from the English colors bands which they had taken into their pay. Applying himself to matters connected with the general administration of the colony, he put on a firm footing the prosperity which had begun to appear. He applied his power specially to the restoration of the culture of the soil; wisely declaring, that the liberty of the blacks could be consolidated only by the prosperity of agriculture. This important averment, spreading among the black chiefs, awoke in them the desire to acquire and to conserve property.

While the English had great difficulty to struggle against the French arms in the West, they were vigorously pressed by Desfourneaux in the North. Four columns surrounded the heights of Vallière, where the enemy, with the aid of some detachments, kept up what they called "La Vendée of Saint Domingo." Henry Christophe, afterwards King of Hayti, powerfully contributed to the success of this expedition. In the South, Rigaud assumed the offensive. Having strongly fortified Les Cayes, he marched to attack Port-au-Prince. He met with a resistance so vigorous, so brave, and so well conducted, that any but a very superior man must have perished. In a sally made by Colonel Markham, at the head of a thousand men, his outposts were carried, and his headquarters plundered. The rout was becoming general, when Rigaud, though urged to save his life by flight, leaped on his horse, and, rallying fifty men, threw himself on the English occupied in pillage, and put many of them to the sword. The plunder was recovered, and Markham, forced to beat a retreat, fell pierced with balls.

L'Ouverture, not slow in sustaining the efforts of Rigaud, sat down before Saint Marc with ten thousand men. Thrice did he assail the town in vain. After prodigies of valor, he was compelled to retire.

Unwilling to derive no advantage from his exertions, Toussaint determined to rescue Mirebalais out of the hands of the Spaniards, by whom it was held. At his voice, the population rose in a mass, and, with his assistance, made him master of the district.

Mirebalais was a most important post. Lying in the mountains on the northeast corner of the Western Department, the district so called consisted of gorges, steeps, and narrow passes, which made almost every part of it a Thermopylæ. The village of St. Louis, also called by the name of the district, commands an immense extent of level country. Favorable to animal life in general, the country abounds in superior horses. A skilful commander, possessed of Mirebalais, therefore, might almost defy attack, and at his pleasure sally forth to wage war in almost any part of the island.

The English, aware of the importance of this position, resolved to get it into their hands. They succeeded in the bold undertaking.

The loss was too heavy to be endured. L'Ouverture, as soon as other duties permitted, made arrangements for the recovery of Mirebalais. He was not in time, however, to prevent the occupants from covering it with fortifications. The command of the district had been intrusted to a French emigrant, the Count de Bruges, whose forces amounted to two thousand English troops of the line, besides a numerous militia. On the 24th of March, 1797, Toussaint L'Ouverture, by means of his lieutenant, Morney, intercepted the high road leading into the country, and, encamping at Block-haus du Gros Figuier, repelled Montalembert, who was advancing into Mirebalais with seven hundred men and two pieces of artillery. The next day, Toussaint drove the English from all their possessions, and, completing the investment of the village, ordered, on the South, the attack of the forts. With such unity of operation and such impetuosity of assault was the attack made that the whole was carried. Conflagration completed what the firearms left unsubdued. Toussaint L'Ouverture passed from eminence to eminence, and surveyed his troops victorious on all sides. A yet more pleasing sight to him was that which he had when he set at liberty two hundred prisoners of all hues, who were suffering under a degrading punishment, and who every moment expected a horrible death from the flames which were approaching the place of their detention.

Pursuing his advantages, L'Ouverture, in a campaign of fourteen days, totally defeated the English, and brought under obedience the entire province. Among his spoils were eleven pieces of cannon, with their ammunition, and two hundred prisoners. As his recompense, Toussaint L'Ouverture received from Sonthonax the appointment of commander-in-chief of the army of Saint Domingo, vacant by the departure of Laveaux. The conquering hero was installed at the Cape, in the presence of the garrison, composed of black troops, and the remains of the white troops. These are the words which he employed on the occasion :— " Citizen Commissioners, I accept the eminent rank to which you have just raised me, only in the hope of more surely succeeding in entirely extirpating the enemies of Saint Domingo, of contributing to its speedy restoration to prosperity, and of securing the happiness of its inhabitants. If to fulfil the difficult task which it imposes, it sufficed to wish the good of the island, and to effect it, in all that depends on me, I hope that, with the aid of the Divine Being, I shall succeed. The tyrants are cast down on the earth ; they will no more defile the places where the standard of liberty and equality ought to float alone, and where the sacred rights of man ought to be recognized.

" Officers and soldiers, if there is a compensation in the severe labors which I am about to enter on, I shall find it in the satisfaction of commanding brave soldiers. Let the sacred fire of liberty animate us, and let us never take repose until we have prostrated the foe."

Lofty now was the position of Toussaint L'Ouverture. Glad

was his heart. His joy did not arise from his own personal elevation. It is true that he had created an army which could beat European troops, and expel them from even the strongholds of Hayti. It is true that in his deeds and warlike achievements he had equalled the great captains of ancient and modern times. But he had not fought for his own aggrandizement; he had done all with a view to an ultimate object. And now that object seemed within his reach. The emancipation of his race was accomplished, therefore did Toussaint rejoice. "The opening" was made; what remained to be done was detail. Alas! such were the appearances, but the appearances proved delusions.

The achievement just set forth gave the final blow to the war. No longer could the English do more than maintain a desultory conflict with scarcely any hope of final success, whatever temporary advantages they might gain. When all but relieved from a foreign enemy, the French authorities began to disagree among themselves. The particulars are too tedious to be repeated. From the colony appeals were made to the Legislature in Paris. The Commissioner, Sonthonax, fearing impeachment, requested to be sent home as a deputy from the colony. If at first sincere, he seems afterwards to have vacillated. Toussaint, however, convinced that his absence would be conducive to the restoration of harmony and the effective prosecution of hostilities, took measures that his request should not fail of effect. But Toussaint, victorious and powerful in the colony, had reason to fear the result of intrigues and plots against himself in the mother country. As a pledge of his honor and a token of confidence, he sent his two sons to France for their education. On their part, the English, suffering greatly from the climate, and making no progress toward the subjugation of the island, employed the utmost of their power to seduce the hostile leaders. Having with little satisfaction to themselves attempted to secure the mulatto interest, they made the bold attempt of seducing Toussaint L'Ouverture himself. Little knowing the character of the man with whom they dealt, they offered, as the price of his subserviency, the title of King of Hayti. The incorruption of Toussaint on the occasion was the more remarkable and worthy, as General Hédouville, sent after the departure of Southonax as the representative of France, treated him with less consideration than was deserved by the man to whom that country owed the restoration of its colony. Toussaint had, indeed, become too powerful perhaps for France, certainly for its deputy, Hédouville. In his anxiety to disembarrass himself of the black chief, that general, by means of his creatures, tried to induce him to embark for the mother country, in order to plead his cause and maintain his interests. Pointing with his hand to a sapling which grew near—" I will go," he said, " when that branch shall form a vessel of sufficient size to carry me thither."

During these unhappy divisions, the English had been losing ground. Worn down and dispirited, they at length began to take decided steps for the evacuation of the island. In the negotiations and measures which this involved, the polemics and distrusts of the French authorities displayed but too strongly their evil effects. Port-au-Prince, however, was surrendered by the English, who shortly afterward found it prudent to place the Môle Saint-Nicholas in the hands of the French. Dissatisfied with the stipulations made by Hédouville, Toussaint repaired to Saint-Marc, and took into his own hands the settlement of the terms of capitulation. Not yet wholly without hope of winning over to English views their most formidable opponent, the English, by their representative, General Maitland, rendered the highest honors to Toussaint L'Ouverture. The attempt met with deserved failure. Toussaint could see through the covered designs of his old foes. He had no faith that the freedom of his race would ensue from English domination; and he knew that their equality before the law had been recognized by France. Faithful to his great idea and final design, he remained superior to the blandishments of English wealth and adulation. After enduring so many fatigues and acquiring so much glory, L'Ouverture retired into the interior of the Artibonite, and took up his abode on the estate called Deschaux, which was situated in the mountains. There **he** flattered himself with the hope of some repose, and there, keeping an eye over the great centres of social movement, he could at any moment, like **the eagle, descend to** any part where his presence was required.

8*

CHAPTER X.

Toussaint L'Ouverture composes agitation, and brings back prosperity —
Is opposed by the Commissioner, Hédouville, who flies to France —
Appeals, in self-justification, to the Directory in Paris.

HAVING reached the commanding position which he held, Toussaint L'Ouverture, with a true patriotism and a wise benevolence, applied himself to the difficult task of healing the wounds of his country. The first task was to induce the planters to resume possession of their estates, and re-commence the tillage of the soil. This he effected in part by persuasion, in part by gentle compulsion; numerous detachments of infantry, traversing the cities, collected together the scattered owners, and conducted them to the plantations. The conduct of the troops employed in the service was as worthy of notice as the obedience of the agriculturists; for, observing the strictest discipline, they showed the greatest respect to property, and conducted themselves toward all with becoming moderation and mildness. The control over these rude natures which this temperance implied was the result of the discipline instituted by Toussaint, and of the love and the fear which his name inspired. Among his signal triumphs this was, perhaps, the most signal. Not by blacks only, but by whites, was this extraordinary man obeyed. Obedience secured Toussaint's protection. Regardless of the color of the skin, he received with favor, and treated with confidence, and promoted with readiness, all whom he had valid reasons for believing sincerely bent on advancing the public good. Disdaining to govern by the rivalry of classes, he aimed to serve the whole, by the means and with the aid of each. Emigrant or creole, black or white, men were treated by him as men, — being placed in the posts for which they were fitted, whether military or civil. If there was a difference in his conduct toward dependents, that difference was not in favor of white men. The injured, he rightly judged, had the first claim to his attention. Generally, however, his administration was impartial,—severely impartial.

It scarcely need be added that he grew in universal estimation. Respected by men in general, his influence became immense; and even the fear or distrust which was secretly nourished against him by some was an acknowledgment of his power. Under Toussaint's benign sway, parties began to melt away and heart-burnings to cease. An unqualified amnesty, which he proclaimed, tranquillized men's minds and reconciled them to the existing state of things.

Nor did the victorious general forget the All-powerful Arm to which he knew that he owed his triumph, and by whose aid only, he was equally assured, he could finish the work he had begun and so far accomplished.

But the Governor disapproved of L'Ouverture's policy. Whether from a difference of view, or from suspecting Toussaint of ambitious designs, Hédouville, though a professed Republican, characterized his administration as "too mild and too full of results." Never having behaved toward the negro captain with cordiality, he now conveyed to Toussaint's ears words of open complaint and covert blame. Toussaint was not to be turned from a course which he had deliberately adopted and found to be most beneficial. Afraid lest Hédouville's power would interrupt that course, or abate its good, he issued proclamations to his troops—his chief basis of reliance—in order to confirm them in their obedience by the strongest of ties, namely, the religious ties to which their susceptible and impulsive natures made them peculiarly sensible. "This," said he, "is the path which we must all follow in order to draw down upon us the blessing of the Lord. I hope you will never depart from it, and that you will punctually execute what follows:—

"The heads of regiments are required to see that the troops join in prayer morning and evening, as far as the service will permit.

" At the earliest review, the Generals Commanding-in-chief will cause high mass to be celebrated, and a *Te Deum* to be sung, in all the places of their several districts, as an expression of gratitude to Heaven for having vouchsafed to direct our last campaigns; for having caused the evacuation of the enemy to take place without effusion of blood; for having protected the return amongst us of many thousand men of every color, who till then had been lost; and, finally, for having restored to the labors of agriculture more than twenty thousand hands. The *Te Deum* will be announced by a salvo of twenty-two pieces of cannon."

Under the effects of words so religious and so just, the credit of Hédouville was greatly lessened. In proportion as L'Ouverture gained ascendency, he sank, until he retained among his supporters only those who were immediately around him, such as his officials, Frenchmen who were foreigners in the colony, and others who, from personal connections with the mother country, desired to maintain its power in the hands of its agents.

The contrast was made greater by the diverse course pursued by the two in regard to the cultivators of the soil. While Hédouville unconditionally declared all the blacks free, Toussaint wisely prefixed to their actual freedom a kind of apprenticeship for five years, on condition of their receiving one-fourth of the produce, out of which the masters were to defray the cost of their subsistence. The plan of the Governor, speciously designed to catch the popular breeze, would have issued in universal disorder. Instead of immediate emancipation, always *\
pregnant with present and future disasters, Toussaint interposed a period of preparation, and in so doing saved the property of the masters, as well as promoted the interests of the servants. So wise and moderate a use of his triumph and his power probably saved Hayti from the terrors of a universal convulsion, and certainly raised him to a high position in the respect of all impartial and judicious men.

* Where the author writes *always* in this sentence, the concurrent voice of history writes NEVER. It is *always* safe to do right. — ED.

Hédouville, aware to what an extent he had lost the public confidence, took measures for provoking a movement contrary to Toussaint, among the men of color. Rigaud he accordingly invited to the seat of government. As a cover, he invited Toussaint also to take part in the conference. But the negro chief was as wary as he was bold; and he may have heard that some time previously officers of Hédouville's staff had offered to seize his person if only their master would put four brave soldiers at their disposal.

Remaining at Port-au-Prince, Toussaint was informed that Rigaud was on his way to the Cape. The commander of that place and several black officers advised Toussaint to intercept and apprehend Rigaud. "I could," he replied, "easily do so; but God forbid. I have need of Rigaud. He is violent. I want him for carrying on war; and that war is necessary to me. The mulatto caste is superior to my own. If I take Rigaud from them, they will, perhaps, find another superior to him. I know Rigaud; he gives up the bridle when he gallops; he shows his arm when he strikes. For me, I gallop also; but I know where to stop; and when I strike, I am felt, not seen. M. Rigaud can conduct insurrections only by blood and massacres; I know how to put the people in movement; but when I appear, all must be tranquil."

A general feeling of uneasiness spread abroad. Fear began to prevail. A counter-revolution seemed at hand. The blacks were uneasy, especially those who had compromised themselves in taking part with the English. The mulattoes were regarded with alarm. In Fort-Saint-Dauphin, a regiment ran to arms, declaring that the whites wished to restore slavery. A combat took place between the black troops and the white troops. The former, being beaten, spread over the open country, which they raised on all sides. Then, once more, conflagration committed its ravages. Many unfortunate whites, taken by surprise on their estates, were slaughtered. The insurgents marched to the Cape. Toussaint hastened to the seat of the insurrection. The blacks were raging as in former days. Suddenly their chief appeared, and all was peaceful. Undertaking to be the exponent of their griefs, he led them to the Cape. The moment he arrived there, the alarm was given by the authorities, who seem to have desired a *rencontre*. The troops were assembled, but the effort proved nugatory. By little and little, the soldiers deserted their posts when they knew that Toussaint was at hand. Hédouville, failing in his *coup d'état*, embarked to return to France. From on board the ship he published a proclamation, in which, being no longer able to profit by the prejudices of color, he sought his account by appealing to national jealousies, and declared that Toussaint L'Ouverture was sold to the English.

The movement was at an end. The plotter was on his way back to France, and the regenerator of his country found himself in a freer field, and possessed of augmented resources. No less single than pure in his aims, Toussaint L'Ouverture rose in general regard and public confidence, even by the contrarieties which the Governor had thrown in his way. By the failure of the recent plot, too, the mulatto interest, considered as hostile to the interest of other classes, received a heavy blow.

As soon as General Hédouville had set sail, the blacks were not only tranquil, but obedient to the eye and the finger of their chief. Every one silently resumed his habitudes. The most perfect calm succeeded the most raging tempest. A *Te Deum* was chanted, and the name of Toussaint L'Ouverture was mingled with the Hallowed Name in the uttered gratitude of thousands. Toussaint was not insensible to the homage, and he desired the complete accomplishment of his mission. But he had seen the edifice he had so carefully and painfully raised put in danger with only too much facility. The mulatto party, though weakened, were still powerful. At their head was Rigaud, who had not shown himself averse to the designs of his caste. Toussaint dreaded a collision. Possibly he himself was a hindrance to a peaceful and permanent settlement. Entertaining no merely personal objects, he gave utterance to a desire to be relieved of his weighty responsibilities. At a moment when, by a bold stroke, he might have set up a throne, and perhaps established a dynasty, he asked for his dismissal. The word called forth a universal remonstrance. The civil and the military authorities, the white, black, and brown inhabitants, the proprietors and the laborers, all combined in laying before him formal addresses, in which they entreated him to remain, to use their own terms, "their father and their benefactor."

But there was a court of appeal. Before that tribunal Hédouville would appear with singular advantage. Toussaint knew the disparity of his means for obtaining a fair hearing; but he resolved to employ such as were at his command. Accordingly he sent Colonel Vincent, one of his secretaries, to explain and justify his conduct before the French Government, then in the hands of the Directory. Colonel Vincent was the bearer of a letter, of which the following contains the principal passages : —

"Toussaint L'Ouverture, General-in-Chief of the army of Saint Domingo, to the Directory of the Republic : —

"CITIZEN DIRECTORS: When, in my last dispatches, I determined to request my dismissal, I did so because, after having collected all the instances of opposition to the principles which the Constitution has established, which your wisdom has maintained, which your energy has defended, — all the instances of opposition, I say, manifested in conduct held by the agent, Hédouville, during the short space of time which he governed this colony, — I foresaw the unhappy event which for an instant disturbed the public tranquillity I had had so much trouble to establish; and I did so after having calculated the consequences of the distance at which he held himself from me, and of which he gave public proofs on several occasions, fearing that my deposition, which he meditated, would be the reward of my long services, of my fidelity, and of my devotedness.

"The incident at Fort-Dauphin realized my apprehensions as to the convulsion for which preparations were made; and the proclamation which the Agent put forth at the moment of his departure has justified my fears regarding the fate he intended for me.

" The most outrageous injury which can be done to a man of honor crowns the vexations which he has made me undergo. By this perfidious act, he causes a vast number of Frenchmen to quit these lands, who had congratulated themselves on their happiness here, and who, faithful to their country, were compelled to sacrifice their interests, rather than become accomplices in the crime of independence of which I was regarded as guilty; he carries with him, especially, the principal authorities, that (as he said on leaving) they may be the irrefragable proof of my duplicity, of my perfidy.

" Doubtless, the first feeling of the Directory, whom I respect, on seeing them unanimously bear witness against me, will be to invoke vengeance on my head; that of the French people, whom I love, to devote me to execration; and that of the enemies of the blacks, whom I despise, to cry out for slavery; but when it shall be known that at the time which I was accused of wishing to sunder this island from France, my benefactress, I repeated the oath of fidelity to her, I take pleasure in believing that the government I own, and my fellow-citizens, will render me the justice I merit, and that the enemies of my brethren will be reduced to silence.

" The Agent, in reality, surrounded himself only with persons in the colony sunk in public opinion, ambitious and intriguing, who caress all the factions which have torn this unfortunate country. A band of young men, of no character and no principles, who came with him, then threw away the mask, and manifested a spirit both anti-national and insulting to me.

" The laborers, who began to taste the sweets of repose in the midst of security, were surprised at the impure sounds which struck their ear and wounded their heart. I became the depositary of their griefs, and I composed their minds by assuring them of the good intentions of the Agent of a benevolent government; but they soon accused me myself of partiality, having become certain that even at the table of the General Agent they were denounced as unworthy the liberty they enjoy, and which they have derived from the equity of France.

" Often did the Agent reproach me with having received emigrants, with violating the constitution, and breaking the law. Whatever may have been the reasons of the continual blame which I received from him in regard to conduct in which I found nothing to reproach myself with, I could not ascertain them, and, persuaded that, from the moment I lost his confidence, I could expect no more good, I asked of you my dismissal. Happy would it have been if it had reached me prior to his departure! He would then have learnt that ambition never was my master, and especially he would not have done me the injury to publish that I desired to terminate my services to France by a crime toward which I was drawn by the men around me who were sold to the English.

" Whoever those may have been of whom I was obliged to make use to assist me in my important occupations, and without whom even with all the means given by education which I have not received, I could not have performed my functions, I will one day prove that no one less than myself merits the reproach laid at my door by my adversaries, namely, that I allowed myself to be governed.

" Could it be laid to my charge that I directed toward the public interests, that I employed for the advantage of the public, activity, talents, and genius? And when my secretaries, whom bonds too sacred unite to their mother country to allow a moment's doubt of their attachment to her, are the sole depositaries of my secrets, the sole confidants of the projects which I could not confine within my own breast, why cast on men who will never influence me the blame of the ridiculous intentions imputed to me, and which, never having entered my heart, again prove that I do not allow myself to be governed by the passions of others? If those passions had directed my steps, I should not have foreseen the event which has just taken place; and, walking like a blind man on my political course, I should have asked you for my dismissal.

" But that step which prudence forced me to take, the only one which could dissipate the storm with which I was threatened, was very far from restoring confidence in the minds of the people of Saint Domingo. The discontent of the laborers had increased by the compulsion of an engagement for three years. That seemed to them a step back to slavery. They called to mind the means proposed by Vaublanc to establish his system in this colony, and they were surprised that when the Directory had punished that conspirator, its Agent should propose the same measures, should prescribe them, should exact their prompt and full execution. This dissatisfaction, which was fostered, was soon shared by the soldiers. By the discharge of more than three thousand men, effected after the evacuation of the West by the English, I had proved how necessary I thought it to cut down the armaments of the military. I was blamed in that operation, and I received the order not to cut down any troop. Nevertheless, on the departure of the English, it was declared that all the black forces ought to be disbanded in order to be sent back to agriculture, and that European soldiers only should be employed in the defence of the coasts. Then distrust entered the soldiers' hearts, and while previously a part of them had taken the hoe without a murmur, they showed aversion toward a measure which they regarded as an attack on liberty.

" Whatever were the grounds of distrust with which I was surrounded, however faithful the counsels I received on all parts from the most sincere friends of the prosperity of Saint Domingo, whatever fears were infused into my mind by the crimes contemplated against my person, I did not hesitate to set out for the Cape, and even endeavored to give a proof of my confidence in the highest authorities, by going unattended, except by an aide-de-camp and a cavalry officer; but, having arrived on the Héricourt plantation, I was met by alarming rumors. I learned that at Fort-Dauphin, the fifth colonial regiment — which contributed so much to the restoration of order, to the purification of La Grande Rivière (the Vendée of Saint Domingo), to the expulsion of the English — had become the victim of the European troops, who formerly had delivered up

to foreign powers the points of the colony which had been
confided to their defence.

"Convinced, then, of the bad intentions of the Government in whose names all those horrors were committed; no
longer seeing any security for any one who had acquired well-
grounded claims to the national gratitude; fearing, with good
reason, for my own life,—I turned back and prepared to go and
wait at Gonaïves official news of an event, the consequences of
which I dreaded. I received a letter from the General Agent,
which confirmed my fears, and in which he ordered me to repair to Fort-Dauphin to aid the citizen Manigat, whom he had
invested with all civil and military power, in the reëstablishment of order and public tranquillity. I then pressed on to
Gonaïves in order to take the escort, of which I had need.
The crimes committed by Frenchmen against my brethren
forced me to this prudential measure. I left Gonaïves with the
fourth regiment; but what was my grief when, on arriving at
the Héricourt plantation, I learned that the rising of the laborers had become general, that all the plain was in arms, and
threatened the Cape with an immediate irruption. Those
who with that design had assembled on the Héricourt estate
surrounded me as soon as I arrived, reproaching me with having deceived them in answering for the good intentions of General Hédouville, and attributed to me the slaughter of their
brethren at Fort-Dauphin, the arrest of some of them, and the
dismissal of General Moyse; and then it was that I received
information of all the details of that unfortunate event. Soon
I learned that the evil was intruding into all the parishes, and
that the people required that General Hédouville should be
sent away, the restoration of General Moyse to his rights, and
the liberation of the officers of the fifth regiment, made prisoners in the affair at Fort-Dauphin, &c.

"Whatever pain I felt at the excesses committed against a
corps, respectable for its services, and against officers whom I
knew always attached to their duties, against a chief who never failed in his attachment to France and to the principles of

liberty,— my own nephew,— I regarded in so alarming an event only the imminent dangers to which the public interests were exposed. I sent on all sides faithful emissaries to calm the agitated minds of men; to announce to them my arrival, and to require of them to do nothing without my orders. I hastened to set myself in opposition to the enterprises of the more senseless, who had already taken possession of the heights of the Cape and of Fort Belair which commands the city. With difficulty could I make my way through the crowds; an immense influx of people, whom the blind desire for revenge had armed, covered all the roads which led to the Cape, and threatened that city with the greatest calamities. Frightened at the abyss, on the brink of which the city stood, I ran to draw it back. In my course, I learned that the General Agent had gone on board the fleet. Surprised at the news, I hastened to the Cape, which I reached with difficulty, after having, sometimes by prayers, sometimes by menaces, stopped the torrent with which it was threatened to be inundated. The astonishment caused by the departure of General Hédouville was changed into grief when I learned that that Agent, alarmed, doubtless, at the dangers to which he had exposed the public weal, and despairing of any longer being able to conserve it, had resolved to go away, and that, to color his pusillanimous flight, he had proclaimed that I was aiming at independence.

"The terror having augmented, more than eighteen hundred persons followed the Agent in his flight. He ordered the cannons to be spiked. The command was being executed, when there arose a cry 'To arms!' The troops drawn out in battle array were moved by the cry; they were pacified by their leaders; had a single musket been fired, the city would have perished.

"Strong in my conscience, I shall not remind you, Citizen-Directors, of all I have done for the triumph of liberty, the prosperity of St. Domingo, the glory of the French Republic; nor will I protest to you my attachment to our mother country, to my duties; my respect to the constitution, to the laws of the

Republic, and my submission to the government. I swear to you I am faithful, and my future conduct, more than all oaths, will prove to you that I shall always be faithful.

"If the defence of my cause, that of the freedom of my brethren, needed cunning and intrigue and manly eloquence, in order to triumph over my enemies, I would give it up and weep over France; but, as I am persuaded that it is sufficient to present the truth for it to be apprehended by the republican government, I am satisfied with setting before you an exposition of my conduct, and of that of General Hédouville, and repose on your justice for the verdict which is to result.

"As soon as I had reëstablished the public tranquillity, I sent to the Commissioner Roume — your delegate in what was formerly the Spanish part of this island — to entreat him in the name of the public safety to come and take the reins of government thrown up by General Hédouville; persuaded that his determination will be conformed to the wishes of all good Frenchmen, I impatiently await his arrival, in order to aid him with all my power in the important functions of his new position."

The appeal of justice and rectitude prevailed. The Directory were satisfied with Toussaint's self-justification. More might have been expected; more ought to have been given. But suspicions began to prevail in France to the disadvantage of the negro emancipator. The purer his conduct, the more heroic his life, the greater was his crime; for his real crime was his power, and that power was the natural and inevitable consequence of his virtuous and high-minded career.

9*

CHAPTER XI.

Civil war in the South between Toussaint L'Ouverture and Rigaud—
Siege and capture of Jacmel.

IN quitting the shores of Hayti, Hédouville threw a torch of discord amidst the excitable population. Not only did he cause alarm by declaring that Toussaint was preparing to betray the colony to the English, but he called forth the slumbering passions of the men of color, by intimating that with them lay the power and the duty of traversing his treacherous designs. He even addressed a letter to their leader, Rigaud, in which he formally set that mulatto General free from his obligations to Toussaint as Commander-in-chief, and requested him to assume the command of the Southern Department. This was nothing less than an invitation to civil strife. A correspondence took place between L'Ouverture and Rigaud. According to what he believed to be his duty, the former acquainted the latter with the departure of Hédouville, and exhorted him to pursue such a course as would promote the general weal. Rigaud, evading the real point at issue, brought into prominence the alleged partiality of Toussaint toward the emigrants, whom he requested him to drive away.

The request, of course, remained without effect, but it served as a pretext to the jealousies of Rigaud. Again did trouble take possession of the popular mind. The fear became the greater because Rigaud urged on Toussaint severity toward the proprietors, whereas the latter had determined to pursue his course of administering equal justice to men of all colors, so long as they proved themselves good citizens. In this state of excitement, Toussaint L'Ouverture invited the Commissioner Roume to repair to the seat of government in order to fill the post vacated by Hédouville. In this step he gave effect to a decree of the Directory. Roume appeared at the Cape on the 12th of January, 1799. Toussaint, though suffering from sickness, repaired thither to confer with him a few days afterward. The two chief authorities in the island came to an amicable understanding after mutual explanations. Entering into the large and philanthropic views of L'Ouverture, Roume pronounced him " a philosopher, a legislator, a general, and a good citizen."

Anxious to scatter the clouds which overhung the horizon, Roume called together the chief captains of the island. In order to excite attention to the conference and commemorate the event, public festivities were celebrated. At the foot of the tree of liberty, planted in the great square, and surrounded by generals, Roume delivered a speech, in which he recommended peace, union, love of the republic, and self-sacrifice. He pronounced eulogies on the army, extolling the success of its arms against the enemies of France, and declared that the most perfect union existed between the generals, Toussaint L'Ouverture, Rigaud, Biassou, Laplume, and the other military chiefs. The following day, business was entered into in earnest. The representative of the French Government requested Rigaud to cede certain portions of the territory which was under his control. The request looked like a concession to Toussaint L'Ouverture. Jealousy sprang into activity in Rigaud's mind. After a warm discussion, and some time for reflection, the mulatto chief gave in his resignation. Roume replied, urging its withdrawal. The request prevailed, and Rigaud set out for the South. On his way, he evacuated Grand Goâve and Petit Goâve, — a portion only of what had been required, — which L'Ouverture caused his troops to occupy. The storm had receded; by no means had it passed away. The colonists rallied around L'Ouverture; for they had not forgotten that it was from the efforts of the free men of color to gain equality of political rights, that the revolution had proceeded, which had changed the face of the island. They stirred up divisions among the blacks and the

men of mingled blood.   On their part, the men of color were
displeased at seeing the supreme command settled in the hands
of an African of pure blood, and flocked around the standard
of Rigaud. The blacks, under the protection of the Government and Toussaint, beheld the gathering clouds not without
excitement, yet in confidence; nor were they unwilling, after
so many victories, to try a last fall with their special foe.

The contest began with extremes; free white men fought
with black slaves. Its intervals have disappeared. The circle
has narrowed. Those who are nearest each other are about to
join in conflict. The black will fight with those who are a
little less black than himself; therefore, this will be the dead-
liest combat of all. The two parties stand and look at each
other like inflamed beasts of prey. Which will make the first
spring?

The mulatto, to the qualities of pride and meanness, adds
singular strength of muscle and impulse of passion. Conscious
of power, he also feels within him boiling emotions. If victory
depended on a dash, he would be master wherever he dwells.
But the very exuberance of his nature precludes caution and
banishes prudence; and in the impetuosity of his rush he incurs
as much peril as he occasions. Impatient of delay, he pays
for momentary advantages by speedy and irretrievable defeat.
Yet the same unbridled will which brings disaster nourishes
vindictiveness; he is therefore ever prepared, if not panting,
for revenge. The fight, consequently, is renewed, but without
a change of result; and so life passes away in extravagant and
disappointed efforts.

The mulattoes of Hayti could not restrain their wounded
feelings. The opposition to the Government broke out at
Corail, a small village in the Southern Department. The men
of color, gaining the upper hand, threw into prison, at Jérémie,
thirty of their prisoners, consisting of one colonist and nine-
and-twenty blacks. Then was reënacted the tragedy of the
Black Hole in Calcutta. The prisoners perished from bad air.
Premeditation was imputed to the mulattoes; of culpable in

consideration and blind passion they were guilty. "In all movements," remarked L'Ouverture, "the blacks are the victims." This dark event rendered the continuance of peace impossible. Both sides prepared for war. Toussaint, with a foresight becoming his position, looked calmly at the probable wants of the island in general. Hayti was indebted for the food of its inhabitants chiefly to importation. The condition of France gave small hope of sufficient supplies. War, too, would suspend the operations of agriculture in the island. He therefore negotiated a commercial treaty with the United States.

The conflict began with an attack by Rigaud's troops on Petit Goâve, the surrender of which had been obtained in the conference at the Cape. The place fell and the colonists were all ruthlessly massacred. Profiting by the success, Rigaud advanced and took up a position against Grand Goâve. Hastening to Port-au-Prince, Toussaint justly accused Rigaud with having first drawn the sword, and made preparations for the campaign. Having called the mulattoes together into the church, he ascended the pulpit and laid bare their bosoms, foretelling his own success and the ruin of their cause. "I see," he said to them,— "I see to the bottom of your souls; you are ready to rise against me, but although all the troops are quitting the West, I leave behind my eye and my arm, — my eye, which will watch you; my arm, which, if necessary, will fall upon you."

A mulatto plot, which extended even to the North, had put the keys of Port-au-Prince into the hands of a traitor. L'Ouverture was a prisoner in a town which he thought his own. But his decision and courage were equal to all crises. He discovered the snare, punished the criminals, and then, with the fleetness and the force of the eagle, flew back over his own territories, and forcing strongholds and capturing towns, went as far to the northwest as Saint Nicholas, which he brought back to its duty. The men of color were smitten with consternation, and many of them, having been captured in the several collisions, suffered indignities the most humiliating. Suddenly

Toussaint returned to the Cape. The guilty thought the hour of their doom was come. The high-minded victor invited the inhabitants to meet him at the church, and there, besides a concourse of people, all the civil and military authorities assembled. The garrison, which consisted of black troops, surrounded the place; and under the guard of a picket of soldiers in the church were the men of color, almost naked, and in extreme dejection. Toussaint L'Ouverture ascended an elevation, pronounced a eulogium on the forgiveness of injuries as the duty of every Christian, and then, proclaiming the pardon and the freedom of all the mulattoes, he distributed clothes and money to them severally, and gave strict injunctions that, on their way to join their families, they should be protected and treated as brothers. This unexpected generosity produced the most lively enthusiasm. As he left the church, benedictions were showered on his head.

While at the Cape, admiration at Toussaint's clemency was universal; the mulatto insurgents in the South only fought the more strenuously, in order to make up by military advantage that which L'Ouverture had gained by wise moderation. No wars are so bitter or so bloody as those of class, caste, and color. The fact was illustrated in this terrible conflict. With such bitterness and ferocity did it rage, that Toussaint was compelled to employ all his influence to recruit his ranks. To the blacks he might look with confidence, as the war was specially for their benefit; but the blacks began to grow alarmed as the sanguinary struggle proceeded. The whites in the North and the West, who had hitherto been exempt from the service, were marshalled at the Cape, and sent into the South, to take part in a contest in which they had only a remote interest. A mute consternation prevailed. Scarcely was the conflict spoken of in the intercourse of private life, and the periodical press transcribed the reports of the several chiefs without permitting themselves to add any comments or reflections. Every one not actually engaged in the warfare feared to compromise himself, lest he should bring on his head the vengeance of the conqueror. Yet prudence did not prevent complications of all kinds, nor could Toussaint's mercy preclude horrors the most distressing. Rigaud, boundless in resources as he was brave and daring, put forth all his energy, and maintained his position at every cost. Toussaint, with a prowess not inferior to Rigaud's, was equally vigilant and equally bold. Yet was he unable to guard against all stratagems. In the recesses of the mountains near Port-de-Paix, as he made his way with few attendants, he found that he had fallen into an ambuscade. A discharge of musketry rattled around his head; his physician fell dead at his feet. The plume of feathers which he wore was shot away, and he himself escaped as if by miracle. Saved from one, he shortly after was exposed to another ambuscade. The shots were directed at his carriage; the coachman was killed; he himself rode tranquilly on horseback a few paces distant. In the midst of perils, Toussaint L'Ouverture persevered. Yet he obtained only partial success. The troops of Rigaud, if fewer in number, were individually superior to the hasty levies of Toussaint, and collectively better disciplined. Many of them had long fought under their chief, and were conversant with all the resources and requirements of the war in which they were engaged. With the country in which the conflict was waged they were intimately acquainted, and of the character of their leader they knew enough to be aware that only defeat would bring discredit or occasion displeasure. Having to overcome such an enemy, Toussaint L'Ouverture found it necessary to put forth his utmost power, the rather as he had to hold possession of a wide extent of country, and that with troops of whom the bulk were of an inferior caste. Painful is it to read the alternations of defeat and victory in this terrible contest, especially as on both sides they were accompanied by acts of cruelty. The only relief that the mind can obtain in going through the now tedious, now revolting details, arises from the reflection that had such amount of effort and such patience of suffering as these events show man to possess been employed, as happily one day they may be employed, in some cause of high benevolence, some undertaking to save and not to destroy men's lives, the results would have been no less satisfactory than glorious indeed. The terror inspired by Rigaud's successes and ferocity drove the laborers from the fields into the forts; from the forts they were driven into the towns; when one town was taken, they escaped into another. Then they assembled together to concert and make attacks. Thus the country was a desert, the cities overflowed. While agriculture was at a stand-still, provisions were often destroyed, and while no supplies came from the country, the dense masses aggregated in the towns experienced want. The want arose to famine in Jacmel, lying on the southern side of the tongue of land which forms the Southern Department. Jacmel, on the seashore, formed the key of the district. It was under the power of Rigaud, commanded by Birot. Resolved to capture the place, which was capable of affording an obstinate resistance, Toussaint himself sat down before it. With the utmost difficulty were the preparations for the siege made. Women and children were employed to convey ammunition. Bands, amounting to six thousand laborers, drew huge pieces of cannon along frightful precipices, and down roads, the most rugged, broken, and dangerous. At length, the troops were collected, and Jacmel was invested, so far as the sea would permit. Soon the harbor also was blockaded. Then the terrors of famine began to be experienced. So intense and various were the sufferings, that the officers at length determined to capitulate. The determination was opposed by the soldiers, who declared resistance still possible. The commander, with two of his staff, embarked in the night and escaped to Cayes. His post was assumed by Gauthier. The siege was pressed with vigor. Post after post was taken. Meanwhile, Rigaud neither came up to aid, nor operated a diversion. Then Petion, apprised of the critical position of the town, determined to assume the perilous command, and, with three vessels and some provisions, succeeded in making his way into the port, under the discharges of fire-arms from the enemy's posts. Entering into the duties he had voluntarily undertaken, he employed all his ability in the defence. But an enemy was at work over whom he had no power. The famine reached such a height, that the inhabitants were compelled to eat the horses belonging to the cavalry. Every green thing was torn up and devoured. Those thought themselves happy who, in their search for food, met with a rat or a lizard. In the public highways, famished men scarcely recognized each other. Frenzy and wailing filled every place. Mothers, worn down by want, fatigue, and woe, lay in the streets, with their dead infants on their exhausted breasts. At length Petion, seeing that further resistance was impossible, resolved to cut his way through the besiegers. In order to inspire his soldiers with his own courage, he tore the flags from the staffs, and commanded his men to bind strips of them round their bodies, so that if they perished they might still be faithful to their colors. Jacmel fell, and its fall was a heavy blow to Rigaud. Having taken possession of Jacmel, Toussaint L'Ouverture addressed to the inhabitants of the Southern Department the following proclamation : —

" CITIZENS : By what fatality is it, that, hitherto deaf to my voice, which invites you to order, you have listened only to the counsels of Rigaud ? How is it possible that the pride of a single person should be the source of your evils, and that to flatter his ambition, you are willing to destroy your families, ruin your property, and bring yourselves into disgrace in the eyes of the whole world ?

"I repeat to you for the third and last time, that my quarrel is not with the citizens of the South, but solely with Rigaud, inasmuch as he is disobedient and insubordinate; whom I wish to bring back to his duties, that he may submit to the authority of a chief whom he can no longer disown. You ought not to have supported in his misdeeds a proud soldier who evidently raised the standard of revolt. You ought to have left me free to act, since I had a right to reprimand and even to punish him. This Rigaud knew well; but, too haughty to bow before the organs of the law, he has employed every means to seduce you and to retain you as accomplices. Consult your conscience; put away all prejudices; you will then easily know that Rigaud has desired to drive into revolt all men of color, in order to make them his partisans and coöperators. I need not remind you of the means he has taken for the purpose, and the resources he has employed to deceive you all. You know as well as I, perhaps better than I, his destructive projects, and all he has attempted to put them into execution; he pretended to command blacks and whites without being willing to be commanded by them. Yet the law is equal for all. Painful experience ought to have torn from your eyes the veil which hides the brink of the precipice. Give, then, close attention to what you are about to do, and the danger which you still run. Reflect on the perils and the calamities which threaten you, and hasten to prevent them. I am kind, I am humane, I open to you my fatherly arms. Come, all of you; I will receive you all; no less those of the South than those of the West, and of the North, who, gained over by Rigaud, have deserted your firesides, your wives, your children, to place yourselves at his side. And Rigaud himself,—that ambitious man,—if he had followed the advice which I gave him, to submit to his lawful superiors,—would he not now be tranquil and peaceful in the bosom of his family? Would he not be firm and untroubled in the command which was intrusted to him? But, mastered by deadly passions, Rigaud has dug a gulf at your feet; he has laid snares which you could not avoid. He wished to have you as partisans in his revolt; and to succeed in his object he has employed falsehood and seduction. If you carefully examine this artful but very impolitic conduct you cannot but declare that Rigaud does not love his color, and that he had rather sacrifice it to his pride and ambition than labor for its happiness by good example and wise counsels. And in truth, citizens, the greater number of those whom he has misled have perished, either in battle, or on the scaffold. Must not the others who persist in this revolt expect a similar fate if they abjure not their culpable error?

You may be well assured that if humanity did not direct the actions of a chief attached to his country as well as to his fellow-citizens, and more disposed to pardon than to punish, the calamity would be still greater. It belongs to you to prevent its augmentation. In consequence, I invite you, citizens, to open your eyes and to give serious attention to the future. Reflect on the disasters which may ensue from longer obstinacy. Submit to lawful authority, if you wish to preserve the South untouched. Save your families and your property.

"But if, contrary to my expectation, you continue to support the revolt raised and propagated by Rigaud, in vain will you reckon on the fortifications he has constructed. The army of Toussaint L'Ouverture, led by generals whose bravery you know, will assail you, and you will be conquered. Then, not without grief, and in spite of my efforts, shall I see that you have been the unhappy victims of the pride and ambition of a single man. I will say more. Desiring to put an end to the evils which have already too long afflicted this unfortunate colony, and wishing to prove to the French nation that I have done everything for the safety and happiness of my fellow-citizens, if Rigaud—though the author of these troubles—presents himself in good faith, and without stratagem, and acknowledges his fault, I will still receive him. But if Rigaud persists, and if he refuses to profit by my offer, do you, fathers, mothers, families,—do you all come. I will receive you with open arms. The father of the prodigal son received his child after he had repented."

This merciful invitation was not without effect on the population of the South. Rigaud himself, however, had gone too far to return. He was committed to the rebellion, and felt both compelled and disposed to abide the result. In order to counteract the loss of Jacmel, and the appeal of Toussaint, he made extraordinary exertions to raise in mass the population under his sway. On his side, L'Ouverture prepared to prosecute his advantages and terminate the disastrous war.

CHAPTER XII.

Toussaint endeavors to suppress the slave-trade in Santo-Domingo, and
thereby incurs the displeasure of Roume, the representative of France
— He overcomes Rigaud — Bonaparte, now First Consul, sends Commissioners to the island — End of the war in the South.

BUT Toussaint L'Ouverture found troubles and hindrances in an unexpected quarter. During the fratricidal war which deluged the South with blood, the horrible traffic of the slave-trade was revived on the east of the island. This commerce, originated by Jean François and Biassou, continued after their disappearance from the political scene, and went on constantly increasing. Young blacks, stolen in the North were conveyed to the city of Saint Domingo, where they were shipped for Porto Rico and Havanah, there to bear the yoke of slavery. Many of the old officers of Jean François pursued this as their only means of subsistence.

Aware that representations had in vain been made against these barbarities at the court of Madrid, and indignant that slavery, when nearly extinguished in its old form, should be revived in a new and even worse one, Toussaint wrote (Dec. 25, 1800), from the walls of Jacmel to the Agent, Roume, urging him, as the only effectual means of putting a stop to the evil, to take possession of the Spanish part of the island, conformably to treaty. Under the pretext that it was necessary to await the arrival of some European troops, Roume postponed the execution of the request. Toussaint was too versed in politics not to be aware that the ostensible postponement was in reality a refusal. He also became aware that Roume's adviser was one who owed no good-will to himself. That person, being invited to give an account of his conduct, emigrated to Porto Rico, —

justifying the suspicion that he had interested motives for promoting the continuance of the infamous traffic.

This event, in which L'Ouverture appears to fresh advantage,* and acted in agreement with the general tenor of his public life, occasioned an estrangement between him and Roume. The Agent had conceived the plan of conquering the English possessions in the West Indies. On an enterprise of such a nature and magnitude, he ought to have consulted, and, if he were willing, employed, the Commander-in-chief. But, either to show his independence of Toussaint L'Ouverture, or to put a public insult on him, he passed by that General, and confided to Marshall Bese the command of an expedition against Jamaica. In order to pave the way, he sent into the island two men of determined character, — a white and a mulatto. Those emissaries were denounced, taken, and hanged. The event interfered with Toussaint's operations; for the English captured a flotilla which he intended for the blockade of Jacmel. From this time, there existed a rupture between Roume and Toussaint. Criminations were exchanged. Each threw impediments in the way of the other. Toussaint could not regard Roume as a sincere friend of his race. Roume affected to believe that Toussaint had sympathies in favor of the English, with whom France was at war. At last, Roume demanded a vessel to convey him to France.

As soon as Toussaint had become master of Jacmel, he proceeded to the Cape, and in an interview with the Agent, reproached him, in the presence of his staff, with being an enemy to the colony and to the liberty of the blacks. He further required him to give an order for the occupation of the East, — resolved to put down the slave-trade, of which that was the centre. Roume refused compliance. The consequence was, that he apprehended the Agent, and sent him to prison. The expedient prevailed. The order was given. Toussaint dispatched General Agé to Santo Domingo, and returned to finish the war in the South. A regular campaign was begun. The rebels were defeated, and abandoned several posts, the retention of which was indispensable to their safety. Rigaud saw his star grow pale. Most of his superior officers abandoned him. Desertion spread through the ranks. On the other side, Toussaint appeared amid his troops, radiant with victory. He brought with him pecuniary resources. With these, he distributed pay among the soldiers; and so, while supplying their wants, gained their confidence, and excited their enthusiasm.

The two armies sat down opposite each other. Skirmishing began. Then serious *rencontres* took place. At last, issue was joined, and the revolters suffered a signal defeat. After this trial of strength, Rigaud might be troublesome, but he could not be formidable. Driven to desperation by his failures, he ordered his men to lay waste the country, and, to use his own words, to take such steps that " the trees should have their roots in the air." His old hands, thinned by war, sickness, and age, became Rigaud's sole reliance. On every side his cause was abandoned by the citizens and the civic authorities. Thus was he reduced to a leader of banditti. He saw his position, and issued this proclamation, — it was his last word to the public : —

" Considering the crisis in which the Department is, owing to the unjust and inhuman war carried on against it by the traitor Toussaint L'Ouverture, from whom no one must expect either safety or honor, I am obliged, in the position I hold, to take the only measures that remain to save the Department : considering, moreover, that proposals for peace, or for suspension of arms, directly concern the executive power, and that, in all cases, it is to the chief of the armed force of the Department that the right belongs of proposing peace or suspending arms, because he ought to seize the moment favorable for proposals of the kind, which, if made in critical junctures, and by those who have not the means of putting a stop to the evil, may imbolden the enemy, and cause calamities he would have avoided.

" For now a year this war has been going on; the popular bodies and the pretended friends of peace have taken no step to stop its course. At the present, when the enemy has had some success, and when terror has taken possession of feeble and timid minds, they fancy that a monster thirsting for human blood, an ungrateful wretch, a traitor toward the Republic, his benefactor, the devastator of Saint-Domingo, the executioner of the parish of Jacmel, the persecutor of all the French Agents, — finally, the slave of the English, — that he only can grant a peace or a suspension of arms. Citizens of the Southern Department, undeceive yourselves, if you think that anything else than arms can save you, while you wait for the intervention of the French Government, to whom those differences between the South and the other departments have been referred. Be well assured, my fellow-citizens, that I have your tranquillity and your happiness too much at heart not to seize all opportunities to procure for you peace or a suspension of arms; and, if the enemy adhere not to the proposals which, in proper time and place, I shall think it my duty to make to him, I shall know how, with the aid of my brave comrades, to make war on him even to extinction. Resume your courage. If he is powerful in numbers and resources, your fellow-citizens, composing the Southern army, possess courage and honor, and will find means to secure your safety.

" Under these circumstances, and employing the powers confided to me, I make these provisional arrangements, which are to be punctually executed; and accordingly ordain: —

" Article 1. The municipal government of the South shall for the future restrict themselves to the simple but useful functions of verifying births, marriages, and deaths; but all municipal deliberations, all assemblies, as well as deputations to the enemy, are interdicted. The municipalities shall only lay before me the wishes of their fellow-citizens, to which I will give replies.

" Article 2. Parochial assemblies may take place after permission has been obtained from the commander of the Southern Department.

" Article 3. Before legal permission is given, if there are meetings, whether of individuals or of parishes, in the cities, or in the country, martial law shall be forthwith proclaimed, and the chief of the armed force of the district is authorized to put his troops in movement to put down the said meetings; he shall begin with mild measures, and then employ severity, if he is forced to it.

"Article 4. The greatest vigilance shall be observed toward the disturbers of the public peace, and against secret disorganizers; the proprietors shall be protected, and their property shall be respected. The national armed police shall be in permanent activity in the interior, and those who shall be denounced for any crime against order and safety shall be apprehended and tried by a council of war, and punished according to the laws."

This manifesto, the spirit of which is even worse than its logic and its grammar, served only to show how undone Rigaud was, and how necessary that all who had any regard for themselves or the public good should abandon the desperate gladiator. His bands, however, were unwilling to yield. Blood, therefore, flowed in streams. The old men of the South are said still to shudder when they think of that conflict, which they designate "the war of the knife," thus showing to what extreme means the combatants resorted in their deadly hatred and murderous strife. The proclamation was scarcely anything more than the half-articulate words of a man who was staggering to his fall. Two more serious conflicts tried, and lost, and Rigaud's star went down below the horizon.

While, during the weeks and months of a long year, these frightful scenes of mutual carnage had been covering one of the finest parts of Hayti with corpses and ruins, the Directory in the mother country, too much occupied with its own divisions and party interests, gave no attention to the distracted colony. A change was at hand. Bonaparte, hastening from Egypt, overturned the Directory, and snatched the reins of power. Having taken his seat, he called around him (Dec. 2, 1799,) those who were thought to be conversant with the condition of the colony, in order to discuss the means of restoring peace within its borders. The representatives of Toussaint and of Rigaud were alike heard. Shortly after, a decree was issued, by which

Vincent, Raymond, and Michel were deputed to Hayti, in order to carry thither the Consular Constitution and a proclamation addressed to the inhabitants. Rigaud was recalled to France. Toussaint L'Ouverture was confirmed in his post as General-in-chief.

The proclamation was far from inspiring confidence or promoting tranquillity among the blacks, since it postponed and deferred to another legislative act the promulgation of the laws which were to govern Hayti. Michel, dissatisfied with the bravery of Toussaint L'Ouverture, returned into France. Raymond, whose mulatto's skin made him an object of suspicion, was ordered to remain at the Cape. Vincent alone was received with confidence. He presented to the Commander-in-chief the new Constitution, a letter written from the Minister of Marine, and the proclamation of the Consuls. In the proclamation were these words: "Brave blacks, remember that the French Republic has given you liberty, and that it only can cause that liberty to be respected." These words, it was ordered, should be inscribed in letters of gold on all the flags of the colonial national guard. Toussaint manifested no haste either to publish the proclamation or embroider the sentence on the colors. How could he promulgate a known falsehood? The Republic had not given freedom to the blacks. The blacks, under their able leader, had extorted freedom from the hands of their masters. Toussaint, who was well informed of the views and intrigues regarding the colony which were nourished in Paris, knew that his ruin had been resolved on before the self-elevation of Bonaparte to the Consulship. Had the ill-feeling passed away? Why, then, had not the First Consul written to him under his own signature? Distrust and disquietude prevailed in the relations of L'Ouverture and the representatives of the new Government in France. It is true that Rigaud was disowned, but Toussaint was not cordially embraced; nor were the rights of the blacks frankly recognized and legally settled.

As soon as he had given audience to Vincent, Toussaint

L'Ouverture set off for the seat of the not yet wholly terminated war. After a few days, he sent for Vincent, in order that the chief civil and military powers should be on the spot. In the hope of bringing the business to an amicable termination, the General induced Vincent, accompanied by a black man and a man of color, to go on a deputation to the revolters, who yet stood out. He put into the hands of the deputies an act of amnesty in favor of all who had taken part in the war, not even Rigaud excepted. The deputies reached Cayes, where Rigaud held his headquarters. The city, exhausted by so long and so disastrous a conflict, heard with pleasure of the object of their mission. Rigaud was quickly informed of the arrival of the deputies. On reading the dispatch, he flew into the most violent passion. The outburst was so violent as to endanger Vincent's life. That Agent, however, was the bearer of a letter from Rigaud's son, to whom he had shown the kindest attentions, and who declared to his father the gratitude he felt in return. The mulatto chief eagerly threw his eyes over the lines. All at once his wrath ceased. But the warrior soon overcame the father. Vexation took the place of vengeance. He would not live; he could not endure to live. Again and again he tried to kill himself. At length he was calmed down, and ere many days he quitted Saint Domingo for the shores of France. Thither he was accompanied by Petion and some of his principal officers. The other mulatto chiefs emigrated to various parts of the archipelago of the Antilles.

Thus terminated the war in the South. With that war every obstacle to the freedom of the blacks disappeared. One after the other had hindrances and opposition been swept out of the way by the strong hand of Toussaint L'Ouverture, the negro champion of the negro race. Against the colonists, against the Spaniards, against the English, against the mulattoes, against the French representatives, and in a measure against blacks themselves, had he, by prudence, perseverance, and prowess, by singleness of aim, by unity of purpose, by personal efforts the most astounding, and a union of skill, caution, and daring rarely equalled, vindicated the freedom of the Africans in Hayti. There was yet a stronger power. Religion, in its relation to the grand work he had undertaken, rose in his breast to enthusiasm. In some sense he was, he believed, God's envoy and God's agent in the fierce and sanguinary struggle. In that conviction he found light and strength which had, to him, the vividness and the authority of what, in a qualified sense, may be called inspiration. Here was the grand secret of his success. He has himself given an outline of his career, which may appropriately find insertion in this place. " At the beginning of the troubles of Saint Domingo, I felt that I was destined to great things. When I received this Divine intimation I was four-and-fifty years of age; I could neither read nor write; I had some Portuguese coins; I gave them to a subaltern of the regiment of the Cape, and, thanks to him, in a few months I could sign my name and read with ease. The revolution of Saint Domingo was taking its course. I saw that the whites could not endure, because they were divided and because they were overpowered by numbers; I congratulated myself that I was a black man. A necessity was laid on me to commence my career. I went over to the Spanish side, where the first troops of my color had found an asylum and protection. That asylum and protection ended in nothing. I was delighted to see Jean François make himself a Spaniard when the powerful French Republic proclaimed the general freedom of the blacks. A secret voice said to me, ' Since the blacks are free, they need a chief, and it is I who must be that chief, foretold by the Abbé Raynal.' Under this feeling I joyously returned to the service of France. France and the voice of God have not deceived me." These words are reported from memory. As depending on the ear and the tongue, they must be received only in their general tenor. Our narrative, which rests on satisfactory vouchers, shows that, long prior to the age of fifty-four, Toussaint could at least read. If taken as indicating the defectiveness of his scholarship even at the time when he began his task, they are, doubtless, substantially correct; and their testimony goes to confirm the unquestionable fact, that not by ordinary human appliances and aids did this extraordinary genius accomplish his meritorious and noble work.*

* The instruction which Toussaint received in boyhood is testified by his son Isaac, in his interesting Notes to the Memoirs he wrote, "Sur l'Expédition des Français sous le Consulat de Bonaparte," appended to Metral's Histoire de l'Expédition des Français à Saint Domingue," Paris, 1825. According to Isaac's testimony, Toussaint when a boy learnt something of Latin and geometry (p. 326.) While yet he was in the service of Spain, Isaac says of him, — " Without having topographical maps of those countries, after the example of captains of the ancient world, — Lucullus, Pompey, Cæsar, — Toussaint made one ; he laid down on paper, according to information given him by people who knew the districts, their extent, their respective distances, the direction of the mountains and of the rivers, and everything remarkable, such as defiles, &c. &c." (p. 329). The skill to form such a map, besides involving reading and writing, gives countenance to the intimation of Isaac Toussaint, that his father had some acquaintance with geometry as well as drawing. Doubtless, the father's scholarship was always quite rudimental.

CHAPTER XIII.

Toussaint L'Ouverture inaugurates a better future — Publishes a general amnesty — Declares his task accomplished in putting an end to civil strife, and establishing peace on a sound basis — Takes possession of Spanish Hayti, and stops the slave-trade — Welcomes back the old colonists — Restores agriculture — Recalls prosperity — Studies personal appearance on public occasions — Simplicity of his life and manners — His audiences and receptions — Is held in general respect.

ON the first of August, 1800, L'Ouverture made his triumphal entrance into Cayes. All official honors were rendered to him. Hearts on every side beat with enthusiastic gratitude toward the general benefactor. He ascended the pulpit and proclaimed the oblivion of wrongs. He complained only of the absence of the mulattoes. The sense of their discomfiture was too recent. Two of their chiefs, however, went to meet him afterward, and he received them in a cordial manner. His aim was to direct men's minds from the dark past to the bright future. On the 17th of the month he put forth his proclamation.

"Citizens, — All the events which have taken place at Saint Domingo during the civil war occasioned by Rigaud are of a nature to merit public attention.

"Now that they are no longer likely to be renewed, it is of importance to the prosperity of the colony, and to the happiness of the inhabitants, to draw the curtain on the past, in order that we may be occupied exclusively in repairing the evils which, of necessity, have resulted from the intestine war brought forth by the pride and ambition of an individual.

"A part of the citizens of St. Domingo have been deceived because, too credulous, they did not sufficiently suspect the snares which had been laid to draw them into their criminal designs. Others have acted in these circumstances according to the impulsion of their hearts. Moved by the same principles as the chief of the revolt, they considered it beneath them to be commanded by a black man. Him they judged it necessary to get rid of, at whatever cost, and they spared nothing to succeed in their object. The ambition of their chief led him to make the country his own. His satellites had at heart nothing so much as to give him aid. For their reward he assigned to them aforehand the offices they were to occupy. They are disappointed in their expectation; and in my quality as the victor, wishing and very ardently desiring to promote the happiness of my native land, penetrated by what is set forth in the Lord's Prayer, 'Forgive us our transgressions as we forgive those who transgress against us,' I have published a proclamation by which I grant a general amnesty. That proclamation is known to you. It has produced the happy result which I promised myself. The Southern Department has returned to its obedience to the laws. Let us forget that bad men had led it away from duty to gratify their criminal passions, and let us now consider only as brothers those who, through their easy faith, dared to turn their arms against the flag of the Republic, and against their lawful chief. I have ordered all citizens to return to their several parishes to enjoy the benefits of this amnesty. Citizens, not less generous than myself, let your most precious moments be employed in causing the past to be forgotten; let all my fellow-citizens swear never to recall the past; let them receive their misled brethren with open arms; and let them in future be on their guard against the traps of bad men.

" Civil and military authorities, my task is accomplished. It now belongs to you to see that harmony is no more troubled. Do not allow the least reproach on the part of any one against those who went astray but have returned to their duty. Notwithstanding my proclamation, keep an eye on the bad, and do not spare them. The man is unjust, he is inclined to evil rather than good. Firmly put down his perverse designs, and never close your eyes on his conduct and his proceedings. Honor should guide you all. The interests of our country require it; its prosperity needs peace, true and confiding peace. Such a peace must be your work. On you solely now depends public tranquillity in Saint Domingo. Take no rest until you have secured it. I expect this from your courage and from your devotion to the French Republic."

The spirit of moderation, the spirit of mercy itself dictated these words. Reference to the late troubles was prescribed by a rigid sense of duty. The reference made in no way exceeds what the occasion demanded, and falls very short of what the evil inflicted by the revolt would have justified. It was of absolute necessity to characterize Rigaud. But how different the tone of Toussaint L'Ouverture compared with the injurious epithets lavished in his proclamation by that mulatto leader against his lawful chief! But even for the bad, L'Ouverture had forgiveness. How terrible a punishment might he now have inflicted on the men of color! Had he been open to the prejudices of caste and skin, he would have let loose on them the desire of retribution, and the thirst for revenge. One word of his, and the race would have been nearly extirpated. Not by their forbearance was he kept from uttering that word; nor by their softened feelings toward the negroes; nor by a confidence that they would no more attempt disturbance; but solely by a regard to his religious duty, and a manly confidence in the right and the merciful.

"My task is accomplished." And yet he had obtained nothing for himself. The military position he held, as it was won by the sword, so was it necessary to the work he had performed. It was a burden rather than a recompense, — a duty and an obligation instead of an honor. Not for himself, but for his country, did he hold the command of the armies of Saint Domingo. "My task is accomplished." It *is*, noble black, — it *is* accomplished, and accomplished well, if only thou lookest to the weal of Hayti. But hast thou no object of thine own? Opposition can no longer hold up its head. Thy foes are prostrate. Every eye is turned to thee. Every heart is fixed on thee.

Hast thou nothing to ask for thyself? The crown and sceptre of Hayti? Nay, frown not. Other successful warriors have taken regal titles as their due. Nor need thou fear opposition. The Agent is weak and disesteemed. Bonaparte is reaping laurels in Italy. England will be prompt to aid thee. Then consider how much thy race needs elevation. What could so much raise them from the dust? Yes, thou must, as thou canst, be King of Hayti; and thy name, glorious for its military deeds, will be more glorious still as the first of a long line of illustrious sovereigns of negro blood.

Instead of troubling himself and others in arrangements for placing on his head the bauble of a crown, Toussaint L'Ouverture turned his attention to the condition of the country. Hayti was not yet wholly in the power of France. Though formally ceded to the French, the eastern part of the isle remained under Spanish rule. Not sincere in his wishes to take possession of Spanish Hayti, Roume had sent forces so inconsiderable, that they were easily defeated. On their return, he revoked his order for its occupation. On learning the fact, L'Ouverture was indignant. Was slavery, then, in its worst form, to be established and acknowledged in Hayti? Was the Government to be an assenting, if not a concurring, party? And were all his own labors and sacrifices to be thus frustrated?—frustrated by low self-interest and base intrigues? Could he, who had conquered freedom for the negroes, allow their children to be kidnapped and transported to strange countries and foreign lands, there to be degraded and ruined? Impossible! Yet such was the alternative if Roume retained possession of the civil government; for he had tried what could be done in this matter with Roume by argument and moral influence. The effort had failed, and now Roume had availed himself of his absence, and his absorption in military duties, to reverse a policy in which they had in council come to an understanding. Besides, he had proved himself unfaithful to France, by virtually surrendering a portion of his rightful possessions. In such hands, power could not be safely trusted. And, doubtless, the Home Government would thank him if Toussaint vindicated his rights and secured its territory.

Actuated by those considerations, Toussaint L'Ouverture arrested Roume, and sent him to Dondon. On the occasion, he issued this address : —

" Toussaint L'Ouverture, General-in-chief of his fellow-citizens.

" The duties of the office held by Citizen Roume were, in his quality of representative of the French Government, to consecrate his moral and physical faculties to the happiness of Saint Domingo and to its prosperity. Very far from doing so, he took counsel only of the intriguers by whom he was surrounded, to sow discord amongst us, and to foment the troubles which have not ceased to agitate society. However, in spite of the calumnies which he has continually thrown out against myself, in his letters to France and Santo Domingo, he shall be protected from every penalty. But my respect for his character must not prevent me from taking the proper steps in order to deprive him of the power of again plotting against the tranquillity which, after so many revolutionary concussions, I have just had the happiness to establish. In consequence, and in order to isolate him from the intriguers who have kept him in their shackles, and to respond to the complaints made in respect to him by all the parishes, the brigadier-general Moyse will supply the said Citizen Roume with two carriages and a sure escort, which, with all respect due to his character, will conduct him to the village of Dondon, where he will remain until the French Government shall recall him to render an account of his administration.

" At Cap-Français, 5 Frimaire (26 November), the ninth year (1800) of the French Republic, one and indivisible.

" The General-in-chief, TOUSSAINT L'OUVERTURE."

Roume remained a prisoner at Dondon for several months, and then was permitted by L'Ouverture to return to France by way of the United States.

11*

As soon as he had removed the impediment, Toussaint L'Ouverture took effectual steps for putting down the slave-trade, and occupying the east of the island. After a few shots, he entered Santo Domingo on the 2d of January, 1801, at the head of 10,000 men, and hoisted the flag of the French Republic on its ramparts, to the salvo of two-and-twenty cannon. He was received at the mansion-house by the chief authorities, who wished him to take, in the name of the Holy Trinity, an oath to govern with wisdom. "Such a course would be proper," he replied, "in an officer appointed by the Court of Madrid, but I am the servant of the Republic. Therefore, I am unable to do what you ask; but I swear solemnly before God, who hears the oath, that I forget the past, and that my watchings and my cares shall have no other object than to render the Spaniards, now become Frenchmen, contented and happy." On the utterance of these words, Don Garcia, the governor, handed him the keys of the city. "I accept them," said Toussaint, "in the name of the French Republic;" and then turning toward the assembly, he added, with an humble voice, "Let us go and thank the Author of all things for having crowned with the greatest success our enterprise, prescribed by treaties and the laws of the Republic." Followed by the Governor and all the Spanish authorities, he went to the cathedral, where a *Te Deum* was chanted in token of gratitude to God.

Thus, from Cape Samana in the East to Cape Tiburon in the West, the power of Toussaint L'Ouverture was everywhere established and acknowledged. Knowing the favorable effects produced on the popular mind by the progress of distinguished personages in the parts under their administration, Toussaint L'Ouverture traversed the Spanish territory and visited the principal places. He was everywhere received with the acclamations of the people, the merry peal of bells, and the thunders of cannon. The clergy, barefooted, came on all sides to give him welcome. He treated them with profound respect. Within a few days he was master of the obedience of the Spaniards as much as of the confidence of the blacks.

The union of the Spanish to the French part of Hayti procured reciprocal advantages, the effects of which soon became apparent. The French gained facility in acquiring horses and mules for the cultivation of the soil, and the Spaniards found enormous gain in the exportation of its animals, flocks, and horned cattle. The black regiments, restrained by Toussaint's powerful hand, had done but little damage in the invasion; and those who were left in garrison put large sums of money in circulation. The elements of French administration, which followed the troops, bestowed on the country new principles and sources of industry and wealth. Magnificent roads were formed. Carriages were then for the first time introduced. Even the horses, under the influence of Toussaint's example, improved their pace. Distances were abridged; time was saved; the minds of the people were awakened from torpor; activity universally prevailed, and commerce and riches began to abound. Amid the general excitement, prosperity, and hope, the enthusiasm toward its cause became greater every day, and Toussaint's name was pronounced with blessings by all tongues.

Having given the command of Santo Domingo to his brother Paul, who had risen by merit to the rank of brigadier-general, Toussaint L'Ouverture returned to the French part of Hayti, and forthwith applied his mind to the condition and wants of the island.

He was thoroughly acquainted with the theatre on which he had to act, and the character of the people subject to his power. He took the wisest measures to develop the powers of the former, and to gain the confidence of the latter. Aware that he had a mass of prejudices to overcome, and the most tangled web of interests to set in order, he mingled discretion with zeal; and, while aiming at the general weal, forgot not the deference that might conciliate, nor failed in the bland and courteous manners that might win. The old colonists he welcomed to his presence without familiarity, and showed respect even to their prejudices, so far as the public good would permit.

The steward of the plantation on which he had himself been a slave vegetated in the United States. L'Ouverture, being informed of the fact, wrote him an invitation to return to Hayti, to put himself "at the head of the interests of their good old masters." The letter, conceived in a friendly and urgent tone, brought back the steward. Toussaint gave him an interview, and among other things said to him, "Return to the plantation; be just and inflexible; see that the blacks do their duty, in order to add, by your prosperity, to the prosperity of the land."

The discontinuance of the war led to the resumption of agriculture. The change from the musket to the hoe was of course gradual; but such was the influence and such the determination of the great black, that erelong the rich cultivable districts began to put on a smiling aspect, promising riches as well as abundance. Had the peace continued, the promise would have been realized in the fullest degree. Forthwith, however, did the culture of the soil, besides providing for the wants of the inhabitants, furnish the public treasury with sufficient resources. Intelligence of the returning prosperity reached foreign lands. The colonists who were scattered up and down in those lands saw a ray of hope, and, notwithstanding what they had undergone in Saint Domingo, notwithstanding their dislike of the predominance of the blacks, they invited and gladly accepted permission to return home and resume possession of their estates. Their letters, coming from various countries, and unanimously expressing confidence in the integrity and the power of the General-in-chief, as well as in the justice and excellence of his administration, greatly contributed to strengthen his hands and confirm his authority. Scarcely could a more satisfactory or a more striking proof be given of the claim of Toussaint to our respect and admiration than is found in the readiness with which this class of men embarked their all in the vessel which he commanded.

The political evils and civil wars that had afflicted Saint Domingo, in causing the expatriation of proprietors, had in many cases occasioned the loss of traces to the succession. Under Toussaint's orders, the property so circumstanced was secured to military chiefs, and was thus restored to cultivation and productiveness. At the same time, regulations were issued by which the laborers on the estates became a sort of co-proprietors. He had, aforetime, thrown his protection over emigrants, and thereby had brought on himself difficulty and suspicion. He now took into his service subaltern officers of emigrant regiments, and offered protection to those who were unwilling to join his forces. Disregarding color and position in his appointments, he sought in his servants and fellow-laborers for those who were most fitted for the duties of the several offices. If his favor was less marked toward any, it was toward those of his own blood; not because he loved them less, but because, having their confidence, he could employ in relation to them a freedom of word and action which might have been misunderstood by others. With his strong and vivid religious sentiments, he was naturally prompted to pay special regard to the priests, and to the interests of religion in general. Nor, environed as he was by men whose senses were the avenues to their affections, did he neglect personal appearance. Studious in his attire, he surrounded himself with a numerous guard, in which were names distinguished in the olden time. When he went forth in public, he was accompanied by a splendid retinue, which fixed and dazzled all eyes. Surrounded by a guard of from fifteen to eighteen hundred men, brilliantly clad, and having for his own personal use a stud containing hundreds of horses, he appeared before the eyes of the people in the exterior of a prince. But, beneath this imposing show, he himself studied the utmost simplicity. Always temperate, he often carried moderation to abstinence. His iron frame received strength chiefly from the deep and full resources of his vigorous mind. Master of his soul, he had no difficulty in mastering his body. While partaking of none but the most frugal diet, with water for his drink, and vegetable preparations for his meat, he rarely slept more than two hours. The whole enegy of his life was absorbed and consumed in the great task which he had undertaken, and which, in truth, demanded more vital power than even he had to bestow. Though advanced in life, he was incessantly in movement, and travelled with a rapidity which defied calculation and excited amazement. Seeing everything with his own eyes, he had little need to rely on the reports of others; and he at once promoted his independence and augmented his power by deriving his policy and his plans from his own knowledge and his own meditations. Little should we expect to see such a person addicted to the labors of the cabinet. Yet, in replying, by means of several secretaries, to two or three hundred letters daily, he seemed to experience a pleasure as lively as that enjoyed by other men in the satisfaction of the senses.

As the Governor of the land, Toussaint L'Ouverture felt it necessary to keep up some kind of state. Like other chief magistrates, he had his receptions of ceremony, as well as his less formal audiences. The union of French vanity and negro love of parade in the foremost people made him feel the importance of requiring due attention to appearances and etiquette. Hence, he instituted what bears the name of "circles," at which all who were invited were expected to be present. These circles were of two kinds,—the greater and the less. To the greater, formal invitations were given. Toussaint himself appeared in the assemblies in the undress uniform of a general officer. His simple attire, in the midst of surrounding brilliancy, contrasted favorably with the dignified tone which he knew how to maintain. When he presented himself, all the company, females as well as males, arose from their seats. Attentive even to the proprieties, he showed his disapproval of any exposure of the person in female dress. On one occasion, he was seen to throw his handkerchief over the bare bosom of a lady, saying, "Modesty is the best charm of the sex." After having made the tour of the hall, and spoken to everybody, he withdrew by the door at which he entered, bowing right and left to the company. The less circles were public audiences, which took place every evening. At these, Toussaint L'Ouverture appeared clad like the ancient proprietors when on their plantations. All the citizens entered the grand saloon, and were, irrespectively of rank and position, addressed by the Governor as convenience served. After having gone round the room, he retired, and took with him into a small apartment in front of his bed-chamber, which he used as a study, the persons with whom he wished to converse more freely and more at length. The greater number of these were the chief whites of the colony. There, seating himself, he requested all others to be seated. Then he proceeded to talk with them of France, of his children, of religion, of his old masters, and of God's grace in giving him liberty, and granting him means for discharging the duties of the post in which he had been placed by the mother country. He also conversed of the progress of agriculture, of commerce, and never of political concerns. He questioned each respecting his own private affairs, and of his family, and appeared to take an interest in the several matters. With mothers, he spoke of their children, and inquired whether they attended to their religious education; and the young he would sometimes briefly examine in their catechism. When he wished to put an end to the audience, he arose and bowed. The company then retired, being attended by him to the door. As they left, he appointed times for special interviews with those who made the request. Then he shut himself up with his private secretaries, and commonly continued his labors far into the night.

In this practical regard to show and parade, L'Ouverture may have been influenced by his own personal defects. Small in person, he was of a repulsive aspect, and, having a difficult utterance, he spoke with as little elegance as grammar. Yet his were words of power, for they came from a strong soul and were the heralds of a resolute will. A man of few words and powerful imagination, he sometimes uttered his ideas in para_ bles — the rather that in such a form he could the more effect- ually imprint them on the minds of the rude natures with which he had to deal. On more occasions than one he took a glass vase, and, having filled it with grains of black maize, he put therein some grains of white maize, and said, "You are the black maize; the whites who would enslave you are the white maize." He then shook the glass, and, placing it before their eyes, he cried, as if inspired, "See the white ones only here and there."

The army Toussaint L'Ouverture kept under the most vigorous discipline. Every breach of duty was severely punished. Even during the civil wars, plunder was restricted as much as possible. He was, however, adored by his soldiers.

Scarcely less was the veneration paid him by other members of Haytian life. He won and enjoyed the esteem of the colonists; he was valued highly by the ministers of religion; by the blacks he was regarded as a messenger of God. Even the mulattoes began to look to him with hope and respect.

The confidence which Toussaint inspired soon produced good effects in the colony. The lands once more cultivated, and cultivated under judicious regulations, became productive, and, as of old, poured forth abundance and wealth. With the spread of industry and the increase of riches, population, which had been greatly diminished in the wars, recovered its impulse and augmented its numbers. A large and prosperous people restored the churches, which had been burnt or allowed to become dilapidated, decorated the cities with fine buildings, enriched the public treasury, cultivated the arts, and erelong indulged in luxury. The general intelligence was raised, and manners were refined. Human nature vindicated itself against his calumniators; for, in a short time, after a period of frightful wasting, the black State of Hayti could endure a comparison with the higher forms of white and European civilization. There was at the Cape, under the name of the Hôtel de la République, an inn, the exterior and interior splendor of which scarcely yielded to the richest establishments of the kind in any part of the world. It was frequented by the principal blacks and by the Americans of the continent. There mere etiquette was unknown; the most perfect equality prevailed. At the same table sat private individuals and the heads of the State, officers of every rank, men of all conditions. It was frequently visited by L'Ouverture, who took his place, without preference, in any vacant seat; for he often said that distinction of rank ought to exist only in the moment of public service.

Travellers who visited the island at the beginning of the present century, warriors who played a part in the events of that epoch, agree in declaring that in the society of Saint Domingo the men were polite and the women easy and elegant; that the relations between the sexes lacked neither attraction nor dignity, and that the prejudices of color seem to have lost their former power. The theatre came into vogue; the greater number of the new actors were blacks, and some of them gave proof of talent in comedy and in pantomime. A taste for music became general; the guitar was specially cultivated. Men of negro and mulatto blood not only formed the bulk of the population, but occupied the higher positions. Even the most important duties of the administration were in their hands. Yet life went forward with ease and efficiency. Religion was honored. Morals were at least not inferior to what they are in white society. The arts were cultivated. The elegancies of life were not unknown. Among men and women who had but recently quitted the brutalizing condition of servitude, an ability and a refinement were observed, which you sometimes look for in vain among men who have the reputation of being highly cultivated.

12

CHAPTER XIV.

Toussaint L'Ouverture takes measures for the perpetuation of the happy condition of Hayti, specially by publishing the draft of a Constitution in which he is named governor for life, and the great doctrine of *Free-trade* is explicitly proclaimed.

THIS happy condition had no guarantee of permanence. True, all was tranquil within the borders of Hayti. One after another had Toussaint L'Ouverture removed hindrances out of the way, until he had succeeded in establishing a universal accord. But would the harmony endure? Its continuance was essential to the full development of the resources of the colony; and, to all appearance, that continuance was the sole prerequisite. As yet, however, there had been no general recognition of the established order. If all were to work for the general good, all must concur in the formation and acknowledgment of a constitution by which the established order might be perpetuated.

In bringing that constitution into existence, and giving it the force of law, three powers must concur. These three powers were the inhabitants of Hayti, France, and Toussaint himself. Self-government was a recognized right of the colony. The concurrence of France was equally an admitted fact in the colonial government, and L'Ouverture held, under the authority of the mother country, the highest functions in the island. When the question of a constitution assumed a practical shape, it became important to determine with which of these three authorities the initiative should lie. Was the colony to look to France? That question involved another: was France sincere in her acknowledgment of negro freedom? France appeared unworthy of trust. The last dispatches on the matter of a code of laws for Hayti wore a suspicious aspect, and were generally disliked. And if France wished to give the colony a good code of laws, had she the power? How could the requisite knowledge be possessed by a legislature which sat thousands of miles distant from those who were to obey the laws? Metropolitan government for colonial dependencies is full of evils, arising not only from ignorance and incompetence, but intrigue and corruption. Besides, Bonaparte was now the sole legislative and the sole ruling power in France. The position which Louis XIV. had fancied himself to possess, when he declared himself to be the state, — "L'état, c'est moi," — the Corsican adventurer had fully realized. The ruling passion of Bonaparte was ambition; his means, resort to force. What had the colony to expect but a *coup d'état* similar to that which had just suppressed the Directory and concentrated all power in the hands of the First Consul? The thought is said to have disturbed the short hours of Toussaint's repose. The probability was, that the conqueror of Italy only waited the moment of necessary leisure, and that moment, as the event afterward showed, might shortly arrive. Undesirable was it, therefore, to leave the initiative with France. The colony itself must act. Indeed, the colony only could act with wisdom and effect. "But in so doing, the colony was setting up for independence." To take the first step in drawing up a constitution cannot be justly so characterized. A draft of a constitution was only a species of petition. Until sanctioned by legislation, it amounted to nothing more than a bill of rights. It did no more than say, "Here is a formal statement of what will suit us, what will consolidate and augment our existing weal, what we entreat you to send back with the seal of your solemn sanction." And were such a step a step toward independence, who can blame it? If the colony had acquired strength enough to run alone, why should it remain in leading-strings? Nay, the desire for independence, if cherished, was a worthy feeling. Such a desire showed that black men could appreciate liberty, and well deserved the degree of freedom they had already gained. The rather was a cautious approach to independence praiseworthy, because tokens were not wanting that Bonaparte, in his ambitious passions, had grown impatient of the ascendency of the great negro Haytian. Resolved to be master of the world, he could not endure a rival power, and watched his opportunity to establish his supremacy in the island. The rather was he desirous of establishing the exclusive rule of France there, because Hayti, he felt, could be made a bulwark for hostile operations against the English power in the West Indies.

Yet was the colony passively and quietly to await the blow? What was this but to invite the blow? Whereas, to propound a constitution, while it ought to give no offence, would prove that the Haytians were sensible alike of their rights and of their power. In the great issue, Toussaint had himself a problem to solve. If, as he had reason to fear, Bonaparte intended his overthrow, was he to submit without an effort? Was he not, as a prudent man and a wise legislator, to enter on such a course as seemed most likely to ward off the blow, and strengthen his own position? As to the necessity of his continuing to hold that position, he could not for a moment doubt. The retention of the position was indispensable to the continuance of the peace in the island. As all mountains had become plains before his energy and determination, so would all be undone if he were removed from the head of affairs; once more the smouldering fires of passion and prejudice would burst into a flame, and a war arise not less bloody and terrific than that which he had so recently brought to a happy conclusion. Yes; there, at the helm, had he been placed by the resistless stream of events, or what to him, nor without reason, seemed the hand of Providence; and there duty, in the clearest and loudest tones, called upon him to remain. This is, in substance, the feeling to which at this time he gave utterance in these terms: "I have taken my flight in the region of eagles; I must be prudent in alighting on the earth; I can be placed only on a rock; and that rock must be a constitutional government, which will secure me power so long as I shall be among men."

Yes; if in any case, certainly in Toussaint L'Ouverture's, was a constitutional dictatorship of indispensable necessity. Rightly did he interpret his position, and well did he understand his duties. This new Moses had brought his people out of Egyptian bondage, and must now give them a code of laws, over the execution of which, for the few remaining years of his life, it is his most solemn duty to watch. Such conduct asks no defence, and admits no excuse. It is positively and highly virtuous, and any other course would have been a betrayal of a sacred duty, a breach of a momentous trust.

Again the hour of temptation has come. The victorious general who commands universal obedience and enjoys universal respect may become a president or a sovereign. The good principle conquers; Satan is dismissed with a rebuke; the crown is refused; the presidency is deliberately chosen.

Does the reader think of Washington, who, when he might possibly have become a king, became a private citizen? We are not sure that Washington's means for establishing a throne in the midst of the high-minded republicans of the Anglo-Saxon race were equal to those which Toussaint possessed among the uncultured and recently liberated Haytians, whom nature made fond of parade, and custom had habituated to royalty. The greater the opportunity, the greater the temptation; nor can he be accounted the inferior man who overcame in the severer trial. Nor must it be forgotten, that while Washington could, with confidence and safety, leave his associates to their own well-tried and well-matured powers of self-government, L'Ouverture had, in comparision, but children to deal with and provide for. Would it have been either prudent or benevolent to retire from the oversight of those children at the very moment when they had ceased to do evil and were learning to do well? Clearly, duty, in the most solemn and emphatic tones, demanded the continuance of that fatherly care which had rescued those babes in intellect from impending ruin, and so far led them toward the attainment of individual strength and social excellence. Yes, Toussaint L'Ouverture, an eagle thou hast proved thyself to be; an eagle's eye shows thee distant but coming realities; may thine eagle's pinion bear thee above danger, and place thee, where thou longest to be, " on a rock," — the rock of a wisely-constituted and well-governed commonwealth! Then, like thy Hebrew prototype, when at last thou descriest the promised land, and while thou contemplatest its fertility and loveliness, thou mayest depart from " among men," falling to sleep in thy lofty eyrie, and buried on the mountain, which shall be at once thy sepulchre and thy monument.

We do not possess the materials to determine whether the idea of drawing up a constitution for Hayti originated with Toussaint L'Ouverture himself, or was presented to him as the proper course by his colonial advisers. The determination of the question is of the less consequence since, beyond a doubt, unanimity prevailed to a very great extent between the General-in-chief and the principal authorities and persons in the island. One party, and but one, evinced repugnance to the measure. The small number who represented the views of Bonaparte in the colony were naturally adverse to the constitution. At their head was Brigadier-General Vincent, who employed the influence which excellence of character justly gave him with L'Ouverture to turn him aside from the project. The effort proved nugatory.

Resolved to persevere in a course which his judgment approved, and his position required, Toussaint L'Ouverture, as possessing the highest authority in the island, called together a council to take into consideration the propriety of drawing up a constitution, and to determine what its provisions should be. The council consisted of nine members. The composition of this deliberative assembly displays the integrity of the General-in-chief. He might have formed it out of his officers. He might have given predominance in it to negro blood. These things, doubtless, he would have done, had he sought his own aggrandizement. But he chose its members among the men of property and intelligence. Of the nine members, eight were white proprietors, and one a mulatto; not a single black had a seat at the council-board. Even the purest patriotism might have required him to place himself at the head of the council. Its president was the white colonist Borgella, who had held the office of Mayor of Port-au-Prince. The constitution, carefully prepared by this council, was presented to Toussaint L'Ouverture, who, having approved it (May 19th, 1800), sent a copy by the hands of General Vincent to Europe. The draft was accompanied by the following letter, addressed to " Citizen Bonaparte, First Consul of the French Republic (16th July)."

" CITIZEN CONSUL:— The Minister of Marine, in the account which he has rendered to you of the political situation of this colony, which I have taken care to acquaint him with in the dispatches which I addressed to him, sent by the corvette *L'Enfant Prodigue*, will have submitted to you my proclamation, convening a central assembly, which, at the moment when the junction of the Spanish part to the French part had made of Saint Domingo one single country, subject to the same government, should fix its destinies by wise laws, framed with special reference to the localities and the characters of the inhabitants. I have now the satisfaction to announce to you, that the last hand has been put to that work, and that the salt is a constitution which promises happiness to the inhabitants of this colony, which has so long been unfortunate. I hasten to lay it before you for your approbation, and for the sanction of the Government I serve. With this view, I send to you Citizen Vincent, general director of fortifications at Saint Domingo, to whom I have confided this precious deposit. The Central Assembly, in the absence of laws, and considering the necessity which exists of substituting the rule of law for anarchy, having demanded that I should provisionally put it into execution, as promising to conduct the colony more rapidly toward prosperity, I have yielded to its desires; and this constitution has been welcomed by all classes of citizens with transports of joy, which will not fail to be manifested afresh, when it shall be sent back invested with the sanction of the Government. With salutations and profound respect.

" Toussaint L'Ouverture."

This constitution, which had been made public and accepted amid solemn formalities and universal joy, was worthy of the cause in which L'Ouverture had risked his life and employed the utmost of his strength. Proceeding on the basis that slavery was abolished and could never more exist in Saint Domingo, and that all men there born were free citizens of the French Republic, it provided that every one, whatever his color, was admissible to all employments, on the special ground that among the citizens there was no other distinction than the distinction of virtue and of ability. Establishing Roman Catholicism as the sole religion to be professed and protected, it recognized the sanctity of marriage by abolishing divorce. It required that agriculture should receive special encouragement, for which purpose measures were to be taken for the increase of the number of laborers. The reins of government it intrusted to one governor, to be appointed for the period of five years, with authority to prolong the term as a recompense for good conduct; and that " in consideration of the important services which General Toussaint L'Ouverture has rendered to the colony, he is named Governor for life, with power to appoint his successor."

One provision we have advisedly omitted in order to bring it into full relief. In a very short sentence the constitution declares *commerce free*. Thus free trade was first proclaimed by the negro chief of Hayti. Is any other proof necessary that Toussaint was more than a successful warrior? more than a social liberator? more than a disinterested patriot? His economical views were large and liberal. They were in advance of their age; how much in advance let the fact declare, that nearly a half a century had to elapse before even England obtained the boon which Hayti not only claimed but decreed.

Yet what was there in Toussaint L'Ouverture which may not be found in other negroes? His sole external advantage was that he received some rudimental instruction in the simple arts of reading and writing. Give that advantage to the myriads of blacks that now vegetate and pine in slavery in the United States, and other practical philosophers will appear among them to vindicate the race by wise laws as well as philanthropy and heroism. But " Oh, it is not safe." Safe? yes, much more safe than is the present course, which does but concentrate the lava of the volcano, which, at no distant day, will burst fort'n, unless precautionary measures are taken, and due preparations be made for lifting slaves into a condition fit for freedom. Surely this lesson is taught in the tenor of the preceding narrative.

BOOK II.

FROM THE FITTING OUT OF THE EXPEDITION BY BONA-
PARTE AGAINST SAINT DOMINGO TO THE SUB-
MISSION OF TOUSSAINT L'OUVERTURE.

CHAPTER I.

Peace of Amiens — Bonaparte contemplates the subjugation of Saint Domingo, and the restoration of slavery — Excitement caused by report
to that effect in the island — Views of Toussaint L'Ouverture on the
point.

THE year 1801 did not close without seeing the peace of
Amiens definitively concluded. By the treaty then signed,
France found herself confirmed in the possessions she had captured during the war, and at liberty to prosecute any enterprise which she might judge required by her position, or likely
to conduce to the confirmation of her power. Her destinies
were in the hands of Napoleon Bonaparte, who, under the modest title of Consul, concealed designs which already looked to
an imperial throne, and ruled the nation and its dependencies
with a sceptre more powerful and more despotic than the sway
of any contemporaneous legitimate monarch. Born with the
qualities which give and insure command, Bonaparte, to a
boundless ambition, added a restless activity which constantly
prompted new efforts, a thirst for dominion, which as constantly demanded new acquisitions, and a jealousy of power
which made rival greatness intolerable. With an evil eye,
therefore, did he regard the high position obtained by Toussaint
L'Ouverture through his wise and generous efforts in the French
colony of Saint Domingo. The brilliancy of his own fame
seemed dimmed in his eyes by the glory achieved by a negro
chieftain who had been a slave.

The termination of the war had left unoccupied in France a
large body of soldiers, who might be dangerous at home, and
whose leaders, in the repose of peace, might trouble his actual
position, or prove impediments to his ambitious designs. Dissatisfied with seeing themselves outstripped by a soldier of fortune,

they were ready for political intrigue rather than civil obedience, and would be most safely employed in a distant expedition in which success would increase the number of his own laurels, and failure issue in their permanent removal out of his path. That the climate in which he thought of employing them was destructive to Europeans, was a consideration which could not deter him, and only added another reason why, on his part, he should decide in favor of the attempt.

Yet, if he left Hayti in the hands of Toussaint L'Ouverture, he would possess, in an army of thirty thousand black troops obedient to their actual commander, the means of countervailing the power of Great Britain in the West Indies, and of controlling its descendants in the United States. The employment, however, of such an ally seemed scarcely compatible with the dignity which he affected; nor was it impossible, if the ruler of Saint Domingo were left undisturbed in his authority, that he might assist the absolute independence of the colony, and either by augmenting his own power or joining the English, inflict a heavy blow on the supremacy of France. Then the question of colonial slavery presented itself for consideration. Should he recognize or nullify the freedom which existed in Saint Domingo? The recognition would bring him no advantage, for Toussaint and his associates considered their work as accomplished. To nullify it would secure on his side the sympathies and coöperation of the colonists who had lost their estates, and who, regretting their past opulence, and believing its recovery impossible in the present state of the island, besieged the cabinet of the Tuileries with importunities for the restoration of slavery. The wise and just held a different language. Even as a matter of policy an expedition to Hayti, they urged, was to be deprecated, for the risk would be very great, and failure would end in disgrace. Those who now held power in the island were men of valor and of great military skill. As administrators of the colony they enjoyed general sympathy and support, and had proved their ability by the prosperity they had called into being. And while it did not become

France, who had gained her own liberty, to suppress freedom in one of her own colonies, it was contrary to the laws of everlasting right to tear from men that freedom which they had purchased with their blood, and, by their moderation, proved they well deserved. These diverse views occupied the minds and dwelt on the tongues of men in Paris, according as position, character, or personal interests swayed their bosoms. The Consul heard them all, and kept shrouded in his own dark breast the design which he meditated and was maturing. At the moment Vincent arrived from Saint Domingo, he presented the constitution to the Consul. Here was the spark which that sombre genius desired. "He is a revolted slave whom we must punish; the honor of France is outraged." In vain was it pleaded before Bonaparte that the adoption or rejection of the constitution lay with himself, and that it contained only the expression of the wishes of Toussaint and his fellow-laborers. Bonaparte was too adroit not to seize, and too skilful not to make the most of, the opportunity. His words, which we have just reported, circulated through Paris, and excited a feeling in favor of war. An expedition was decided on. And the popular fervor was increased when the Consul declared in the senate that Toussaint was a brigand chief whom it was necessary to bring to justice. One voice was raised against the undertaking, —a voice in the high places of authority. The minister Forfait, a man of high character, attempted to dissuade Bonaparte by setting before him a picture of the inevitable calamities of such an enterprise. He was silenced by the answer, "There are sixty thousand men that I want to send to a distance."

And so, from the most unworthy considerations, an armament against a peaceful and flourishing state is to be speedily fitted out. Yet the adventurers call themselves Christians. What but robbery on a large scale is such conduct? And who can believe that the man who decreed that robbery had in his heart any genuine love of liberty?

Once more, Toussaint L'Ouverture, must you take the buckler and draw the sword. The hero of Europe, and panting for conquests in another world, comes against you. Once more must the broad, rich plains of your native land resound with the clash of hostile armies, and run with human blood. A cloud is on your countenance. Yet let it pass away. Take courage, noble heart! The coming struggle is only another step in the path of freedom. Necessary is the step, or you would not have to take it. And if the effort is painful, and the prospect dark, weigh well the magnitude of the issues. On the fields of Hayti the battle of your race will be fought out. It is before the eye, not of a few islanders, but of the world, that you are about to try your strength with the Gallic gladiator, and settle the question, once for all, whether Africans are men or brutes, worthy of freedom, or doomed to servitude. Success? No, the settlement of the question depends not on success. You will perish in the combat, yet will you win; your cause will triumph even over your grave. Be just, and fear not.

Meanwhile, rumors and intelligence brought to Hayti produced sinister impressions, and disturbed the public mind. It appeared probable that slavery would be maintained in the French colonies of Martinique and Cayenne, and that at Saint Domingo France would make an effort for its restoration. Fears began to prevail, disturbances were threatened. Every eye turned to Toussaint L'Ouverture. On his part, he was not without forebodings, which recently had grown into apprehensions. He had written to the Consul, and received no reply. He felt himself humiliated. At times, tears stole from his eyes when he thought of the possibility that Bonaparte meant to undo all that he had done; foreseeing the long train of calamities which would ensue from such an attempt, he was now and then for an instant unmanned, and spoke hasty words. "Bonaparte," he said, "is wrong not to write to me; he must have listened to my enemies, otherwise would he refuse me proofs of his satisfaction? Me, I say, who have rendered greater services to France than any other general? The English and Spanish Governments treat with more regard the generals who have signalized themselves by services of the first order." His fears and his vexation became greater, and affected his demeanor in a more marked manner, when he heard that preliminaries of peace between England and France had been signed at London. Peace in Europe he saw foreboded war to Hayti.

What now should be his course? . Should he anticipate the blow, and prepare for it by proclaiming the independence of the colony? By rousing its inhabitants to resistance, and marshalling his forces with his own ability and vigor, he might repel even the attack of France when at peace with the world. And right would such a policy have been. Not impossibly it would have proved successful. But L'Ouverture was not prepared to adopt it. Equal to the demands on his courage and energy which a determination of the kind would make, he was not equal to the requisite demands on his sense of justice. Hayti was a French colony;—as a French colony it had gained its freedom. A free republic would not sanction its subjugation; and should Bonaparte attempt to wrest "the rod of empire" out of his own hands, he had better lose his power than forfeit his self-respect. Any way, the duty of the moment was clear; he must calm men's minds. For that purpose he issued a proclamation (18th December, 1801), which, among other things, declared that it was necessary to receive the orders and the envoys of the mother country with respect and filial regard. Yet, while he encouraged obedience, he could not be insensible to the possibility that resistance might be his duty. He was, therefore, under an obligation to foster the means of resistance, and not only to appear confident himself, but to keep up the spirits of his soldiers. This twofold state of mind is seen in words which he uttered from time to time, as in these: "A well-educated child owns submission and obedience to his mother; but if that mother becomes so unnatural as to seek the ruin of her child, the child must look for justice with Him to whom vengeance belongs. If I must die, I will die as a brave soldier, as a man of honor. I fear no one."

It did not escape the eye of those who, having access to the President, narrowly watched him, that the agitation of his mind

13*

increased, and had risen to a great height. Catching alarm from these symptoms, some began to take measures for quitting the island. One of the most distinguished creoles of Port-au-Prince, and who afterwards settled in France, was of the number. He one day asked Toussaint in private for a passport, in order to proceed to the mother country. The unexpected request disturbed the President. Hastening to the door, to ascertain if he could reckon on their not being disturbed, he speedily returned and asked, looking his companion fixedly in the face, "Why do you wish to go away? You, whom I esteem and love?" "Because I am white, and because, notwithstanding the good feelings you have for me, I see that you are on the eve of being the irritated chief of the blacks, and that within these few days you are no longer the protector of the whites, since you have just sent out of the island several for having expressed joy that the Europeans were about to come to Saint Domingo." "Yes," replied Toussaint, with warmth; "they have had the imprudence and folly to rejoice at such news, as if the expedition was not destined to destroy me — to destroy the whites — to destroy the colony. In France I am represented as an independent power, and therefore they are arming against me, — against me, who refused General Maitland to establish my independence under the protection of England, and who always rejected the proposals which Sonthonax made on the subject. Since, however, you wish to set out for France, I consent to it; but, at least, let your voyage be useful to the colony. I will send by you letters to the First Consul, and I will intreat him to listen to you. Make him acquainted with me; make him acquainted with the prosperous state of the agriculture and the commerce of the colony; in a word, let him know what I have done. It is according to all that I have done here that I ought, and that I wish, to be judged. Twenty times have I written to Bonaparte, to ask him to send civil commissioners, to tell him to despatch hither the old colonists, whites instructed in administering public affairs, good machinists, good workmen; he has never replied. Suddenly he avails himself of the peace, (of which he has not deigned to inform me, and which I learn only through the English,) in order to direct against me a formidable expedition, in the ranks of which I see my personal enemies, and people injurious to the colony, whom I sent away. Come to me within four-and-twenty hours. Very ardently do I wish that you and my letters may arrive in time to make the First Consul change his determination, and to make him sensible that in ruining me he ruins the blacks,— he ruins not only Saint Domingo, but also all the Western colonies. If Bonaparte is the first man in France, Toussaint is the first man in the Archipelago of the Antilles." After a moment of reflection, he added, in a firm tone, " I was going to treat with the Americans and the English to procure me twenty thousand blacks from the coast, but I had no other object than to make soldiers of them for France. I know the perfidy of the English. I am under no obligation to them for the information they give me as to the expedition coming to Saint Domingo. No! never will I arm for them! I took up arms for the freedom of my color, which France alone proclaimed, but which she has no right to nullify. Our liberty is no longer in her hands; it is our own! We will defend it or perish."

CHAPTER II.

Bonaparte cannot be turned from undertaking an expedition against Toussaint — Resolves on the enterprise in order chiefly to get rid of his republican associates in arms — Restores slavery and the slave-trade — Excepts Hayti from the decree — Misleads Toussaint's sons — Despatches an armament under Leclerc.

IN vain was it that Vincent, who had attempted to dissuade Toussaint against the adventure of a constitution, now employed his honest and prudent arguments to turn aside Bonaparte from the intended expedition against Saint Domingo. Disregardful of the effect which his advice might have on himself, he urged on the Consul that the victorious warriors of Europe would lose their energy, together with their strength, under the climate of the Antilles; that such a climate would annihilate the army, even if the ascendency of Toussaint L'Ouverture over the inhabitants did not succeed in destroying it by arms; he added the consideration of the probability that the English would openly or secretly endeavor to traverse his object, and frustrate his attempt. To the last remark Bonaparte answered, " The cabinet of St. James's has been disposed to set itself in opposition to my sending a squadron to Saint Domingo; I have notified it, that if it did not consent, I would send to Toussaint unlimited powers, and acknowledge him as independent. It has said no more to me on the point." If this is correct, England, it may be presumed, was influenced by fear for the effects of such a recognition on her neighboring slave colony of Jamaica. Thus does wrong support wrong. Having effected nothing in conversation, Vincent addressed to the Consul a written document, in which, after setting forth the means of defence which the colony possessed, he said, " At the head of so many resources is a man the most active and indefatigable

that can possibly be imagined. It may be strictly said that he
is everywhere, and especially at the spot where sound judgment and danger would say that his presence is most essential;
his great moderation, his power, peculiar to himself, of never
needing rest; the advantage he has of being able to resume
the labors of the cabinet, after laborious journeys, of replying
to a hundred letters every day, and of habitually fatiguing five
secretaries; more still, the skill of amusing and deceiving everybody, carried even to deceit,—make him a man so superior to all
around him that respect and submission go to the extent of
fanaticism in a very great number of persons; it may be affirmed, that no man of the present day has acquired over an
ignorant mass the boundless power obtained by General Toussaint over his brethren in Saint Domingo; he is the absolute
master of the island; and nothing can counteract his wishes,
whatever they are, although some distinguished men, of whom,
however, the number among the blacks is very small, know and
fear the extent to which his views proceed." Bonaparte was
displeased at the frankness of these representations, and banished Vincent, their author, to the island of Elba, whither, at a
later period, he was himself to be banished.

Resolved to disembarrass himself of the veterans in union
with whom he had gained his renown, but who now from their
strong republican sympathies blocked up his way to the imperial throne, he called a council to deliberate on the most effectual means to be taken in order to bring Toussaint under his
yoke. The members of the council were, of course, Bonaparte's
creatures. Their desire to please the real sovereign of the
land was stronger than their professed attachment to liberty.
The councillors recommended the employment of force in order
to reëstablish slavery; a large number proposed that, for the
sake of terror, those whom they characterized as "the guilty"
should be decimated. The Bishop of Blois, Gregory, that immortal friend of the cause of the blacks, had not given his
opinion. "What do you think on the matter?" asked the
council. "I think," he replied, "that the hearing of such

speeches suffices to show that they are uttered by whites; if these gentlemen were this moment to change color, they would talk differently." The restoration of slavery was resolved in the legislative body by a vote of two hundred and twelve against sixty-five. Such was the love of Frenchmen for liberty, for the rights of man, for the rights of their fellow-citizens, for the freedom of the black population of Hayti. The determination of itself justifies the course pursued by Toussaint L'Ouverture. His constitution may prove an ineffectual guarantee of the hardly-earned liberties of his color, but clearly it afforded the only feasible chance of perpetuating the good he had wrought out.

On the 20th of May, 1801, Bonaparte published the infamous decree which placed the French colonies in the state in which they were before the year 1789, and which, authorizing the slave-trade, abrogated all laws to the contrary. This execrable measure marks the real character of the Corsican adventurer, and hands his name down to posterity covered with disgrace. Soon, however, did he find that in an evil hour he had over-stepped the limits of prudence; and therefore he put forth another decree which hypocritically excepted Saint Domingo and Guadeloupe, " because these islands are free, not only by right, but in fact, whilst the other colonies are actually in slavery, and it would be dangerous to put an end to that state of things."

The preparation of the public mind for the unjust and wicked attempt to put down liberty in Saint Domingo was aided by the less obvious but powerful efforts, not only of the colonists in general, but by the mulattoes who dwelt at Paris, of whom Rigaud may be considered as the head. Overcome and exiled by Toussaint, Rigaud panted for revenge. In that vindictive sentiment, he well represented his race, who could not forgive the black President for having extorted the freedom of his color out of their hands.

There were in Paris two young men who looked on the arrangements for the expedition which they saw everywhere proceeding with anxiety and alarm. These were Isaac and Placide

L'Ouverture, sons of the liberator of Hayti, whom, as a testimony of his confidence, and a pledge of his fidelity, their father had sent to Paris for their education. They both resided in the College La Marche, of which Coasnon was the principal. The Consul judged it politic to throw a veil over their eyes. Intending to destroy the father, he had no scruples of conscience about deluding the sons. Coasnon, their teacher, being gained over, assured the young men that the French Government had none but pacific views. A few days afterward he received a letter from the Minister of Marine, apprising him that the Consul wished to see and converse with his pupils before their departure. Repairing to the minister's residence, they received in the presence of Coasnon a confirmation of his statement that the intentions of the Government were of a friendly nature. They were then conducted to Bonaparte, who, the better to conceal his real purposes, received them in a flattering manner. Having ascertained which of the two was Toussaint's own son, he said to him, "Your father is a great man ; he has rendered eminent services to France. You will tell him that I, the first magistrate of the French people, promise him protection, glory, and honor. Do not think that France intends to carry war to Saint Domingo. The army which it sends thither is destined, not to attack the troops of the country, but to augment their numbers. Here is General Leclerc, my brother-in-law, whom I have appointed Captain-General, and who will command that armament. Orders have been given for you to arrive at Saint Domingo a fortnight before the fleet, to announce to your father the coming of the expedition." On the next day, the delusion was carried still farther, for the Minister of Marine, as a kind of practical assurance how well Toussaint and his children stood with the highest authorities, entertained the young men at a magnificent repast; and shortly after, in order to complete the farce by an appeal to negro vanity, he, in the name of his government, presented to them a superb suit of armor, and a rich and brilliant military costume.

It scarcely needs be stated that the promise that the youths should have time to assure their father of the pacific intentions of France was not observed. Having answered its momentary purpose it was openly and deliberately violated. The real design of all this collusion was that, misled by the reports of his sons in Paris, Toussaint L'Ouverture might be taken off his guard. Alas! that in the crisis of his fate he should have given credit to men who blushed not to deal in falsehood.

It has already appeared, from the Consul's own words, that he had chosen Leclerc, who was the husband of his sister Pauline, to be at the head of the expedition. Bonaparte was well pleased to have the opportunity of separating himself from Leclerc, whom he regarded as a relative little worthy of his present and his future greatness. The obscure birth of Leclerc, in the small town of Pontoise, disquieted his pride. Every day there came to Paris persons of low condition who gave themselves out as relatives of the Consul's sister. That sister possessed so rare a beauty that Canova reproduced her features in his statue of Venus Victrix, — *Victorious Venus*. To personal charms she added subtlety and grace of mind. Her looks awakened desires in the most indifferent hearts. She gathered around her all the artifices of voluptuousness. In her furniture she was luxurious; elegant in her personal decorations, and choice in the persons attached to her suite. She was attended by painters, musicians, and buffoons. Pauline accompanied her husband in the expedition. Leclerc was small in stature, but he had vivacity of mind and grace of manner. In countenance he was thought to bear some resemblance to the Consul. Though he had shown some courage and perseverance in the campaigns of the Alps and the Rhine, he was little else than the blind instrument of his brother-in-law, whom he imitated in war as well as in peace, with a closeness which betokened a contracted intellect. From such a man was expected the final settlement of the long quarrel of color in Saint Domingo.

The preparations for the armament were made in different ports. No expense was spared. Holland, then under the domination of France and Spain, kept in alliance with it by fear, furnished ships. The fleet, when collected, was composed of twenty-one frigates, and thirty-five vessels of war. It had on board all the best sailors of France, and was commanded by Villaret Joyeuse. In December, 1801, portions of it left the ports of Brest, Rochefort, and Lorient. The rest were to sail from other points. The ocean was covered with ships in order to punish a contumacious slave! The magnitude of the equipment is a measure of Toussaint's power. This fleet bore to Hayti one of the most valiant of armies. The Alps, Italy, the Rhine, and the Nile resounded with the exploits of the veterans who formed its strength. They now left lands which boasted of their civilization, to carry chains to a people who, uncultured though they were, had vindicated their freedom, and used that freedom wisely.

As soon as the fleet had anchored off Cape Samana, at the eastern end of Saint Domingo, Leclerc numbered his sea and land forces, including others which he expected. They amounted to sixty ships and more than thirty thousand men, commanded by generals and captains of experience and renown. Among them were men of color who had become illustrious in the sanguinary struggle for emancipation. There was found Rigaud, whose valor had disputed the laurel with Toussaint himself. There was found Pétion, who, under a mild physiognomy, bore a lofty spirit. He was destined to found and govern a republic in the island he took part in invading. There was found Boyer, his illustrious successor, who, by a treaty with the king of France, was one day to secure the permanent independence of his native land.* All these mulatto chiefs had consented to second the expedition with their council, their courage, and their example. On the other side, the forces of Toussaint consisted at most of sixteen thousand men; five in the North, four

---

* Boyer was a man of talent, but I cannot understand why he should be called illustrious. The treaty with France was characterized at the time, by many of the best men of Hayti, as an act of abject cowardice. Certainly, there was nothing illustrious in it: it may have been politic, but it was not heroic; for it was signed under threats of bombardment. — ED.

14

in the West, four in the South, and three in what was formerly the Spanish territory. These troops, thus scattered, were, however, commanded by captains well trained to mountain warfare; all were animated by the love of freedom, which they cherished the more because they had acquired it at the cost of labor, peril, and bloodshed. Everywhere the Haytian army would find auxiliaries; soldiers, women, children, citizens, had all lived in the camps of the civil wars. Full of recollections of their former servitude, they were ready to perish sooner than submit.

The gathering of the fleet at Samana took several weeks. The effect of a sudden descent was lost. On hearing that a fleet was approaching the island, Toussaint L'Ouverture threw the bridle over his horse's neck, and galloped to Cape Samana to reconnoitre the squadrons. Unversed in marine affairs, he at first took the manœuvring for hesitation. But, as the vessels anchored in their several places, having never seen so large a fleet before, he was struck with astonishment, and feeling for a moment discouraged, he exclaimed to his officers, " We must perish. All France is coming to Saint Domingo. It has been deceived ; it comes to take revenge and enslave the blacks."

Convinced as he was of the hostile designs of the armament, Toussaint could not deny that its heralds had announced friendship. As little did he possess the right of making war against the forces of the country to which he professed allegiance. Had he already proclaimed the independence of Hayti, he would have been relieved from the perplexity of a dubious position. Even had he at this last moment proclaimed independence, he would have been saved from the evils of vacillation. But being neither at peace nor at war with his assailants, he labored under a great disadvantage. However, he made such arrangements as his unhappy position permitted. To act on the defensive was compulsory on him in the circumstances, and probably such a policy was every way the best. Should the armament prove really hostile, should it attack the island, then resistance must be made; and if defeat ensued, there were the mountains for a retreat, and a succession of strongholds where an almost unlimited defence might be maintained.

At length the fleet put itself in movement. After having detached Kerverseau to go and take possession of the city of Saint Domingo, Leclerc directed the armament in three divisions against three principal points; Fort Dauphin, and the city of the Cape in the North, and Port-au-Prince in the West. The island was thus invested. No declaration of war was made, no negotiations were opened. The squadrons sailed to the several points as if they approached a friendly shore, and as a matter of course entered friendly harbors. Nor could they be challenged. Toussaint possessed no vessels, and if he had vessels, was he not a French subject, and were these not French ships and French commanders?

It was not possible for Isaac and Placide L'Ouverture any longer to doubt the nature of the errand on which the armament had been sent. They drew up, in writing, remonstrances which they presented to Leclerc, who, doubtless, smiled in his thoughts at their easy faith.

CHAPTER III.

Leclerc obtains possession of the chief positions in the island, and yet is not master thereof — By arms and by treachery he establishes himself at the Cape, at Fort Dauphin, at Saint Domingo, and at Port-au-Prince — Toussaint L'Ouverture depends on his mountain strongholds.

THE main squadron, under the immediate direction of Leclerc, proceeded to act against the Cape. Sent on an errand of duplicity, the commander meant war, yet was obliged to feign peace. His aim was, if possible, to obtain possession of the Cape, under the cover of friendship. Surely, admission into a French port could not be denied to French forces. In order to effect his purpose, he sent Lebrun, aide-de-camp of the admiral Villaret Joyeuse, on shore, to announce his intention of landing his troops. Lebrun was conducted to General Christophe, who held the place on behalf of the insular authorities. As Lebrun passed along, he, as if by accident, let fall a number of proclamations, intended to serve the cause of Bonaparte by stirring up the inhabitants. Having put his papers into the hands of Christophe, he received for answer, " Without the orders of the Governor-General, Toussaint L'Ouverture, who at present is in the Spanish part, I cannot receive the squadron and the troops which are on board." Lebrun whispered in the ear of Christophe, that General Leclerc was the bearer of splendid tokens of the favor of the Government toward him. "No, sir," was the prompt and decided reply, " I cannot listen to any proposition without the orders of the Governor. The proclamations you bring breathe despotism and tyranny. I shall go and administer to my soldiers an oath to maintain our liberty at the peril of their lives." The proclamation covertly published by Lebrun, was not wholly without effect. A deputation of citizens waited on Christophe to impress on him the responsibility he took on himself in withstanding the orders of the mother country. He replied that he was a soldier; that he acknowledged as his supreme chief only Toussaint L'Ouverture; that nothing proved to him that a squadron over which they saw foreign banners float had been sent by the mother country; that France would have taken other means to cause its commands to be acknowledged, and that it would have sent them by an envoy, and not by foreign squadrons. He ended by declaring, that if Leclerc, who called himself Captain-General, persisted in his resolution to enter the Cape, he would set the whole in flames rather than the ships should anchor in the harbor. However, he permitted a deputation of the city to go on board Leclerc's ship, and entreat a delay of two days, in order that Toussaint might be consulted. The General assured the deputies, that France, full of affection for the colony, had made every arrangement for its happiness; he set forth in a few words the great and benevolent projects which the mother country had for Toussaint L'Ouverture, whose sons it sent back after having educated them with the greatest care; he announced that he brought General Christophe proofs of the public gratitude, and remarked how monstrous would be the ingratitude of which those two chiefs seemed disposed to render themselves guilty. He added, that the conduct of General Christophe having caused him to fear that he would employ the delay asked for in order, by drawing together his forces, to secure the success of the meditated resistance, he could not postpone the entrance of the squadron, and that he should make his arrangements in the space of half-an-hour, — time sufficient to enable General Chrisophe to repair the disgrace of his revolt by prompt submission. Christophe remained unmoved by the allurements and the threats of the French commander, though supported by the following letter : —

"I learn with indignation, Citizen-General, that you refuse to receive the French squadron and army which I command, un-

14*

der the pretext that you have not any order from the Governor-General.

"France has made peace with England, and its Government sends to Saint Domingo forces able to subdue rebels, if rebels are to be found in Saint Domingo. As to you, Citizen-General, I avow that it would give me pain to reckon you among rebels. I warn you that if this very day you do not put into my possession the Forts Picolet, Belair and all the batteries of the coast, to-morrow at dawn fifteen thousand men shall be disembarked. Four thousand at this moment are landing at Fort Liberté, eight thousand at Port Republican; you will find my proclamation joined to this communication; it expresses the intentions of the French Government; but, remember, whatever esteem your conduct in the colony has inspired me with, I hold you responsible for whatever may take place.

"The General-in-chief of the army of Saint Domingo,
and Captain-General of the colony.
(Signed) "LECLERC."

The letter, and the tone of the Captain-General served only to inflame the spirit of resistance, which had time to gather strength, because the squadron, not being able to procure pilots, was obliged to gain the open sea without being able to land the troops. Christophe mustered the soldiers of the line and made them swear to conquer or die, conformably to the proclamation of Toussaint L'Ouverture, dated the 18th of December, 1801. The proclamation of Leclerc, intended to win over the civil authorities and the inhabitants, assumed a more pacific character, and promised to all the soldiers and functionaries of the colony, whatever their color, the confirmation of their rank and their offices. Smitten with fear, some of the civil authorities endeavored to prevail with Christophe, but he was not a man to be easily overcome.

That chief, born in the island of Grenada, first an emancipated slave, then an innkeeper, a tradesman, and a cattle-dealer, ended by becoming a king. To the advantage of great height he added that of a majestic carriage and an eye full of fire. He had a strong soul, adorned with civic, domestic, and military virtues. His prudence led him to trust little to fortune. He was active, patient, and temperate. Without having been instructed in the schools, he spoke with ease and grace; he took peculiar pleasure in diverting his guests by the recital of adventures or his valorous exploits. He was moreover liable to contrasts of temper which indicated the fiery impulses of his character. Some of his excellences he lost when seated on a throne. When the messenger of Leclerc urged him to surrender the city, he replied with *hauteur*, "Go and tell your General that the French shall march here only over ashes, and that the ground shall burn beneath their feet." He afterward wrote his determination in these terms, — "The decision of arms can admit you only into a city in ashes, and even on these ashes I will fight still!" Inexorable to the entreaties of treacherous natives, he was assailed by the following proclamation from Bonaparte, which they received from the hands of Leclerc, and put into circulation.

"THE FIRST CONSUL TO THE INHABITANTS OF SAINT DOMINGO.

" Whatever your origin and your color, you are all Frenchmen; you are all free and equal before God and before men.

" France, like Saint Domingo, has been a prey to factions, and has been torn by civil war and by foreign war; but all is changed; all nations have embraced the French, and have sworn peace and friendship toward them; all Frenchmen likewise have embraced each other, and have sworn to be friends and brothers; do you embrace the French, and rejoice at again beholding your brethren and your friends from Europe. The Government sends to you the Captain-General Leclerc; he brings with him large forces to protect you against your enemies and against the enemies of the Republic. If you are told, ' Those forces are destined to rob you of your liberty,' reply, ' The Republic will not allow that liberty shall be taken from us.'

" Rally round the Captain-General; he brings you abundance and peace; rally round him. Whoever shall dare to separate himself from the Captain-General, will be an enemy to his country, and the wrath of the Republic will devour him as the fire devours your dried sugar-canes.

" Given at Paris, at the Government Palace, the 17th Brumaire, in the tenth year of the French Republic (8 Nov., 1801).

" The First Consul,

(Signed) " BONAPARTE."

This proclamation was not of a nature to inspire confidence in men whom servitude had made habitually distrustful. The words of the Consul appeared those of a master who alternately employs promises and threats. The people of the Cape had no need of being assured of a liberty which they actually enjoyed; and that wrath presented under the image of the conflagration of their harvests looked, in their eyes, like a token of slavery. All declared that they would rather perish than return to servitude. While time was thus spent in useless words, the war had begun without any negotiation with Toussaint, whether an order to that effect had been given by the Consul, that he might strike terror into the inhabitants, or whether Leclerc considered that promptitude was the best means of commanding obedience. Rochambeau, who had been sent against Fort Dauphin, attacked the place by land and by sea. Everything soon yielded to French valor. The blacks fled, but in flying set the city on fire. At the sight of the flames, Rochambeau slaughtered all the prisoners, whom he treated as revolters. The bay of Mancenille was stained with the blood of many unarmed blacks, whose crime was that they had shouted, " No whites! no slavery!"

Afraid lest Christophe should carry his threat into execution and set the city on fire, Leclerc resolved to take the enemy in the rear by landing his forces in the Bay of Acul. But the movement of the vessels and the noise of the cannon spread on all sides tumult and alarm. Burning plantations announced that flames would soon rise from the town. Christophe, threatened by sea and by land by two bodies of foes, determined to set fire to the Cape. After distributing torches to his soldiers, and to all who were devoted to so sacred a cause, he called the Almighty Protector of liberty to witness that he was driven to extremity, and commenced the conflagration with his own residence, decorated in a costly manner by the arts of luxury. An ocean of flames rose in the air; roofs fell in all on fire; and in those flames the black man saw the preservation of his liberty. The appearance of the fleet, the blood of blacks and whites flowing on two parts of the coast, terror, confusion, the loss of so much wealth, awoke in all hearts the former furies of freedom and slavery. At the sight of the flames, which changed night into day, those passions painted themselves on white as well as black countenances. But no cries, no complaints were heard. Only fingers were pointed to the high lands above the Cape where freedom might find an asylum. The flight took place in silence, as if vengeance was deferred in order to be more terrible. An explosion of a powder magazine crowned that work of courage and despair. The flames of the conflagration were seen nearly at the same time by the French fleet and by Toussaint L'Ouverture, who arrived in the neighborhood from Santo Domingo, and who then regretted that he had not lost his life in the plains of the Artibonite when he fought for France and for his country; so great was his grief. He showed compassion to a multitude of old men, women, and children, who were scattered on all the roads, and who were flying through the mountains. How embarrassing his position: the Cape and Fort Dauphin had been treated as hostile cities.

Christophe, who had set on fire his own house and the city, manifested a generosity too rare in war; fearing lest, in the confusion and the tumult of the conflagration, some two thousand whites with their wives and children might become victims of his men, he conducted them into a place of safety. After abandoning the Cape, Christophe joined Toussaint, and con-

jointly they raised fire and flames everywhere. At the request
of his chief, Christophe took up a position at La Grande Rivière, while Toussaint himself went toward the plain of the
North. Both were thus immediately above the invading forces.
The latter, in proceeding to his post, found himself face to face
with the advanced guard of Leclerc, and passed through a most
terrible fire. His cloak was riddled with balls, and his horse
was wounded. Reaching Mornay, he received a letter from
Rochambeau, who sought to set off his glory by affectations
of pity. "I did not expect," he said, "that my soldiers in arriving here would have to dye their bayonets in the blood of
their brothers and their friends." Toussaint L'Ouverture found
it desirable to quit Mornay, and, passing through Ennery, where
was his wife with a part of his family, made his way toward
Gonaïves in the West. While Leclerc and Rochambeau were
conquering in the North towns which were in ashes, their co-
operator, General Boudet, in the West, was seeking by stratagem as much as by force to take possession of Port-au-Prince.
That city, built of wood, was the rival of the Cape. Agé, who
was intrusted with its defence, had not a soul proof against
treachery. But alongside of him there served a captain worthy of "the good old times." Lamartinière possessed a heroic soul ; his firmness, his courage, and his patience could not
be surpassed. With a handful of soldiers, he was capable of
resisting the efforts of an army. When the surrender of the
city was demanded, the reply was the same as that which had
been given at the Cape, only the threat of carnage was sub-
joined to the threat of conflagration. "If," replied the blacks,
— "if the French disembark before we can be informed of the
resolution of Toussaint, three cannon-shot, repeated from
mountain-top to mountain-top, shall be the signal for the conflagration of our homes, and for the death of those who may
endeavor to make us slaves."

Not without disgust, nor without fear, did Boudet who had
gained renown in the Antilles by wresting Guadeloupe from the
hands of the English, land near Lamentin, distant about a

league to the west of Port-au-Prince. At the appointed signal, flames arose on all sides. Frightful disorder prevailed in the town. The blacks, dreading slavery, pursued the whites through the streets, and even searched for them in hiding-places. At the recollection of the evils of their past servitude, marks of which many of them still bore in their mutilated bodies, they saw in the whites only pitiless masters, and slew them unsparingly, or carried them away as hostages into the mountains. A large number of women, children, and old men sought in a church an asylum against the rage of their former slaves, who, in spite of the sanctity of the place, were on the point of sacrificing them as victims to their liberty; but a priest appeared, and called out for mercy; presenting the sacred utensils of the altar, and assuaging the wrath of the assailants, he saved the lives of the trembling and helpless crowd; but the raging men hastened away to find, in less hallowed places, whites on whom they might effectually wreak their terrible vengeance. Boudet, unused to the terrors that arose on every hand, exhorted his soldiers to mercy. "My comrades," he said, "you must regard these people as fellow-citizens; this is no foreign land, it is your country. Do not make use of your arms; uncover your breasts to them, in order that those who follow us may have the right to avenge us." By the treachery of its defenders, he obtained possession of Fort Bizoton, by which his progress might have been long stopped. Agé was thinking of surrendering the city itself; but Lamartinière, indignant at a second instance of perfidy, called into action, for its defence, all his resolution. At the council-board, he blew out the brains of a captain of artillery who refused the keys of the arsenal. So daring a stroke put an end to indecision and enkindled courage; he drew after him four thousand men to the gate of Leogane, where a redoubt, armed with six pieces of artillery, defended the town. Death was spread in the ranks of the French, who advanced slowly, uncertain of the use they should make of their arms. Soon their ardor burned up; they rushed across the moat, threw themselves into the city, and preserved it from the threatened conflagration.

Lamartinière, less afflicted at his defeat than at not having reduced Port-au-Prince into ashes, hastened to intrench himself in Croix-des-Bouquets, a little to the north; a position surrounded by moats cut in a very hard soil. There he was waited for by Dessalines, who had come up too late to defend the city. That chief, who had the West under his command, was of a bold, turbulent, and ferocious spirit; now from revenge, now from ambition, he imbrued his hands in the blood of both white men and black men. Hunger, thirst, fatigue, and loss of sleep he seemed made to endure as if by a peculiarity of constitution. His air was fierce, his step oblique, his look sanguinary. His face, furrowed with incisions, indicated the coast of Africa as his birthplace. Under that terrible aspect he concealed an impenetrable dissimulation. His barbarous eloquence lay in expressive signs rather than in words. What is strange in his destiny is, that he was a savage, a slave, a soldier, a general, and died, when an emperor, under the dagger of a Brutus. When he learnt that Port-au-Prince had escaped from conflagration, he turned pale, scolded, and roared with wrath.

Boudet, intending to follow up his victory, flew to Croix-des-Bouquets, where he was awaited by those two formidable chiefs. But Dessalines understood his business too well to encounter the French general in set battle array. Knowing how by bold and rapid movements to deceive as well as escape from an enemy, he outflanked Boudet, and getting in his rear, set on fire Leogane, a charming city built on a promontory, before the invaders could arrive in the vicinity. The flames which destroyed that city rejoiced the soul of the barbarian, but did not console him for the escape of Port-au-Prince; he meditated fresh conflagrations.

While the North and the West were theatres of fire and carnage, the East and the South submitted without the endurance of calamity. General Kerverseau, on presenting himself before Santo Domingo, found the inhabitants the more disposed to receive him, because in perilous missions in Santo Domingo, he had acquired a reputation for prudence and honor. Kerverseau was not a great general, but a good man, modest and mild; respected by parties, he enjoyed much popularity. Paul L'Ouverture, who commanded the city, refused to yield without instructions from Toussaint, his brother. Negotiations, nevertheless, were opened, but they came to a stop when the news arrived that all was in flames in other parts. Then Kerverseau invested Santo Domingo by sea and land. Paul, meanwhile, had written for instructions to his distinguished brother. Toussaint sent a dispatch commanding him to destroy the city if he was unable to hold it against his adversary. But, fearing the message might fall into the hands of Kerverseau, he sent another, which recommended conciliation. These communications, intercepted by Spaniards who had taken sides with the French, fell into the hands of the besieging general. Kerverseau conveyed to Paul the message which bore a friendly character. Paul, importuned by the townsmen, admitted his assailant, and joined his ranks. Thus fell Santo Domingo, and with it there passed under the power of France a portion of Toussaint's forces.

The Southern province, inhabited chiefly by mulattoes, and being the scene of Rigaud's revolt, was not likely to offer a stern resistance. Its commander, Laplume, no sooner heard that the French were masters of the Cape and Port-au-Prince, than he resolved to submit to the authority of the mother country. His troops, mostly of his own blood, cherished no friendly recollections toward Toussaint, by whom they had been subdued, and were easily induced by their leader, who painted to them vividly the evils of civil war, and read the proclamation of the Consul, whose power, genius, and glory he extolled, to join him in taking place side by side with the assailants of the constitutional rights of the island. Thus, the strong points of Hayti were in the hands of Leclerc.

At the Cape and at Fort Dauphin in the North, at Santo Domingo in the East, at Cayes in the South, and at Port-au-Prince in the West, the French invader had succeeded in taking up strong positions. In vain had Toussaint L'Ouverture organized the best resistance in his power. The enemy were on the island. True, some of the places they held were only heaps of ruins. Nevertheless, they had effected a landing. The island, however, was not in their possession. Neither arms nor treachery had subdued the natives. Toussaint well knew that the seaports could not withstand so formidable an assault. But he knew also that a country which is full of mountains is inexpugnable. For the desultory warfare of the mountains he prepared himself, and, backed by the population at large, men of his own blood, he defied defeat, and felt confident that time and the climate would unstring the arm, and lay waste the spirits as well as the frames of his assailants. Even one advantage he had gained; for, whereas, at the first, the islanders knew not whether they had to expect peace or war, their leader, consequently, could fully prepare for neither : now, at length, the cloak was stripped off, and to all eyes it was clear that the only alternative was victory or servitude.

On his part, Leclerc, though victorious, did not deceive himself with the notion of having accomplished his work. On the contrary, in view of the facts to which we have just adverted, he was aware that he had everything but the first step to accomplish. The Spartacus of Hayti was on his own mountains supported by a whole people able and ready to resist to the utmost. How was Leclerc to succeed ? How could a desultory warfare in ravines and on precipices, in recesses and in mountain fastnesses, be either carried on or brought to a desirable issue against what was not in name but literally *a levy en masse?* A different method must be tried. So long as Toussaint L'Ouverture was at the head of those predatory bands, the consequences of victory would be only a little less beneficial than those of defeat. But treachery has power, and treachery of the basest kind was put into action.

CHAPTER IV.

General Leclerc opens a negotiation with Toussaint L'Ouverture by means
of his two sons, Isaac and Placide — the negotiation ends in nothing —
the French Commander-in-chief outlaws Toussaint, and prepares for a
campaign.

BEFORE he was yet informed of the success of the expedition in the East, the South, and the West, Leclerc, well
aware that in Toussaint L'Ouverture he had to do with an
enemy not easy to overcome, resolved, when now he had himself taken up a firm position in the North, to put into play a
method of operation from which he expected a decisive and
immediate result. Vincent, who foresaw the terrible wasting
that the European troops would have to endure under the
tropics, advised the Consul to send back, partly as hostages,
and partly as mediators, the sons of Toussaint, — and so take a
means for bringing the colony into subjection, both more sure
and less costly than the appeal to arms. This advice he urged
specially on the ground that, as Toussaint had strong domestic
feelings, he would not be able to stand out against the influence
which the return of the young men, after a long absence, would
exert on their father in favor of the Consul's designs. Accordingly, the Captain-General, having sent for the youths, who had
remained on board the fleet, spoke to them of the calamities
which had befallen the island, urged the necessity of a speedy
accommodation, and reminded them of the letter written to
their father by the First Consul. "I have," he added, "the
greatest hope of coming to a good understanding with your
father; he was absent; he could not command the resistance.
You must carry to him the First Consul's letter; let him know
my intentions, and the high opinion I entertain of him." It

was somewhat late to set on foot a friendly negotiation. But
the hour was well-timed, since the delay had given Leclerc a
footing in the island, if it had not also served, as intended, to
show Toussaint L'Ouverture the inutility of opposition to the
will of Bonaparte. The young men felt that their mission of
peace should have preceded hostilities; but they felt, also, a
very strong desire to see their parents and their home; nor
were they wholly without a hope that even yet a pacific arrangement might be made. They therefore gladly accepted
the embassy, and set out for Ennery, their father's dwelling-
place, accompanied by their tutor, M. Coasnon. Behind them
they left a horrible image of civil war, — old men, women, children, flying from fire and sword; everywhere alarm and consternation. Soon they came into view of peaceful scenes, the
work of their father's genius, — cultivated fields, abundant
crops, happy families. There was a land of desolation; here
a land of prosperity. On their route they saw many inhabitants, but not one soldier. As soon as it was known who they
were, crowds came out to greet them with acclamations; they
were surrounded, welcomed, embraced, and questioned. Their
object? It was to convey friendly assurances to their father.
The news was gladly heard. Nevertheless, doubt soon resumed
the ascendency. Those were, indeed, the sons of their venerated chief; they had been sent back unhurt; it was a token for
good; yet, why announce peace by cannon-balls? Why land
on a friendly shore with a charge of bayonets? Along the
whole route, the same eagerness to see and welcome the youths
was displayed. Delight for a moment took the place of terror.
The family had been warned of the approach of the young men.
At last, about nine o'clock in the evening of the second day
after the departure from the Cape, their mother, accompanied
by a few friends, came, with the aid of torch-light, to receive
them in the midst of an immense crowd. It is more easy to
conceive than describe the tender scenes which passed that
evening in the home of Toussaint L'Ouverture. After the
mother had for the moment indulged all her emotions in regard

to her sons, she turned to their preceptor, whose care and trouble she acknowledged in the fullest and warmest terms. All the family, for a short hour, forgetting the common miseries of their country, gave way to the sweetest and most joyous sentiments. Duty had prevented Toussaint himself from taking his place in this affecting interview. But, at eleven o'clock in the evening of the next day, the sound of a trumpet and the rattling of horses' feet announced his arrival. On his entrance, Isaac and Placide threw themselves passionately on his neck. Their father long held them pressed closely to his heart, while tears streamed down his hardy cheeks. M. Coasnon was sent for, to whom L'Ouverture expressed the high sense of his obligation for the attentions he had bestowed on the young men, thanking him for having accompanied them into the bosom of their family, — though he was sorry that their arrival took place in the midst of war, the cause of which, he said, was unknown to him, and which he had in no way expected. Then M. Coasnon presented to him the Consul's letter, to which was suspended by a silk cord the State seal, — the whole enclosed in a golden casket. The epistle was as follows: —

"TO CITIZEN TOUSSAINT, GENERAL-IN-CHIEF OF THE ARMY OF SAINT DOMINGO.

" CITIZEN-GENERAL, —

" The peace with England, and all the Powers of Europe, which has just placed the Republic on the summit of power and greatness, gives the Government the opportunity of occupying itself with the colony of Saint Domingo. We send thither Citizen-General Leclerc, our brother-in-law, as Captain-General, as First Magistrate of the colony. He is accompanied by forces sufficient to cause the sovereignty of the French people to be respected. In these circumstances, we have pleasure in hoping that you will prove to us and to all France the sincerity of the sentiments you have constantly expressed in the different letters that you have written to us.

" We have conceived an esteem for you, and we take pleas-

15*

ure in recognizing and proclaiming the services which you have rendered to the French people. If its banner floats over Saint Domingo, it is to you and the brave blacks that we owe it.

" Called by your talents and the force of circumstances to the highest post, you have destroyed civil war, put reins on the persecution carried on by ferocious men, restored to honor religion and the worship of God, — from whom all things proceed.

" The constitution you have formed, while containing many good things, contains some which are contrary to the dignity and the sovereignty of the French nation, of which Saint Domingo forms a portion.

" The circumstances in which you found yourself, surrounded by enemies, while the mother country could not succor you nor send you provisions, rendered legitimate articles of that constitution which otherwise could not be legitimate; but now, when circumstances are so happily changed, you will be the first to pay homage to the sovereignty of the nation which counts you in the number of her most illustrious citizens, both for the services which you have rendered, and for the talents and force of character with which nature has endowed you. Conduct contrary to this would be irreconcilable with the idea which we have formed of you. It would cause you to forfeit the numerous rights you have to the gratitude of the Republic, and would dig before your feet a precipice, which, in causing your own ruin, might contribute to the ruin of those brave blacks whose courage we love, and whose rebellion we should be sorry to find ourselves compelled to punish.

" We have made known to your children and their preceptor the sentiments which animate us, and we send them back to you.

"Assist the Captain-General with your counsels, your influence, and your talents. What can you desire? The freedom of the blacks? You know that in all the countries where we have been, we have given freedom to the nations who did not possess it. Respect, honors, fortune? After the services which you have rendered, and which in this juncture you may render, with the special sentiment we entertain toward you, how can you be uncertain as to the respect, the fortune, and the homage which await you?

"Let the people of Saint Domingo know that the solicitude which France has always felt for their happiness has often been powerless through the imperious circumstances of war; that men come from the continent to agitate the island and support factions, were the products of the factions which distracted the mother country; that henceforth peace, and the strength of the Government, will secure the prosperity and the freedom of the colony. Tell them, that if to them liberty is the first of blessings, they cannot enjoy it except as French citizens, and that every act contrary to the interests of the mother country, to the obedience which they owe to the Government, and to the Captain-General, which is its delegate, would be a crime against the national sovereignty, which would eclipse their services, and render Saint Domingo the theatre of a destructive war in which parents and children would slay each other.

"And you, General, reflect, that if you are the first of your color that has reached such a height of power, and that has gained distinction by bravery and military talents, you are, also, before God and us, the person who is responsible for the conduct of the inhabitants of the colony.

"If there are evil-disposed persons who tell the individuals that have played the principal parts in the troubles of Saint Domingo that we have come to investigate what they have done during the times of anarchy, assure them that we shall inquire only as to their conduct in this last circumstance; that we shall search into the past only to discover the deeds which have made them distinguished in the war against the Spaniards and the English, who were our enemies.

"Reckon unreservedly on our esteem, and conduct yourself as he ought who is one of the principal citizens of the greatest nation in the world.

" The First Consul,

(Signed)   " BONAPARTE."

Toussaint L'Ouverture, after running his eyes rapidly over this compound of cajolery and menace, was about to reply, when his sons and. M. Coasnon spoke to him of the handsome reception they had had from the Consul, and the magnificent promises he had made them; they also did justice in setting forth the assurance given them by Bonaparte, that the army commanded by Leclerc was not sent to Saint Domingo with hostile views; adding, that it was the desire of that general to enter into an accommodation with Toussaint L'Ouverture. Then the liberator of Hayti said in reply, " You, M. Coasnon, you, whom I consider as the preceptor of my sons, and the envoy of France, must confess that the words and the letter of the First Consul are altogether in opposition to the conduct of General Leclerc; those announce peace, — he makes war on me.

" General Leclerc, in falling on Saint Domingo as a clap of thunder, has announced his mission to me only by the burning of the capital, which he might have avoided; by the capture of Fort Dauphin, and the landing on the coast of Limbé effected by main force.

" I have just been informed that General Maurepas has been attacked by a French division, which he has repulsed; that the commander of Saint Marc has forced two French vessels which cannonaded that city to put to sea. In the midst of so many disasters and acts of violence, I must not forget that I wear a sword. But, for what reason is so unjust, so impolitic, a war declared against me? Is it because I have delivered my country from the plague of foreign and civil conflict; that with all my power I have labored for her prosperity and her splendor; that I have established order and justice here? Since these actions are regarded as a crime, why are my children sent to me, in such a juncture, to share that crime?

" As for the rest, if, as you tell me, General Leclerc frankly desires peace, let him stop the march of his troops. He will preserve Saint Domingo from total subversion, and will tranquillize minds exasperated by his system of aggression and invasion. I will, M. Coasnon, write him a letter having this tenor, which you, my two children, and M. Granville, the tutor of my younger son, shall put into his hands."

The conversation was prolonged far into the night. Toussaint remarked on the inconsistency of recognizing him as Commander-in-chief of Saint Domingo, at the very time that he was assailed by an overpowering force. He could not suppress the indignation which he felt at the thought that his children were offered to him as the price of his surrender. He bade M. Coasnon take them back to General Leclerc, because, at every hazard, he owed the sacrifice of his life to the freedom of his fellow-citizens. The father struggled with the liberator, and brought a flood of tears from his eyes. The liberator overpowered even the father, and exacted the sternest regard to public duty.

In two days the letter was ready. On the night of February 11th, 1802, the appointed messengers were despatched with the communication. As they travelled toward the Cape, M. Granville acquainted M. Coasnon with the irritation that prevailed among the blacks. The life of the unfortunate whites hung by a thread, and, at any moment, a word would be sufficient to sunder the slender tie. In his reply, Toussaint reproached Leclerc with having come to displace him by means of cannon shot; with not having delivered to him the letter of the First Consul, until three months after its date; and with having, by hostile acts, rendered doubtful the rights and the services of his color. He declared that those rights imposed upon him duties that were superior to those of nature; that he was prepared to sacrifice his children to his color, and that he sent them back that it might not be supposed they were bound by his presence. He ended by saying, that, being more distrustful than ever, he required time in order to decide the course which remained for him to take.

Leclerc hastened to send back the young men with a reply, in which he invited Toussaint to come and concert with him means for putting a stop to the public disorders; giving him his word that the past should be sunk in oblivion; that he, Toussaint, should be treated with the greatest distinction; and that, if he complied with the request, he should that moment be proclaimed the first lieutenant of the Captain-General of the colony. Leclerc finished his epistle by stating that, though he had precise instructions not to discontinue warlike operations if he found it necessary to commence them, yet, in the hope of a good understanding, he would condescend to an armistice of four days, but, that delay over, he would, by a proclamation, declare Toussaint an enemy of the French nation, and put him beyond the pale of the law.

The allurement was too weak; the threat was impotent. Duty with Toussaint was superior to every other consideration. He could be neither bought nor intimidated. Irritated by this ultimatum he resolved to employ all his energies for the maintenance of the liberties he had achieved. Yet had he no wish to involve his sons in the issue. He, therefore, after announcing to them his final resolution, declared that he left them free to choose between France and their father; that he did not blame their attachment to the mother country; but that his color stood between him and France; that he could not compromise the destinies of his color by placing himself at the mercy of an expedition, in which figured several white generals, as well as Rigaud, Pétion, Boyer, Chanlatte, and others, all his personal enemies; that the order not to cease from fighting to negotiate, showed that France had more confidence in its arms than in its rights; that a confidence of such a nature indicated the despotism of mere force; and that if no practical regard was paid to the rights of the blacks while they had some power, what would their condition be when he and his should be powerless?

His sons threw themselves into his arms, imploring him to yield. Their tears and their caresses failed to move him. Remaining inflexible, he merely repeated, "My children, make your choice; whatever it is, I shall always love you." At length his own son Isaac, detaching himself from his father's arms, exclaimed, " Well, behold in me a faithful servant of France, who can never resolve to bear arms against her." Placide, Isaac's uterine brother, manifested indecision. Toussaint, petrified, gave his paternal benediction to Isaac, whom he gently put away from him. Meanwhile Placide, overpowered, threw himself on his father's neck, and sobbing, said, " I am yours, father; I fear the future; I fear slavery; I am ready to fight against it; I renounce France." Immediately L'Ouverture invested him with the command of a battalion of his guard, whom, a few days after, he led against the invaders. With all Toussaint's affection for his own son, Isaac, he was unable to bring himself to offer the least opposition to his joining the French. A mother's tenderness, however, knows no claims but those of natural affection, and, impelled by that powerful sentiment, Toussaint's wife succeeded in causing Isaac to change his determination. The young man wrote that he was prevented from returning to the Cape by his mother's urgent entreaties.

This scene, which was reported to Leclerc, sufficed to prove to him the failure of the device by which the parents were to be enslaved through their attachment to their children. Most unworthy purpose ! What a terrible thing is war ! How blind is ambition ! A thirst for self-aggrandizement, when supported by power and sustained by position, confounds right and wrong, desecrates the holy, disowns moral obligation, and spreads wasting and woe through families, cities, and nations.

Further attempts at accommodation were made. Toussaint offered to prevent resistance, if Leclerc would communicate to him the instructions he had received from the First Consul, and stop the advance of the French troops. Toussaint added, that should Leclerc continue to press forward, he would repel him by force of arms. A deputation of the natives waited on the French commander. To their solicitations, Leclerc insolently replied, that he was the brother-in-law of the First Consul, that he had the bayonets on his side, and that he would take Toussaint before he had his boots off. Full of himself, and fancying that he was about to become the Bonaparte of America, he issued to the inhabitants of Saint Domingo the following proclamation : —

HEADQUARTERS OF THE CAPE, le 28 Pluviose, an 10.
(17th February, 1802.)

"INHABITANTS OF SAINT DOMINGO,

"I have come hither, in the name of the French Government, to bring you peace and happiness; I feared I should encounter obstacles in the ambitious views of the chiefs of the colony; I was not in error.

"Those chiefs who announced their devotion to France in their proclamations, had no intention of being Frenchmen; if they sometimes spoke of France, the reason is that they did not think themselves able to disown it openly. At present, their perfidious intentions are unmasked. General Toussaint sent me back his sons with a letter in which he assured me that he desired nothing so much as the happiness of the colony, and that he was ready to obey all the orders that I should give him.

"I ordered him to come to me; I gave him an assurance that I would employ him as my lieutenant-general: he replied to that order by mere words; he only seeks to gain time.

"I have been commanded by the French Government to establish here prosperity and abundance promptly; if I allow myself to be amused by cunning and perfidious ciruumlocutions, the colony will be the theatre of a long civil war.

"I commence my campaign, and I will teach that rebel what is the force of the French Government.

"From this moment, he must be regarded by all good Frenchmen residing in Saint Domingo only as an insensate monster.

"I have promised liberty to the inhabitants of Saint Domingo; I will see that they enjoy it. I will cause persons and property to be respected.

"I ordain what follows: —

"Article 1. — General Toussaint and General Christophe are outlawed; every good citizen is commanded to seize them, and to treat them as rebels to the French Republic.

"Article 2. — From the day when the French army shall have taken up quarters, every officer, whether civil or military, who shall obey other orders than those of the Generals of the army of the French Republic, which I command, shall be treated as a rebel.

"Article 3. — The agricultural laborers who have been led into error, and who, deceived by the perfidious insinuations of the rebel Generals, may have taken up arms, shall be treated as wandering children, and shall be sent back to tillage, provided they have not endeavored to incite insurrection.

"Article 4. — The soldiers of the demi-brigades who shall abandon the army of Toussaint, shall form part of the French army.

"Article 5. — General Augustin Clervaux, who commands the Department of the Ciboa, having acknowledged the French government, and the authority of the Captain-general, is maintained in his rank and in his command.

"Article 6. — The General-in-chief of the Staff will cause this proclamation to be printed and published.

"The Captain-General commanding the army of Saint Domingo.   (Signed)   " LECLERC."

This is plain language. Leclerc could speak so as to be understood, when it suited his purpose.

Toussaint L'Ouverture, on his part, was not dismayed by the threatening storm. The greater the danger the loftier was his spirit; he reviewed his guard, and acquainted them with General Leclerc's imperious determination. "General," they shouted with one voice, "we will all die with you."

16

CHAPTER V.

General Leclerc advances against Toussaint with 25,000 men in three divisions, intending to overwhelm him near Gonaïves — The plan is disconcerted by a check given by Toussaint to General Rochambeau in the Ravine Couleuvre.

THE Captain-General of the French army, having mustered all his disposable forces in the North, and received a reinforcement of seven thousand men, commenced operations in three divisions, amounting in all to five-and-twenty thousand men. One division, commanded by General Rochambeau, set out from Fort Dauphin to march to Saint Michel; the second, led by Desfourneaux, advanced from Limbé to occupy Plaisance; and the third, under General Hardy, marching to the centre, went to take possession of Marmelade. These three divisions were, together with Boudet, who was to proceed from Port-au-Prince, to effect a junction at Gonaïves in order to surprise Toussaint in his headquarters there, and put a speedy termination to the war. In proportion as the French army forced its way into the interior of the country, which was broken by mountains, gorges, and defiles, the conflict became more and more difficult. The soldiers were vexed and harassed at having to do with a flying enemy, who, constantly fighting in ambush, inflicted wounds or death as if from an invisible cause, with perfect impunity to themselves, whether from the speed with which they fled into well-known retreats, or from the height of the mountains, on which the sun burnt with a heat intolerable to Europeans. In these marches, which were rather difficult than long, the soldiers suffered from hunger, thirst, and extreme lassitude; and after the perils and penalties of the ocean, they found on the land, instead of repose or glory, a warfare in which victory brought no honor, and defeat entailed deep disgrace; and in which victory was purchased by intolerable endurance, and defeat was made afflicting by contempt for the foe, and disastrous by the revenge which that foe could on his own soil so easily take. In quitting Fort Dauphin, Rochambeau traversed the country called Ouanaminthe, passed round the north of La Grande Rivière, climbed the black mountain of Gonaïves, and descended toward the savannas of La Desolée.

The division commanded by Desfourneaux took possession of the district of Plaisance, which was treacherously delivered to him by its commander without striking a blow.

The division under Hardy scaled and captured the formidable position at Boispin, and carried at the point of the bayonet Marmelade, which was defended by Christophe.

The theatre of the war lay accordingly on the chain of the mountains which separate the North from the West, and which overtop the heights of Dondon, Villière, and the black mountain of Gonaïves. In those places Toussaint had concentrated his inferior army in order to prevent the French, who had landed on three points of the coast, from concerting their operations, and from surrounding his own troops, overwhelming him at once with all their sea and land forces.

The situation of Toussaint had become perilous, environed as he was on all sides by advancing foes. The peril, however, was neither unexpected nor unprovided for. Rochambeau was near Lacroix, lying in the mountains in a line between Esther and Gonaïves. In order to descend into the plains, he must pass through the ravine Couleuvre. This ravine was a narrow gorge flanked by precipitous mountains, covered with wood, and which swarmed with armed black laborers.

Rochambeau, by a movement in this direction, seemed likely to effect great results. He might render himself master of the person of Madame Toussaint, of her sister and her two nieces, who had just arrived at Lacroix. He might also cut off Toussaint's connection with Dessalines and Belair, and so bring the contest to an end by one blow. It was then necessary for

Toussaint to prevent the advance of Rochambeau, unless he was willing to be the next morning attacked by all Leclerc's army, in a semicircle, of which the coast, off which lay vessels of war, would have been the diameter. Leaving General Vernet, therefore, in command of his troops at Gonaïves, he put himself at the head of a squadron and of the grenadier battalion of his guard, and marched to his habitation at Lacroix. Not finding his wife and family on his arrival, he inquired where they were, and at what distance Rochambeau might be. He could learn nothing more exact than that, at the news of the enemy's approach, the ladies had sought shelter in the forest. Toussaint, having surveyed the district, made his arrangements for attack. To stop or retard the foe, he closed the defile with trees that were felled and thrown across the narrow path. In the flanks of the two mountains he placed ambuscades that were to fall on the French on their sides and in their rear, at the same time that he would assail them in front, thus surrounding them every way. For fear of being discovered, he lighted no fire during the night. Accompanied by one of his aide-de-camps and two laborers, he went forward to reconnoitre. One of his guides, having pushed on venturously, fell into the midst of an outpost belonging to Rochambeau. Captured, he was put to death without being able even by a cry to warn Toussaint of the proximity of his foes. Having learned all he could, that general rejoined his band, gave orders for battle, and addressed to the soldiers the following speech : —

" You are going to fight against enemies who have neither faith, law, nor religion. They promise you liberty, they intend your servitude. Why have so many ships traversed the ocean, if not to throw you again into chains ? They disdain to recognize in you submissive children, and if you are not their slaves, you are rebels. The mother country, misled by the Consul, is no longer anything for you but a step-mother. Was there ever a defence more just than yours ? Uncover your breasts, you will see them branded by the iron of slavery. During ten years, what did you not undertake for liberty? Your masters slain or put to flight; the English humiliated by defeat; discord extinguished; a land of slavery purified by fire, and reviving more beautiful than ever under liberty; these are your labors, and these the fruits of your labors; and the foe wishes to snatch both out of your hands. Already have you left traces of your despair; but for a traitor, Port-au-Prince would be only a heap of ruins; but Léogane, Fort-Dauphin, the Cape, that opulent capital of the Antilles, exist no longer; you have carried everywhere consuming fires, the flambeaux of our liberty. The steps of our enemies have trodden only on ashes; their eyes have encountered nothing but smoking ruins, which you have watered with their blood. This is the road by which they have come to us. What do they hope for? Have we not all the presages of victory? Not for their country, not for liberty do they fight, but to serve the hatred and the ambition of the Consul, my enemy, — mine because he is yours; their bodies are not mutilated by the punishments of servitude; their wives and their children are not near their camps, and the graves of their fathers are beyond the ocean. This sky, these mountains, these lands, all are strange to them? What do I say? As soon as they breathe the same air as we, their bravery sinks, their courage departs. Fortune seems to have delivered them as victims into our hands. Those whom the sword spares will be struck dead by an avenging climate. Their bones will be scattered among these mountains and rocks, and tossed about by the waves of our sea. Never more will they behold their native land; never more will they receive the tender embraces of their wives, their sisters, and their mothers; and liberty will reign over their tomb."

On his side, Rochambeau, too much accustomed to treat the Africans with pride and contempt, nevertheless, thought it prudent to encourage his men by telling them that this day would raise their glory to the highest pitch, since there would be no part of the world which would not be a witness of their triumph; that the Tiber, the Nile, and the Rhine, where they had

16*

conquered very formidable adversaries, resounded with the echoes of their exploits; that now they had to combat slaves, who, not daring to look them in the face, were flying on all hands; and that they had not come thousands of miles from home to be overcome by a rebellious slave.

As soon as the day broke, Toussaint's advanced guard, in passing a river, encountered the advanced guard of Rochambeau, which was on its march. Then the action began. The impetuosity of the attack was checked by the bravery of the resistance. The troops in ambush pressed forward on the flanks and in the rear of the French, who everywhere presented a bold front to the assailants. The retrenchment having been opened, the conflict became bloody and obstinate. Now the victory inclined to this side, now to that. The uncertainty did but inflame the courage of both. Toussaint was, then seen to brave a thousand perils. Some of his grenadiers yielding a little before the French impetuosity, a young officer called back their powers by these words, "What! you desert your general!" That moment he put himself at the head of a platoon of grenadiers, and, ascending an eminence which commanded Rochambeau's right wing, annoyed him with a destructive fire. At this moment an officer of dragoons having informed Toussaint that his wife and family were behind a mountain not far from the place of action, he replied, "Do you see that they take the road to Esther; I must here perform my duty." His duty he did perform. Regardless of himself, he encouraged his men when they vacillated, and ever again led them into the fight. With such fury did the conflict rage that arms were thrown aside, and combatants, seizing each other, struggled for ilfe and death. The field of battle was covered with the slain. A decisive effort was necessary. Putting himself at the head of his grenadiers, Toussaint rushed to the attack, and drove Rochambeau over the river, where, in the morning, the fight had begun. He then returned, and took up a position on his side of the stream.

The issue remained undecided; but Toussaint had rescued his

family and stopped the impetuous career of Rochambeau. He had also gained time, while Christophe, by a vigorous defence, retarded the advance of Desfourneaux and of Hardy. Thus had he saved himself from being surrounded on the plain of Gonaïves. Like a man of genius, he had chosen the place and the time of the combat, and in a crisis obtained great advantages.

Retiring toward his centre, Toussaint pitched his camp on the banks of Esther. There, surrounded by his soldiers and his family, and covered with a cloak, he had only a plank on which to sit and to sleep. He passed the greater part of the night in despatching orders written with his own hand, and in going from post to post. The next day he sent his wife and family to the mountain known by the name of Grand Cahos, which runs in a line with the Artibonite. His visit to Esther, however, was only for a temporary purpose. He was too good a soldier to meet the concentrated forces of the enemy in a level country, where, with all his valor, he would not have been able to prevent his comparatively diminutive army from being crushed. His ability to offer any effectual resistance had arisen from the judgment he had employed in making the mountains the seat of the warfare. Justified in this policy by the success which he had gained, he determined to evacuate Esther, and to collect troops in another mountainous stronghold, still more favorable than that in which he had defeated Rochambeau.

A review of the operations of Toussaint L'Ouverture, from the point at which our narrative has arrived, shows that the method of his warfare consisted in passive or active resistance, which, after spreading fire and devastation before the enemy's march, withdrew from the coast and made the mountains its centre and its bulwark. That this plan was carefully weighed and well laid out, may be presumed from a knowledge of Toussaint's character. It was also carried into effect as thoroughly as circumstances permitted. If, in any respect, it failed, the failure was owing to no remissness on the part of the great chief. The following letters, written by him at the beginning of the campaign, may serve to illustrate and confirm these observations, and may conduce to the reader's acquaintance with the character of our hero.

" LIBERTY.   " EQUALITY.

" The Governor-General to General Dessalines, Commander-in-chief of the army of the West.

HEADQUARTERS GONAÏVES, Feb. 8, 1802.

" There is no reason for despair, Citizen-General, if you can succeed in removing from the troops that have landed the resources offered to them by Port Republican. Endeavor, by all the means of force and address, to set that place on fire; it is constructed entirely of wood; you have only to send into it some faithful emissaries. Are there none under your orders devoted enough for this service? Ah! my dear General, what a misfortune that there was a traitor in that city, and that your orders and mine were not put into execution.

" Watch the moment when the garrison shall be weak in consequence of expeditions into the plains, and then try to surprise and carry that city, falling on it in the rear.

" Do not forget, while waiting for the rainy season which will rid us of our foes, that we have no other resource than destruction and flames. Bear in mind that the soil bathed with our sweat must not furnish our enemies with the smallest aliment. Tear up the roads with shot; throw corpses and horses into all the fountains; burn and annihilate everything, in order that those who have come to reduce us to slavery may have before their eyes the image of that hell which they deserve.

" Salutation and Friendship,

(Signed)   " TOUSSAINT L'OUVERTURE."

" Toussaint L'Ouverture, Governor of Saint Domingo, to Citizen Domage, Brigadier-General, commanding the district of Jérémie.

HEADQUARTERS, SAINT MARC, the 9th of Feb., 1802.

" I send to you, my dear General, my aide-de-camp, Chancy.

He conveys to you the present communication, and will tell you from me what I have charged him to make known to you.

"The whites of France and of the Colony, united together, wish to take away our liberty. Many vessels and troops have arrived, which have seized the Cape, Port Republican, and Fort Liberté.

"The Cape, after a vigorous resistance, has fallen; but the enemy found only a city and country of ashes; the forts were blown up, and everything has been burnt.

"The town of Port Republican was surrendered to them by the traitor Agé, as well as Fort Bizoton, which yielded without striking a blow, through the cowardice and the treachery of Bardet. The General of Division, Dessalines, at this moment maintains a cordon at Croix des Bouquets; and all our other places are on the defensive.

"As Jérémie is very strong through its natural advantages, you will maintain yourself in it, and defend it with the courage which I know you possess. Raise the laborers in a mass, and infuse into them this truth, namely, that they must distrust those who have received proclamations from the whites of France, and who secretly circulate them in order to seduce the friends of liberty.

"I have ordered Laplume, Brigadier-General, to set on fire the City of Cayes, the other towns, and all the plains, in case he is unable to withstand the enemy's force, and then all the troops of the different garrisons, and all the laborers should go to Jérémie to augment your band. You will take measures with General Laplume, for the due execution of these things. You will employ the women engaged in agriculture in making depôts of provisions in great abundance.

"Endeavor as much as you can to send me news of your position. I reckon entirely on you, and leave you absolutely master, to do everything in order to save us from the most frightful yoke.

"Wishing you health,

"Salutation and Friendship,

(Signed)   "TOUSSAINT L'OUVERTURE.

CHAPTER VI.

THE district into which Toussaint L'Ouverture had sent his family was that to which he meant to transfer his resistance. The mountain range which he resolved to occupy and entrench bears the name of Artibonite, and is divided into two districts, the one called the Grand Cahos, the other the Petit Cahos. These mountains, over which he spread his army, are intersected with deep ravines and precipitous outlets, at every one of which a handful of brave men could arrest an army. The principal entrance was defended by Crête-à-Pierrot, a redoubt which blocked up the pass, and which the English had constructed when they invaded the West.

In passing toward the new seat of war, where he was joined by his chief generals, Toussaint was suddenly attacked with a burning fever. His mind, however, so far mastered his body that he scarcely abated his activity, and formed designs of the greatest daring, in making arrangements for attacking the enemy in the rear. Ill as he was, he set out to survey the district, and arrived in time to prevent the demolition of Crête-à-Pierrot, which had been abandoned, and which Dessalines had ordered to be razed. He then proceeded to add to its strength. He supplied it with water and food as precautions against a siege. He placed in it a garrison, and gave the command to Dessalines. Having called the officers together, he harangued them thus· "Children,—yes, you are all my children, from Lamartinière, who is white as a white, but who knows that he has negro blood in his veins, to Monpoint, whose skin is the same as mine,—I intrust to you this post. Take measures for its defence." The officers declared that he might rely on them, living or dead.

To more destructive hands than those of Dessalines, this important post could not have been confided. In his retreat, that ferocious monster had dragged away from their homes all the whites he could seize, whom the sword and the musket had spared. These were conducted to Verettes, Mirebalais, and Petite Rivière, towns lying along the banks of the Artibonite. There were renewed the frightful scenes of the first insurrection. At the sight of the conflagration which reduced into ashes the villages and the fields at the foot of Mount Cahos, where Toussaint had entrenched himself, a vast carnage was made of the whites. Four hundred men were massacred at Mirebalais and Petite Rivière. In no place was the slaughter so terrible as at the village of Verettes. At the nod of Dessalines, men who had been slaves, and who dreaded the new servitude with which they were threatened, slew seven hundred of the poor wretches that Dessalines had dragged after him. The daughter breathed her last on the bosom of her expiring mother. The father was unable to save the son; the son was unable to save the father. There a sister died in the arms of a brother; here, a nurse tried to make her body a means of defence for her infant; her milk and her blood flowed in one stream. Farther on, old men in vain implored pity from their former slaves, whom they called on by name to bring back the remembrance of past acts of kindness. Whole families were thus bathed in blood. More frightful and more atrocious still was the sight when sons slew their fathers, thus revenging themselves for the black blood of their mothers, and the neglect and disavowal of their fathers. So great was the fury of the blacks and mulattoes that they even wreaked their rage on domestic animals which belonged to the planters. Thus the banks of the Artibonite were covered with fire and blood. Before the arrival of the French expedition, all there was peaceful, prosperous, and happy.

The French felt deep compassion when, on coming up, they beheld at Verettes so many victims who still remained unburied, and who retained the attitudes in which they perished, as if to paint an awful picture of the evils of slavery. They there saw the arm of one victim locked in that of another; hand grasped in hand; faces fixed on the same object; father, mother, children grouped together,—a family even in death; young women who in the last moments forgot not they were women; bodies which had served as useless ramparts to friendship and to filial and paternal love. The scenes were horrible. Nor was their horror abated by the fact that ravages scarcely less atrocious had been committed by the white invaders. A little before, the bay of Mancenille had smoked with innocent blood. And on more than one occasion had prisoners been slain in bands, in order to strike alarm into the defenders of their native soil. All the blacks, however, were not barbarians. Many, moved by pity or gratitude, saved the lives of unfortunate colonists. Some concealed them in the mountains, and supported them by what they took in hunting. Others led them, through by-paths, into districts occupied by the French. There were blacks who, to prevent suspicion on the part of pursuers, covered their white friends with leaves and branches, and counterfeited drunkenness when they thought there was special danger of discovery. Calamities, public and private, so numerous and so terrible, were more than human strength could endure, and under their pressure, some persons lost their reason and others committed suicide. What a complication of sorrows,—all caused by slavery.

Having provided for the defence of the country of the Artibonite, and directed Belair to occupy the mountains of Verettes, Toussaint proceeded to execute his daring plan of taking Leclerc in the rear in order to operate a diversion in favor of the Artibonite lines, and to reanimate the courage of the North. With a small but resolute force, Toussaint ascended the defiles, and the chain of mountains which separate the Artibonite from the district of Saint Michael. In vain was General Hardy detached in pursuit of him by Leclerc, whose army was in movement to attack Crête-à-Pierrot. Toussaint appeared at Ennery, and the French garrison which Leclerc had left there fled at his approach to Gonaïves. He presented himself before Gonaïves, and might have captured it, had he chosen. He was satisfied with alarming the garrison, which was on the point of embarking on board a frigate that was in the roads. Having attained his end, he returned to Ennery, where he organized battalions of militia, who were employed to guard and defend the country. This work finished, he betook himself to Marmelade. There he sent an order to Christophe, who was at Petite-Rivière, to return promptly into the North, where, in the forest of Grande Rivière, there had, without the French being aware of it, been formed a considerable depôt of arms and ammunition. From Marmelade, Toussaint went to Plaisance. On his arrival, he proceeded to reconnoitre a fort situated on a height. A few hours after, he placed himself at the head of two companies of grenadiers and captured it. The following day, he divided his troops into two bodies. Taking the command of the right wing, he marched to meet Desfourneaux, who was coming up to attack him. He bore up against the impetuosity of the French troops, who were much more numerous than his own, and at length succeeded in putting them to flight. Sending, in the moment of action, an aide-de-camp to learn how things went on in the left wing, he was led to believe that Desfourneaux was manœuvring so as to circumvent him. Thereupon he left the right to the care of Colonel Gabarre, and with a few men hurried to the point of danger. Among the European troops he recognized the uniform of the Ninth Saint Domingo regiment. Advancing quite alone to within five or six paces of the regiment, which easily recognized their proper commander, he said, "Soldiers of the ninth, will you dare fire on your general and on your brethren?" The words fell like a thunder-clap on the soldiers; who forthwith were on their knees, and, but for the European troops, who began to fire, they would have joined Toussaint. Seeing the peril of their general, Toussaint's forces defended him against the Europeans. He escaped through the thick of a fire which was very destructive. A young officer, bearing a letter from Dessalines to the Governor of the island,

17

received a mortal blow at the moment that he delivered it, and expired in Toussaint's arms. From that letter the General-in-chief learned that his aid was urgently required at Crête-à-Pierrot; thither, therefore, he repaired.

The French had been drawing their strength under the foot of the mountains of Cahos. As they made their way, they beheld the ravages committed by the enemy. Traces of fire and death appeared everywhere. Here and there they met a great number of colonists wandering in the woods and hanging on the sides of the rocks, with their wives and children, having escaped from death only by chance or flight. The soldiers restored to them hope, and promised them revenge. The sight of these unhappy people, whose clothes were in rags, their cries, their moanings, the horror with which they were stricken, inflamed the minds of their rescuers, and prepared them for any atrocities. Without scruple and without pity, they massacred the herds of blacks whom the fate of war had thrown into their hands; two hundred they immolated at the Fort of Mount Nolo; a little further on, six hundred fell beneath their murderous hands. Thus carnage was added to carnage, and black blood flowed to avenge white blood. The savage and torn sides of Mount Cahos, the odorous banks of the Artibonite, offered the spectacle of barbarity opposed to barbarity, and war was only prolonged assassination. These are the horrible devastations of slavery.

No graves were dug, no mounds were raised for sepulture. Dessalines had prohibited interment in order that the eyes of his assailants might see his vengeance even in the repulsive remains of carnage. It is said that the monster slew a mother for having buried her son. The French, carried away by the movements of the war, gave no attention to the religious duty of burial, so that the dead bodies became food for dogs, vultures, and crocodiles; and their bones, partly calcined by the sun, remained scattered about, as if to mark the mournful fury of servitude and lust of power.

Fortune seemed to smile on Leclerc. He lost no time in

announcing to his brother-in-law his success, which he failed not to exaggerate, — entire battalions that had joined his ranks, the two provinces of the South and the East subdued, all the maritime cities in his power, — such were the heads of his triumphant report. He described Toussaint L'Ouverture as a party-chief, sullen, violent, fanatical, hateful, breathing only fire and slaughter; he called him a barbarian, an unnatural father, sacrificing his children to his passion for revolt, a mere fugitive slave, devoured by remorse, abandoned, and pursued. This news, which gave the Consul joy, delighted the colonists who had remained in France, and revived the cupidity of the slave-dealers whose vessels had for six years remained in harbor unproductive.

When, however, Bonaparte began seriously to reflect on all that had taken place, his satisfaction was not a little diminished. It was true that he held under his domination the South rich in manufactures and the East fertile in pasturage. But what had he conquered? Lands in ashes. Port-au-Prince had miraculously escaped from the incendiary torch. But what a sight in other parts! Those barbarians do not place the keys of their cities at the feet of their conquerors. Toussaint, designated a bandit, is a formidable General in his mountains. The Consul applies himself to study that remarkable man. He is the soul of the war, and him he must reach, seize, and put in chains. That accomplished, what then? He must attach to himself the men of mixed blood, who are already partly his. Then discord must be disseminated. The black in revolt will be overcome by the subjugated black. This was the Consul's policy. These were his means for bringing the island into subjection. To this purpose, and for these results, he wrote to Leclerc. But suddenly the war took a new aspect.

Twelve thousand men, the bravest soldiers of the Republic, are assembled near Petite Rivière to put down a revolted slave! Rochambeau, Hardy, Debelle, generals of great skill and high powers, are stopped in a ravine by a handful of revolted slaves! their passage is barred, their valor rendered nugatory by a few men whom they despise! Officers and soldiers, who have gained victory and renown against the first troops of Europe, perish in huge numbers under the blows of half-civilized blacks. So much do the issues of war depend on opportunity; so dear is freedom; so odious is servitude.

The first division which came up to the attack of Crête-à-Pierrot was that of Debelle. As soon as the French troops were seen in the redoubt, Dessalines opened the gates. " The gates have been opened," he said, "for those who do not feel themselves courageous enough to die; while there is yet time, let the friends of the French depart; they have nothing but death to look for here." After having sent away all whom sickness or fear made desirous of going, he spread a train of gunpowder as far as the first gate, and, seizing a torch, exclaimed, " Now for the first fire; I will blow up the fort, if you do not defend it." During these things, the French were advancing, preceded by a herald (4th March, 1802). The herald held a letter in his hand. Dessalines ordered his men to fire. The herald fell dead. Firing began on both sides in real earnest. For several hours it continued without an interval. The French rushed forward with their usual bravery and enthusiasm, but it was only to meet death. The moment they were within reach, the batteries were opened and the ground was strewed with dead. The General-in-chief, Debelle, was grievously wounded, as well as Brigadier-General Devaux. The division was compelled to fall back with the loss of four hundred men.

This defeat deeply affected the mind of Leclerc, who was then at Port-au-Prince. Was his victorious career, then, to be delayed by a single stronghold? Not without apprehension he hastened to the scene of action. He brought with him the division of Boudet. While the troops were assembling, a scout of Toussaint's, in his zeal to ascertain all he could, entered their camp, pretending to be a deserter. In the midst of his guard, General Boudet questioned the man. When the former asked him how many whites he had put to death, the latter with well-feigned fear, appeared overwhelmed. In the twinkling of an eye, having learnt the condition of the French, he leaped from his horse. Boudet, the first to observe the movement, attempted to seize him, and had his thumb nearly bitten off. The man got away, slipped beneath the horse's legs, overthrew the soldiers who attempted to stop him, ran toward the Artibonite, plunged into the stream, and escaped amid a shower of balls. Arrived on the opposite bank, he appeared to have been struck, for he fell as if his thigh was broken. The presence on the other side of the river of a reconnoitring party of the foe prevented pursuit. The black scout, who had the rank of captain, appears to have been carried off by his friends.

Among the troops which now advanced to the attack, there were Rigaud and Pétion. True to his instructions, Leclerc added to the skill of the white soldiers the fury and the animosity of mulatto blood.

In the interval which had elapsed since the first attack, Dessalines had erected a new fort on an eminence which commanded that on which stood the famous Crête-a-Pierrot. The new redoubt, though hastily constructed, was to witness the defeat of the Consul's boastful brother-in-law.

The French, in advancing, surprised a camp of blacks who were asleep. They fell on them; the blacks ran toward the fort and the French pursued them. Those who could not enter the fort threw themselves into the moat. Immediately the fort opened its fire and mowed down the assailants. General Boudet received a wound. At the moment when his division was on the point of perishing, that of Dugua came up. Forthwith, that general was struck. Only one general officer kept the field. Then the blacks rushed to the charge. The French retreated. In the retreat, Leclerc himself, who came up with reinforcements, received a serious contusion. This second attack cost the Captain-General eight hundred men.

In their retrograde movement, the Europeans had opportunities of ascertaining how entirely the population was in enmity against them. On the plantations, they saw the laborers watching their movements. Those laborers exchanged shots with the soldiers who flanked the column. If a party of scouts were detached, they fled; as soon as the scouts retired, they reappeared. The French army inspired only terror.

A third attack was to be made. The stronghold was regularly invested. Fresh troops had come up. All that ability, experience, labor, and prowess could contribute was set in vigorous action.

While the operations for the blockade were proceeding, the French soldiers heard from the strongholds the words of the very songs to which they had themselves marched against the enemies of liberty in Europe. The effect was singular and deep. " What! those black men the injured, and we the injurers! those black men the oppressed, and we the oppressors! Are we, then, no longer the servants and patrons of liberty? The Republic gives freedom; we are fighting for servitude." Such impressions were little likely to increase the efficiency of republican soldiers. Their duty they continue to do, but services higher than a mere sense of duty can command, were now required.

By degrees, the works were completed and brought into play against the redoubt. Partial successes were obtained. Encouraged by these, Rochambeau thought himself able to carry a battery, which he had for a moment silenced, by one blow. He lost three hundred men in the useless attempt. Then a constant cannonade was commenced. From the 22d to the 24th of March, it was carried on with great activity. The redoubt was in the greatest peril.

At this time a black man and a black woman were captured. Suspected to be spies, they were subjected to the severest punishment. The man said he was blind; nothing but the whites of his eyes were to be seen. Only in leaning on the aged negress, his companion, did he appear able to walk. She affected to be deaf. Scarcely anything but groans and sobs could the cruellest treatment extort from them. At length, compassion prevailed. They were bid go about their business. They had dreadfully suffered, and seemed unable to move. Not before they were threatened to be shot did they attempt to walk.

They were conducted beyond the outlying sentinels. When fairly out of the reach of their enemies, they began to dance, and instantly darted off for the fort, where they were received. They conveyed to its commander intelligence of the approach of Toussaint L'Ouverture.

That very night (March 24) an attack was made on the French lines which was repulsed only with difficulty and loss. That attack was led by Toussaint himself, who had conceived a project worthy of his own genius. Having reason to think the North could for some time give him no more trouble, and afraid lest Crête-a-Pierrot might be carried by storm, he hastened to the Artibonite, intending with a few trusty soldiers to penetrate to Leclerc's headquarters, make him prisoner, and ship him off to France. To aid him in his daring plan, a feint was made in the attack of which we have just spoken. And the captured fugitives were sent to encourage the garrison to hold out.

The stratagem was too late. Lamartinière, who had taken the command with his accustomed bravery, had done and endured everything that man can do and endure. With his soldiers he patiently bore hunger, thirst, sickness, exhaustion, and the prospect of death at any moment. With their aid, he performed prodigies of heroism. But stone walls are not proof against cannon-balls and bombs. The forts were defended against thousands of brave Frenchmen, even when falling into ruins. But the hour at length came. Then, when resistance was vain, the commander resolved to cut himself a passage through the ranks of his enemies. He escaped from the hands of 12,000 men, not having lost half his garrison, and leaving to his assailants only the dead and the wounded amid a heap of ruins.

CHAPTER VII.

Shattered condition of the French army — Dark prospects of Toussaint — Leclerc opens negotiations for peace — Wins over Christophe and Dessalines — Offers to recognize Toussaint as Governor-General — Receives his submission on condition of preserving universal freedom — L'Ouverture in the quiet of his home.

DEARLY had the reduction of Crête-à-Pierrot been bought by the French. The loss deeply afflicted the Captain-General, who induced his subordinates to make it appear as slight as possible, remembering the contemptuous terms in which he had spoken of Toussaint and his forces, and well dreading the moral effect on the inhabitants of the island.

After the capture of this stronghold, Leclerc took measures for reëstablishing his communications. He ordered Rochambeau's division to open them by forming a junction at Gonaïves with Desfourneaux ; and directed Hardy, with his forces, to make for the Cape. The latter division were compelled to form for themselves a road with their arms in their hands. Under the impression that the invaders had suffered a total defeat, Hardy had with him only bands of fugitives who hastened to the Cape in order to fly by sea from the island, while on the whole line of his march, he encountered opposition from regular troops or armed laborers. But for the courage of the soldiers who were kept under discipline, and the judgment and energy of the commanders, the whole division would have perished. From four to five hundred men were lost on the route.

While the divisions of Rochambeau and Hardy proceeded toward the North, that of Boudet, under the command of General Lacroix, was commanded to return to Saint Marc in order to attack Belair, who up to that time had remained in observation on the heights of Matheux, which stand to the southeast of that post, between it and Mount Cahos. We give a report of the undertaking, in the words of its leader: —

"We climbed the heights by the sources of Mount Ronis. I had often heard speak of a 'carabined road,' but I was, I avow, far from forming an idea of the obstacles which I had to overcome in order to open the carabined road of Matheux. Yet was I expert in work of the kind, having a year before opened the passage of Splugen. In the memorable campaign of the army of reserve, I had also traced, round Fort Bard, routes on peaked mountains declared impassable. I had conveyed cannon by those roads, thus executing an enterprise till then regarded as impossible. That path round Fort Bard threw down the barrier which stood against the fortune of the First Consul; by that road the army of reserve gained the plains of Piedmont and reconquered Italy on the field of Marengo. Precipices and road accidents are everywhere the same; but in the Alps the bushwood is at least accessible, and the trees are of a determinate height, while in America the former are fine mountains and the latter colossal masses which you can scarcely take in in one view, and which you can displace only by strength of arm and length of time. I doubt whether I could have been able to gain the plateau of Matheux if Belair had added the efforts of his resistance to the obstacles of the locality in which he was.

"After the most fatiguing march, I at last arrived at Matheux. Belair had quitted the plain the previous evening to join Dessalines on Mount Cahos.

"I wrote to him, suggesting that he should imitate the examples of Generals Clervaux, Paul L'Ouverture, and Maurepas, and announcing that I was authorized by the Captain-General to guarantee to him and to his officers their military rank. He answered that he blindly followed the authority of Toussaint L'Ouverture, recognized governor for life, by the constitution of the colony, and by his numberless services, which France seemed disposed to disown.

" The lofty position of Matheux presented to us the aspect
of the champaign lands of France ; we there found its atmosphere ; the lungs of our soldiers dilated ; we were agile ; on
the contrary, the blacks, whom we had as auxiliaries, wore a
shrunk appearance. In the different gorges of the mountain,
we delivered from five to six hundred persons who had fled
thither from Saint Marc and the neighboring lands. Hardy
and Rochambeau had set at large a thousand fugitives in Mount
Cahos.

" I collected on Matheux a large number of horses, mules,
and horned cattle, which Belair had got together. Two days
after, I began to march toward Port-au-Prince. A letter was
brought me from General Boudet, who, directing me to conduct
his division to that city, requested that I would make a proces-
sional entrance into it, and that in so doing, I should make the
troops appear as numerous as possible, in order to efface from
the minds of the men of color in the West the impressions they
had received as to the extent of our loss. I put the troops into
two ranks : our sections marched at great distances ; all our
officers were on horseback ; artillery ready for the field was
sent to meet me ; I distributed it in the column with the baggage ; and our entrance produced the moral effect which we
expected." *

Nothing can more clearly show the valorous resistance made
by Toussaint L'Ouverture than the frank confessions made by
this respectable writer of the disorganized and weakened condition of the French troops after the capture of Crête-à-Pierrot.
Scarcely able to keep the field or effect a retrograde movement,
the decimated and shattered armies of Leclerc could not be
allowed, except when tricked out in this fashion, to return to
the capital of the island. What impudence, then, was that
which described the great African leader as a mere chief of
banditti ! and what did that leader want but the support of
some European power, friendly to human freedom, in order to

* " Mémoires pour servir à l'histoire de la Révolution," &c., Vol. ii. p.
172, seq.

establish on a permanent basis that constitution which had been so wisely constructed, and that liberty which had been purchased at so large a price, and of which the Haytian negroes had proved themselves so worthy? Alas! such a friendly power did not exist. England and the United States were both committed to the support of slavery; and the great war of the African world had to be fought out by Toussaint alone. Well was the conflict sustained, and though the immediate result was adverse, the strife, we trust, will not have to be renewed. If the plains, the mountains, and the ravines of Saint Domingo say nothing effectually on behalf of negro rights, surely they cry with so loud a voice, declaring the horrors of a war of " bloods," that even fear will suffice to break the bonds of the slave!

From the ruins and carnage of Crête-à-Pierrot, L'Ouverture hastened to the recesses of Mount Cahos, whither he had ordered the brave defenders of that post to follow him. They, as well as he, needed a few days' repose. And there, where he had for some time formerly dwelt, he met his wife and family, and in their society enjoyed a short tranquillity. Of this brief leisure he availed himself to write to Bonaparte in order to explain to him the conduct of General Leclerc and to ask him to send another to take his place, into whose hands he might resign the command of the island.

This was an hour for calm reflection Toussaint L'Ouverture did not let slip. Thoughtful by nature, he now, by the force of circumstances, was drawn to the consideration of his past career and his present position. He had effected much. At one time, he thought he had achieved the permanent freedom of his color. But, alas! the constitution had not been ratified. In defence of that solemn national act, he had not only again and again risked his life and nearly forfeited all he possessed, but he had given many a severe lesson to its assailants, and taught them to respect and fear a man whom they disgracefully attempted to enslave. Yet amid these triumphs, the final success of his undertaking seemed now to recede into distant mists.

The present was dark and gloomy. Leclerc, with shattered forces, was still strong, and should the army now under his command be annihilated, it could easily be replaced by the inexhaustible resources of France. Yet, so long as he himself lived, he was bound to labor in the sacred cause he had undertaken. With the past full in his view, he could not despair. Any way it is for man to deserve, as it is for God to give, success.

Instead of sinking beneath his sense of the great loss suffered by the destruction of Crête-à-Pierrot, Toussaint, after a brief interval, resumed hostile operations with an active energy, not surpassed even in his days of triumph. He had indeed disappeared from the view of his foes, but it was only to deceive them by false and rapid marches, to prepare ambuscades, to harass them on their flanks and in the rear; to make them sink under the fatigue, hunger, thirst, and want of sleep he compelled them to undergo. Now he covered his flight by deserts and by flames to make their victory more baneful than ordinary defeat; now he waited for his prey in a defile, always doing much, by the force of his genius, to carry the warfare beyond all acknowledged rules. Christophe in the North Dessalines in the West, supported his adroit and rapid movements. At the sound of the church-bells, he sent forth from the pulpit a manly and magical eloquence, which painted to the eye and impressed on the heart the horrors of servitude and the delights of liberty, and preached a religion which, acknowledging all men as brothers, disclaimed and condemned slavery, and made his soldiers feel that in fighting for freedom they fought on the side of God and Christ. His sermon over, he resumed the soldier and the general, disappeared, flew, reappeared, and seemed almost as if he possessed a species of omnipresence. All the time he had an army at his command, though where they were, or what the number and resources of his troops, was hidden to all but himself and a chosen few; while, by means as sure as they were hidden, he learnt all that took place among his assailants. Moved by his authority, his spies and scouts, now in appearance blind, deaf, lame, and now beggars or fugitives, made light of toil, peril, and torture in a service which religion, as well as civil obedience, seemed to them to exact.

The different bodies of the French army, who believed Toussaint ruined, if not dead, felt his blows on every side. As they returned to the Cape, or to Port-au-Prince, he disturbed them, beat them, worried them, alike in their communications, in their attacks, in their marches, in their retreat. Everywhere he carried alarm and dread. When the soldiers entered the Cape, Toussaint appeared in its suburbs. The city required both walls and defenders. The blacks, if they appeared to be friends, proved to be enemies in reality. With all dispatch, Leclerc raised anew the fortifications of a town in which, more than ever, the party of servitude and the party of liberty disputed and contended. In that war no man knew his neighbor; you lived side by side with your enemy; you slept under the same roof; you ate at the same table with him, and yet you knew him not; for there were blacks on the side of the Consul, and there were whites on the side of Toussaint. At length, arms were taken up. The ships supplied cannon, and the sailor was brought on shore to fight. Only the more vigor did Toussaint put forth, and the city was about to become his prey when fresh troops arrived from France, and the black hero thought it prudent to retire.

The position of Leclerc had become one of extreme difficulty. By painful experience he had learned with what singular enemies he had to contend. Of what use was it to continue a war in which victories cost so much and were so readily effaced by reverses? Already had he lost five thousand men in battle; a like number, sick or wounded, were in the hospitals. Besides, the war offered no reward. What glory was there even in totally subjugating semi-barbarian blacks? Conquest, instead of enriching the soldier, only carried him into burning towns or desert mountains. The army murmured; the climate was intolerable; the work they had to perform was repulsive. " The

18

Consul," they said, "has sent us here to perish, companions though we are of his achievements and sharers in his glory."

These, and similar complaints, which reached the ears of the captain of the expedition, occasioned him lively disquietude, the rather because his army was attacked by a malady which, bad as it was, threatened to become more deadly; and although he expected fresh troops, scarcely would all suffice to keep the population in order, to say nothing of the exigencies of war. He had, it is true, many blacks under his banners, but could he count on their fidelity? Did he not know that their chiefs, who showed the most zeal and devotion, were wrapped in impenetrable dissimulation, and that he kept them obedient only by reiterated promises of liberty.

The people of color appeared to him more devoted, but had they not, in preceding wars, passed now into the party of the whites, and now into that of the blacks, as much from inconstancy as for the sake of liberty? The barbarous chiefs, however, who were his enemies, gave him most concern; Christophe, filled with prowess and intrepidity; Dessalines, that savage Achilles, of unequalled courage and fury; Toussaint, who by his prolific genius was capable of everything, who escaped only to reappear, who everywhere caused foes to spring up under the feet of his army, as if they were born of the mountains.

Reflecting on these things, — counting his losses, surveying his disappointments, measuring his enemies, calculating his difficulties, and forecasting his prospects, — Leclerc came to the determination that he should act wisely if he tried what could be done in the way of negotiation. Should the attempt fail, he would have gained time; should it succeed, he would have put an end to a doubtful and disastrous war.

Among the heads of the hostile army, Christophe had shown the least aversion to accommodation. With him, Leclerc commenced his negotiations; he intimated to Christophe that as the mother country would unquestionably give legal confirmation to the abolition of servitude, the war was useless and without an object, and that the sole obstacle to peace being the ambition of Toussaint, he would arrange with him in order to arrest that chief in the most secret manner possible. Instead of becoming the instrument of that perfidy, Christophe replied in language and tones of virtue, saying that to arrest his friend, his companion, his chief, would be to betray at once friendship and honor, as well as his country; and that a treason so disgraceful could not for a moment be entertained by him. He ended his letter with these words: " Show us the laws which guarantee our liberty, then Toussaint, my brethren, myself, — all of us, — will with joy throw ourselves into the arms of our mother country. How could we believe the Consul's words, brought to us as they were amid demonstrations of war? Excuse," he added, " the fears and the alarm of a people which has suffered so much in slavery. Give it grounds of confidence if you desire to terminate the calamities of Saint Domingo; then, forgetting the past, we shall in security enjoy the present and the future."

Struck with the wisdom and energy of this reply, Leclerc felt that it was more than ever necessary to put away all idea of slavery, which could be restored only in very different circumstances. With this view he dealt freely in protestations. The Consul, he urged, could not have proposed laws for a country with which he was not acquainted; but in the name of the Supreme Being, the avenger of falsehood, he affirmed that the liberty of the blacks was the basis of the laws which would be passed.

An interview ensued, and, in reliance on the protestations and the oath of Leclerc, Christophe went over to the French with twelve hundred men, surrendering the mountains of Limbé, Port-François, and Grande Rivière, with an immense amount of warlike stores.

Christophe immediately sought an interview with Toussaint, and, among other things, remarked that Leclerc appeared very sorry at having undertaken the war, that he had done so in the persuasion that he could soon bring it to a successful termination, and that, being now disabused of that error, was desirous of concluding a peace ; adding that, at the express request of the Captain-General, he wished to converse with Toussaint on the subject.

On his part, Toussaint complained that Christophe had listened to overtures from the enemy, contrary to military discipline, since he had no authority from his superior officer. Before leaving, Christophe put into the hands of Toussaint a letter from Leclerc. Prevented, at the moment, from reading the communication, Toussaint did not learn till after Christophe's departure, that he had gone over to the French. The regret which he felt gave place to astonishment, and astonishment was succeeded by indignation. He sent for Adjutant-General Fontaine, the chief of his staff, and to him alone communicated the contents of the letter, directing him to go to Christophe, and command him to repair to the headquarters at Marmelade, in order to explain his conduct. The traitor affected compliance. Many of his officers, on hearing of the mission of General Fontaine, declared that they had been misled. On his return, that officer reported the surrender of Port-François and other places. Toussaint L'Ouverture assembled his chief officers, and announced to them the extraordinary event. Christophe's conduct appeared to them no less incomprehensible than blameworthy. The news having spread among the people and the soldiers, they burst forth in reproaches against him, and by a spontaneous movement assembled around Toussaint's dwelling to assure him of their fidelity and devotedness.

In this conjuncture, the hope of an approaching peace, which for a moment even Toussaint had indulged, vanished wholly. The warlike spirit became universal, together with indignation at the treachery. All swore to die for their chief, because in so doing they would die for liberty. Toussaint's orders flew on all sides in order to prevent or abate the consequences of the perfidy. He still had, in the West and in the North, faithful battalions and devoted districts. The less his resources became, the more grand did his character appear. Had fortune, then, abandoned him ? Could he no longer look to the highest of all powers, whose work he had undertaken, and by whose hand he had been guided and protected? Was his country, after all, to fall under the dishonorable yoke of servitude? Adversity crushes only ordinary men. Toussaint took courage even from despair.

Shortly, he learned that Dessalines had imitated Christophe and joined the ranks of the enemy. This was the second heavy blow. Toussaint did not so much regard the individual loss of these two leaders, nor the loss of the troops they carried with them, nor the loss of the lands they commanded, as the loss of his own influence which must ensue, and the perplexity in which he found himself as to who was and who was not trust-worthy. His best captains, — Christophe, Dessalines, Laplume, Clervaux, his two brothers, his nephew were in the camp of his foes. Where could he be sure to find men worthy of his confidence?

Under these circumstances it was that Leclerc put every means into action in order to induce Toussaint to come to an accommodation. The Captain-General was the more desirous of such a result because, though he knew that Toussaint's power was broken, he knew also that the population at large were wholly alienated from his own Government, and might at any moment be roused to a resistance more determined and more sanguinary than what they had made already. With a view to appease the hardly suppressed ill-humor, Leclerc had sent Rigaud out of the island, hoping thereby to gain some favor with the blacks. The effect on the whole was inconsiderable. Even after their treachery, the negro chiefs were idols, while Frenchmen were objects of indifference or detestation. This contrasted feeling was observed, and is spoken of by an eye-witness thus : —

" On arriving at the Cape, I had occasion to make very serious reflections. I saw many of our general officers in full uniform pass by; the inhabitants, no matter what their color, showed no sign of exterior deference. Suddenly I heard a noise, — it was General Dessalines; he came for the first time

18*

to pay his respects to the Captain-General Leclerc. The population of both sexes and of all colors rushed to meet him; they fell down at his approach. I was saddened rather than revolted. Dark and painful ideas accompanied me to the mansion of the General-in-chief In the antechamber I found General Dessalines. The horror he inspired me with kept me at a distance from him. He asked who I was, and came to me, and without looking me in the face, said, in a rough voice, 'I am General Dessalines; in bad times, General, I have heard you much spoken of.' His bearing and his manners were savage; I was surprised at his words, which announced assurance rather than remorse. The barbarian must have felt himself powerful, or he would not have dared to take that attitude." *

Once before had Leclerc made an attempt to bring Toussaint to treat. The attempt failed. A second effort had a different result. To Leclerc's overture, Toussaint in substance replied, "I am powerful enough to burn and ravage, as well as to sell dearly a life which has not been useless to the mother country." But with bootless destruction such a mind as Toussaint's could not be satisfied. For a great object he had taken up arms; if that object could be secured by peaceful means, his duty was clear. This view, on which his own mind had for some time been dwelling, was enforced by the representations and advice of persons around him, whose fidelity and courage gave them a right to be heard. Toussaint became less indisposed to listen to terms of accommodation. Leclerc proposed, as the principal conditions of peace, to leave in Toussaint's hands the government of Saint Domingo, to hold by his side the office of delegate from France, and to employ Toussaint's officers according to their rank. "I swear," he said, "before the face of the Supreme Being, to respect the liberty of the people of Saint Domingo."

Toussaint L'Ouverture replied, "I accept everything which is favorable for the people and for the army; and, for myself, I wish to live in retirement."

* Mémoires, &c., par Lacroix, ii. 191, 2.

Noble resolution! resolution worthy of all thy previous conduct, thou noble-hearted man! All for others, nothing for thyself! Yet had he now the option of retaining supreme power in the island, sanctioned and guaranteed by French authority. And out of that supreme power, were he ambitious, he might have carved a crown. But didst thou think that thy frank disinterestedness might be turned to thy own ruin? The possibility could hardly have escaped thy sagacious and foreseeing mind. Nevertheless, rather wilt thou incur any personal risk than prolong the horrors of this war, which every day becomes more fratricidal and more disastrous!

As a consequence of this accommodation, an interview between Toussaint and Leclerc was agreed on. It was proposed that they should meet on a spot in the mountains of Mornay. Learning that the place had given rise to suspicions, Toussaint magnanimously resolved to repair to the Cape. His journey was a triumph. Everywhere crowds pressed and prostrated themselves before the hero. They hailed him as their friend; they hailed him as their liberator; for in their acclaim they bore in mind that the liberty for which he had fought was sanctioned and secured by the Captain-General's solemn oath. His arrival at the Cape was announced by salvos from both the sea and the land forces. The multitude surrounded him with demonstrations of love and veneration; the mother pointed him out to her child, and girls strewed his path with flowers. Leclerc received him in his mansion, situated near the sea. During the interview, four hundred horsemen, who had accompanied Toussaint, stood near, drawn up in order and with bare sabres. To the Captain-General Toussaint was no longer a fanatical slave in revolt, and condemned to death, nor was he an unnatural father. The Consul's brother-in-law took pains to laud his good faith and his magnanimity. He dwelt with emphasis on the reconciliation thus ratified, which would restore prosperity to the colony. He repeated his oath in presence of the chiefs of the two armies. "General," he said, "one cannot but praise you and admire you when one has, as you have done, borne the burden of the government of Saint Domingo. Your presence in this city is a proof of your magnanimity and your good faith. Our reconciliation will make this island, of which you are the restorer, bloom again ; and will consolidate its new institutions, which are the fundamental basis of the liberty and the happiness of all."

" When the people of Saint Domingo," replied L'Ouverture, " triumphed in a war foreign both in relation to France and to themselves, they never thought that they should ever have to resist their natural protector. If explanations had preceded your arrival in this island, the cannon would not have been fired, except to welcome the envoy of a great power, and you would, on reaching these shores, have seen no other lights than *feux de joie.* You knew for certainty that I was at Santo Domingo. There was still time to send me news of your mission. When you were before the Cape, General Christophe begged you to grant him delay sufficient to acquaint me with the fact that a French squadron was on our shores ; you might reasonably have acceded to his request, instead of reducing the people to despair by your threats, and exposing your army on the crater of a volcano."

Leclerc admitted that pilots, whom he had taken near the bay of Samana, had assured him that Toussaint L'Ouverture was at Santo Domingo. " But I am the brother-in-law of the First Consul; I am Commander-in-chief of a French army, and consequently in position and rank superior to General Christophe, and I did not think it consistent with my dignity to stop before a brigadier-general, and to listen to all his allegations."

" Nevertheless," rejoined Toussaint, " you waited for four days, and you will agree that some days more would not have done an injury to your honor, since, according to the words and the letter of your brother-in-law, you are intrusted with only a pacific mission. It seems to me that by patience you would have served equally France and Saint Domingo."

" It is true ; but I was not master of myself. Let us retain no recollection of the past; all shall be repaired. Let us,

General, rejoice at our union. Your sons, the officers who have accompanied you, as well as the generals and officers of my army, who are here, must be witnesses of our common gladness." At these words the door of the hall opened, and at Leclerc's invitation all the persons who were in the next apartment entered and took their places. In their presence the Captain-General renewed his oaths. During this exchange of words, Leclerc, pressing Toussaint as to the reduced condition of his resources, asked him where he could have obtained arms to continue the war. In a truly Lacedemonian manner the hero replied, " I would have taken yours."

Presently there entered a fine boy who leapt on the neck of Toussaint L'Ouverture, — it was his youngest son. During the war he had been lost by his father, and carried off by the French. Taken to the Cape, he was consigned to the care of his tutor; and now, as a touching pledge of friendship, he had been restored to his father, who was deeply affected by thus recovering his beloved child.

In returning from this conference, in the details of which we learn on how insignificant causes depend peace and war with all their mighty issues, Toussaint L'Ouverture passed through the posts of the French army, in the midst of the acclamations of the soldiers, the militia, and the people, who crowded around him; and under salvos of artillery, entered Marmelade, where the commander received him at the head of his own troops. The day following, he addressed the grenadiers and the dragoons of his guard. Having spoken to them of the peace, and shown them that it could not be violated except by perjury, he praised their courage, and thanked them for the love and devotedness they had displayed toward himself, and solemnly declared that the recollection of their deeds would forever remain engraven on his mind. In order to testify to them his satisfaction, and at the same time take his farewell, he embraced all their officers. Those brave and hardy veterans could not restrain their tears, and the soldiers were sad and inconsolable. Toussaint then took the road for Ennery, which he had chosen for his residence. When near it, he was surrounded by crowds of people, who shouted out, " General, have you abandoned us ?"

" No, my children," he answered ; " all your brethren are under arms, and the officers of all ranks retain their posts."

When Toussaint L'Ouverture had fixed himself in the fertile and delightful valley of Ennery, to enjoy the repose of private and domestic life, he found occupation a necessity, and employed his energy in repairing and improving the dwellings of the inhabitants, and dispensing around him other benefits. Though retired from the world, he was not forgotten. Generals and other officers of the French army, and strangers from distant lands, came to visit him, and were welcomed with an affability which was a part of his nature. Exempt from fear and disquietude, he lived in the bosom of his family as if he had been guarded by an army. He rode over the country, and was everywhere greeted with tokens of respect.

With the cessation of hostilities, bands of black troops descended from the mountains, and the two armies mingled together as brothers. Freedom rendered friends those whom slavery had made deadly enemies. The population laid down their arms to engage in the labors of the field. The dwellings, which the fear of servitude had burned down, rose again under the reign of liberty. With a view to confirm the peace, the captain of the expedition put into the hands of Christophe the police of the North, and into Dessalines the police of the West. The cities which had been consumed were rebuilt. Vessels soon filled the ports. Commerce began once more to flourish. Everything promised a smiling future. Songs were heard, and dances were seen in the villages. The whole country offered a proof how happy this world would be but for the disturbances occasioned by human passions.

BOOK III.

FROM THE RAVAGES OF THE YELLOW FEVER IN HAYTI
UNTIL THE DEPORTATION AND DEATH
OF ITS LIBERATOR.

CHAPTER I.

ERELONG, the natural consequences of the ravages which had been carried over the country, and of the abstraction from agriculture of a large portion of the population, were felt in scarcity of provisions, the rather that Saint Domingo did not abound in articles of human food of a superior kind. This scarcity was augmented by the necessity of supporting out of he public magazines a large number of soldiers; for, though the European part of the army was much reduced, a large number of blacks and men of color had been thrown on the government stores. Shortness of food, and the high prices which ensue, are specially trying to a government of force. Complaints began to spread among the native population, and not without difficulty were the servants of the State supplied with the necessaries of life.

Application for aid was made to the governors of foreign possessions in the neighborhood. The Spaniards furnished supplies with chivalrous generosity; but those supplies were very far from being sufficient. The English, who had not anticipated the success of the French arms, and saw that success with uneasiness, refused to give succor. From Americans a similar answer was received. The conduct of their agents disclosed the regret which their governments felt in not finding at Saint Domingo, under the French sway, the commercial advantages which they enjoyed while it was ruled by Toussaint L'Ouverture. The state of the island, combined with the native politeness of the French character, caused attentions to be paid to

foreign ships and visitors, which were interpreted into tokens of
a sense of civil and political weakness. This adverse impression found its way into the minds of the blacks, so that the spirit
of the colonial army became increasingly difficult to manage.
Thus what at first was the Captain-General's power proved a
source of weakness and embarrassment. To provide a remedy,
he attempted to incorporate the colonial troops with the reinforcements that came from France, but the prejudices of Europeans rendered the plan all but nugatory. Yet, if it was
dangerous to have entire large bodies of blacks, it was not less
dangerous to discharge and dismiss them at once. Leclerc had
no resource but time, and sought to govern by dividing. Accordingly, he took care to employ black soldiers only in small
detachments, and regarded even desertion with satisfaction.
He could not, however, feel at ease unless he knew that the
blacks were resuming their agricultural labors; and, though in
sending them back to the plantations, he received assistance
from some of their chiefs, he was made sensible of the want of
such an influence as that which Toussaint L'Ouverture had
exerted before the war, and effected his purpose only on a
limited scale.

These difficulties, however, though in themselves not small,
were inconsiderable compared with those which sprang from a
terrible malady with which the island, and especially its European inhabitants, was now visited. The yellow fever, which
had already proved destructive, broke out with great violence
at the same time at Port-au-Prince and at the Cape. It appeared there in a form unusually repulsive and deadly. It
seized persons who were in good health, without any premo-
nition. Sometimes death was the immediate consequence.
Happy those who were immediately carried off! Ordinarily
it was slow in its progress as well as frightful in its inflictions.
The disorder began in the brain, by an oppressive pain accompanied or followed by fever. The patient was devoured with
burning thirst. The stomach, distracted by pains, in vain
sought relief by efforts to disburden itself. Fiery veins streaked

the eye; the face was inflamed, and dyed of a dark, dull-red color; the ears from time to time rang painfully. Now mucous secretions surcharged the tongue, and took away the power of speech; now the sick man spoke, but in speaking had a foresight of death. When the violence of the disorder approached the heart, the gums were blackened. The sleep, broken, or troubled by convulsions or by frightful visions, was worse than the waking hours, and when the reason sank under the delirium which had its seat in the brain, repose utterly forsook the patient's couch. The progress of the fire within was marked by yellowish spots, which spread over the surface of the body. If, then, a happy crisis came not, all hope was gone. Soon the breath infected the air with a fetid odor, the lips glazed, despair painted itself in the eyes, and sobs, with long intervals of silence, formed the only language. From each side of the mouth spread foam, tinged with black and burnt blood. Blue streaks mingled with the yellow over all the frame. Death came on the thirteenth day, though more commonly it tarried till the seventeenth. All remedies were useless. Rarely did the victims escape.

The malady produced a general melancholy. Its depressing effects were visible in the troops who had not yet been stricken with the fever. You saw the men regard each other with furtive glances, and in deep yet ominous silence; their arms looked tarnished; their steps were heavy and slow. Unconquerable in the field, they already felt themselves the victims of destiny. When undergoing review, the men, scarcely expecting to see each other again, affected a foolish gayety, the real character of which was betrayed by a bitter smile, or took leave of each other sadly, as pilgrims, through suffering, to the dark shores of the eternal world.

The city of the Cape then presented one of those sights which are rare in the history of human calamities. Scarcely had a part of the buildings destroyed by the conflagration been hastily reconstructed, when the town and the hospitals were filled with the sick and the dying. The chief hospital, situated on a height which overhangs the city, having been burnt down, consisted now only of large sheds covered with sugar-canes. Therein the patients were for the most part laid in straw, unprovided with necessary appliances, exposed now to the fury of storms, now to torrents of rain, and now to the burning rays of the sun. Those remaining in the city were better protected and cared for, but breathing an impurer air, and deprived of breezes by the mountains, they suffered scarcely less, and died as certainly.

Military discipline disappeared; the common soldier had the same authority as the general, and each general acknowledged no authority except his own. Men spoke no more of combats, of exploits, of glory. The heart of the soldier sank within him. Even the funeral knell ceased its mournful sounds; the common calamity crushed the sense of religious observance. In the midst of disorder and confusion, death heaped victims on victims. Friend followed friend in quick succession; the sick were avoided from the fear of contagion, and for the same reason the dead were left without burial. Despair alone remained in activity, —fierce despair; for the dying man could cast his eye on neither friend nor nurse, and had to suffer and expire in terrific solitude or more terrific companionship. The country, the mountains, the sea, afforded no place of refuge. The troops that were removed to a distance from the towns were not the less attacked. Their camp was transformed into a hospital. Soldiers died under trees laden with fruit, and under plants breathing perfumes. The ships of war and merchant vessels lost their crews. Eight-and-forty passengers from Bordeaux expired in disembarking at the Cape. Terrified at the destruction, some, on nearing the island, went on board vessels that were quitting its infected shores, yet perished, smitten by the poisoned air. Four thousand men who came in Dutch vessels perished. Fear multiplied the victims.

When the malady was in all its force, human passions manifested their guilty excesses. Virtue was disregarded when it no longer offered an earthly reward. Some sought distraction and relief to their wretchedness in gambling and in voluptuousness; violence and adultery became common. Others endeavored to drown their torments in reckless intoxication; others, again, attired in military costume, which at such a moment was simply ridiculous, threw insult at the disease, and braved death, either in satirical gayety or in buffooneries, or in roars of silly laughter. The words "Ah! the funny fellow," became a derisive phrase to indicate a poor wretch that was trying to laugh or trick away his calamity. Others, again, deep sunk in guilt, sought to deceive Death in the arms of a mistress or in perfumed baths. While all around was perishing, songs were heard from the sea. They were the attempts of men who thus tried to cheat themselves into momentary joy. The nearer men were to eternity, the more greedy they were of the pleasures of earth.

Pauline, the wife of Leclerc and the sister of the Consul, did not renounce her voluptuous habits in the midst of so terrible a plague. In the hope of breathing a less infected air, she had gone to a country house, on the declivity of a pleasant hill which overhung the sea. Here she passed her hours in pleasure and luxury. She saw die around her officers whose incense she had welcomed, but for whose sufferings she showed no concern, — intent only on putting away all unpleasant objects, and seizing with avidity on sources of gratification. Now she caused herself, like a queen, to be borne in a palanquin through the most beautiful scenes of nature; there would she, for hours together, dwell, in contemplating the ocean and its delightful shores, loaded with the luxuries of tropical vegetation; now she plunged into the depths of odoriferous forests, and surrendered herself to the captivating reveries of love; and now she sailed on the sea, accompanied by courtiers, musicians, and buffoons, as if she would sustain the character of Venus rising from the waves.

What is still more remarkable is that she took pains to defy the malady by festivities, in which she gathered around her dancing, music, pleasure, and voluptuousness; there she drew on herself admiration by her wit, her graces, her beauty, and

19*

the ravishing tenderness of her looks. But around and in those festivities, Death bore his funeral torches. The balls which she ceased not to give took place on the brink of the grave. The dancers of to-night were dead on the morrow. But the more joyous did she affect to appear. "These," she said, "are our last moments; let us pass them in pleasure."

As the disorder raged in other places as well as in the cities of the Cape and Port-au-Prince, there died every day, on land and on sea, not less than from three to four hundred persons. More and more irregular in its symptoms and its course, the fever baffled and defied the skill of the physicians, who died together with their patients.

The little attention which at first was paid to funeral rites became less and less, and soon was wholly discontinued. The dead bodies were put on the outside of the doors and carried off by night. If anything could excite compassion, it was to see on some of those livid frames the scars of wounds received in the battles of Europe, where *he* had gained his fame who sent those warriors and heroes to die on a distant, foreign, and deadly shore. As it was necessary to remove the dead as soon as they had breathed their last, some were carried off while yet alive; groans were heard in the heaps of abandoned corpses, and from the putrid mass some rose and returned to take their place among the living. As very many bodies were tossed into the sea, the waves bore them up and down the harbor, or left them on the shore, painful mementos to spectators, and food for birds and beasts of prey, while they added to the foul infection with which the atmosphere was burdened.

During the prevalence of these accumulated disasters, the black population, proof against the pest, remained faithful to the peace which had been forced on them and their venerated chief. Had they chosen to rise, the whole expedition would have perished. Their virtue was more than abstinence from self-avengement. With characteristic hospitality, they received sick persons into their homes, and gave them unlooked-for aid; they did more: they gave them tears and sympathy, — seeing in them not Frenchmen and asssailants, but sufferers. There were other benefactors. Sisters of Charity, truly worthy of the. name, went from street to street, and from bed to bed, ministering with tenderness and skill to the sick, the despairing, and the departing. Womanly love was almost the only virtue that maintained itself erect. When all other remedies had proved vain, that noble affection showed itself fertile in resources, nor was it the less respectable because in the extremity it resorted to fetish practices which had their origin in Africa. More simple and even more touching was that manifestation of it which compelled young women to follow their lovers to their graves, —

"Amid the faithless only faithful found."

It is terrible to think that some of these worthy women may afterward have been repaid with slavery.

At length, when the summer heats had reached their height, the malady redoubled its fury, and broke down alike benevolence and virtue. Then was the harvest of death. According to authentic tables, there died fifteen hundred officers, twenty thousand soldiers, nine thousand sailors, and three thousand persons who loosely hung about the skirts of the army in quest of employment or fortune. Not fewer than fourteen generals lost their lives in the plague. Of that number was Debelle, whose virtues made him regretted alike by foes and friends; Dugua, an intrepid and joyous old man, whose hairs had grown gray on the borders of the Nile; Hardy, who had displayed rare courage in the victories and the reverses of the expedition. Almost incredible is it that there died seven hundred medical men, worthy, for the most, of high praise, such was their courage, their patience, their devotedness.

The malady changed the character of the army. Those who survived, experiencing a long and difficult convalescence, became habitually depressed, morose, or exasperated. Some had their memory weakened; some remained broken down or crippled for life. Discipline was restored with difficulty. Even news from home brought little pleasure, and gave only a transient relief; and communications with France were intercepted, in order, so far as possible, to conceal from the mother country the awful loss which she had endured.

Such was the terrible punishment which fell on the predatory expedition sent by the Corsican adventurer against the hero and patriot of Saint Domingo.

And can there be a more decisive proof of anything than we have here of the honor of Toussaint L'Ouverture? The necessity of the French was his opportunity. With what ease now might he have mustered those blacks which were in Leclerc's way, and extorted from his enfeebled hands the sovereignty of the island. That Toussaint remained quiet at Ennery disproves the base insinuations which were fabricated expressly for his ruin.

CHAPTER II.

Bonaparte and Leclerc conspire to effect the arrest of Toussaint L'Ouverture, who is treacherously seized, sent to France, and confined in the Chateau de **Joux** ; partial risings in consequence.

IF the establishment in Saint Domingo of the authority of France had been the object of the expedition, the present settlement of its affairs would have been left to unfold its resources, and the blessings of the existing peace would have been permanent. All opposition had been put down. Mutual explanations had been given. With one exception, the leaders of the blacks held rank and power in the French army. Toussaint L'Ouverture, the only exception, was engaged in rural pursuits and acts of beneficence. Leclerc was sole master in the island. Hayti was now at least a colonial dependency of France. And if there were evils or obstacles which he could not at the moment put away, they were nothing more than such as promised to disappear before good government, aided by the healing and reformatory hand of Time. Even through the tempest of the plague, tokens of coming serenity were readily discerned. But the occupation of the island was only the first act in the drama.

The intelligence of the ravages of the fever in Saint Domingo shocked the mind of Bonaparte, though he had foreseen and even premeditated the calamity. One obstacle which lay in his way to the imperial throne had been removed. So far the expedition had not proved nugatory. There were two other obstacles. One was the freedom of the blacks. Such freedom, in the Consul's eyes, was licentiousness. It was, moreover, incompatible with his designs. If Saint Domingo remained free, the other French colonies must and would be free.   In their emancipation the colonial system would be endangered, nay, would soon be lost; for freedom was the precursor of independence : and if the colonies became independent, what strongholds would France possess in the West Indies to check the growing power of England ; and where would be its outposts to keep the United States in good behavior ? Even more important were those dependencies when considered as pastures for the powerful and the aspiring around the Consul's person.   Let the colonies be reduced into servitude ; then would they naturally enter as constituent parts in an empire under governors with more than the power of ordinary princes, who, with Bonaparte at their head, would form a regular and august political hierarchy, and so lay the basis of a dominion which might extend widely over both hemispheres, if not in time comprehend the civilized world.   To the ambitious Corsican the prospect was enchanting.   The herds of Haytian negroes must be sent back into slavery.

This resolution he knew could not be carried into effect so long as Toussaint L'Ouverture lived on the island.   His existence there was the second great impediment.   That impediment, too, the Consul determined to remove.   The determination was the more readily formed because the world had come to regard Toussaint as a sort of rival to Bonaparte.   The phrase became current which designated the one " the first of the blacks," and the other " the first of the whites."   Comparisons were made between the two which the First Consul always found offensive, and which were not always to the First Consul's advantage.   Was his bright star to pale before the fiery meteor of a slave ?   Besides, that slave had not been easily subdued ; he had all but overcome and destroyed the soldiers of Egypt and Italy.   When peace was concluded, it was difficult to say whether the assailant or the assailed was in the worse condition.   This manly and effective resistance Bonaparte could not forgive.   It would have been less intolerable, had it been made by Europeans ; but to come from negro slaves — it was an unpardonable offence.   Yes, Bonaparte hated Toussaint, and resolved to effect his destruction. His arrest was the first point to be gained. With Toussaint in his hands, everything else he judged would be easy.

The First Consul was not to be deterred by the consideration that such a step could not be taken without dissimulation and perfidy. The end covered, if it did not justify, the means, in his eyes. In Leclerc he had a ready and passive instrument. Nor was the Captain-General without his own reasons for the contemplated apprehension. The hatred borne by the master had taken possession of the servant's soul. Little satisfaction did he feel in a peace which a hard fate had induced him to seek and conclude. The popularity of the negro chief caused him to be an object of fear with Leclerc. In the war, the chief glory had been gained by his foe, and now that foe, having become his rival, eclipsed Leclerc in the estimation of the natives of nearly all classes and all opinions. He had, moreover, — and he knew he had, — injured, deeply injured, Toussaint L'Ouverture, and injury invariably begets a hatred in proportion to its own intensity. Besides, the original plan, which so far had been successful, remained to be completed. Leclerc, in consequence, was well disposed to execute the Consul's will.

Without waiting for express directions in a matter on which he well knew the mind of Bonaparte, the Captain-General began to prepare the way for the final act. For this purpose he spoke of Toussaint, not as an independent power who had of his own accord laid down arms and declined the highest post in the colony, but as a revolter who had been outlawed and condemned to death, but pardoned as an act of grace on his own part. Consulting him as to the disposition of the troops, so as to prevent suspicion, he sought occasions which, in extorting complaints from him, might form the grounds of a disagreement, and so afford pretexts for his seizure. Two frigates anchored off Gonaïves. The soldiers no longer paid Toussaint military honors. The plot was dimly seen by friends, who advised the black hero to be on his guard. Some went so far as to recommend him to take measures for his personal security. He replied, " For one to expose one's life for one's country when in peril is a sacred duty ; but to arouse one's country in order to save one's life, is inglorious."

In order to give some color to the contemplated arrest, Leclerc complained that Toussaint's body-guard had not been wholly disarmed. Toussaint replied that he had given orders for its disbandment, and advised the Captain-General to proceed mildly in bringing that result about. Impatient of contradiction, Leclerc employed force, and with difficulty succeeded. In this opposition an excuse was found for filling the district of Ennery with European troops. The inhabitants complained. Toussaint L'Ouverture became the medium for making those complaints known. " This was exactly what was wanted," says one who knew Leclerc's designs.

On the 7th of June, General Brunet wrote to Toussaint L'Ouverture the following letter : —

BRUNET, GENERAL OF DIVISION, TO THE GENERAL OF DIVISION, TOUSSAINT L'OUVERTURE.

"HEADQUARTERS AT THE PLANTATION OF GEORGES,
18 Prairial, An. X.

" The moment, Citizen-General, has come to make known to General Leclerc, in an incontestable manner, those who may deceive him in regard to yourself; they are calumniators, since your sentiments tend only to bring back order in the district which you inhabit. It is necessary to render me aid in order to restore the communication with the Cape, which was yesterday interrupted, since three persons have been murdered by a band of fifty brigands, between Ennery and Coupe-à-Pintade. Send toward those places faithful men, whom you will pay well ; I will be accountable for the outlay. There are, my dear General, arrangements which we ought to make in concert, which it is impossible to treat of by letter, but which an hour's conference would terminate. Had I not to-day been overwhelmed with business, I would myself have brought the answer to your letter. Occupied as I am, I must beg you to come to my residence. You will not find there all the pleasures which I would wish to welcome you with, but you will find the frankness of an honorable man, who desires nothing but the happiness of the colony and your own happiness. If Madame Toussaint, whom I shall have the greatest pleasure to become acquainted with, could accompany you, I should be gratified; if she has occasion for horses, I will send her mine. Never, General, will you find a more sincere friend than myself. With confidence in the Captain-General, and friendship toward all under him, you will enjoy tranquillity.

" I cordially salute you,

" BRUNET."

Now here is a piece of consummate villany. This man, who signs himself Brunet, who calls himself a man of honor, and who would have run any one through who should have thrown on that honor the slightest doubt, — this man, who probably went to church, and heard mass and professed Christianity, or who, at any rate, did not in private pick pockets or cut throats, this man deliberately sits down and employs his ingenuity in fabricating a tissue of lies in order to ensnare to his ruin an innocent patriot, the liberator of his country. Every word in this diabolical composition is selected with a view to deceive. By implication, inuendo, and direct averment, the tissue of falsehoods goes forward to its end. " You are, you know, alleged to be less quick than might be wished. False, doubtless. Now you may prove how false by acting in concert with me. Come hither, and so convict your calumniators; let the Captain-General see how earnest you are for the furtherance of public tranquillity." This is a dexterous movement. To remind Toussaint that he was suspected was to prepare him for the offered means of exculpation. An innocent man, from a consciousness of his innocence, and a guilty man, in order to affect and display such consciousness, would alike be inclined to accept the expedient. Then for this honorable man, who does not

20

invent, but merely employs groundless suspicions, he himself is quite confident that his victim is calumniated. "No, in coming to me, you come to a friend who knows the real facts, and so is fully aware of what you have done and are doing to tranquillize the country. But, notwithstanding your efforts, disturbances exist. These must be put a stop to. I have said I have confidence in you; I now show it, for I ask you to take the requisite measures." Excellent Jesuit! Yes, the way to beget confidence is, you well know, to show confidence. But how show confidence so much as by employing a man to put down the very evils he is accused of causing? Surely this, if anything, would make him feel that he is trusted, or at any rate show him how desirable, even for his own bad purposes, if he has bad purposes, it is that he should act as if he felt that he is trusted.

"Then as to the cost of these efforts, we will settle that when we meet." Yes, it is a small affair of business between two generals of division, — nothing more, — some brigands to exterminate, some expense to be incurred, — all to be amicably talked of when the two friends are taking a glass of wine together, and to be ended by an order for payment on the public purse. What more simple, what more natural, what more straightforward? None but one deeply versed in deceit could have thought of treachery.

But the tricks are not exhausted. "We must have an interview. For that purpose I intended to come and see you. I had ordered my horse and an escort; but really I cannot leave; I am nailed to the spot. I must throw myself on your goodness; pray, come; I will do all I can to make you comfortable; and bring your wife with you on this little excursion, — a mere party of pleasure. Shall I send my own horses to convey her and her domestics? What! do you hesitate? — still hesitate? Ah! take care you fail not to confide in the Captain-General. Distrust on your part may justify distrust on his part. Insinuations are best repelled by confidingness. And, you know, trust in Leclerc involves friendship toward me. Yes, you must come; you will come."

In this wily epistle there is only one mistake, but it is a serious one. Brunet declares that he is an honorable man. Over this declaration, you, Toussaint, surely paused. Here the cunning hand displays its cunning. Yet thy guileless nature will not entertain a distrust. In general, the epistle has a fair seeming. You will accept the invitation. Suspicion of treachery is dishonorable to him who entertains it. And had not Toussaint, when the clouds were really dark, gone to the Cape? And did not a friendly arrangement ensue? The oath of Leclerc remained in force. And here was an opportunity not only to benefit his neighbors, but to purge himself from any suspicions which weak men, or designing men, had raised. As to the rumors of peril to himself, the timid always abound in illusions of their own fabrication. A brave man never fears danger, and a wise man is not very careful to shun danger. Besides, the civilities of hospitality have their claims. Clearly, on the whole, there was no valid reason against going, and many valid reasons for going. Toussaint had intended to go to Gonaïves before he received Brunet's letter. He was on his way thither; he turned not back when the invitation was put into his hands.

Proceeding on his journey, he met Brunet on the plantation called Georges, where the General was waiting for him. For some time they conversed together. Then Brunet begged to be excused, and left the room. The next moment there entered from eighteen to twenty officers, with drawn swords and pistols in their hands. Toussaint L'Ouverture took them for assassins, and arose. He drew his sabre, resolved to sell his life dearly. Then the colonel, who was at the head of the band, seeing that he waited for them with intrepidity, advanced toward him with his sword lowered, and said, " General, we have not come here to attempt your life. We have merely the order to secure your person." At these words, Toussaint put his sword back into the scabbard, saying, " The justice of Heaven will avenge my cause."

Those prophetic words have had accomplishment; those prophetic words will have accomplishment; nor ever will they be fulfilled until slavery is blotted out of America, and is known no more in the world.

From the plantation where he was arrested to Gonaïves, troops had been placed from distance to distance along the road. At midnight, the prisoner was taken on board a French frigate, called the "Creole." The officer who commanded the ship was touched, even to tears, at the lot of that victim of the basest treachery. They sailed for the Cape, where Toussaint was transferred to the Hero, which waited for them off the port. "Adieu, Captain," said the captive, on leaving the Creole; "I shall remember you till my last sigh." When he reached the Hero, he found in his arms St. Jean L'Ouverture, the very son, who, on a brighter day, had been restored to him by Leclerc. Placide L'Ouverture was arrested next day. Isaac was at Ennery. Ignorant that his father had been seized, he was tranquilly reading, about seven o'clock in the morning, when he was startled by a brisk firing, followed by alarming cries. Hastening from the room, he beheld laborers, women, and children, running hither and thither in terror, and from three to four hundred French soldiers firing on them in pursuit. A servant urged him to fly. He feared that evil had befallen his father, but remained. Forthwith he was arrested. The officer told him that his father had been embarked, and that he had orders from General Brunet to apprehend him and all the family; adding that he should not have fired on the people, had they not attempted to bar his passage. The money and the papers belonging to Toussaint L'Ouverture were taken possession of. The house was rifled; insolence was added to robbery. Madame Toussaint and her niece were carried off. " Only a heart of stone," says Isaac L'Ouverture,* who has described the whole scene, "could fail to be softened by the tears and the lamentations of the men, the women, and the children who were present, and who deplored her (Madame Toussaint's) lot, when she was forever quitting her country, a part of her family, and her

* "Mémoires d'Isaac, fils de Toussaint L'Ouverture," &c., p. 300.

abode, which was the abode of beneficence and hospitality. Those men, those women, and those children, in the excess of their grief, expressed their fears and their regrets with deep sensibility. "Madame," cried they, "are you leaving us? Shall we never see each other again?" Then, addressing the commanding officer, they added, "Ah, at least, sir, don't kill her, don't kill her children!"— they all believed that Toussaint L'Ouverture himself was dead. That woman who was worthy of those marks of attachment and love quitted her home without taking anything with her.

Madame Toussaint and her son Isaac and her niece were conducted to the Cape, and put on board the Hero. The vessel forthwith set sail for France. It is related that, in fixing, for the last time, his straining eyes on the mountains made memorable by his exploits, Toussaint L'Ouverture exclaimed, "They have only felled the trunk of the tree (of the freedom of the blacks); branches will sprout, for the roots are numerous and deep."

And in that confidence, thou large-hearted man, dost thou sail over that waste of waters; saddened, but not overwhelmed. Thou carriest the cause of thy color in thy soul, and, with a mind replete with Christian principles and affections, thou neither doubtest nor despondest. Twenty-five days hast thou to live on the sea, uncertain of thy own fate; but with such knowledge of thy oppressors as must have occasioned dark forecastings. To thy own view, however, thy past is bright. Not for thyself, but for others hast thou toiled and bled; and those others are the outcast, the ignorant, the injured, and the lost. True disciple of thy Galilean Master, bear up in the recollection of his load and his persecutions,— yet heavier than thine. And now, in the hour of darkness, find and acknowledge thy glory, in that which heathen France accounts thy shame. Not on man's judgment dost thou rely. Not by a local tribunal wilt thou be judged. The wide earth will take cognizance of what thou didst attempt and achieve, and pronounce thee a benefactor, not of thy color only, but of thy

20*

kind. Regret not the president's chair, left vacant in thy beloved mother country, nor let men's ingratitude and perfidy sour thy feelings. From high motives thou wroughtest for a high purpose ; and that purpose, though not in thine own way, will be attained. Be greater, by patience in the day of thy weakness, than thou wast in the day of thy power by thy valor; and thy name will pass down to posterity, encircled with undying fame. Listen to that solemn voice in thine own heart which tells thee that Hayti will be free.

On the voyage, Toussaint was denied all intercourse with his family. He was confined constantly to his cabin, and the door was guarded by soldiers with fixed bayonets. Uncertain as to his fate, yet apprehensive of a very dark future, he determined to make a solemn appeal to Bonaparte, and prepared the following epistle : —

"ON BOARD THE HERO, 1 Thermidor, an X. (12th July, 1802.)

"GENERAL TOUSSAINT L'OUVERTURE TO GENERAL BONAPARTE, FIRST CONSUL OF THE FRENCH REPUBLIC.

"CITIZEN FIRST CONSUL: I will not conceal my faults from you. I have committed some. What man is exempt? I am quite ready to avow them. After the word of honor of the Captain-General who represents the French Government, after a proclamation addressed to the colony, in which he promised to throw the veil of oblivion over the events which had taken place in Saint Domingo, I, as you did on the 18th Brumaire, withdrew into the bosom of my family. Scarcely had a month passed away, when evil-disposed persons, by means of intrigues, effected my ruin with the General-in-chief, by filling his mind with distrust against me. I received a letter from him which ordered me to act in conjunction with General Brunet. I obeyed. Accompanied by two persons, I went to Gonaïves, where I was arrested. They sent me on board the frigate Creole, I know not for what reason, without any other clothes than those I had on. The next day my house was exposed to pillage; my wife and my children were arrested; they had nothing, not even the means to cover themselves.

"Citizen First Consul: A mother fifty years of age may deserve the indulgence and the kindness of a generous and liberal nation. She has no account to render. I alone ought to be responsible for my conduct to the Government I have served. I have too high an idea of the greatness and the justice of the First Magistrate of the French people, to doubt a moment of its impartiality. I indulge the feeling that the balance in its hands will not incline to one side more than to another. I claim its generosity.

"Salutations and respect,
"TOUSSAINT L'OUVERTURE."

When he wrote this high-spirited letter, in which the writer characteristically shows his concern for others more than for himself, — and the tone of which contrasts favorably with that which his oppressor, when fallen, and on the point of quitting Europe for Saint Helena, addressed in true French melodramatic style to the English people, — Toussaint obviously had no idea of the extent of the perfidy to which he was about to fall a victim. He had been seized and carried off, but only, as he thought, that he might be confronted with his maligners, and have a fair trial in France. All he requested, therefore, was an impartial hearing, assured that the even hand of Justice would repair the injuries he had suffered. Little did he then foresee the dreadful end to which he had been destined by the Consul's blind ambition.

While on board the Hero, Toussaint wrote also to Admiral Décrès, Minister of Marine and of the Colonies: —

"CITIZEN-MINISTER: I was, with all my family, arrested by the order of the Captain-General, who, nevertheless, had given me his word of honor, and who had promised me the protection of the French Government. I venture to claim both its justice and its good-will. If I have committed faults, I only ought to suffer the punishment of them.

"I beg you, Citizen-Minister, to employ your interest with the First Consul, on behalf of my family and myself.

"Salutation and respect,

(Signed)   "TOUSSAINT L'OUVERTURE."

This simple and dignified letter is reported to have drawn tears from the eyes of the minister. That minister felt the contrast between the dark designs of Government and the unsuspicious tone of the communication. "Justice!" As well ask mercy from tigers; as well seek grapes on a bramble-bush.

As soon as the vessel arrived at Brest, the First Consul, glad to have so formidable an enemy in his hands, gave free course to his resentment. Without paying any respect to Toussaint's character, fame, services, or former position, he, consulting only his fears and selfish interests, tore him from his family, and began the persecution which was to end in a most painful death. Toussaint was immediately hurried on shore. On the 13th of August, the maritime provost of Brest, at five in the morning, sent an officer of police and four men to transfer the negro chief from the vessel. On the deck only was he permitted to have an interview with his wife and children, whom he was to meet no more in this life. Only his servant was he allowed to take with him. When in the boat, he bade a last adieu to Madame Toussaint, to Isaac, to Saint-Jean, who then remained on board the Hero, and extended his hand to Placide, whom a cruel policy at the same moment was tearing from the arms of his mother, and was conveying on board the corvette La Naïade to Belle Isle en Mer. In the evening, Placide learnt of the removal of his father from the Hero. Previously, he had sent the following letter to him, which was found under Toussaint's pillow : —

"BREST ROADS, 24 Thermidor.

"MY DEAR FATHER AND MOTHER, —

"I am on board the brig La Naïade. As yet, I am ignorant of my lot. Perhaps I shall never see you again. In that I do not accuse my destiny. No matter where I am, I entreat you to take courage, and **sometimes to think of me.** I will send you news of myself if I am not dead ; give me news of yourselves if you have an opportunity. I am very well situated. I am with persons who are very good to me, and who promise to continue so. Isaac and Saint-Jean, do not forget your brother ! I shall always love you. Many kind thoughts to you all; embrace my cousins for me. I embrace you as I love you.

"Your son,

(Signed) "PLACIDE L'OUVERTURE."

When he thus rudely broke up this amiable and interesting family, the First Consul did not foresee that one day he would be torn away from his wife and son. Curious coincidence in the destiny of the oppressed and that of the oppressor ! Bonaparte was repaid in his own coin, nor in this instance merely : others have presented themselves in our narrative. But what a "superfluity of naughtiness" have we here ! Why are all the members of the L'Ouverture family involved in their father's ruin ? And if stern policy required their deportation from Hayti, why are wife and children separated from their natural head, and why should the aged captive be denied the companionship of her who was the choice of his youth, became the comfort of his adult age, and might still have supported his overladen heart to bear his troubles ? Was she severed from him expressly to exasperate his feelings and augment his woes, making his load heavier, the more surely and the more speedily to put an end to his existence ? Oh, the depth of wickedness with which what is called policy is chargeable ! Reader, be not hoodwinked by general terms. Policy would be nothing without politicians, and when statesmen lose their manhood in statecraft, and perpetrate, in their public capacity, wherein they have power, deeds which they dare not attempt in their individual capacity, wherein they are weak, then do they contract a criminality which should make them abhorred by all good men, and which is a virtual forfeiture of the tenure by which they hold their high position. Office does not change the char-

acter of realities. What is the painful reality here? It is
nothing less than theft. Toussaint L'Ouverture was stolen.
The First Consul was a man-stealer. He was more, he was a
burglar; he broke into Toussaint's house, and, having ransacked
and plundered it, he stole the family, after having perfidiously
carried off its head. And, having stolen father, mother, and
children, he not only separated them one from the other, but
murdered, at least, the father. This is plain speaking. At
least, it is intended to be so. Crime does not appear crime in
men's eyes, unless it is branded as crime. Therefore do I declare and proclaim, that Bonaparte and his accomplices were,
and forever remain, guilty of man-stealing, robbery, and murder, in their treacherous, violent, and most wicked conduct
toward this virtuous household.

Madame Toussaint and her children were conveyed to Bayonne, where they were placed under the supervision of General
Ducos. L'Ouverture, with his servant, Mars Plaisir, was put
on shore at Landerneau, where they were taken in charge by
two companies of cavalry. Compelled to quit immediately,
Toussaint in one carriage and Mars in another set out for Paris
under a strong guard. At Guingamp, some officers of the
Eighty-second, who had served under Toussaint L'Ouverture's
orders, prevailed on the commander to stop the cavalcade that
they might enjoy the opportunity of saluting their old General.
The permission was accorded. This was the only solace that
the captive enjoyed on the French soil. He reached Paris on
the 17th of August, and was immediately imprisoned in the
Temple. Thence, without any interview with Bonaparte or
his ministers, and without the slightest explanation, he was hurried away into the Department of Jura, and consigned to the
dungeons of the Castle of Joux. Singular caprice of what is
called history: at that very hour the same prison held in chains
Rigaud, the rival and foe of Toussaint. Separated in the busy
hours of public life, Toussaint and Rigaud were united by misfortune. And yet the union was little more than nominal, for
they were too powerful, even in a dungeon, to be allowed to

confer together. Suffering deserves compassion even when it cannot command respect. Therefore, I leave Rigaud to his endurance, without commenting on his guilt in joining Leclerc's marauding enterprise. Rigaud and Toussaint, the first a man of color, the second a negro, but for your skin, or rather but for European prejudice against your skin, you would not have come to your present unhappy condition. You are dark in hue, therefore are you persecuted. Distinguished representatives of your respective races, there are still men who deal in the like of you as they deal in pigs, in poultry, in flocks, and in herds, and there are others who justify this traffic in human flesh on the ground that your epidermis contains a coloring-matter of a somewhat deeper shade than their own. Yes, to this issue the question comes at last. How long, O reason, shall so patent and flimsy a pretext prevail? A brown complexion, commonly called white, insures and justifies personal immunity and personal freedom; a rather deeper brown, and a complexion of a somewhat sable tinge, insures and justifies the loss of personal liberty, and therein the loss of all the rights, privileges, and possibilities of manhood. Nay, more; the former may buy and sell, oppress, maim, mutilate, brand, scourge, imprison, and even kill the latter; and that, too, not only with perfect impunity, but with all the high bearing of unquestionable right. The relation of master and slave, when reduced to its last link, is the relation of simply more or less in the hues of the skin, of which the varieties are so very numerous, and which extend from the fair Circassian to the raven-black negro. Where, in this minutely graduated scale, is the point at which liberty ends, and slavery begins? And who has fixed that point? And on what authority? In truth, slavery in its origin and in its essence is simply man-stealing, is robbery of the very worst kind; it is the strong preying on the weak; it is the law of the bludgeon, the bayonet, the fetter, the prison, the ship, the gallows. Bonaparte, in carrying off Toussaint L'Ouverture, did no more than his African prototypes in power did before him, and, alas! continue to do to the present hour. One and all, he as well as they, and they not more than he, are robbers and plunderers. What, then, are those who purchase the stolen goods? And what they who grow rich and fatten on the system? Let men, then, renounce the Christian name, or change from the top to the bottom a "domestic institution," which, having piracy and theft for its basis, and violence for its support, stands in flagrant contradiction to the clearest precepts, the simplest doctrines, and the fundamental principles, of the gospel.

As soon as the carrying off of L'Ouverture was known in St. Domingo, General Belair, in the mountains of Saint Marc; Colonel Sans-Souci, at Valière; the chief of the battalion of Noel, at Dondon, took up arms as by one accord, and set in movement the population of those districts. The latter made his way as far as Ennery, overcoming all opposition in his route, and augmenting his troops at every step. A multitude of men and women who followed him, at the sight of the French garrison, made the hills of Ennery resound with their cries of woe, indignation, and vengeance. Sans-Souci had no sooner drawn his sword than he was arrested, as well as General Baradat, by Christophe, sent to the Cape, and embarked for France. Belair was at the head of considerable forces, when Dessalines, who was despatched from the Cape against him, came into the mountains of Saint Marc, and requested a colloquy. Belair, hoping that the interview might bring a similarity of sentiments to light, acceded to the request. He thus fell into the snare laid against him by Dessalines. He was arrested, and, with his wife, conveyed to the Cape, where they were both shot. Thus perished General Charles Belair, the victim of his devotion to Toussaint, and of his confidence in Dessalines. A model of friendship, with bravery and military talents he united the qualities which make a good and amiable man. Toussaint, well pleased with his conduct when he was his aide-de-camp, once said to him, "Charles, you have acted to-day like Labienus." "General," he replied, "I hope I shall be more faithful to you than Labienus at last proved to Cæsar." The hope became a reality. Other less distinguished, but worthy and faithful, friends of Toussaint L'Ouverture, impelled to espouse his cause, suffered death in ways which soldiers account disgraceful.

Society exacts from bad men an account of their deeds, and bad men, unable to give a satisfactory account, feel it necessary to put forth, at any cost, colorable pretexts. Leclerc could not endure the voice of public opinion, even as it existed in Saint Domingo. He had treacherously seized, and hastily sent from the island, one who had been both its hero and its pacificator. The evil work given him to perform by his brother-in-law, he had fully executed. Yet did he fear men's tongues. As a palliation of the misdeed, he set abroad a statement that Toussaint was plotting against the peace of the island. What was the evidence ? A fabrication. Two letters, said to be written by Toussaint, and intercepted, were put into circulation. The fraud has come down to these days; it is so clumsy as to bear its own condemnation on its front. If the authenticity of these letters were ascertained, they prove nothing to Toussaint's disadvantage. Even the most tortuous interpretation could not extract from them a valid suspicion. But their broken and scattered words only show to what extremities their fabricators were driven, in the fear of detection. And, so far as their sense can be made out, neither the ideas nor the style correspond with the warm, energetic, rapid, and figurative manner of Toussaint L'Ouverture. The fabricator was some poor, mean creature, who was utterly unable to give to his wretched composition the most superficial mark of that genius which appears in all that we possess of Toussaint's writing or dictation. . However, the fragments in some way served their purpose, in turning attention from Leclerc's perfidy to the allegation of evil designs on the part of his victim. Even if the evidence were less worthless than it is, the presumption would be against the Captain-General, who shunned a public investigation and condemned unheard a man to whom he had solemnly pledged his honor.

The blacks, guided by a simple sense of right and justice, gave no credence to the alleged conspiracy, and saw the blood of innocent men and women shed with alarm and indignation. At the same time, they lost all trust in Leclerc ; for had they not seen their Liberator seized and sent away, contrary to the obligations of an oath, the claims of a solemn compact, and the sacred rights of hospitality ?

CHAPTER III.

Leclerc tries to rule by creating jealousy and division — Ill-treats the men of color — Disarms the blacks — An insurrection ensues, and gains head, until it wrests from the violent hands of the General nearly all his possessions — Leclerc dies — Bonaparte resolves to send a new army to Saint Domingo.

AS the news of the deportation of Toussaint L'Ouverture spread abroad, secret and deep discontent began to prevail, which threatened disturbance, if not disaster. In vain Leclerc tried to prevent these consequences of his own misdeeds by a slow, concealed tyranny. He created division among the black chiefs by insinuating into their violent natures rivalry, jealousy, and hatred; he set the ambition of one in opposition to the moderation of another; now he brought into contrast this man's fidelity with that man's want of fidelity; mingling adroitly together praises and enticements, favors and disgrace, encouraging and rewarding mutual accusations. Special pains did he take to revive the old animosities between the blacks and the men of color, — animosities which in reality were only a consequence of the difference in the servitude to which they were in common subject. As a result of this Machiavellian policy, many officers of black and of mixed blood were persecuted, imprisoned, or banished to a distance. Of this number was Rigaud, next to Toussaint the most renowned of all. He was arrested in the port of Saint Marc, whither he had been sent as if to take a command. In his indignation, he threw his sword into the sea to prevent its being sullied by traitors. He was sent to France, and, curiously enough, was, as we have seen, cast into the prison which held Toussaint L'Ouverture. Lamartinière, who had displayed the virtues of a champion of liberty behind the walls of Crête-à-Pierrot, was massacred in an ambuscade. Thus was manifested the hatred of the colonists against men whom they could not endure to see in the enjoyment of freedom. That hatred was fostered by the Consul and by his representative, Leclerc. Of special consequence did the Captain-General consider the disarming of the blacks; but the step was one of extreme difficulty. Men, whose passions are excited, and whose future is uncertain, do not easily surrender their arms. Cajolery and mutual distrust were put into action; the result was, that thirty thousand muskets were collected and laid up in the common armory. But in the midst of the operation discontent was displayed, menaces were uttered, sedition was fostered, risings took place; the Government was compelled to employ vigor as well as adroitness. Troops were set in movement, blacks who were in subjection were employed against others who were ripe for revolt; some sullenly gave up their arms, others hid them, waiting their opportunity. Ferocious bands were formed, who practised all kinds of atrocities. The disarming succeeded best in the South; in the West it was very partial; the colored population, distrustful and disquieted, especially since the deportation of Rigaud, betook themselves to the mountains; then most unjust and injudicious severities were exercised; suspicion sufficed for the infliction of death; the scaffolds were loaded with victims of both sexes, and of all ages. Several of the wives of the officers of the seventh colonial brigade were publicly executed. After capturing Belair, Dessalines slaughtered three hundred blacks and men of color in the vale of the Artibonite, to avenge the death of some European soldiers massacred within the country under his command. Meanwhile, an impression had been obtaining prevalence that the disarming and other offensive measures were parts of a system intended to issue in the restoration of slavery. Some imprudent colonists, whom experience of evil had not taught anything but revenge, uttered in one of their assemblies the old maxim, — " No slavery, no colony." The alarm caused thereby was augmented by news that slavery had been restored in other French dependencies, and that even the slave-trade was resumed. Under the growing fears and distrust, some applied to purchase their freedom. The request was refused by their former owners. " We are then," said mothers of families, with tears in their eyes, — " we are then about to fall back into slavery." To prevent the calamity, the blacks made such preparation as they could. Circumstances were in their favor: a malady which had gone far to destroy the army and the fleet; the rainy season, which was at hand, not less baneful to the whites than favorable to the blacks; the asylum of the mountains, where their foes would pursue them almost in vain. Full of fear, yet full of courage, they spoke to each other words of exhortation: " Do they expect to find slaves in us? Why did they not leave us at large in our forests? Was Africa, our native land, weary of us? Have our rivers been dried up? Did not our flocks, our fields, did not hunting and fishing, suffice for our wants? We learned no other wants but at the price of our liberty; they have deceived us in our simplicity by poisoned gifts. Were not our feet accustomed, unshod, to walk over burning sands; and did not our uncovered heads brave the fires of the torrid zone? Our skin, given by Nature to enable us to live near the sun, performed the office of garments fabricated by luxury. Was not the limpid wave of our fountains preferable to the liquors which cause brutal fury? To enjoy the sweet manifestations of friendship, the guileless smile of our children, the caresses of a mother who, during three years, nurtured us with her milk; to trouble neither our own lot nor the lot of others; to pass our life without fear and without desires, as a river of a tranquil and uniform flow, — such were the precious advantages of which we have been robbed by our enemies." While thus they inflamed each other by fancy pictures of their ancestral mode of life, they drew a too true and a very painful contrast in adverting to their actual condition. Here a man held forth his arm, mutilated by a barbarous monster; there another pointed to his leg, eaten into by the links of an iron chain; others drew attention to the scars left by the driver's thong; women uncovered their breasts, which showed

21*

traces of the branding iron, — the breasts which had suckled their masters' children. And then, with what pride did they turn to the blessings of freedom ? "Heaven, in its pity, has given us a new country in this land of exile, of grief, and of shame ; shall it be torn from us ?"

Soon the standard of revolt was raised. At first the banner was unfurled by obscure men who occasioned little solicitude. But civil wars are pregnant with great leaders. In the mountains of Saint Domingo there were always tribes of untamed Africans, who had thrown off the yoke of slavery. At the head of one of these tribes was Lamour de Rance, an adroit, stern, savage man, half-naked, with epaulettes tied by a cord for his only token of authority. At home in the mountains, he passed from one to the other with something of the ease of one of their own birds. Toussaint himself had in vain pursued him in those retreats whose proper inhabitants are wild beasts; that chief acknowledged no other authority than that which Nature gave, in no way thinking or caring about monarchy or republicanism. His tender of obedience to the Government had been a matter of mere form. His dress, his manners, his character, his mode of fighting, at the Cape, where he just showed himself, were objects of curiosity and amusement with the French army. A greater insult could not be given than to ask this savage warrior for his arms. Were they not the protectors of his life ? He avenged the insult by carrying fire and sword over the highlands in the vicinity of Port-au-Prince. In the plain of Léogane he reduced to ashes more than a hundred plantations; he carried off the laborers, and inflicted barbarous cruelties on the whites.

The revolt extended. In the North, as well as in the South and the West, it broke out and spread devastation. As reports of these insurrections got abroad at the Cape and Port-au-Prince, consternation increased. News was eagerly sought after, though almost always the source of fresh anxiety. Some reported that they had seen on fire the mountains which overhang Port-au-Prince; others that Lamour de Rance had reduced to ashes the plantations of Léogane. This day brought intelligence that Sans-Souci was in arms at Vallière; the next, that Noël had seized Dondon and Sylla Plaisance. "You have heard that Macaya raises the country around Port-de-Paix?" "No; but a band of insurgents is spreading terror in the island of Tortue." More lamentable still were the narratives which some had to give, how their brothers, their wives, their children, had been massacred with an incredible refinement of cruelty.

The general alarm was exaggerated by the colonists, who, forgetful of the share they had had in causing it, and that but for them there would have been no conquest of the island, no violation of oaths, no intention of restoring slavery, accused (as is the custom of such men) their destiny, the Government, Heaven, every object but themselves, the real sources of all these evils. "Heaven, then," they said, "has not ceased to persecute us; have we not suffered enough during ten years of exile and misery? Shall we always be driven into flight, or be massacred by our ferocious slaves? Was there ever a similar succession of reverses and misfortunes? Are we not the most unfortunate of men? Our slaves are before our eyes kindling incendiary torches, and twice have we seen our plantations and our towns burned to the ground. Why does not the Government act with decision? Why leave us to certain and speedy destruction?" Then they invoked the aid of the black chiefs who remained attached to their party, and who replied to them only by a fierce silence or by dissimulation. But always allowing themselves to be borne away by vengeance, they surrounded the Captain-General with their pernicious counsels, and he, instead of employing clemency and mildness, made use only of arms and punishments. In the cities scaffolds were raised which were bathed in the blood of the blacks. They even executed women and children, whose only crime was that they had brothers, fathers, or husbands, among the revolters; they were accused of corresponding with them, — the penalty of such intercourse was death. Port-au-Prince, in consternation at the ravages of Lamour de Rance, became the special theatre of executions. All suffered death with intrepidity, calmness, and resignation. The more numerous the executions, the more extensive were 'the desertions. Instead of terrifying, they exasperated; they fed the insurrection, though they intended to suppress it.

While the scaffolds were crowded with victims, Leclerc applied to Dessalines for assistance. He went to the Cape and renewed his protestations of fidelity and devotedness. Cruel as false, the monster declared that he thirsted for the blood of the revolters. In a moment when his indignation had gained the mastery, and the agitation of his members manifested more rage than even his words, the General-in-chief said to him in transport, " The troops which I expect from France will give me the power of striking a terrible blow." " There shall be," shouted Dessalines, in fury, " a general earthquake!" A Government that stimulates and employs such wretches condemns itself and forfeits its authority. Instead of carrying on the war honorably, Dessalines pretended to entertain feelings in favor of the revolt. By this means it was that he entrapped General Belair

While Dessalines was subduing Mount Cahos, Leclerc ordered Rochambeau to punish Lamour de Rance; but the troops who went in pursuit of him saw only vast fields of fire which covered his flight. When circumstances suggested, the barbarians sheltered themselves in the heart of precipitous mountains, which were to them fortifications stronger than any which the art of man ever constructed. All that could be done was to oppose some limit to the ravages of the foe in the West and the South, the frontiers of which two provinces he had laid waste.

At the same time the captain of the expedition, seconded by Christophe and Maurepas, employed all his efforts both to put down the sedition in the Isle of Tortue, and to arrest the progress of the revolt in the North. But Sans-Souci was an African not less agile than Lamour de Rance. He also covered his flight with deserts and flames; he did not, however, fear to try actual combat. Twice he defeated the troops sent against him.

Meanwhile, the black generals still attached to the French preserved only a suspected fidelity, and barely concealed their disquietude. Christophe, afraid of being arrested like Toussaint, did not accept Leclerc's invitation to a banquet until he had directed his troops to be in readiness for a sudden blow. An officer who sat next him at table took pleasure in filling his glass. Christophe, suspecting an evil design, turned to him in rage, and said, "Dost thou know, thou little white thing, that if I had drunk the wine which thou pouredst out for me, I should have desired to drink thy blood and that of thy general?" These words caused great agitation among the guests. Leclerc reproached Christophe with what he called Toussaint's treason, and commanded the officers of his guard to run to arms. "Vain is it to call your soldiers," the chief replied; "mine are under arms, and with a single word I can make you a prisoner; but, as to my betraying you, learn to know me. I remain subject to you as I was to Toussaint; had he said to me, 'Hurl this island into the sea,' I would have done my best. This is the way I obey or command. The faith of oaths and treaties, — security of person, — sacred rights of hospitality, — have not all been violated by your cruel policy? Prison, banishment, death, are the rewards of those whose blood flows for our liberty. No longer are you around me, friends, soldiers, heroes of our mountains! And thou, Toussaint, the pride of our race, the terror of our enemies, — thou whose genius led us from slavery to liberty, — thou whose hand adorned peace with lovely virtues, — thou whose glory fills the world, — they have put thee in irons like the vilest criminal! But what is there in common between you, Captain-General and Toussaint? Your name came amongst us only as his who turned parricidal arms against the representatives of your country. It is this crime, doubtless, that the Consul wished to reward in giving you the government of Saint Domingo." These were bold words to be spoken at the Governor's table.

The guests looked astounded.   Leclerc, alarmed in his inmost soul, affected composure.

In truth the condition of the colony was lamentable.   The fever continued its wasting career.   The Government every day lost power, while its enemies increased.   Suspicion and alarm opened on every hand.   This state of things finds a good description in the words of an eye-witness.   Thus does General Pamphile de Lacroix speak : " I was invited to the heights of the Cape by General Boudet, whom the General-in-chief was sending to France to acquaint the Government with the true condition of the island.   At the house of General Boudet I found Generals Clervaux and Christophe.   I asked them the cause of the progress of the insurrection.   The latter replied, ' You are a European, and you are young ; you have fought merely in the armies of the mother country ; you, consequently, cannot have any prejudices regarding slavery.   I will therefore speak to you with frankness.   The revolt grows because distrust is at its height.   If you had our skin, you would not, perhaps, be so confiding as myself, who am intrusting my only son, Ferdinand, to General Boudet that he may be educated in France.   I make no account of the brigands who have given the signal for the insurrection.   The danger lies not there; the danger is in the general opinion of the blacks; those of Saint Domingo are frightened because they know the decree of the 30th Floréal, which maintains slavery and the slave-trade in the colonies restored to France by the treaty of Amiens. They are alarmed at seeing the First Consul reëstablish the old system in those colonies.   They are afraid lest the indiscreet talk that is heard here on all sides should find its way to France, and suggest to the Government the idea of depriving the blacks of Saint Domingo of their liberty.'   In order to pique his self-love, I asked him how it was that he, who had so much influence in the South, should not have found troops sufficiently devoted to put Sans-Souci into his hands.   His reply struck me : ' If Sans-Souci was a soldier, I might get hold of him ; but he is a mean and cruel brigand, who has no scruple to kill whomsoever he suspects; he knows when to fly, and he knows how to cover his flight with the deserts which he leaves behind him. He goes about the affair better than we did at the time of your disembarkation. If, then, instead of fighting, our system of resistance had consisted in flight, and in well alarming the blacks, you would never have been able to overtake us. So said old Toussaint; no one believed him. We possessed arms; the pride of making use of them was our ruin. These new insurgents follow the system of Toussaint; if they persist in it we shall have difficulty to reduce them.'

" General Christophe urged me not to return that evening to Fort Dauphin; saying, that the revolters, having attacked his posts in the plain, were probably informed of my journey. I thanked him; but, urging that the danger would be greater to-morrow, I said that I should return as soon as I had seen the General-in-chief. General Leclerc acquainted me with his melancholy situation, congratulating himself in seeing none but bandits among the new chiefs of the insurrection, and added, that, in the feeble state of the forces of the mother country, he was glad to find the generals of color still faithful to France. On my way to Saint Michel, I stopped at General Christophe's, who, hearing discharges of fire-arms in the mountains, repeated his request that I would not that evening press on to Fort Dauphin. I persisted in my intention. He then ordered six of his guides to accompany me. 'Bear in mind,' he said to them repeatedly, ' that you are escorting a general whom I esteem and love.'

" We set out. Of a sudden, the guides, who led the way with torches, stopped before a detachment of thirty blacks, who had concealed themselves in a ditch. Forthwith one heard the words, ' Halt! stop! halt!' Shots succeeded. The commanding officer meanwhile recognized in Don Diego Polanco, who was with me, an old friend. We were saved. But I had seen reason to believe that the chiefs of the colonial troops and the colored generals had communications with the insurgents.

"Too frequently did the Europeans speak of the reinforcements captured from France for the blacks not to perceive the need in which we stood of them."

The news of the events which had taken place at Guadeloupe, the maintenance of slavery at Martinique, indiscreet talk, and insinuations from foreigners, fomented distrust in the minds of the black chiefs. The words which the First Consul had addressed to the Abbé Grégoire, at an official presentation at the Institute, were repeated in the colony : "From what is taking place in Saint Domingo, I wish the friends of the blacks throughout Europe had their heads covered with mourning crape." The words struck men's imaginations. The minds of the blacks and of the men of color were at the height of disquietude when the frigate Cocarde entered the roads, having on board blacks sent from Guadeloupe ; many of them in the night jumped into the sea, swam to shore, and by their reports made the alarm still greater. At the same time, some men of color, also from Guadeloupe, brought to Saint Domingo information that the slave-trade in that island comprehended their caste. Here were dark presages of what might be expected in Saint Domingo. The fidelity of the chiefs of the colonial troops was from that hour irrevocably shaken.

General Clervaux, who had recently condemned Charles Belair to death, first threw off the mask by deserting. The evening before, being at Madame Leclerc's, he had said in a fit of passion, "I was free formerly ; only to new circumstances do I owe it that I have raised up my reviled color ; but if I fancied that here the restoration of slavery would ever be thought of, that instant I would become a brigand."

Judge, if you can, of the position of Captain-General Leclerc ; he knew the danger, he could not prevent it. The crews were not sufficient for the service of the ships. The garrison of the Cape did not comprise more than two hundred Europeans ; there were in it fifteen hundred colonial soldiers. On the night of the 13th-14th of September (1802), Pétion, that coolly audacious chief, threw all into confusion at the Cape, spiked the guns, and disarmed the European cannoniers." *

Two days after, Clervaux and Pétion made an attack on the Cape, but failed to capture it. So well were they received by Brigadier Anhouil that, thinking they were opposed by the fresh troops expected from France, they drew off their forces, which, if pressed forward, must have been overwhelming, so superior were they in number to the defenders of the colonial metropolis. At the moment of the attack, Leclerc, as a measure of precaution, sent on board vessels in the harbor, whose crews had been greatly reduced by the fever, detachments of the colonial soldiers who had remained at the Cape. The sailors, panic-struck, cried out, " Let us kill those who may kill us." They fell on the black soldiers, and ruthlessly drowned of them more than a thousand.

Then Christophe, already prepared for defection, and lately standing, to use his phrase, *as a benevolent spectator*, — in other words, watching the right moment, — joined Clervaux. A few days after, Dessalines threw himself into opposition.

The insurrection became general. The entire population was the enemy of France. The mother, the daughter, the child, as well as the father and the brother, all were soldiers. The woods were their camps, dens their dwellings; the mountains their ramparts; they found their food in the spontaneous products of the earth; they transmuted into arms the instruments of agriculture. Stones hurled from the rocks served them instead of artillery. They threw their whole life into assaults, combats, and ambuscades. A new future was before them. " Death or liberty ! " again became their rallying cry. Everywhere the insurgents repulsed, and laid waste the enemies of their freedom. They captured Port-de-Paix, Gonaïves, Fort Dauphin. In the evacuation of the last place, General de Lacroix was obliged in his extremity to destroy powder and provisions to the value of two millions of francs. Escaping by sea to the Cape, he lost in the short voyage sixty-six sick persons,

* Mémoires, vol. ii. 224, seq.

22

who were thrown into the sea. The first words which Leclerc addressed to him on landing them were, " General, what have you done? You bring a colored population four times more numerous than your Europeans; you do not know then that they are tigers, serpents, that you bear in your bosom."

Leclerc felt that the colony was escaping out of his hands. Of all his conquests there remained only, in the North, the Cape, and Môle Saint-Nicholas, and in the West, Port-au-Prince, and Saint Marc. But for the colonists, who then appeared with arms in their hands, all was over.

At the prospect the Captain-General was greatly alarmed. He looked everywhere for succor. In his perplexity, he sent to an enemy's camp to beg the aid of Christophe, offering him honors and riches. Christophe contented himself with replying that he was rich and honored enough in possessing liberty himself, and in securing the liberty of his color.

Shortly, Christophe put himself at the head of the insurgents, and proceeded to attack the Cape. Then was Leclerc on the land side shut up within the walls of the capital. Scarcely did he possess vessels sufficient for flight.

Such was the condition of Hayti, when, in the first of November, 1802, the Captain-General, worn down by fatigue and pains, and overwhelmed with vexation, disappointment, and despair, breathed his last as the final result of a sickness which had long threatened to prove fatal. A little before his death, he expressed his regret for the errors committed by himself in the government, — regret now utterly vain, — errors which had proved disastrous to all the great interests of the colony. Nor less disastrous to France was this iniquitous expedition. Of four-and-thirty thousand warriors, twenty-four thousand had perished, and eight thousand were in the hospitals; scarcely more than two thousand were fit for service.

Amid this thick darkness, and surrounded by these vengeful penalties, the Captain-General passed to a tribunal before which diversities of skin are unknown. Leclerc wanted neither sense nor manners. He possessed an easy eloquence which threw light on the discussions of his council-chamber. But he was little acquainted with the human heart, and was unable to interpret the peculiar character of Africans. In war he was active, uncertain, and presumptuous. Blindly obedient to the wishes of the First Consul, he made peace consist of a complication of troubles, divisions, treachery, and violence. By these deplorable crimes, he was reduced to the state of impotence which has been described. As he had none of the qualities of a great commander, a funeral oration pronounced in his honor, before a few soldiers, who had escaped from the fever and the sword, was a mere harmonious assemblage of idle words.

Pauline, Leclerc's wife, affected the marks of extraordinary mourning, but she betrayed appearances by choosing for her companion one of the most handsome men of the army, and returned to her ordinary habits of luxury, pleasure, and voluptuousness. After having had her husband's body embalmed, she crossed the sea to France. When her vessel appeared at Marseilles, the inhabitants, at the sight of the Consul's sister, a widow, so young, in tears, manifested their sorrow by decorating the port and the streets with crape and funereal garlands. The tokens of sadness had been commanded, but they had some reality, for many of them had seen her grow up to adolescence within their walls.

In mournful procession she entered Paris. Brothers, sisters, and wives, then shed true tears at the remembrance of sons, brothers, and husbands, whom they had lost in the expedition. Pauline herself let some tears fall when she saw her brother, who embraced her with joy and tenderness. Then she spoke to him eloquently of Saint Domingo as a land of fire, blood, and desolation. The Consul heard her in silence, and said, "Here is all that remains of that fine army, — the body of a brother-in-law, of a general, my right arm, a handful of dust; all has perished, all will perish. Fatal conquest! cursed land! perfidious colonists! a wretched slave in revolt! These are the causes of so many evils." He concealed from himself for a moment that he had sent away so many brave warriors that they might not throw their bayonets across the road to the imperial throne, whither he was urged by his impetuous desires.

Soon his mind arose from that dejection, and in the immensity of the future which his genius embraced, he regarded the calamities of Saint Domingo only as an unlucky but useful incident. Had he not thrown into prison Toussaint, the chief and the soul of the revolt? The fever had nearly consumed its fuel; Rochambeau, whose character he knew, would terrify the island into obedience. Those wandering bands of insurgents, without a head, without union, divided among themselves, would desert the mountains to enjoy the pleasures of the cities. Besides, did he not possess the two heads of Saint Domingo, — the South and the Spanish territory? Had he no more soldiers, no more ships? Let twenty thousand men fly over the ocean. Thus Bonaparte prepared for the loss of a second army. Blind ambition, reckless of its means, reckless of the misery it occasions! Meanwhile, the First Consul deposited Leclerc's corpse, amid much pomp, in the Panthéon, and erected statues to his memory. The greater the calamities of Hayti, the more he endeavored to efface the recollection of them by show and pomp, and by the aid of those arts which ought to transmit to posterity the memory only of truly great men.

CHAPTER IV.

Rochambeau assumes the command — His character — Voluptuousness, tyranny, and cruelty — Receives large reinforcements — Institutes a system of terror — The insurrection becomes general and irresistible — The French are driven out of the island.

AFTER the death of Leclerc, the command of Hayti passed into the hands of Rochambeau. That General was deformed in body, but of a robust constitution; his manner was hard and severe, though he had a propensity to voluptuousness. In his youth he had, under the eyes of an illustrious father, served the cause of independence in North America. He lacked neither ability nor experience in war. He possessed tender, domestic, and friendly affections. His good qualities would have accompanied him to the tomb if he had not been called to the government of Saint Domingo. Regarding virtue as both lovely and requisite in private life, he judged it useless and even dangerous in public affairs, as if the laws of eternal justice depended on position and circumstances. Misled by this gross delusion, he feared not to give himself up to acts of violation, spoliation, and cruelty of all kinds. Blaming the tardy and hesitating administration of his predecessor, he resolved to employ all the resources of terror in order to establish his authority.

Masters who had been impoverished by the freedom of the slaves saw with joy Rochambeau succeed a chief, who, according to circumstances, espoused or betrayed their personal interests. But the blacks were disquieted when they knew that he had taken the helm. Independently of the massacre he had committed in the Bay of Mancenille, they remembered that when merely a general, he had not scrupled to degrade them with the punishment of the lash; but what caused them greater alarm were some words addressed in a tone of pleasantry to their wives at a festivity which he had given at Port-au-Prince. "You," he said, "are invited to dance at your interment." A hall hung with black, and lighted up by funeral torches, seemed to them the image of their approaching sanguinary end.

Despotism and sensuality have often been companions. In Rochambeau the one sharpened the appetite for the other, as though greediness of bodily pleasure welcomed the zest arising from the sight of bodily pain. No small part of his time Rochambeau passed at table, or on sofas with creole females, worshippers of pleasure as well as most cruel toward their slaves. They spoke to him constantly of chains, prisons, the scourge and other punishments, in the midst of games, laughter, caresses, and senseless gratifications with which they intoxicated his soul. As his policy inclined him to violence, he willingly allowed himself to be overcome by the fascinations of these women, as well as by irritated proprietors, who continually pointed him to their houses in flames, and their slaves in revolt in the mountains. Thus did he listen only to counsels of hatred enforced by contempt and vice.

The fever had changed the character of the army. The heart of the soldier was worn by regret, fatigued by misfortune, and filled with trouble; no longer had the noise and glitter of arms, encampments, war, and victory any attractions for him. A bitter and savage melancholy had succeeded to the hilarity and joy of courage and hope. Even officers of rank were seen to disown authority and to favor a revolt, which they judged legitimate. But Rochambeau, who required a blind submission, dismissed those the firmness of whose soul he doubted; thus giving free course to tyranny in order to oppose an effectual remedy to the evils he wished to put down.

Up to this time, punishment and violence had been covered with a veil. Toussaint had not been arrested except as a result of a pretended conspiracy; a military tribunal had condemned Charles Belair. Those who had suffered death had been taken with arms in their hands, or had kept up communications with the insurgents. In truth, many women and children were in the number of the victims, but they were at least implicated by some accusation, and it was through fear rather than cruelty that disarmed soldiers had been drowned at the Cape. But from this time there was no longer any study of appearances; law, judges, and tribunals were ceremonies too circuitous and too tardy.

Meanwhile, Rochambeau, who received in different detachments fresh troops, to the number of 20,000 men, sent them under different circumstances against the revolters, whom he drove away from the country around Port-au-Prince, Môle Saint-Nicholas, and the heights which overhung the Cape. As he was most eager to signalize his command by some victory, he retook Fort Dauphin and Port-De-Paix, without any memorable action. This was the term of his success. The blacks, without regret, abandoned fortresses which to them seemed contemptible in comparison with their rocks. But in the degree in which they were repulsed at one point, they extended toward another, so that they only acquired accessions of strength. But what was more for their encouragement and advantage was that they were furnished with arms by English vessels. Rochambeau thought that there was no surer means to repress their ardor than to affright them by some extraordinary punishment.

The sea off the Cape was chosen to be the theatre of an execution, unparalleled in what is called civilized life. For fear that Maurepas, who had gained distinction under Toussaint L'Ouverture, after having embraced the side of France, should join the insurgents, Leclerc had written to him to come by sea, with his family and his troop, to take the command of the Cape, which he destined for him as a reward for his services. No sooner had he arrived than he and his soldiers were seized and disarmed. Rochambeau ordered preparations to be made for a barbarous punishment in order to put the negro general to death, with his troop, consisting of 400 blacks. It was also put in deliberation whether death should be inflicted on his children, in order to prevent them from rising up to avenge their father.

After having been bound to the mast of a vessel, Maurepas was frightfully insulted. His wife, his children, and his soldiers were brought to be drowned under his eyes. The executioners were astounded when they beheld a father fix his dying eyes by turns on his children, his wife, and his companions in arms, undergoing a violent death; while they, on their part, turned their eyes away from a father, a husband, a general, whose countenance was disfigured by the tortures he was enduring. After being made to contemplate each other's sufferings, they were all tossed into the ocean. They died without complaining in a manner worthy the champions of liberty. With a reversal of the order of nature, the father died last; he also suffered most.

Thus died Maurepas, whose character was a compound of frankness and severity. Thrice had he repulsed the French at the gorge of Trois-Rivières; he had at once the glory and the misfortune to go over to the French with victorious arms. The elevation of his soul equalled his valor. He preserved a tender feeling for the master whose slave he had been; he caused funeral honors to be paid to that master, and when his grave had been negligently prepared, he threw off his upper garment in order to perform the pious office properly. Among men of his own blood he was a powerful chief. A spirit of order and justice prevailed in his life. His riches, which were considerable, were given up to pillage. It would almost seem as if so much excellence were subjected to so much ignominy, expressly to show that while black men are capable of any virtue, white men are capable of any crime. Certainly, my narrative is replete with instances which, beyond a question, prove that moral as well as mental excellence is independent of the varieties of color.

This brutal punishment, preceded by vile perfidy, filled the camps of the insurgents with horror. That horror was augmented when Rochambeau, at the Cape, put to death five hundred prisoners. On the place of execution, and under the eyes of the victims, they dug a large hole for their grave, so that the poor wretches may be said to have been present at their own funeral.

Dessalines, burning to avenge Maurepas and his fellow-soldiers, rushed like a lion on the Cape, and, in his impetuous and terrible march, he surrounded and made prisoners a body of Frenchmen, who, at the post called Belair, defended the approach to the city. Then, with branches of trees, that ferocious African raised, under the eyes of Rochambeau, five hundred gibbets, on which he hanged the same number of prisoners. Of these victims of vengeance, the greater number had been the Consul's companions in arms; they had assisted that bad great man to acquire his pretensions to a throne, and for their reward they had been sent out of his way to suffer an ignominious and painful death at the hands of a savage.

Rochambeau, who occupied himself less and less with war, continued to plunge into the delights of the table, and of voluptuousness with courtesans and wives of colonists, who never ceased to stimulate his tyranny, and exact from him the restoration of their slaves. Then, while the insurrection, in the name of liberty, made head in the mountains, on the plains suspicion converted everything into crime. If you went abroad, you joined the revolters; if you stayed at home, you were waiting for them; if you manifested joy, you took pleasure in the public calamities; if you appeared sad, you grieved over the reverses of the revolt; if you wrote letters, you corresponded with the enemy; if you talked, you spread sedition; if you were observed to listen, you were a spy; if you failed to salute a white, you insulted a master; bravery was dangerous, weakness was complicity, innocence was stratagem. Interpretations were put on a gesture, a smile, a sigh; silence was accused of sedition, and even thoughts had no asylum in their last refuge, — the human heart.

Such is the character of the tyranny which under the slightest pretext and often by mere hazard, threw its toils round a multitude of victims without distinction of age or sex to effect their ruin. The number of sufferers was greatly augmented because colonists by a species of rivalry denounced the peaceful slaves of other colonists, so that it became almost the sole business of Rochambeau to order or even to devise punishments; the sea and the land were covered with them. The unfortunate blacks were bound together and then thrown into the sea to perish; if they came up to the surface and made their way to the shore, they were in sport pursued and massacred. The executions were varied: now the blacks were beheaded, now they were dragged down into the depths by the weight of a shot tied to their feet; and now they were stifled by sulphur on shipboard.

Among the number of these victims were female priests, who worshipped African fetish idols. That veneration for the gods of their fathers was punished with death; so little does unbelief guarantee toleration. A French General, touched with compassion at the approaching death of one of these superstitious but well-meaning women, implored that her life might be spared. Rochambeau, taking into his hands the pigmy idols of her worship, said, " How can I save the life of one who worships these?" Yet, during the fever, these very women had bestowed every attention on sick French soldiers. Unhappy women! their charity had no other recompense than the punishment which is reserved for the vilest crimes. Base ingratitude of the commander! Here, again, on which side is the moral superiority? Oh, civilization, what crimes have been committed in thy name! Ye weak ones, whose " feeble knees" a Christian authority commands Christian men to strengthen (Heb. xii. 12), how have indignities and woes been heaped on your heads, simply because ye were weak, not only by sceptics and scoffers, but even by professed believers in a divine religion!

The numerous executions which began at Cape City soon extended to other places. Port-au-Prince had its salt waters made bloody, and scaffolds were erected and loaded within and without its walls, The hand of tyranny spread terror and death over the shores of the North and the West. As the insurrection became more daring, it was thought that the punishments had not been either numerous enough, violent enough, or various enough. The colonists counselled and encouraged vengeance as if it was their wealth.

All human passions were let loose. Never was such a spectacle of ferocity beheld. The calm, concentrated, impassible revolt which followed the death of Leclerc had committed only particular acts of revenge; but at the sight of punishments so numerous and so horrible, insurrection roared and raged on all sides. Men, scarcely anything else than barbarians, made the mountains resound with this death-song:—

> " Open, ye sepulchres of our ancestors; ye dusty bones, shudder;
>   Vengeance! vengeance! reply the tombs and all nature."

With shouts of joy they ran to battle, and, impatient to avenge their color, they seized the enemies of their liberty, and cast them to the earth to perish. The South was once more on fire.

At the same time, at the Cape, at Fort Dauphin, at Port-de-Paix, at Saint Marc, at Port-au-Prince, and all along the shores, everywhere were whips, crosses, gibbets, funeral-piles; and soldiers, colonists, sailors engaged in slaying, strangling, drowning human beings, whose only crime was their refusal to go back into slavery. Some had their bodies lacerated by the scourge; then they were fastened to posts in the vicinity of a marsh, that they might be devoured, half-alive, by blood-sucking insects. Others were literally burnt alive, as if they had been martyrs for religion. Death thus appeared before the negro in its two most terrible aspects,—extreme slowness and extreme rapidity. Others in greater number perished in the sea or on the scaffold. In the country, trees, loaded with flowers and breathing perfumes, served as gallowses, as if to put in broad contrast the goodness of God and the vileness of man. Countries created for peace, happiness, and joy were thus desolated by human passions scarcely less baneful to those who fostered and indulged them than to those against whom they raged.

On the countenance of those who were led to death shone a

anticipation of the liberty which they felt was about to grow on a land watered with the blood of their caste. They had the same firmness, the same resignation, the same enthusiasm as distinguished the martyr of the Christian religion. On the gibbets, in the flames, in the midst of tortures, scarcely was a sigh to be heard; even the child hardly shed tears. The words "our country," "freedom," breathed quietly from their dying lips. They often encouraged each other to bear death manfully. A black chief, named Chevalier, hesitated when he saw the instruments of his punishment. "What!" said his wife, "thou knowest not how sweet it is to die for liberty!" and, without allowing herself to be touched by the executioner, she took the rope and ended her days. A mother said to her daughters who were going to execution, "Be glad; you will not be mothers of slaves."

The strength of soul which the blacks showed in their tortures was so surprising that the whites ascribed the cause to some peculiarity of organization. It was pretended that the fibres of the blacks contracted with so much force that the sufferers became insensible to pain. Thus, by vain suppositions, an effort was made to rob the victims of the glory of their death. If the question was to make them slaves, then they were not men; if the cruellest punishments were to be inflicted on them, then they did not suffer. If they were not men, why make them do the work of men? If they did not suffer, why impose the punishments? Beasts may do the work which was laid on beings who were not men; and sufferings not felt were inefficacious both as punishments and examples. But when did tyranny lack a pretext, or cruelty lack a palliation? In this case, the pretext and the palliation did but throw the enormity of the injustice into relief.

Ordinary expedients were too tame, or too slow, or not sufficiently efficacious. History was ransacked for others. Children, women, and old men were confined in sacks and thrown into the sea: it was the punishment of parricides among the Romans. It was ascertained that three centuries before, in that same country, Spaniards had employed dogs to run down the innocent savages. Frenchmen of the nineteenth century rejoiced that they had at their command a resource so effectual, and, I must add, so diabolical. Rochambeau, however, sent a vessel to the isle of Cuba to purchase dogs whose nature, under man's training, made them fit for the work of hunting human beings. When this ship appeared at the fort of the Cape, wives of the colonists went to receive them on the shore, and made the air resound with cries of joy; they put garlands on their necks, and strewed their path with flowers. Some degraded themselves so far as to cover those instruments of their vengeance with kisses. To what extravagances does slavery lead! An experiment must be made. In the court-yard of a convent a sort of amphitheatre was erected, which was filled with a multitude panting for negro blood. The victim was bound to a post. The dogs, sharpened by extreme hunger, were no sooner let loose than they tore the poor wretch to pieces. The raging animals disputed with each other the palpitating members, and the ground was dyed with human blood and canine foam. A report spread among the blacks, that, at the last groan of that pitiable creature, the heavens opened and received his soul.

This kind of death, with circumstances more or less frightful, became common, until cruelty, dispensing with all forms, disdainfully cast human beings to the dogs, who were kept in packs near the city; and when the appetite of the animals, satisfied with human flesh and gore, refused any longer to destroy, the sword finished the bloody work: showing that man's passions surpass in atrocity those of wild beasts. Indeed, language failed of terms to describe the crimes which the lust of unjust power perpetrated. New expressions were invented. The drowning of two or three hundred human beings was called "a good haul;" death on a gallows was "a step upward;" to be torn in pieces by dogs was "to enter the arena." Some executioners gained celebrity; the name of Tombarel long continued to make men shudder. The sea and the rivers were stained with blood. The numbers of victims were so considerable that the inhabitants refused to eat fish, lest they should feed on blood of their own color.

Many blacks, of whom some had witnessed these atrocities, and others, who, in the confusion, had, by swimming or flight, escaped from the hands of the executioners, went to join the ranks of the insurgents in different places. Often, under the shade of a tree, or under the point of a rock, these fugitives might be seen recounting to their companions the punishment they had witnessed, or suffered. How great soever the cruelty, it was exaggerated in their hyperbolical phraseology. The crowd listened with intense curiosity, silence, and horror; often the narrators were interrupted by questions respecting the fate of a child, or a sister, who had died on the gibbet, or had been tossed into the sea. At these frightful accounts, the auditors shed tears, but they were tears of vengeance. Some shouted, "Shall we go down into our tombs without having avenged them? No! their bones would repulse ours." Others, by gestures and cries, not satisfied with having carried fire and sword over the lowlands, stirred each other up to deeds of carnage and devastation. Vengeance of a certain barbaric grandeur burst forth. In listening to one of these narratives, Paul L'Ouverture, the brother of Toussaint, learned that, without any reason, his wife, who lived at the Cape, in the peace of her own home, had been drowned. He fell into a madness of revenge which grief nourished, and which nothing appeased. He captured, near Fort Dauphin, a shipwrecked vessel, on board of which were thirty French passengers. He took them, and having led them to one of the principal entrances to Cape City, he pitilessly immolated them all to the manes of his innocent wife, taking pains to put on a post an inscription, which stated that the death of a beloved partner had extorted from his grief a vengeance worthy of a proud, loving, and deeply afflicted soul. Truly, indeed, is revenge blind as well as ruthless. Who can describe, who can dare to contemplate, the evils of slavery? Sixteen of the bravest generals of Toussaint L'Ouverture, chained by the neck to the rocks of an uninhabited island, breathed their last miserable sigh after wasting away during seventeen days. These abominable cruelties are not wholly without relief. Captains of ships, instead of casting the innocent victims, put into their hands for the purpose, into the sea, supported them at their own expense, and landed them on some of the neighboring islands, or on some remote shore of Saint Domingo. None showed more humanity than Mazard, who employed as much zeal in saving victims as others did in destroying them. " I have," he said, " deceived your tyrants; my heart is lacerated to see the land and the sea covered with victims; go into the mountains, rejoin your people, that posterity may learn that savages dragged to servitude have founded a new state ; but pity men's passions, and leave your revenge to time, to remorse, to Heaven."

All the sea-captains did not act with the same elevation of soul. They did, indeed, save the blacks from death, but their conduct was dictated by a base avarice ; they took them and sold them as slaves in some neighboring island. On one of these occasions, the Governor of Porto-Rico made this fine reply : " If they are slaves, I will not purchase them ; if they are free men, you have not the right to sell them."

Nor was the army without examples of virtue. There were generals who, indignant at so many cruelties, uttered remonstrances, or disobeyed inhuman commands. Allix, who commanded at Port-au-Prince, refused ten thousand shot intended to be fastened to the feet of victims to freedom. This act of disobedience, which was really a virtue, Rochambeau punished by banishment. Other officers were punished for similar offences. Truly did the forcible eloquence of the Africans characterize the war as " a War of Cannibals."

Suddenly the South, which had been tranquil, awoke at the noise of the punishments which sent from the North and the West corpses to float on its shores. That province was peopled chiefly by men of color, who possessed great wealth, and who showed themselves less than in other parts enemies of the whites, with whom, notwithstanding the force of prejudice, they were united by marriage. When they saw that they themselves were not spared any more than the blacks, they ran to arms. The revolt began in the district of Petit-Troux, where, under the pretext of a conspiracy, of which nothing has ever become known, they had drowned Boudet, who had delivered up the Fort Bizoton at the attack of Port-au-Prince. That punishment revolted public opinion the more because it involved ingratitude. The revolt became general as soon as it had been resolved to put to death, in the city of Cayes, inhabitants of color, who were in the police service, and who were charged with betraying signs of discontent. But how could punishment be inflicted on so many in silence? Recourse was had to the sea. The men were seized, disarmed, put into a ship, murdered, and thrown by night into the waves. But womanly love could not be blinded. Women, who had heard the voice of the carnage, demanded, with tears in their eyes, that the massacre of their brothers and their husbands should not go unpunished. Then there appeared on the stage a new man named Ferrou. Highly esteemed in peace, he was terrible in war. He was not a barbarian; his vengeance had some dignity. After having raised the country, he ordered all the colonists to be arrested, and to be conducted safe and sound to the village Coteaux, situate not far from the sea, where his people had been destroyed. Not expecting clemency, the captives disdained supplication and prepared for death. Ferrou addressed to them these words full of pride and bitterness: "Cruel whites, you hesitate not to sacrifice to your hate those who in this land are your defenders. Of what use is it that we are allied to you by the sweet and sacred bonds of nature, for our wives are your mothers and daughters? Not fearing the crime of parricide, you imbrue your hands in our blood. From this spot behold that sea in which, during a frightful night, under the pale light of the stars, you drowned a band of our people. What was their crime? To love you and to serve you. The winds and the waves bear back to us their livid bodies. They are brothers, husbands, companions, faithful friends in servitude, in war, in freedom. A just resentment commands us to sacrifice you; but go across that blood-stained sea, and join your own color; behold in us enemies but not executioners." Ferrou then sent them in a vessel to Cayes, and forthwith made his arrangements for marching against the city.

Informed of this revolt, provoked by imprudent attacks, Laplume precipitately returned from the frontiers of the South, where he was engaged in checking the ravages of the terrible Lamour de Rance. Scarcely had he got back when he discovered the smoke of Ferrou's camp, in the vicinity of Port-au-Prince. He fell on him and compelled him to retreat into the rugged mountains called La Hotte, whose decomposing rocks, breaking and bursting under men's feet, throw them into their abysses. But Ferrou knew the safe ways. Those he chose, and from them he rushed down to make an irruption into the plains near the town, Petit Goave. The body of troops employed in the defence of that city was in part composed of people of color, and partly of Frenchmen. The former joined the devastator, the latter took to flight.

In order the more effectually to keep his eye on the insurrection which now covered three provinces, Rochambeau had fixed his residence at Port-au-Prince, still drawing after him a great number of women, with all the equipage of effeminate luxury. As soon as he had learned the disastrous news, he sent Nétervood by sea to recapture the city of Petit Goave. As he did not doubt of success, he gave his lieutenant a pack of hounds partly to pursue the insurgents with, and partly to devour the prisoners. Nétervood hastened on his errand, and made an attack. But the enemy, setting the city on fire, entrenched themselves in a fort, whence they dealt death on their assailants. Nétervood received a mortal wound in the midst of his soldiers, who were fast perishing, being placed between a burning town and a powerful stronghold. Flight by sea was the only resource; and the dogs, in the confusion dispersing abroad, added to the dangers and disgrace of the defeat. Thus Nétervood, eager for peril and combat, lost his life in the flower of his youth, in the dishonorable cause of slavery.

Bands of insurgents, inflamed by victory, occupied the long chains of mountains which run through the southern province. They formed communications, one with another, and at their convenience and their pleasure rushed down into the plains in torrents which carried away whatever was before them. Dessalines put himself at the head of that great movement. Two powerful chiefs, Geffrard and Cangé, passed from the North to the South. They joined Ferrou, and in unison hastened across the mountains to ravage the fertile lands of Cavaillon, of Saint Louis, and of Cayes. Then they carried devastation over those of Jérémie.

These events threw consternation into the soul of Rochambeau. The insurrection threatened to pluck out of his hands the southern provinces. He had at first sent six hundred men to Laplume for the defence of Cayes; but that weak supply proving insufficient, he immediately directed toward Jérémie vessels which were bringing from France a reinforcement of two thousand men. One moiety of these men reached Jérémie and without delay prepared to set out for their destination. But from the peaks of his rocks Ferrou saw them, watched them, and prepared to cut them to pieces. Scarcely were the French ten miles from Jérémie, when they fell into an ambuscade. After a sanguinary conflict, they were routed. A frightful slaughter ensued. The few that escaped hurried back to Jérémie, where they spread the utmost alarm.

The other moiety, who landed at Tiburon, were also taken in an ambuscade and cut to pieces near Coteaux. The few who escaped took refuge in Cayes, into which six hundred other soldiers had thrown themselves, who were to have formed a junction with the two defeated divisions.

Wherever the insurrection reigned, scaffolds were erected. The cities of Cayes and Jérémie were afflicted with numerous executions, which drew more closely the bonds between the blacks and the colored population, and more and more secured success to the cause of freedom.

Laplume, seeing that all was lost, embarked for France, where he died, without leaving means for the interment of his remains.

Rochambeau, on the brink of despair, made new efforts to put a stop to the insurrection. He took special pains to withstand the ravages of Dessalines, whom in a proclamation he threatened to flog to death as the meanest of slaves. Men only laughed at the folly. Nevertheless, he succeeded in protecting from the continual incursions of that brute the plain Cul-de-Sac, and Mirebalais, which furnished provisions to Port-au-Prince. At the same time he guaranteed the environs of the Cape from the frequent attacks of Christophe.

Meanwhile, Rochambeau experienced increasing difficulties in the low state of his exchequer. He sought remedies in stock-jobbing, and in exactions of all kinds. He drew on the United States bills to a very large amount, which his Government refused to honor. He levied large contributions on cities that were half ruined. He imprisoned opulent persons, who obtained their liberation only by paying large sums of money. Some had even to give up their property altogether. He attempted to justify these exactions by pleading the necessities of the public service. But he alienated the hearts of those who through interest remained attached to his party to such a degree that, after having lost a second army, destroyed thousands of poor victims, and wasted much money, he fell into the same state of distress, misery, and abandonment as that in which Leclerc was a short time before his death; with this difference, that under the latter the South had not been polluted or devastated by insensate passions and internecine war.

Rochambeau's efforts to stay the insurrection were utterly futile. Like a vast conflagration, it extended from the South to the North. If it went out at one point, it blazed up in another. Soon the war changed its seat. Masters on land, the Africans commenced hostilities on the seas, which they carried on the more advantageously because they were protected by the English. In light boats, with the aid of the tide and of oars, they went up and down the rivers, passed from the mountains into the ocean, and from the ocean into the mountains, spreading terror wherever they appeared.   They attacked ships, massacred the passengers, and loaded themselves with plunder, which they carried back into their rocky fastnesses.   Woe to the French who sailed toward those deadly shores.   Two vessels from Havre and from Nantes fell into their hands.   All on board were slaughtered.   As on land so on water; the insurgents could not be reached.   They hid their boats in forests; dispersed, reassembled, defying alike the soldiers and the ships of war; and, almost with impunity, pursued at will their destructive career.

At the sight of an insurrection which was master both on land and on the sea, Rochambeau was seized with an alarm that he in vain endeavored to conceal.   The Consul, who rewarded success only, was to be feared by a man who was overwhelmed in failure.   Of what use so many victims, so many tortures, so many gallowses, so many drownings, so many raging hounds? All this serves only to illustrate the strength of the insurrection, and the hopelessness of his cause.   The moment that the General-in-chief was no longer in a state to make head against the rebellion, it began to insult and brave him, even in the cities which were his last places of refuge.   His temper became more and more disquiet and fierce.   The shades of his victims appeared to him in his dreams.   Now he cried out that he would make Saint Domingo a vast cemetery, where at least slavery should bear sway.   Now he declared he would reëstablish liberty, which his cruelties had made only more precious to the inhabitants.   Then, but too late, he grew angry at the artifices of the women who had him in their toils, and at the colonists who had misled him by their selfish counsels.   Yet did he think it necessary for the security of his troops to continue the system of terror.

A situation so deplorable could no longer be kept concealed from Bonaparte.   Rochambeau sent deputies to Paris, who reported that the revolt, somewhat calm after the death of Le-

clerc, having become active again, had spread from the North
to the South ; that Rochambeau, in order to stop its progress,
had employed the force of arms and the utmost terror ; that
these remedies had proved powerless ; that the insurrection,
animated by a fanatical spirit of liberty, had broken down every
embankment ; that at the head of the insurrection appeared in
the West Dessalines, Christophe in the North, and in the South
Ferrou ; that after having laid waste the interior, the insurgents
ravaged the coasts like pirates ; that the colonists were in a
state of extreme affliction, at seeing so great an armament overwhelmed with reverses ; and that the only means of safety was
another expedition.

Another expedition was impossible.   Already had a bad feeling
arisen between France and England.   Soon the latter power
declared war against the former.   This rupture gave the finishing blow to the French cause in Hayti.   On land, Rochambeau's troops were invested by the insurgents.   At sea the
English were supreme.   Nevertheless, the French general
maintained himself in his post with an intrepidity which would
have done honor to a good cause.   The sufferings of the besieged became extreme ; rarely have woes equal to theirs been
experienced.   Rochambeau has related how pitiable was the
existence of himself and comrades during this period, when
placed between death and life ; they appeased their hunger as
well as they could by eating their horses, mules, asses, and even
their dogs,— yes, the very hounds they had obtained in order to
run down their foes.

Things remained in this condition until the middle of November (1803) ; then the besiegers forced some of the exterior
works, and prepared for a new attack.   The inflexibility of the
French commander was at length obliged to give way.   Well
did he know that an assault, if made, must succeed, and he
feared to fall into the hands of his furious assailants.   He offered to capitulate.   The offer was accepted.   On the 19th of
November, the articles were signed.   The treaty stipulated that
the French should evacuate Cap François at the end of ten

days, with all their artillery, ammunition, and magazines; that they should withdraw to their vessels with the honors of war and the guarantee of their private property; that they should leave their sick and wounded in the hospitals, whom the blacks should take care of until they were well, and that then they should be sent to France in neutral vessels. These conditions were more favorable than the invading army had a right to expect. The day on which this convention was signed, the French general sent two officers to treat with the commander of the English squadron for the evacuation of the Cape. The offered conditions were rejected. Others were proposed, which Rochambeau found inadmissible. His refusal had for its ground the hope that the season would soon compel the English to retire from 'the vicinity of the Cape, and so render his escape possible. Vain expectation. On the 30th of November, the standard of the blacks waved over the Cape. Rochambeau felt compelled to throw himself on the mercy of the English. At the moment when the ships in which he had taken refuge were about to be sunk by red-hot balls prepared by the negroes, the ægis of Britain was thrown before them, and a frightful massacre was prevented. A short agreement having been hastily drawn up, Dessalines was informed that the vessels had surrendered to the arms of His Britannic Majesty. Not without difficulty did the vengeful and ferocious Dessalines consent to allow his prey to be thus plucked out of his hands. Shortly, a favorable breeze having sprung up, the three frigates and seventeen small craft that formed the French fleet at the Cape set sail, according to the convention, under the French flag; then having tacked, they struck their colors and surrendered. The prisoners of war amounted to eight thousand.

Saint Marc, Cayes, Jérémie, Saint Nicholas, the Spanish territory, were successively abandoned by the French. The departure of the troops in the different cities was a painful scene. Families of the colonists and many other persons lacked vessels to fly from the fury of the irritated blacks. Wives and children were separated from their husbands and their fathers.

The shores resounded with cries and lamentations. On land these were about to fall into the hands of persons who had been their slaves; on sea those were about to become prisoners to the English. A number intrusted their lives and their fortunes to fragile barks.

As they sailed from the island, Rochambeau, the soldiers, and the colonists saw the tops of the mountains glow with fire. Aforetime the blaze had been kindled for war and devastation; now the blacks lighted up their highlands in token of their joy. Freedom had been wrested out of the hands of their foes. Every heart beat with the thought. The dark past was wholly gone; the future was radiant with hope. "Freedom! freedom!" ran in joyous echoes from mountain-top to mountain-top till the whole island shouted "Freedom!"

Thus ended this deplorable expedition. In less than two years, sixty thousand persons fell; fifteen hundred were officers of superior rank; eight hundred were medical men; three-and-thirty thousand were soldiers, of whom not a sixth perished in battle. The attempt at subjugation cost the blacks more than twelve thousand men, of whom about four thousand found death at the hands of executioners of various kinds.

CHAPTER V.

Toussaint L'Ouverture, a prisoner in the Jura Mountains, appeals in vain to the First Consul, who brings about his death by starvation — Outline of his career and character.

WHILE the cause of independence, forced at length on the aspirations of the natives of Hayti, was advancing with rapid strides amid all the tumult of arms and all the confusion of despotic cruelties, Toussaint L'Ouverture pined away and died in the dark, damp, cold prison of Joux.

The Castle of Joux stands on a rock. On one side, the river Doubs flows at its base; on the other, the road of Besançon, leading into Switzerland, gives the stronghold the command of the communications between that country and France. The Château de Joux, built by the Romans, for their convenience in marching into Gaul, extended in the Middle Ages by the Lords of Joux, purchased by Louis XI., king of France, became under Louis XIV. a state prison. There Mirabeau suffered incarceration, in virtue of a *lettre-de-cachet*.

Toussaint L'Ouverture carried with him into his dungeon the conviction that he was to undergo a trial. In this conviction he sustained his soul. He felt confident of a triumph. His enemies he knew were numerous and powerful. The Consul, he suspected, feared as much as hated him. Yet what was his crime? Had not his authority emanated from the supreme power in France? By that power his position and his acts had been sanctioned. And if even he had offered resistance to the expedition, that opposition had been covered by an act of indemnity proclaimed by Leclerc. If solemn asseverations meant anything, if reiterated oaths retained their validity, he could stand before any tribunal in full confidence of an honorable acquittal.

But the First Consul was far from intending to give his prisoner the advantages of a trial. A trial was a public appeal to the great principles of law and right. In such an issue Bonaparte knew very well who would be the loser. There was another, and, for his purpose, a safer way. Toussaint was advanced in years. He had been accustomed to active pursuits. He was an African, and had lived only in tropical regions. His days, therefore, could be only few, and their number would be much abridged by confinement in a foul prison, under a chilling climate. Could he hold out through the coming winter ? If he survived too long — why, other prisoners had passed away secretly ; power has its secret strings and its swift remedies.

By a series of cunningly devised and coolly executed measures, Toussaint L'Ouverture was, ere many months, brought to his grave.

All communication with the outer world was forbidden him. He received no news of his wife and family. He passed his days alone with his servant ; the presence of that faithful domestic was a support to him. That solace was taken away, and Toussaint was left alone. Yet was he not alone, for God was with him. In prayer his soul rose hourly to his Maker, and he received constantly new effusions of comfort and strength. Religious thoughts and observances carried his mind back to the country for which he had sacrificed everything. There, in imagination, he again saw the chapel where he and his family were wont to worship, and while the hymns of praise went up from its neatly-formed roof, he was drawn into sympathy with the worshippers, and, with a moved heart and liquid voice, he joined his thanksgiving with theirs. Day by day, and often hours together, was he on his knees, seeking aid and finding support at the footstool of the heavenly grace, where never mortal knelt in vain.

But time passed on, and there were no signs of the expected trial. Hope sustained against hope began at last to fail. What! was he then a prisoner for life? If so, his sufferings, if severe, would not be long. Already he felt the chills of the nights of autumn, — there alone, in that cold, dreary dungeon, no fire, little clothes, no companion, — those long, pinching nights. And then the winds began to blow hollow and loud, as if they announced a worse time coming. How soon ? How long ? The winter must be at hand ; his captivity may extend through its whole course ; but can it endure, can life stretch out till the genial breath of Spring return ?

One day, in the midst of Toussaint's gloomy solitude, a visitor was announced. A visitor ! what if it were his son Isaac ! or if not he, perhaps an officer of justice to announce the coming trial. No; it was Cafarelli, aide-de-camp to the First Consul. " Oh, then, here is an order for liberation ; the prison-doors will fly open, and I shall once more see my wife and children !" Alas, poor heart, no ! the man comes from one whose soul is meaner than his own. Bonaparte thinks it a pity the treasures he fancies you have buried should be lost ; and though he does not intend to give you your freedom as the price of the disclosure, yet he sends his aide-de-camp to trick you into some kind of confession on the point, which he may turn to account, and in the result of which, if it is enough, he may find some compensation for the millions he has lavished in St. Domingo in making you his captive.

Toussaint, great in misfortune, gave for his reply, " I have lost something very different from money." Yes, thou hadst lost the liberty thou didst once enjoy; and, peradventure, in a moment of sorrow thou thoughtest thou hadst lost the sacred cause in which thou hadst put thy soul.

But mark this Consul's mean spirit. He had his victim there cooped up only too safely in that humid and infected prison. Still he was unsatisfied. Possibly the prisoner had money. If so, why, its hiding-place must be ascertained ere his lips are sealed in the silence of death. " Go, then, Cafarelli, get the secret out of the old negro, and then he may be allowed to die."

Toussaint would not resign himself to his fate without an effort. There was only one tribunal, and that tribunal was a perjured one. Yet an appeal might have some effect. The following letter was therefore written : —

In the dungeon of Fort Joux, this 30 Fructidor, an xi.
(17th September, 1802.)

" GENERAL, AND FIRST CONSUL,

" The respect and the submission which I could wish forever graven on my heart — [*here words are wanting as if obliterated by tears*]. If I have sinned in doing my duty, it is contrary to my intentions; if I was wrong in forming the constitution, it was through my great desire to do good; it was through having employed too much zeal, too much self-love, thinking I was pleasing the Government under which I was; if the formalities which I ought to have observed were neglected, it was through inattention. I have had the misfortune to incur your wrath, but as to fidelity and probity, I am strong in my conscience, and I dare affirm, that among all the servants of the state no one is more honest than myself. I was one of your soldiers, and the first servant of the Republic in St. Domingo; but now I am wretched, ruined, dishonored, a victim of my own services; let your sensibility be moved at my position. You are too great in feeling and too just not to pronounce a judgment as to my destiny. I charge General Cafarelli, your aide-de-camp, to put my report into your hands. I beg you to take it into your best consideration. His honor, his frankness have forced me to open my heart to him.

" Salutation and respect,
" TOUSSAINT L'OUVERTURE."

Days passed away, and no notice was taken of this epistle. The report of which it speaks was either suppressed or neglected. Dead to pity, Bonaparte watched for the consummation of the villany he had designed. It was customary to allow the commander of the prison five francs (about four shillings) a day for the subsistence of each prisoner; the First Consul wrote that three were sufficient for a revolter. More than sufficient for thy base purpose! Didst thou remember those words when thou didst beat thyself against the bars of thy own cage in the island of St. Helena, complaining daily of a table which, compared with thy allowance to "the first of the blacks," was a banquet of delicacies to "a dinner of herbs!"

While the process of gradual starvation was going forward, its unconscious victim, outraged by his sufferings, wrote this spirited epistle to his persecutor : —

In the dungeon of Fort Joux, this 7 Vendémiaire, an xi.
(20th September, 1802.)

"GENERAL, AND FIRST CONSUL,

"I beg you, in the name of God, in the name of humanity, to cast a favorable eye on my appeal, on my position, and my family; direct your great genius to my conduct, to the manner in which I have served my country, to all the dangers I have run in discharging my duty. I have served my country with fidelity and probity; I have served it with zeal and courage; I have been devoted to the Government under which I was; I have sacrificed my blood and a part of what I possessed, to serve my country, and in spite of my efforts, all my labors have been in vain. You will permit me, First Consul, to say to you, with all the respect and submission which I owe you, that the Government has been completely deceived in regard to Toussaint L'Ouverture, in regard to one of its most zealous and courageous servants in Saint Domingo. I labored long to acquire honor and glory from the Government, and to gain the esteem of my fellow-citizens, and I am now, for my reward, crowned with thorns and the most marked ingratitude. I do not deny the faults I may have committed, and for which I beg your pardon. But those faults do not deserve the fourth of the punishment I have received, nor the treatment I have undergone.

"First Consul, it is a misfortune for me that I am not known to you. If you had thoroughly known me while I was at St. Domingo, you would have done me more justice; my heart is good.

I am not learned; I am ignorant; but my father, who is now blind,* showed me the road of virtue and honor, and I am very strong in my conscience in that matter; and if I had not been devoted to the Government, I should not have been here, — that is a truth! I am wretched, miserable, a victim of all my services. All my life I have been in active service, and since the revolution of the 10th of August, 1790, I have constantly been in the service of my country. Now I am a prisoner with no power to do anything; sunk in grief, my health is impaired.

"I have asked you for my freedom that I may labor, that I may gain my subsistence and support my unhappy family. I call on your greatness, on your genius, to pronounce a judgment on my destiny. Let your heart be softened and touched by my position and my misfortunes.

"I salute you, with profound respect,
(Signed)   "Toussaint L'Ouverture."

Alas! the First Consul *has* pronounced judgment, and the consequent sentence the prisoner is even now undergoing. That sentence is "slow death!" And then as you, Toussaint, shake with the cold of the northern blast, or sink overcome with sorrow on the moist, foul floor of your cell, or refuse with loathing the unsavory food; and as your limbs part with their strength, and your heart flutters in debility, and your blood becomes thin and poor, and as you look to the winter's frost, snow, hail, and storm, with a vague distress and dismal forebodings, — in each step of the process of slow death the Consul's verdict goes into execution, and another day, or another week, is taken from the brief number that remain to you.

Yet well and noble is it, that under the depression of your unhappy condition, while your heart sinks with the sinking of your ill-supported frame, — it is well and noble that you descend to no mean flatteries, that you descend to no unworthy supplica-

* Gaou-Guinou, Toussaint's father, died in 1804, having completely lost his sight. He is said to have left the world uttering curses against white men.

tions, and that, retaining your own high manly spirit, you protest your innocence, proclaim your services, and charge your enemies with ingratitude.

Toussaint L'Ouverture then began to compose with his own hand a document, in which he entered into a systematic defence of his conduct. This document, the orthography of which is said to have been defective, was couched in correct and sometimes eloquent terms. By permission of the governor of the castle, it was copied by Martial-Besse, then one of his prisoners, and on the 2d of October it was transmitted to the First Consul. The document contained the following passages :—
" General Leclerc employed toward me means which have never been employed toward the greatest enemies. Doubtless, I owe that contempt to my color; but has that color prevented me from serving my country with zeal and fidelity? Does the color of my body injure my honor or my courage? Suppose I was criminal, and that the General-in-chief had orders to arrest me, — was it needful to employ a hundred carbineers to arrest my wife and children, to tear them from their residence, without respect, and without regard for their rank, their sex; without humanity and without charity? Was it necessary to fire on my plantations and on my family, to ransack and pillage my property? No! My wife, my children, my household, were under no responsibility, — have no account to render to Government; General Leclerc had not even the right to arrest them. Was that officer afraid of a rival? I compare him to the Roman Senate, that pursued Hannibal even into his retirement. I request that he and I may appear before a tribunal, and that the Government bring forward the whole of my correspondence with him. By that means, my innocence, and all I have done for the Republic, will be seen.

" First Consul, father of all French soldiers, upright judge, defender of the innocent, pronounce a decision as to my destiny: my wound is deep, apply a remedy to it: you are the physician; I rely entirely on your wisdom and skill."

These appeals to the justice, honor, and humanity of the

First Consul proved abortive. Bonaparte's mind was made up. His ear, therefore, was closed. Toussaint spoke to a foregone conclusion; his words were encountered by a fixed determination. That determination was so fixed, and so well known, that no one dared to speak in favor of the oppressed and doomed hero. Fear of the supreme magistrate occupied all minds around him, and gave to his will the force of law.

That precipitate and iron mind found the process of slow murder too slow. Solitude, cold, and short fare were tardy in their operation. Their natural tardiness was not abated by the presence with the captive of his faithful servant. Mars Plaisir was therefore taken away by an express order of the Government. In parting from him, Toussaint L'Ouverture said, " Carry my last farewell to my wife, my children, and my niece. Would I could console thee under this cruel separation: be assured of my friendship and of the remembrance which I shall always preserve of thy services and of thy devotedness."

Toussaint, thou art still the same, still self-forgetful, still mindful of thy wife and family. The disinterested benevolence which made thee a patriot, and which the prospect of supreme power could not bribe into subjection, remains unchilled by the cold of the Jura Mountains, and unsuppressed by bodily weakness, and unperverted by ingratitude and perfidy.

Mars Plaisir was loaded with chains and sent to Nantes, where he was put in prison. But unwelcome truths make their way through bars and walls; therefore was the good servant specially guarded and watched, lest, before his master's demise, he should disclose facts that might prove troublesome, or set in motion instruments that might traverse the designs of the tyrant.

The progress made in Hayti by the assertors of the national independence kept Bonaparte in a constant state of solicitude. He could not conceal from himself that the escape of Toussaint from his dungeon was a possible event He was well aware that his reappearance in Saint Domingo would make the reduction of the inhabitants impossible. Nay, the mere knowledge of his being still alive, while it encouraged the hope of his yet taking the lead of the soldiers of independence, served to keep up the courage of the insurgents, and to augment the difficulties of Rochambeau. His death, therefore, seemed to Bonaparte urgently necessary. Affairs were hurrying to a crisis in the West Indies. A blow must be struck. The trunk of the insurrection, the First Consul had it in his power to pluck up and destroy: at least so he thought. Therefore the order went forth, " Cut it down : root it up." The manner was worthy of the deed.

The governor of the castle was chosen for the perpetration of the crime. Scarcely was he a man for the work. He had scruples of conscience. But nothing short of plenary obedience would be accepted. Besides, it was not a question of the dagger or the bowl. All that was wanted was a more decided system of privation. And that system he scarcely needed to work actively. When a prisoner is kept in close confinement, and must be got rid of, you have only to reduce his means of subsistence until death ensues as a matter of course. And if the process is too slow, it may be accelerated by a little well-timed neglect. To an attenuated and famished frame, the want of nutrition for a few days brings certain death. Let the ordinary pittance of supply then be forgotten, and your end is gained. And who shall dare to call an act of oblivion by the foul and offensive name of murder ?

The Governor twice took a journey to Neufchâtel, in Switzerland. The first time he intrusted the keys of Toussaint's cell to Captain Colomier, whom he appointed to fill his place in his absence. Colomier visited the noble prisoner, who spoke to him modestly of his own glory, but with indignation of the design imputed to him of having wished to deliver Saint Domingo up to the English. His emaciated and feeble hands were engaged in writing a paper intended to disprove that groundless charge. The officer found Toussaint in a state of almost absolute privation. A little meal was his only food, and that he had to prepare himself in a small earthen jug. But Coloıııer had a heart: he pitied the destitution of a man who had had at his command the opulence of Saint Domingo. His humanity made him unfit for his office, and ascertaining that the captive accounted the want of coffee among his chief privations, he ventured at his own risk to furnish a small supply.

When the Governor returned, he found that Toussaint L'Ouverture was still alive. In a short time he took a second journey to the same town, and for the same purpose; and, as he suspected that Colomier's good nature had interfered with his duty, he said to him, on leaving, with a disquieted countenance, " I intrust to you the guardianship of the castle; but this time I do not give you the keys of the dungeons; the prisoners have no need of anything."

The Governor returned on the fourth day. Toussaint was no more. He ascertained the fact. Yes, there he is, — dead; no doubt whatever, — dead and cold. He had died of inanition. And see, if you have courage to look on so horrible a sight, — the rats have gnawed his feet!

The work is done — the crime is perpetrated. Bonaparte's will *is* law: his word is death. But murder is a word of evil sound. The world, with all its depravity, has a moral feeling, and that moral feeling it is impolitic to outrage. A veil must be thrown over the assassination.

" Toussaint is dead; " — " how came he by his death ? "

The Governor, on learning that his captive had breathed his last, carried some provisions into his dungeon. Who now can say that Toussaint had been starved to death ? He died in the midst of abundance. This was the Governor's own plea. But he deprived that plea of its effect by his eagerness to obtrude and make the most of it; and he betrayed his guilt by his looks and manner. Yes, he was distressed at Toussaint's sudden departure, — he bewailed the event. But hypocrisy ever overacts its part. Besides, the governor was not thoroughly depraved; and that which he would have men regard as the sadness of a virtuous heart in mourning, they saw to be the ragings of a conscience smitten with a sense of guilt; his cheeks put on a livid paleness; his steps were hasty and uncertain; his eyes were wild. Yes, here is a man deeply suffering under the stings of remorse. His nervous and agitated efforts' to make it clear — very clear, beyond a question — that Toussaint has died of a natural cause, demonstrate that he knows more than he dares reveal, and has contracted a guilt that he would fain conceal even from his own eyes. But the keys of the dungeon were in his possession; and the words, "The prisoners want nothing," and the food recently carried thither; these facts — known to our authority,* and known to Captain Colomier, and known to other inmates of the castle — declare that murder has been committed. Yes; now we see why Mars Plaisir has been sent away. And now we see why this remote, solitary, wild, and freezing prison has been chosen. And now we see why Toussaint L'Ouverture was entrapped. The series of crimes is consummated.

Still the question returns, "What will be the opinion of the world?" Medical men were called in. The head was opened; the brain was scrutinized. "It is apoplexy," the authorities said; and apoplexy was set down in the formal report made as to the cause of Toussaint's death. Possibly so; but what produced the apoplexy? Ask Captain Colomier, — ask the mayor of the district. They were both required to state that death had taken place by some cause different from hunger, and they both refused!

Yes; what was the opinion of the world? The world believed and declared that there had been foul play. That belief gained prevalence in Saint Domingo, and added fuel to the flames of wrath which, without this new brand, burned with intensest fierceness, consuming the French army, and making their longer stay in the island an impossibility.

Thus, in the beginning of April, in the year 1803, died Toussaint L'Ouverture. A grandson of an African king, he passed the greater number of his days in slavery, and rose to be a

* See particularly Métral's "Histoire de l'Expédition des Français à Saint Domingue," p. 201, seq.

soldier, a general, a governor. He possessed a rare genius, the efficiency of which was augmented by an unusual power of self-concealment. His life lay in thought and in action rather than in words. Self-contained, he was also self-sufficing. Though he disdained not the advice of others, he was in the main his own council-board. With an intense concentration of vitality in his own soul, he threw into his outer life a power and an energy which armed one man with the power of thousands, and made him great alike in the command of others and in the command of himself. He was created for government by the hand of Nature. That strength of soul and self-reliance which made him fit to rule also gave him subjects for his sway. Hence it was that he could not remain in the herd of his fellow-slaves. Rise he must, and rise he did; first to humble offices, then to the command of a regiment, and then to the command of " the armies of Saint Domingo."

To the qualities which make an illustrious general and states-man, there were added, in Toussaint's soul, the milder virtues that form the strength and the ornament of domestic life. Great as he was in the field and in the cabinet, scarcely less great and more estimable was he as a husband and a father. There his excellences shone without a shade. The sacrifice of his sons to the duty which he owed to his country only illustrates the intensity of a patriotism which could extort so precious a possession from a father's hands.

But he had learned his duty from the lips of One who taught men to make the love of children and parents subordinate to the love of himself; and assured that he had in some special manner been called and sent to set the captive free, he, in a native benevolence of character which the gospel enriched, strengthened, and directed, concentrated all the fine endowments of his soul on the great work of negro emancipation in the island of his birth.

His mind appeared in his countenance and his manner, yet only as if under a veil. His looks were noble and dignified, rather than refined; * his eyes, darting fire, told of the burning elements of his soul. Though little aided by what is called education, he, in the potency of his mind, bent and moulded language to his thoughts, and ruled the minds of others by an eloquence which was no less concise than simple, manly, and full of imagery. As with other men of ardent genius, he fused ideas into proverbs, and put into circulation sayings that are reported to be still current in his native land.

But, after all, he was greater in deed than he was in word. Vast was the influence which he acquired by the mere force of his silent example. His very name became a tower of strength to his friends and a terror to his foes. Hence his presence was so impressive that none approached him without fear, nor left him without emotion.

If the world has reason to thank God for great men, with special gratitude should we acknowledge the divine goodness in raising up Toussaint L'Ouverture. Among the privileged races of the earth, the roll of patriots, legislators, and heroes is long and well filled. As yet there is but one Toussaint L'Ouverture. Yet how many of the highest qualities of our nature did that one unite in himself. But his best claim to our respect and admiration consists in the entire devotion of his varied and lofty powers to the redemption of his color from degrading bondage, and its elevation into the full stature of perfect manhood.

I do not intend to paint the Haytian patriot as a perfect man. Moral perfection once appeared on earth. It is not likely to have appeared a second time among the slaves of Hayti. Toussaint has been accused of harshness and cruelty. I am not prepared to affirm that the charges are without foundation. But it is equally true that his enemies have done their utmost to point out stains in his character. Unfortunately, the means for a thorough investigation are wholly wanting. It has also been said that he was an adept at dissimulation. But secrecy in his

* All the likenesses of Toussaint L'Ouverture which I have seen, except one, have the disadvantage of being profiles.

circumstances was both needful and virtuous ; and, if the study of secrecy on his part was undue, let the failing be set down against him at its full value. It has even been intimated that when in power he yielded to the fascinations of the accomplished creole women of the Cape. But the intimation, faint and indirect as it is, rests on no solid grounds. In truth, it was impossible that a man of the origin and aims of Toussaint L'Ouverture should have escaped the shafts of calumny, and, after all due abatements are made, enough of excellence remains to command our admiration and win our esteem.

While, however, the world has seen but one Toussaint L'Ouverture, this history sets forth many black men who were possessed of great faculties and accomplished great deeds. And though the instance of their chief only shows what an elevation men with a black skin may possibly attain, there are in the general tenor of this narrative proofs very numerous and irrefragable that, in the ordinary powers and virtues which form the texture and ornament of civilized life, an African origin and negro blood involve no essential disqualification.

Very clear, certainly, has it appeared, that whether in its rights, its wrongs, its penalties, or its rewards, Justice — the ever-living daughter of the eternal God, and the ever-present and ever-active administratrix of divine Providence — knows nothing whatever of the distinctions, the prejudices, the dislikes, or the preferences of color. An injury done to a European ceases not to be an injury when the sufferer is an African. Nor are breakers of God's laws punished with less severity within the tropics than they are in the temperate zones. Slavery, which is the essence and the concentration of injustice, — Slavery, which from its foundation to its top-stone is one huge and frightful accumulation of wrongs, of wrongs the hugest and the direst, — Slavery, which is the worst form of treachery to man and treason against God, entails vengeance the most terrible, the most awful ; vengeance not less sure than dreadful. Alas ! that in the scourge the innocent should suffer as well as the guilty. The thought would sink the mind in grief, were

25

it not attended by the conviction that "the hour cometh" when the righteous shall shine as stars in the firmament forever and ever.

The family of Toussaint L'Ouverture received the news of his death with the deepest grief. They wept and wailed, and refused to be comforted because he was not.

Under a pretence that they contemplated escape, those innocent persons were transferred from Bayonne to Agen, where they found friends worthy of themselves.

When Saint Jean L'Ouverture heard of his father's death, he declared that he should not long survive him. The saying was too true. The effects of the climate on a naturally weak constitution brought him to the tomb ere he had quitted the period of youth. His death almost caused the death of his female cousin, from whom he received in his sickness the most tender and vigilant cares.

Shortly after, the family succeeded in obtaining the favor that Placide L'Ouverture should quit his place of detention and reside with them at Agen.

Madame Toussaint L'Ouverture, who was beloved and revered alike by her husband and her children, survived that husband and her youngest son for several years, without being able to overcome the grief which their loss occasioned, and which was so deep and constant as to undermine her faculties. She died in 1816, in the arms of her sons, Placide and Isaac L'Ouverture.

The history of L'Ouverture, placed by the side of the history of Bonaparte, presents a number of striking parallels. Both born in a humble position, they raised themselves to the height of power by the force of their genius and the intense energy of their character. Both gained renown in legislation and government as well as in war. Both fell the moment they had obtained supreme authority. Both were betrayed by pretended friends, and delivered into the hands of embittered foes. Both were severed from their families. Both finished their lives on a barren rock.

The parallels have their contrasts. Toussaint L'Ouverture fought for liberty; Bonaparte fought for himself. Toussaint L'Ouverture gained fame and power by leading an oppressed and injured race to the successful vindication of their rights; Bonaparte made himself a name and acquired a sceptre by supplanting liberty and destroying nationalities, in order to substitute his own illegitimate despotism. The fall of Toussaint L'Ouverture was a voluntary retirement from power, accompanied by a voluntary renunciation of authority, under circumstances which seemed to guarantee that freedom the attainment of which had been the sole object of his efforts; the fall of Bonaparte was the forced abdication of a throne which was regarded as a European nuisance, and descent from which was a virtual acknowledgment that he had utterly failed in the purposes of his life. In the treachery which they underwent, on one side, Toussaint L'Ouverture was the victim and Bonaparte the seducer; and on the other side the former suffered from those who had been his enemies, the latter from those who in profession were his constant friends. And in the rupture of their domestic ties, Bonaparte was the injurer, Toussaint L'Ouverture the injured.

Nor is it easy to bring one's mind to the conclusion that retribution was wholly absent in the facts to which allusion has just been made. The punishment is too like the crime to be regarded as accidental. Toussaint's domestic bereavement was requited by Bonaparte's domestic sorrows. The drear solitude of the Castle of Joux was experienced over again at Saint Helena by him who inflicted the penalty. Strange to say, it was a friend of the negroes — namely, Admiral Maitland — that conducted the Corsican to his prison. And as if to make the correspondence the more complete, and the retribution the more potent, by an exchange of extreme localities, the man of the temperate regions was transferred to the tropics, to atone for his crime in transferring the man of the tropics to the killing frosts of the temperate regions. Resembling each other in several points of their calamities and pains, the two differed in that

which is the dividing line between the happy and the wretched;
for, while, with Bonaparte, God was a name, with Toussaint
L'Ouverture, God was at once the sole reality and the sovereign good.

BOOK IV.

MEMOIR OF TOUSSAINT L'OUVERTURE, WRITTEN BY HIMSELF.

MEMOIR OF TOUSSAINT L'OUVERTURE, WRITTEN BY HIMSELF.

MEMOIR

OF

GENERAL TOUSSAINT L'OUVERTURE.

WRITTEN BY HIMSELF.

IT is my duty to render to the French Government an exact account of my conduct. I shall relate the facts with all the simplicity and frankness of an old soldier, adding to them the reflections that naturally suggest themselves. In short, I shall tell the truth, though it be against myself.

The colony of Saint Domingo, of which I was commander, enjoyed the greatest tranquillity; agriculture and commerce flourished there. The island had attained a degree of splendor which it had never before seen. And all this — I dare to say it — was my work.

Nevertheless, as we were upon a war footing, the Commission had published a decree ordering me to take all necessary measures to prevent the enemies of the Republic from penetrating into the island. Accordingly, I ordered all the commanders of the sea-ports not to permit any ships of war to enter into the roadstead, except they were known and had obtained permission from me. If it should be a squadron, no matter from what nation, it was absolutely prohibited from entering the port, or even the roadstead, unless I should myself know where it came from, and the port from which it sailed.

This order was in force, when, on the 26th of January, 1802, a squadron appeared before the Cape. At that time I had left

295

this town to visit the Spanish part, Santo Domingo, for the purpose of inspecting the agriculture. On setting out from
Maguâna, I had despatched one of my aides-de-camp to Gen.
Dessalines, Commander-in-chief of the departments of the West
and South, who was then at St. Marc, to order him to join me
at Gonaïves, or at St. Michel, to accompany me on my journey.

At the time of the squadron's appearance, I was at Santo
Domingo, from which place I set out, three days after, to go to
Hinche. Passing by Banique, arriving at Papayes, I met my
aide-de-camp Couppé and an officer sent by Gen. Christophe,
who brought me a letter from the general, by which he informed
me of the arrival of the French squadron before the Cape, and
assured me that the General-in-chief commanding this squadron
had not done him the honor to write to him, but had only sent
an officer to order him to prepare accommodations for his forces;
that Gen. Christophe having demanded of this officer whether
he was the bearer of letters to him or of dispatches for the
General-in-chief, Toussaint L'Ouverture, requesting him to
send them to him, that they might reach him at once, this officer
replied to him, that he was not charged with any, and that it
was not, in fact, a question concerning Gen. Toussaint. "Surrender the town," he continued; "you will be well recompensed;
the French Government sends you presents." To which Gen.
Christophe replied, " Since you have no letters for the General-
in-chief nor for me, you may return and tell your general that
he does not know his duty; that it is not thus that people present themselves in a country belonging to France."

Gen. Leclerc having received this answer, summoned Gen.
Christophe to deliver the place to him, and, in case of refusal,
warned him that on the morning of the next day he should
land fifteen thousand men. In response to this, Gen. Christophe
begged him to wait for Gen. Toussaint L'Ouverture, to whom
he had already sent the intelligence, and would do so the second
time, with the greatest celerity. In fact, I received a second
letter, and hastened to reach the Cape, in spite of the overflowing of the Hinche, hoping to have the pleasure of embracing

my brothers-in-arms from Europe, and to receive at the same time the orders of the French Government; and in order to march with greater speed, I left all my escorts. Between St. Michel and St. Raphaël, I met Gen. Dessalines and said to him, "I have sent for you to accompany me on my tour to Port-de-Paix, and to Môle; but that is useless now. I have just received two letters from Gen. Christophe, announcing the arrival of the French squadron before the Cape."

I communicated to him these letters, whereupon he told me that he had seen from St. Marc six large vessels making sail for the coast of Port Républicain; but he was ignorant of what nation they were. I ordered him then to repair promptly to this port, since it was possible that Gen. Christophe having refused the entrance of the Cape to the general commanding the squadron, the latter might have proceeded to Port Républicain in the hope of finding me there; should this prove true, I ordered him, in advance, to request the general to wait for me, and to assure him that I would go first to the Cape in the hope of meeting him there, and in case I should not find him there, I would repair at once to Port Républicain to confer with him. I set out for the Cape, passing by Vases, the shortest road. On arriving upon the heights of the Grand Boucan, in the place called the Porte-Saint-Jacques, I perceived a fire in the town on the Cape. I urged my horse at full speed to reach this town, to find there the general commanding the squadron, and to ascertain who had caused the conflagration. But, on approaching, I found the roads filled with the inhabitants who had fled from this unfortunate town, and I was unable to penetrate farther because all the passages were cannonaded by the artillery of the vessels which were in the roadstead. I then resolved to go up to the Fort of Bel-Air, but I found this fort evacuated likewise, and all the pieces of cannon spiked.

I was, consequently, obliged to retrace my steps. After passing the hospital, I met Gen. Christophe, and asked him who had ordered the town to be fired. He replied that it was he. I reprimanded him severely for having employed such rigorous measures. "Why," said I to him, "did you not rather make some military arrangements to defend the town until my arrival?" He answered, "What do you wish, general? My duty, necessity, the circumstances, the reiterated threats of the general commanding the squadron, forced me to it. I showed the general the orders of which I was the bearer, but without avail." He added, "that the proclamations spread secretly in the town to seduce the people, and instigate an uprising, were not sanctioned by military usage; that if the commander of the squadron had truly pacific intentions, he would have waited for me; that he would not have employed the means which he used to gain the commander of the Fort of Boque, who is a drunkard; that he would not in consequence have seized this fort; that he would not have put to death half of the garrison of Fort Liberty; that he would not have made a descent upon Acul, and that, in a word, he would not have committed at first all the hostilities of which he was guilty.

Gen. Christophe joined me, and we continued the route together. On arriving at Haut-du-Cap, we passed through the habitations of Breda as far as the barrier of Boulard, passing by the gardens. There I ordered him to rally his troops, and go into camp on the Bonnet until further orders, and to keep me informed of all the movements he made. I told him that I was going to Héricourt; that there, perhaps, I should receive news from the commander of the squadron; that he would doubtless deliver to me the orders of the Government; that I might even meet him there; that I should then ascertain the reasons which had induced him to come in this manner; and, that, in case he was the bearer of orders from the government, I should request him to communicate them to me, and should in consequence make arrangements with him.

Gen. Christophe left me then to repair to the post which I had assigned to him; but he met a body of troops who fired upon him, forced him to dismount from his horse, plunge into the river, and cross it by swimming.

After separating from Gen. Christophe, I had at my side Adjutant-General Fontaine, two other officers, and my aide-de-camp, Couppé, who went in advance; he warned me of the troops on the road. I ordered him to go forward. He told me that this force was commanded by a general. I then demanded a conference with him. But Couppé had not time to execute my orders; they fired upon us at twenty-five steps from the barrier. My horse was pierced with a ball; another ball carried away the hat of one of my officers. This unexpected circumstance forced me to abandon the open road, to cross the savanna and the forests to reach Héricourt, where I remained three days to wait for news of the commander of the squadron, again without avail.

But, the next day, I received a letter from Gen. Rochambeau, announcing "that the column which he commanded had seized upon Fort Liberty, taken and put to the sword a part of the garrison, which had resisted; that he had not believed the garrison would steep its bayonets in the blood of Frenchmen; on the contrary, he had expected to find it disposed in his favor." I replied to this letter, and, manifesting my indignation to the general, asked to know, "Why he had ordered the massacre of those brave soldiers who had only followed the orders given them; who had, besides, contributed so much to the happiness of the colony and to the triumph of the Republic. Was this the recompense that the French Government had promised them?"

I concluded by saying to Gen. Rochambeau, that "I would fight to the last to avenge the death of these brave soldiers, for my own liberty, and to reëstablish tranquillity and order in the colony."

This was, in fact, the resolution I had taken after having reflected deliberately upon the report Gen. Christophe had brought me, upon the danger I had just run, upon the letter of Gen. Rochambeau, and finally upon the conduct of the commander of the squadron.

Having formed my resolution, I went to Gonaïves. There I communicated my intentions to Gen. Maurepas, and ordered him to make the most vigorous resistance to all vessels which should appear before Port-de-Paix, where he commanded; and, in case he should not be strong enough, — having only half of a brigade, — to imitate the example of Gen. Christophe and afterward withdraw to the Mountain, taking with him ammunition of all kinds; there to defend himself to the death.

I then went to St. Marc to visit the fortifications. I found that the news of the shameful events which had just taken place had reached this town, and the inhabitants had already fled. I gave orders for all the resistance to be made that the fortifications and munitions would allow of.

As I was on the point of setting out from this town to go to Port-au-Prince and the southern part to give my orders, Captains Jean-Philippe Dupin and Isaac brought me dispatches from Paul L'Ouverture, who commanded at Santo Domingo. Both informed me that a descent had just been made upon Oyarsaval, and that the French and Spaniards who inhabited this place had risen and cut off the roads from Santo Domingo. I acquainted myself with these dispatches. In running over the letter of Gen. Paul and the copy of Gen. Kerverseau's to the commander of the place of Santo Domingo, which was enclosed in it, I saw that this general had made the overture to the commander of the place, and not to Gen. Paul, as he should have done, to make preparations for the landing of his force. I saw also the refusal given by Gen. Paul to this invitation, until he should receive orders from me. I replied to Gen. Paul that I approved his conduct, and ordered him to make all possible effort to defend himself in case of attack; and even to make prisoners of Gen. Kerverseau and his force, if he could. I returned my reply by the captains just mentioned. But foreseeing, on account of the interception of the roads, that they might be arrested and their dispatches demanded, I gave them in charge a second letter, in which I ordered Gen. Paul to use all possible means of conciliation with Gen. Kerverseau. I charged the captains, in case they should be arrested, to conceal the first letter and show only the second.

My reply not arriving as soon as he expected, Gen. Paul sent another black officer with the same dispatches in duplicate. I gave only a receipt to this officer, and sent him back. Of these three messengers two were black and the other white. They were arrested, as I had anticipated; the two blacks were assassinated in violation of all justice and right, contrary to the customs of war; their dispatches were sent to Gen. Kerverseau, who concealed the first letter, and showed to Gen. Paul only the second, in which I had ordered him to enter into negotiations with Gen. Kerverseau. It was in consequence of this letter that Santo Domingo was surrendered.

Having sent off these dispatches, I resumed my route toward the South. I had hardly set forward when I was overtaken by an orderly, coming up at full speed, who brought me a package from Gen. Vernet and a letter from my wife, both announcing to me the arrival from Paris of my two children and their preceptor, of which I was not before aware. I learned also that they were bearers of orders for me from the First Consul. I retraced my steps and flew to Ennery, where I found my two children and the excellent tutor whom the First Consul had had the goodness to give them. I embraced them with the greatest satisfaction and ardor. I then inquired if they were bearers of letters from the First Consul for me. The tutor replied in the affirmative, and handed me a letter which I opened and read about half through; then I folded it, saying that I would reserve the reading of it for a more quiet moment. I begged him then to impart to me the intentions of the Government, and to tell me the name of the commander of the squadron, which I had not yet been able to ascertain. He answered, that his name was Leclerc; that the intention of the Government toward me was very favorable, which was confirmed by my children, and of which I afterwards assured myself by finishing the letter of the First Consul. I observed to them, nevertheless, that if the intentions of the Government were pacific and good regarding me and those who had contributed to the happiness which the colony enjoyed, Gen. Leclerc surely had not followed nor executed the orders he had received, since he had landed on the island like an enemy, and done evil merely for the pleasure of doing it, without addressing himself to the commander or making known to him his powers. I then asked Citizen Coisnon, my children's tutor, if Gen. Leclerc had not given him a dispatch for me or charged him with something to tell me. He replied in the negative, advising me, however, to go to the Cape to confer with the general; my children added their solicitations to persuade me to do so. I represented to them, "that, after the conduct of this general, I could have no confidence in him; that he had landed like an enemy; that, in spite of that, I had believed it my duty to go to meet him in order to prevent the progress of the evil; that he had fired upon me, and I had run the greatest dangers; that, in short, if his intentions were as pure as those of the Government which sent him, he should have taken the trouble to write to me to inform me of his mission; that, before arriving in the roadstead, he should have sent me an advice-boat with you, sir, and my children, — that being the ordinary practice, — to announce their arrival, and to impart to me his powers; that, since he had observed none of these formalities, the evil was done, and therefore I should refuse decidedly to go in search of him; that, nevertheless, to prove my attachment and submission to the French Government, I would consent to write a letter to Gen. Leclerc. I shall send to him," I continued, " by Mr. Granville, a worthy man, accompanied by my two children and their tutor, whom I shall charge to say to Gen. Leclerc, that it is absolutely dependent upon himself whether this colony is entirely lost, or preserved to France; that I will enter into all possible arrangements with him; that I am ready to submit to the orders of the French Government; but that Gen. Leclerc shall show me orders of which he is bearer, and shall, above all, cease from every species of hostility."

In fact, I wrote the letter, and the deputation set out. In the hope that after the desire I had just manifested to render my submission, order would again be restored, I remained at

Gonaïves till the next day. There I learned that two vessels had attacked St. Marc; I proceeded there and learned that they had been repulsed. I returned then to Gonaïves to wait for Gen. Leclerc's reply. Finally, two days after, my two children arrived with the response so much desired, by which the general commanded me to report in person to him, at the Cape, and announced that he had furthermore ordered his generals to advance upon all points; that his orders being given, he could not revoke them. He promised, however, that Gen. Boudet should be stopped at Artibonite; I concluded then, that he did not know the country perfectly, or had been deceived; for, in order to reach Artibonite, it was necessary to have a free passage by St. Marc, which was impossible now, since the two vessels which had attacked this place had been repulsed. He added, further, that they should not attack Môle, only blockade it, since this place had already surrendered. I replied then plainly to the general, " that I should not report to him at the Cape ; that his conduct did not inspire me with sufficient confidence ; that I was ready to deliver the command to him in conformity with the orders of the First Consul, but that I would not be his lieutenant-general." I besought him again to let me know his intentions, assuring him that I would contribute every-thing in my power to the reëstablishment of order and tran-quillity. I added, in conclusion, that if he persisted in his inva-sion, he would force me to defend myself, although I had but few troops. I sent him this letter with the utmost despatch, by an orderly, who brought me back word, " that he had no reply to make and had taken the field."

The inhabitants of Gonaïves then asked my permission to send a deputation to Gen. Leclerc, which I accorded to them, but he retained the deputation.

The next day I learned that he had taken, without striking a blow and without firing a gun, Dondon, St. Raphaël, St. Michel and Marmelade, and that he was prepared to march against Ennery and Gonaïves.

These new hostilities gave rise to new reflections. I thought that the conduct of Gen. Leclerc was entirely contrary to the intentions of the Government, since the First Consul, in his letter, promised peace, while the general made war. I saw that, instead of seeking to arrest this evil, he only increased it. "Does he not fear," I said to myself, "in pursuing such conduct, to be blamed by his Government? Can he hope to be approved by the First Consul, that great man whose equity and impartiality are so well known, while I shall be disapproved?" I resolved then to defend myself, in case of attack; and in spite of my few troops, I made my dispositions accordingly.

Gonaïves not being defensible, I ordered it to be burned, in case retreat was necessary. I placed Gen. Christophe, who had been obliged to fall back, in the Eribourg road, which leads to Bayonnet, and withdrew myself to Ennery, where a part of my guard of honor had repaired to join and defend me. There I learned that Gros-Morne had just surrendered, and that the army was to march against Gonaïves with three columns; one of these, commanded by Gen. Rochambeau, purposing to pass by Couleuvre and come down upon La Croix, to cut off the road from the town and the passage of the bridge of the Ester.

I ordered Gonaïves to be burned, and, ignorant of Gen. Rochambeau's strength, marched to meet the column, which was making for the bridge of the Ester, at the head of 300 grenadiers of my guard, commanded by their chief, and of sixty mounted guards. We met in a gorge. The attack commenced at six o'clock in the morning with a continuous fire which lasted until noon. Gen. Rochambeau began the attack. I learned from the prisoners I took that the column numbered more than 4,000 men. While I was engaged with Gen. Rochambeau, the column commanded by Gen. Leclerc reached Gonaïves. After the engagement at La Croix, I proceeded to the bridge of the Ester, with artillery, to defend the place, intending to go thence to St. Marc, where I expected to make a desperate resistance. But, on setting out, I learned that Gen. Dessalines, having arrived at this place before me, was obliged to evacuate it and retire to Petite Rivière. I was obliged, after this manœuvre, to slacken my march in order to send in advance the prisoners taken at La Croix, and the wounded to Petite Rivière; and I determined to proceed there myself. When we reached Couriotte, in the plain, I left my troops there, and went in advance alone. I found all the country abandoned.

I received a letter from Gen. Dessalines, informing me that, having learned that the Cahos was to be attacked, he had gone to defend it. I sent an order to him to join me at once. I caused the ammunition and provisions which I had with me to be put in Fort L'Ouverture at the Crête-à-Pierrot. I ordered Gen. Vernet to procure vessels which would contain water enough to last the garrison during a siege. On the arrival of Gen. Dessalines, I ordered him to take command of the fort and defend it to the last extremity.

For this purpose I left him half of my guards with the chief-of-brigade, Magny, and my two squadrons. I charged him not to allow Gen. Vernet to be exposed to fire, but to let him remain in a safe place to superintend the making of cartridges. Finally, I told Gen. Dessalines that while Gen. Leclerc was attacking this place, I should go into the Northern part, make a diversion, and retake the different places which had been seized; by this manœuvre, I should force the general to retrace his steps and make arrangements with me to preserve this beautiful colony to the Government.

Having given these orders, I took six companies of grenadiers commanded by Gabart, chief of the fourth demi-brigade, and Pourcely, the chief-of-battalion, and marched upon Ennery. I found there a proclamation of Gen. Leclerc, pronouncing me an outlaw. Confident that I had done no wrong with which to reproach myself, that all the disorder which prevailed in the country had been occasioned by Gen. Leclerc; believing myself, besides, the legitimate commander of the island, — I refuted his proclamation and declared him to be outlawed. Without loss of time I resumed my march and recaptured, without violence, St. Michel, St. Raphaël, Dondon, and Marmelade. In this last place I received a letter from Gen. Dessalines, announcing that Gen. Leclerc had marched against Petite Rivière with three columns; that one of these columns, passing by the Cahos and the Grand-Fonds, had captured all the treasures of the Republic coming from Gonaïves, and some silver which the inhabitants had deposited; that it was so heavily loaded with booty it was unable to reach its destination, and had been obliged to turn back to deposit its riches at Port-Républicain; that the two other columns, which had attacked the fort, had been repulsed by the chief-of-brigade, Magny; that Gen. Leclerc, having united his forces, had ordered a second attack, which had likewise been repelled by himself, Dessalines, who had then arrived. Apprised of these facts, I moved upon Plaisance and captured the camp of Bidouret, who held this place. This camp was occupied by troops of the line. I assaulted all the advanced posts at the same time. Just as I was going to fall upon Plaisance, I received a letter from the commander of Marmelade, which gave me notice that a strong column from the Spanish part was advancing upon this latter place.

I then moved promptly upon this column, which, instead of advancing upon Marmelade, had marched upon Hinche, where I pursued, but was unable to overtake it. I returned to Gonaïves, made myself master of the plain surrounding the town, ready to march upon the Gros-Morne to succor Gen. Maurepas, whom I supposed must be at Port-de-Paix, or else retired to the mountains where I ordered him to encamp, not knowing that he had already capitulated and submitted to Gen. Leclerc.

I received a third letter from Gen. Dessalines, who reported that Gen. Leclerc, having ordered a general assault and been repulsed, had determined to surround the place and bombard it. As soon as I learned the danger with which he was threatened, I hastened to move my troops there to deliver him. Arrived before the camp, I made a reconnoissance, procured the necessary information and prepared to attack it. I could, without fail, have entered the camp by a weak side which I had discovered,

and seized the person of Gen. Leclerc and all his staff; but at
the moment of execution, I received information that the garrison, failing of water, had been obliged to evacuate the fort. If
the project had succeeded, my intention was to send Gen. Leclerc back to the First Consul, rendering to him an exact account of his conduct, and praying him to send me another person worthy of his confidence, to whom I could deliver up the
command.

I retired to Grand Fonds to wait for the garrison of Crête-à-
Pierrot and to unite my forces. As soon as the garrison arrived,
I inquired of Gen. Dessalines where the prisoners were whom
he had previously told me were at the Cahos. He replied that
a part had been taken by Gen. Rochambeau's column, that
another part had been killed in the different attacks that he
had endured, and that the rest had escaped in the various
marches which he had been obliged to make. This reply evinces the injustice of imputing to me the assassinations which
were committed, because, it is said, as chief, I could have prevented them; but am I responsible for the evil which was done
in my absence and without my knowledge?

While at Gonaïves (at the commencement of hostilities), I
sent my aide-de-camp, Couppé, to Gen. Dessalines, to bid him
order the commander of Léogane to take all the inhabitants,
men and women, and send them to Port Républicain; to mus-
ter all the armed men he could in that place, and prepare himself for a most vigorous resistance in case of attack. My aide-
de-camp, Couppé, bearer of my orders, returned and told me
that he had not found Gen. Dessalines, but had learned that
Léogane had been burned, and that the inhabitants had escaped to Port Républicain.

All these disasters happened just at the time that Gen. Leclerc came. Why did he not inform me of his powers before
landing? Why did he land without my order and in defiance
of the order of the Commission? Did he not commit the first
hostilities? Did he not seek to gain over the generals and
other officers under my command by every possible means?

Did he not try to instigate the laborers to rise, by persuading them that I treated them like slaves, and that he had come to break their chains? Ought he to have employed such means in a country where peace and tranquillity reigned?—in a country which was in the power of the Republic?

If I did oblige my fellow-countrymen to work, it was to teach them the value of true liberty without license; it was to prevent corruption of morals; it was for the general happiness of the island, for the interest of the Republic. And I had effectually succeeded in my undertaking, since there could not be found in all the colony a single man unemployed, and the number of beggars had diminished to such a degree that, apart from a few in the towns, not a single one was to be found in the country.

If Gen. Leclerc's intentions had been good, would he have received Golart into his army, and given to him the command of the 9th demi-brigade,—a corps that he had raised at the time that he was chief of battalion? Would he have employed this dangerous rebel, who caused proprietors to be assassinated in their own dwelling-places; who invaded the town of Môle-Saint-Nicolas; who fired upon Gen. Clerveaux, who commanded there; upon Gen. Maurepas and his brigade commander; who made war upon the laborers of Jean-Rabel, from the *Moustiques* and the heights of Port-de-Paix; who carried his audacity so far as to oppose me when I marched against him to force him to submit to his chief, and to retake the territory and the town which he had invaded! The day that he dared to fire upon me, a ball cut the plume from my hat; Bondère, a physician, who accompanied me, was killed at my side, my aides-de-camp were unhorsed. In short, this brigand, after being steeped in every crime, concealed himself in a forest; he only came out of it upon the arrival of the French squadron. Ought Gen. Leclerc to have raised likewise to the rank of brigade commander another rebel, called L'Amour Desrances, who had caused all the inhabitants of the Plain of Cul-de-Sac to be assassinated; who urged the laborers to revolt; who pillaged all this part of the island; against whom, only two months before the arrival of the squadron, I had been obliged to march, and whom I forced to hide in the forests? Why were rebels and others amicably received, while my subordinates and myself, who remained steadfastly faithful to the French Government, and who had maintained order and tranquillity, were warred upon? Why was it made a crime to have executed the orders of the Government? Why was all the evil which had been done and the disorders which had existed imputed to me? All these facts are known by every inhabitant of St. Domingo. Why, on arriving, did they not go to the root of the evil? Had the troops which gave themselves up to Gen. Leclerc received the order from me? Did they consult me? No. Well! those who committed the wrong did not consult me. It is not right to attribute to me more wrong than I deserve.

I shared these reflections with some prisoners which I had. They replied that it was my influence upon the people which was feared, and that these violent means were employed to destroy it. This caused me new reflections. Considering all the misfortunes which the colony had already suffered, the dwellings destroyed, assassinations committed, the violence exercised even upon women, I forgot all the wrongs which had been done me, to think only of the happiness of the island and the interest of the Government. I determined to obey the order of the First Consul, since Gen. Leclerc had just withdrawn from the Cape with all his forces, after the affair of Crête-à-Pierrot.

Let it be observed that up to this time I had not been able to find an instant in which to reply to the First Consul. I seized with eagerness this momentary quiet to do so. I assured the First Consul of my submission and entire devotion to his orders, but represented to him " that if he did not send another older general to take command, the resistance which I must continue to oppose to Gen. Leclerc would tend to increase the prevalent disorder."

I remembered then that Gen. Dessalines had reported to me that two officers of the squadron — one an aide-de-camp of

Gen. Boudet, the other a naval officer, accompanied by two dragoons, sent to stir up a rebellion among the troops — had been made prisoners at the time of the evacuation of Port-au-Prince. I ordered them to be brought before me, and, after conversing with them, sent them back to Gen. Boudet, sending by them a letter with the one which I had written to the First Consul. Just as I was sending off these two officers, I learned that Gen. Hardy had passed Coupe-à-l'Inde with his army, that he had attacked my possessions, devastated them, and taken away all my animals, among them a horse named Bel-Argent, which I valued very highly. Without losing time, I marched against him with the force I had. I overtook him near Dondon. A fierce engagement took place, which lasted from eleven in the morning till six in the evening.

Before setting out, I had ordered Gen. Dessalines to join the troops which had evacuated Crête-à-Pierrot, and go into camp at Camp-Marchand, informing him that after the battle I should proceed to Marmelade.

Upon my arrival in that place, I received the reply of Gen. Boudet, which he sent me by my nephew Chancy, whom he had previously made prisoner.

That General assured me that my letter would easily reach the First Consul, that, to effect this, he had already sent it to Gen. Leclerc, who had promised him to forward it. Upon the report of my nephew, and after reading the letter of Gen. Boudet, I thought I recognized in him a character of honesty and frankness worthy of a French officer qualified to command. Therefore I addressed myself to him with confidence, begging him to persuade Gen. Leclerc to enter upon terms of conciliation with me. I assured him that ambition had never been my guide, but only honor; that I was ready to give up the command in obedience to the orders of the First Consul, and to make all necessary sacrifices to arrest the progress of the evil. I sent him this letter by my nephew Chancy, whom he kept with him. Two days after, I received a letter sent in haste by an orderly, announcing to me that he had made known my intentions to Gen. Leclerc, and assuring me that the latter was ready to make terms with me, and that I could depend upon the good intentions of the Government with regard to me.

The same day, Gen. Christophe communicated to me a letter which he had just received from a citizen named Vilton, living at the Petite-Anse, and another from Gen. Hardy, both asking him for an interview. I gave permission to Gen. Christophe to hold these interviews, recommending him to be very circumspect.

Gen. Christophe did not meet this appointment with Gen. Hardy, for he received a letter from Gen. Leclerc, proposing to him another rendezvous. He sent me a copy of this letter and of his reply, and asked my permission to report himself at the place indicated; which I granted, and he went.

Gen. Christophe, on his return, brought me a letter from Gen. Leclerc, saying that he should feel highly satisfied if he could induce me to concert with him, and submit to the orders of the Republic. I replied immediately that I had always been submissive to the French Government, as I had invariably borne arms for it; that if from the beginning I had been treated as I should have been, not a single shot would have been fired; that peace would not have been even disturbed in the island, and that the intention of the Government would have been fulfilled. In short, I showed to Gen. Leclerc, as well as to Gen. Christophe, all my indignation at the course which the latter had pursued, without orders from me.

The next day, I sent to Gen. Leclerc my Adjutant-General Fontaine, bearer of a second letter, in which I asked for an interview at Héricourt, which he refused. Fontaine assured me, however, that he had been well received. I was not discouraged. I sent the third time my aide-de-camp, Couppé and my secretary Nathand, assuring him that I was ready to give up the command to him, conformably to the intentions of the First Consul. He replied, that an hour of conversation would be worth more than ten letters, giving me his word of honor that he would act with all the frankness and loyalty that could be expected of a French general.　At the same time a proclamation from him was brought me, bidding all citizens to regard as null and void that article of the proclamation of Feb. 16, 1802, which made me an outlaw.　"Do not fear," he said in this proclamation, "you and your generals, and the people who are with you, that I shall search out the past conduct of any one ; I will draw the veil of oblivion over the events which have taken place at Saint Domingo ; I imitate, in so doing, the example which the First Consul gave to France on the 11th of November.　In future, I wish to see in the island only good citizens.　You ask repose ; after having borne the burden of government so long, repose is due you ; but I hope that in your retirement you will use your wisdom, in your moments of leisure, for the prosperity of Saint Domingo."

After this proclamation and the word of honor of the general, I proceeded to the Cape.　I submitted myself to Gen. Leclerc in accordance with the wish of the First Consul ; I afterward talked with him with all the frankness and cordiality of a soldier who loves and esteems his comrade.　He promised me forgetfulness of the past and the protection of the French Government.　He agreed with me that we had both been wrong.　"You can, General," he said to me, "retire to your home in perfect security.　But tell me if Gen. Dessalines will obey my orders, and if I can rely upon him ? "　I replied that he could ; that Gen. Dessalines might have faults, like every man, but that he understood military subordination.　I suggested to him, however, that for the public good and to reëstablish the laborers in their occupations, as they were at the time of his arrival in the island, it was necessary that Gen. Dessalines should be recalled to his command at Saint Marc, and Gen. Charles Belair to L'Arcahaye, which he promised me should be done.　At eleven in the evening, I took leave of him and withdrew to Héricourt, where I passed the night with Gen. Fressinet, and set out the next morning for Marmelade.

The third day after, I received a letter from Gen. Leclerc,

bidding me discharge my foot-guards and horse-guards. He addressed to me also an order for Gen. Dessalines; I acquainted myself with it and sent it to Gen. Dessalines, telling him to comply with it. And that I might the better fulfil the promises that I had made Gen. Leclerc, I requested Gen. Dessalines to meet me half-way between his house and mine. I urged him to submit, as I had done; I told him that the public interest required me to make great sacrifices, and that I was willing to make them; but as for him, he might keep his command. I said as much to Gen. Charles, also to all the officers with them; finally, I persuaded them, in spite of all the reluctance and regret they evinced, to leave me and go away. They even shed tears. After this interview, all returned to their own homes. Adjutant-General Perrin, whom Gen. Leclerc had sent to Dessalines with his orders, found him very ready to comply with them, since I had previously engaged him to do so in our interview. As we have seen, a promise was made to place Gen. Charles at L'Arcahaye; however, it was not done.

It was unnecessary for me to order the inhabitants of Dondon, St. Michel, St. Raphaël and Marmelade to return to their homes, since they had done so as soon as I had taken possession of these communities; I only advised them to resume their usual occupations. I ordered also the inhabitants of Plaisance and the neighboring places, to return home and begin their labor, too. They expressed fears that they might be disturbed. Therefore I wrote to Gen. Leclerc, reminding him of his promise, and begging him to attend to their execution. He replied, that his orders were already given upon that subject. Meanwhile, the commander of this place had divided his forces and sent detachments into all the districts, which had alarmed the laborers and compelled them to flee to the mountains. I proceeded to Ennery and acquainted Gen. Leclerc with these things, as I had promised him. In this town I found a great many laborers from Gonaïves, whom I persuaded to return home. Before I left Marmelade, I ordered the commander of that place to restore the artillery and ammunition to the commander of Plaisance, in conformity to the desire of Gen. Leclerc. I also ordered the commander at Ennery to return the only piece of artillery there, and also the ammunition, to the commander of Gonaïves.

I then employed myself in rebuilding my houses which had been burned. In a house in the mountains, which had escaped the flames, I had to prepare a comfortable lodging for my wife, who was still in the woods where she had been obliged to take refuge.

While engaged in these occupations, I learned that 500 troops had arrived, to be stationed at Ennery, a little town, which, until then, could not have had more than 50 armed men as a police force; and that a very large detachment had also been sent to St. Michel. I hastened to the town. I saw that all my houses had been pillaged and even the coffers of my laborers carried off. At the very moment when I was entering my complaint to the commander, I pointed out to him the soldiers loaded with fruit of all kinds, even unripe fruit; I also showed him the laborers who, seeing these robberies, were fleeing to other houses in the mountains. I gave an account to Gen. Leclerc of what was going on, and observed to him that the measures which were being taken, far from inspiring confidence, only increased distrust; that the number of troops which he had sent was very considerable, and could only be an injury to agriculture and the inhabitants. I then returned to my house in the mountains.

The next day I received, in this house, a visit from the commander at Ennery, and I saw very clearly that this soldier, instead of making me a visit of politeness, had come to my house merely to reconnoitre my dwelling and the avenues about it, that he might seize me the more easily when he received the order to do so. While talking with him, I was informed that several soldiers had gone with horses and other beasts of burden to one of my residences near the town, where a god-daughter of mine was residing, and had taken away the coffee and other provisions found there. I made complaint to him; he promised me to put a stop to these robberies and to punish severely those who had been guilty of them. Fearing that my house in the mountains inspired only distrust, I determined to remove to that very house which had just been pillaged, and almost totally destroyed, but two hundred paces from the town. I left my wife in the house which I had prepared for her. I was now occupied in laying out new plantations to replace those which had been destroyed, and in preparing necessary materials for reconstructing my buildings. But every day I experienced new robberies and new vexations. The soldiers came to my house in such large numbers that I dared not have them arrested. In vain I bore my complaints to the commander. I received no satisfaction. Finally, I determined, though Gen. Leclerc had not done me the honor to answer my two former letters upon this subject, to write him a third, which I sent to him at the Cape by my son Placide, for greater security. This, like the others, elicited no reply. But the chief of the staff told me that he would make his report. Some time after, the commander, having come to see me again, one afternoon, found me at the head of my laborers, employed in directing the work of reconstruction. He himself saw my son Isaac drive away several soldiers who had just come to the gate to cut down the bananas and figs. I repeated to him the most earnest complaints. He still promised to stop these disorders. During three weeks that I stayed in this place, I witnessed daily new ravages; every day I received visits from people who came as spies, but they were all witnesses that I was engaged solely in domestic labors. Gen. Brunet himself came, and found me occupied in the same manner. Notwithstanding my conduct, I received a letter from Gen. Leclerc, which, in place of giving me satisfaction in regard to the complaints which I had made to him, accused me of keeping armed men within the borders of Ennery, and ordered me to send them away. Persuaded of my innocence, and that evil-disposed people had deceived him, I replied that I had too much honor to break promises which I had made, and that when I gave up the command to him, it was not without reflection ; that, moreover, I had no intention of trying to take it back. I assured him, besides, that I had no knowledge of armed men in the environs of Ennery, and that for three weeks I had been constantly at work on my own place. I sent my son Isaac to give him an account of all the vexations I suffered, and to warn him that if he did not put an end to them, I should be obliged to leave the place where I was living, and go to my ranche in the Spanish part.

One day, before I received any answer from Gen. Leclerc, I was informed that one of his aides-de-camp, passing by Ennery, had told the commander that he was the bearer of an order for my arrest, addressed to Gen. Brunet. Gen. Leclerc having given his word of honor and promised the protection of the French Government, I refused to believe the report; I even said to some one who advised me to leave my residence, that I had promised to stay there quietly, working to repair the havoc that had been made ; that I had not given up the command and sent away my troops to act so foolishly now; that I did not wish to leave home, and if they came to arrest me, they would find me there ; that, besides, I would not give credence to the calumny.

The next day I received a second letter from Gen. Leclerc, by my son whom I sent to him, which read thus: —

" ARMY OF ST. DOMINGO,
" HEADQUARTERS AT CAP FRANÇAIS, June 5, 1802.

" THE GEN.-IN-CHIEF TO GEN. TOUSSAINT :—

" Since you persist, Citizen-General, in thinking that the great number of troops stationed at Plaisance (the Secretary probably wrote Plaisance by mistake, meaning Ennery) frightens the laborers of that district, I have commissioned Gen. Brunet to act in concert with you, and to place a part of these troops in the rear of Gonaïves and one detachment at Plaisance. Let the laborers understand, that, having taken this measure, I shall punish those who leave their dwellings to go to the mountains. Let me know, as soon as this order has been executed, the results which it produces, because, if the means of persuasion which you employ do not succeed, I shall use military measures. I salute you."

The same day I received a letter from Gen. Brunet, of which the following is an extract: —

"ARMY OF SAINT DOMINGO,
"HEADQUARTERS AT GEORGES, June 7, 1802.

"BRUNET, GEN. OF DIVISION, TO THE GEN. OF DIVISION, TOUSSAINT L'OUVERTURE:

"Now is the time, Citizen-General, to make known unquestionably to the General-in-chief that those who wish to deceive him in regard to your fidelity are base calumniators, and that your sentiments tend to restore order and tranquillity in your neighborhood. You must assist me in securing free communication to the Cape, which has been interrupted since yesterday, three persons having been murdered by fifty brigands between Ennery and Coupe-à-Pintade. Send in pursuit of these murderers men worthy of confidence, whom you are to pay well; I will keep account of your expenses.

"We have arrangements to make together, my dear General, which it is impossible to do by letter, but which an hour's conference would complete. If I were not worn out by labor and petty cares, I should have been the bearer of my own letter to-day; but not being able to leave at this time, will you not come to me? If you have recovered from your indisposition, let it be to-morrow; when a good work is to be done, there should be no delay. You will not find in my country-house all the comforts which I could desire before receiving you, but you will find the sincerity of an honest man who desires only the prosperity of the colony and your own happiness. If Madame Toussaint, whom I greatly desire to know, wishes to take the journey, it will give me pleasure. If she needs horses, I will send her mine. I repeat, General, you will never find a sincerer friend than myself.

27*

" With confidence in the Captain-General, with friendship
for all who are under him, and hoping that you may enjoy
peace,   I cordially salute you.
             (Signed)   " BRUNET.

" P. S.   Your servant who has gone to Port-au-Prince passed
here this morning; he left with his passport made out in due
form."

That very servant, instead of receiving his passport, was
arrested, and is now in prison with me.

After reading these two letters, although not very well, I
yielded to the solicitations of my sons and others, and set out
the same night to see Gen. Brunet, accompanied by two officers
only.   At eight in the evening I arrived at the General's house.
When he met me, I told him that I had received his letter, and
also that of the General-in-chief, requesting me to act with
him, and that I had come for that purpose; that I had not
brought my wife, as he requested, because she never left home,
being much occupied with domestic duties, but if sometime,
when he was travelling, he would do her the honor of visiting
her, she would receive him with pleasure.   I said to him that,
being ill, my stay must be short, asking him, therefore, to finish our business as soon as possible, that I might return.

I handed him the letter of Gen. Leclerc.   After reading it,
he told me that he had not yet received any order to act in
concert with me upon the subject of the letter; he then excused himself for a moment, and went out, after calling an officer to keep me company.   He had hardly left the room when
an aide-de-camp of Gen. Leclerc entered, accompanied by a
large number of soldiers, who surrounded me, seized me, bound
me as a criminal, and conducted me on board the frigate
Créole.

I claimed the protection which Gen. Brunet, on his word of
honor, had promised me, but without avail.   I saw him no
more.   He had probably concealed himself to escape my well-
merited reproaches.   I afterward learned that he treated my

family with great cruelty; that, immediately after my arrest, he sent a detachment of troops to the house where I had been living with a part of my family, mostly women, children, and laborers, and ordered them to set it on fire, compelling the unhappy victims to fly half-naked to the woods; that everything had been pillaged and sacked; that the aide-de-camp of Gen. Brunet had even taken from my house fifty-five ounces of gold belonging to me, and thirty-three ounces belonging to one of my nieces, together with all the linen of the family.

Having committed these outrages upon my dwelling, the commander at Ennery went, at the head of one hundred men, to the house occupied by my wife and nieces, and arrested them, without giving them time to collect any of their effects. They were conducted like criminals to Gonaïves and put on board the frigate Guerrière.

When I was arrested, I had no extra clothing with me. I wrote to my wife, asking her to send me such things as I should need most to the Cape, hoping I should be taken there. This note I sent by an aide-de-camp of Gen. Leclerc, begging that it might be allowed to pass; it did not reach its destination, and I received nothing.

As soon as I was taken on board the Créole, we set sail, and, four leagues from the Cape, found the Héros, to which they transferred me. The next day, my wife and my children, who had been arrested with her, arrived there also. We immediately set sail for France. After a voyage of thirty-two days, during which I endured not only great fatigue, but also every species of hardship, while my wife and children received treatment from which their sex and rank should have preserved them, instead of allowing us to land, they retained us on board sixty-seven days.

After such treatment, could I not justly ask where were the promises of Gen. Leclerc? where was the protection of the French Government? If they no longer needed my services and wished to replace me, should they not have treated me as white French generals are always treated? They are warned

when they are to be relieved of their command; a messenger
is sent to notify them to resign the command to such and such
persons; and in case they refuse to obey, measures are taken
to compel them; they can then justly be treated as rebels and
sent to France.

I have, in fact, known some generals guilty of criminally
neglecting their duties, but who, in consideration of their character, have escaped punishment until they could be brought before superior authority.

Should not Gen. Leclerc have informed me that various
charges had been brought against me? Should he not have
said to me, "I gave you my word of honor and promised you
the protection of the Government; to-day, as you have been
found guilty, I am going to send you to that government to
give an account of your conduct"? Or, "Government orders
you to submit; I convey that order to you"? I have not been
so treated; on the other hand, means have been employed
against me which are only used against the greatest criminals. Doubtless, I owe this treatment to my color; but my color,
— my color, — has it hindered me from serving my country
with zeal and fidelity? Does the color of my skin impair my
honor and my bravery?

But even supposing that I was a criminal, and that Government had ordered my arrest, was it necessary to employ a hundred riflemen to arrest my wife and children in their own home,
without regard to their sex, age, and rank; without humanity
and without charity? Was it necessary to burn my houses,
and to pillage and sack my possessions? No. My wife, my
children, my family had no responsibility in the matter; they
were not accountable to the Government; it was not lawful to
arrest them.

Gen. Leclerc's authority was undisputed; did he fear me as a
rival? I can but compare him to the Roman Senate, pursuing
Hannibal to the very depths of his retreat.

Upon the arrival of the squadron in the colony, they took advantage of my absence to seize a part of my correspondence,

which was at Port-Républicain; another portion, which was in one of my houses, has also been seized since my arrest. Why have they not sent me with this correspondence to give an account of my movements? They have taken forcible possession of my papers in order to charge me with crimes which I have never committed; but I have nothing to fear; this correspondence is sufficient to justify me. They have sent me to France destitute of everything; they have seized my property and my papers, and have spread atrocious calumnies concerning me. Is it not like cutting off a man's legs and telling him to walk? Is it not like cutting out a man's tongue and telling him to talk? Is it not burying a man alive?

In regard to the Constitution, the subject of one charge against me: Having driven from the colony the enemies of the Republic, calmed the factions and united all parties; perceiving, after I had taken possession of St. Domingo, that the Government made no laws for the colony, and feeling the necessity of police regulations for the security and tranquillity of the people, I called an assembly of wise and learned men, composed of deputies from all the communities, to conduct this business. When this assembly met, I represented to its members that they had an arduous and responsible task before them; that they were to make laws adapted to the country, advantageous to the Government, and beneficial to all, — laws suited to the localities, to the character and customs of the inhabitants. The Constitution must be submitted for the sanction of the Government, which alone had the right to adopt or reject it. Therefore, as soon as the Constitution was decided upon and its laws fixed, I sent the whole, by a member of the assembly, to the Government, to obtain its sanction. The errors or faults which this Constitution may contain cannot therefore be imputed to me. At the time of Leclerc's arrival, I had heard nothing from the Government upon this subject. Why to-day do they seek to make a crime of that which is no crime? Why put truth for falsehood, and falsehood for truth? Why put darkness for light and light for darkness?

In a conversation which I had at the Cape with Gen. Leclerc, he told me that while at Samana he had sent a spy to Santo Domingo to learn if I was there, who brought back word that I was. Why did he not go there to find me and give me the orders of the First Consul, before commencing hostilities? He knew my readiness to obey orders. Instead of this, he took advantage of my absence at St. Domingo to proceed to the Cape and send troops to all parts of the colony. This conduct proves that he had no intention of communicating anything to me.

If Gen. Leclerc went to the colony to do evil, it should not be charged upon me. It is true that only one of us can be blamed; but however little one may wish to do me justice, it is clear that he is the author of all the evils which the island has suffered, since, without warning me, he entered the colony, which he found in a state of prosperity, fell upon the inhabitants, who were at their work, contributing to the welfare of the community, and shed their blood upon their native soil. That is the true source of the evil.

If two children were quarrelling together, should not their father or mother stop them, find out which was the aggressor, and punish him, or punish them, if they were both wrong? Gen. Leclerc had no right to arrest me; Government alone could arrest us both, hear us, and judge us. Yet Gen. Leclerc enjoys liberty, and I am in a dungeon.

Having given an account of my conduct since the arrival of the fleet at St. Domingo, I will enter into some details of previous events.

Since I entered the service of the Republic, I have not claimed a penny of my salary; Gen. Laveaux, Government agents, all responsible persons connected with the public treasury, can do me this justice, that no one has been more prudent, more disinterested than I. I have only now and then received the extra pay allowed me; very often I have not asked even this. Whenever I have taken money from the treasury, it has been for some public use; the governor (*l'ordonnateur*) has used it as the service required. I remember that once only, when far from home, I borrowed six thousand francs from Citizen Smith, who was governor of the Department of the South.

I will sum up, in a few words, my conduct and the results of my administration. At the time of the evacuation of the English, there was not a penny in the public treasury; money had to be borrowed to pay the troops and the officers of the Republic. When Gen. Leclerc arrived, he found three millions, five hundred thousand francs in the public funds. When I returned to Cayes, after the departure of Gen. Rigaud, the treasury was empty; Gen. Leclerc found three millions there; he found proportionate sums in all the private depositories on the island. Thus it is seen that I did not serve my country from interested motives; but, on the contrary, I served it with honor, fidelity, and integrity, sustained by the hope of receiving, at some future day, flattering acknowledgments from the Government; all who know me will do me this justice.

I have been a slave; I am willing to own it; but I have never received reproaches from my masters.

I have neglected nothing at Saint Domingo for the welfare of the island; I have robbed myself of rest to contribute to it; I have sacrificed everything for it. I have made it my duty and pleasure to develop the resources of this beautiful colony. Zeal, activity, courage, — I have employed them all.

The island was invaded by the enemies of the Republic; I had then but a thousand men, armed with pikes. I sent them back to labor in the field, and organized several regiments, by the authority of Gen. Laveaux.

The Spanish portion had joined the English to make war upon the French. Gen. Desfourneaux was sent to attack Saint Michel with well-disciplined troops of the line; he could not take it. General Laveaux ordered me to the attack; I carried it. It is to be remarked that, at the time of the attack by Gen. Desfourneaux, the place was not fortified, and that when I took it, it was fortified by bastions in every corner. I also took Saint-Raphaël and Hinche, and rendered an account to Gen. Laveaux. The English were intrenched at Pont-de-l'Ester; I drove them from the place. They were in possession of Petite Rivière. My ammunition consisted of one case of cartridges which had fallen into the water on my way to the attack; this did not discourage me. I carried the place by assault before day, with my dragoons, and made all the garrison prisoners. I sent them to Gen. Laveaux. I had but one piece of cannon; I took nine at Petite Rivière. Among the posts gained at Petite Rivière, was a fortification defended by seven pieces of cannon, which I attacked, and carried by assault. I also conquered the Spaniards intrenched in the camps of Miraut and Dubourg at Verrettes. I gained a famous victory over the English in a battle which lasted from six in the morning until nearly night. This battle was so fierce that the roads were filled with the dead, and rivers of blood were seen on every side. I took all the baggage and ammunition of the enemy, and a large number of prisoners. I sent the whole to Gen. Laveaux, giving him an account of the engagement. All the posts of the English upon the heights of Saint Marc were taken by me; the walled fortifications in the mountains of Fond-Baptiste and Délices, the camp of Drouët in the Matheux mountains, which the English regarded as impregnable, the citadels of Mirebalais, called the Gibraltar of the island, occupied by eleven hundred men, the celebrated camp of l'Acul-du-Saut, the stone fortifications of Trou-d'Eau, three stories high, those of the camp of Décayette and of Beau-Bien, — in short, all the fortifications of the English in this quarter were unable to withstand me, as were those of Neybe, of Saint Jean de la Maguâna, of Las Mathas, of Banique and other places occupied by the Spaniards; all were brought by me under the power of the Republic. I was also exposed to the greatest dangers; several times I narrowly escaped being made prisoner; I shed my blood for my country; I received a ball in the right hip which remains there still; I received a violent blow on the head from a cannon-ball, which knocked out the greater part of my teeth, and loosened the rest. In short, I received upon different occasions seventeen wounds, whose honorable scars still remain. Gen. Laveaux witnessed many of my engagements; he is too honorable not to do me justice: ask him if I ever hesitated to endanger my life, when the good of my country and the triumph of the Republic required it.

If I were to record the various services which I have rendered the Government, I should need many volumes, and even then should not finish them; and, as a reward for all these services, I have been arbitrarily arrested at St. Domingo, bound, and put on board ship like a criminal, without regard for my rank, without the least consideration. Is this the recompense due my labors? Should my conduct lead me to expect such treatment?

I was once rich. At the time of the revolution, I was worth six hundred and forty-eight thousand francs. I spent it in the service of my country. I purchased but one small estate upon which to establish my wife and family. To-day, notwithstanding my disinterestedness, they seek to cover me with opprobrium and infamy; I am made the most unhappy of men; my liberty is taken from me; I am separated from all that I hold dearest in the world, — from a venerable father, a hundred and five years old, who needs my assistance, from a dearly-loved wife, who, I fear, separated from me, cannot endure the afflictions which overwhelm her, and from a cherished family, who made the happiness of my life.

On my arrival in France I wrote to the First Consul and to the Minister of Marine, giving them an account of my situation, and asking their assistance for my family and myself. Undoubtedly, they felt the justice of my request, and gave orders that what I asked should be furnished me. But, instead of this, I have received the old half-worn dress of a soldier, and shoes in the same condition. Did I need this humiliation added to my misfortune?

When I left the ship, I was put into a carriage. I hoped then that I was to be taken before a tribunal to give an account of my conduct, and to be judged. Far from it; without a moment's rest I was taken to a fort on the frontiers of the Republic, and confined in a frightful dungeon.

It is from the depths of this dreary prison that I appeal to the justice and magnanimity of the First Consul. He is too noble and too good a general to turn away from an old soldier, covered with wounds in the service of his country, without giving him the opportunity to justify himself, and to have judgment pronounced upon him.

I ask, then, to be brought before a tribunal or council of war, before which, also, Gen. Leclerc may appear, and that we may both be judged after we have both been heard; equity, reason, law, all assure me that this justice cannot be refused me.

In passing through France, I have seen in the newspapers an article concerning myself. I am accused in this article of being a rebel and a traitor, and, to justify the accusation, a letter is said to have been intercepted in which I encouraged the laborers of St. Domingo to revolt. I never wrote such a letter, and I defy any one to produce it, to tell me to whom it was addressed, and to bring forward the person. As to the rest of the calumny, it falls of itself; if I had intended to make war, would I have laid down my arms and submitted? No reasonable man, much less a soldier, can believe such an absurdity.

ADDITION TO THE MEMOIRS.

If the Government had sent a wiser man, there would have been no trouble; not a single shot would have been fired.

Why did fear occasion so much injustice on the part of Gen. Leclerc? Why did he violate his word of honor? Upon the arrival of the frigate Guerrière, which brought my wife, why did I see on board a number of people who had been arrested with her? Many of these persons had not fired a shot. They were innocent men, fathers of families, who had been torn from the arms of their wives and children. All these persons had shed their blood to preserve the colony to France; they were officers of my staff, my secretaries, who had done nothing but by my orders; all, therefore, were arrested without cause.

Upon landing at Brest, my wife and children were sent to different destinations, of both of which I am ignorant. Government should do me more justice: my wife and children have done nothing and have nothing to answer for; they should be sent home to watch over our interests. Gen. Leclerc has occasioned all this evil; but I am at the bottom of a dungeon, unable to justify myself. Government is too just to keep my hands tied, and allow Gen. Leclerc to abuse me thus, without listening to me.

Everybody has told me that this Government was just; should I not, then, share its justice and its benefits?

Gen. Leclerc has said in the letter to the minister, which I have seen in the newspaper, that I was waiting for his troops to grow sick, in order to make war and take back the command. This is an atrocious and abominable lie: it is a cowardly act on his part. Although I may not have much knowledge or much education, I have enough good sense to hinder me from contending against the will of my Government; I never thought of it. The French Government is too strong, too powerful, for Gen. Leclerc to think me opposed to it, who am its servant. It it is true, that when Gen. Leclerc marched against me, I said several times that I should make no attack, that I should only defend myself, until July or August; that then I would commence in my turn. But, afterward, I reflected upon the misfortunes of the colony and upon the letter of the First Consul; I then submitted.

I repeat it again: I demand that Gen. Leclerc and myself be judged before a tribunal; that Government should order all my correspondence to be brought; by this means my innocence,

and all that I have done for the Republic will be seen, although
I know that several letters have been intercepted.

First Consul, father of all soldiers, upright judge, defender
of innocence, pronounce my destiny.   My wounds are deep;
apply to them the healing remedy which will prevent them
from opening anew; you are the physician; I rely entirely upon your justice and wisdom!

NOTES AND TESTIMONIES.

I.

THE following is the view taken of the struggle for negro freedom by CHRISTOPHE; the passage is quoted from a manifesto, published in 1814, by that warrior, then King of Hayti, and threatened with a new invasion by the whites.

"We have deserved the favors of liberty, by our indissoluble attachment to the mother country. We have proved to her our gratitude.

"At the time when, reduced to our own private resources, cut off from all communication with France, we resisted every allurement; when, inflexible to menaces, deaf to proposals, inaccessible to artifice, we braved misery, famine, and privation of every kind, and finally triumphed over our enemies both within and without.

"We were then far from perceiving that twelve years after, as the price of so much perseverance, sacrifice, and blood, France would deprive us in a most barbarous manner of the most precious of our possessions, — liberty.

"Under the administration of Governor-General Toussaint L'Ouverture, Hayti arose from her ruins, and everything seemed to promise a happy future. The arrival of General Hedouville completely changed the aspect of affairs, and struck a deadly blow to public tranquillity. We will not enter into the detail of his intrigues with the Haytian General, Rigaud, whom he persuaded to revolt against the legitimate chief. We will only say, that before leaving the island, Hédouville had put everything into confusion, by casting among us the firebrands of discord, and lighting the torch of civil war.

"Ever zealous for the reëstablishment of order and of peace, Toussaint L'Ouverture, by a paternal government, restored their original energy to law, morality, religion, education, and industry. Agriculture and commerce were flourishing; he was favorable to white colonists, especially to those who occupied new possessions; and the care and partiality which he felt for them went so far that he was severely censured as being more attached to them than to people of his own color. This negro wail was not without reason; for some months previous to the arrival of the French, he put to death his own nephew, General Moise, for having disregarded his orders relative to the protection of the colonists. This act of the Governor, and the great confidence which he had in the French Government, were the chief causes of the weak resistance which the French met with in Hayti. In reality, his confidence in that Government was so great, that the General had disbanded the greater part of the regular troops, and employed them in the cultivation of the ground.

"Such was the state of affairs whilst the peace of Amiens was being negotiated; it was scarcely concluded, when a powerful armament landed on our coasts a large army, which, attacking us by surprise, when we thought ourselves perfectly secure, plunged us suddenly into an abyss of evils.

"Posterity will find a difficulty in believing that, in so enlightened and philosophic an age, such an abominable enterprise could possibly have been conceived. In the midst of a civilized people, a horde of barbarians suddenly set out with the design of exterminating an innocent and peaceable nation, or at least of loading them anew with the chains of national slavery.

"It was not enough that they employed violence; they also thought it necessary to use perfidy and villany,—they were compelled to sow dissension among us. Every means was put in requisition to carry out this abominable scheme. The leaders of all political parties in France, even the sons of the Governor Toussaint, were invited to take part in the expedition. They, as well as ourselves, were deceived by that *chef-d'œuvre* of

perfidy, the proclamation of the First Consul, in which he said
to us, 'You are all equal and free before God and the Republic ;' such was his declaration, at the same time that his private
instructions to General Leclerc were to reëstablish slavery.

"The greater part of the population, deceived by these fal-
lacious promises, and for a long time accustomed to consider itself as French, submitted without resistance. The Governor so
little expected the appearance of an enemy that he had not
even ordered his generals to resist in case of an attack being
made; and, when the armament arrived, he himself was on
a journey toward the eastern coast. If some few generals
did resist, it was owing only to the hostile and menacing manner in which they were summoned to surrender, which compelled them to respect their duty, their honor, and the present
circumstances.

"After a resistance of some months, the Governor-General
yielded to the pressing entreaties and the solemn protestations
of Leclerc, ' that he intended to protect the liberties of every
one, and that France would never destroy so noble a work.'
On this footing, peace was negotiated with France; and the
Governor Toussaint, laying aside his power, peaceably retired
to the retreat he had prepared for himself.

"Scarcely had the French extended their dominion over the
whole island, and that more by roguery and deceit than by force
of arms, than they began to put in execution their horrible system of slavery and destruction.

"To hasten the accomplishment of their projects, merce-
nary and Machiavellian writers fabricated fictitious narratives,
and attributed to Toussaint designs that he had never entertained. While he was remaining peaceably at home, on the
faith of solemn treaties, he was seized, loaded with irons, dragged away with the whole of his family, and transported to
France. The whole of Europe knows how he ended his unfortunate career in torture and in prayer, in the dungeon of the
Château de Joux.

"Such was the recompense reserved for his attachment to

France, and for the eminent services he had rendered to the colony.

"At the same time, notice was given to arrest all suspected persons throughout the island. All those who had shown brave and enlightened souls, when we claimed for ourselves the rights of men, were the first to be seized. Even the traitors who had most contributed to the success of the French army, by serving as guides to their advanced guard, and by exciting their compatriots to take vengeance, were not spared. At first they desired to sell them into strange colonies; but, as this plan did not succeed, they resolved to transport them to France, where overpowering labor, the galleys, chains, and prisons, were awaiting them.

"Then the white colonists, whose numbers have continually increased, seeing their power sufficiently established, discarded the mask of dissimulation, openly declared the reëstablishment of slavery, and acted in accordance with their declaration. They had the impudence to claim as their slaves men who had made themselves eminent by the most brilliant services to their country, in both the civil and military departments. Virtuous and honorable magistrates, warriors covered with wounds, whose blood had been poured out for France and for liberty, were compelled to fall back into the bonds of slavery. These colonists, scarcely established in the possession of their land, whose power was liable to be overthrown by the slightest cause, already marked out and chose in the distance those whom they determined should be the first victims of their vengeance.

"The proud and liberty-hating faction of the colonists, of those traffickers in human flesh, who, since the commencement of the revolution, had not ceased to impregnate the successive Governments in France with their plans, their projects, their atrocious and extravagant memorials, and everything tending to our ruin, — these factious men, tormented by the recollection of the despotism which they had formerly exercised at Hayti, a prey to their low and cruel passions, exerted all their efforts to repossess themselves of the prey which had escaped from their clutches. In favor of independence under the constitutional assembly, terrorists under the Jacobins, and, finally, zealous Bonapartists, they knew how to assume the mask of any party, in order to obtain place and favor. It was thus, by their insidious counsels, they urged Bonaparte to undertake this iniquitous expedition to Hayti. It was this faction who, after having advised the expedition, furnished the pecuniary resources which were necessary, by means of subscriptions which were at this time commenced. In a word, it was this faction which caused the blood of our compatriots to flow in torrents, — which invented the exhausting tortures to which we were subjected; it is to these colonists that France owes the loss of a powerful army, which perished in the plains and marshes of Hayti; it is to them she owes the shame of an enterprise which has fixed an indelible stain on the French name.

"Immediately, the greater part of the people took up arms for the preservation of life and liberty. Even this first movement alarmed the French, and appeared to General Leclerc so important as to cause him to summon a special meeting of the colonists, in order to adopt measures suitable to bring about a better state of affairs; but these colonists, far from desisting from their atrocious principles, notwithstanding the imminence of the danger, unanimously exclaimed, ' If there is no slavery, there is no colony !'

"Members of the council, it was in vain that we raised our voices to prevent the total ruin of our country; in vain we represented to them the horrible injustice of again casting so many free men into slavery; in vain (for we knew the spirit of liberty which animated our compatriots) we denounced this measure as the certain ruin of the country, and that it would detach it forever from France : it was all in vain. Convinced that there no longer remained any hope of conciliation, and that we were compelled to choose between slavery and death, then, with our weapons in our hands, we undeceived our compatriots, whose whole attention was directed toward us, and we unanimously seized our swords, resolved either to drive those tyrants from the land forever, or to die.

"General Leclerc had already announced the conquest of the island, and had received from almost all the maritime towns of France (where resided the chief advocates of slavery) letters of congratulation on his pretended conquest. Ashamed of having given rise to such deceitful hopes, mortified at not being able to achieve the detestable enterprise, and mistrusting the approach of another terrible war, despair shortened his days and dragged him down to the grave.

"Amid this long tissue of crimes which marked the administration of General Leclerc, we will merely point out his conduct toward the Haytian General, Maurepas, which could not but excite the commiseration even of the most cold-hearted. Maurepas, a man of gentle and agreeable manners, esteemed by his fellow-citizens for his integrity, was one of the first to join the French, and rendered them the most signal services. Nevertheless, he was suddenly carried off to Port-au-Prince, and taken on board the admiral's vessel, which was then at anchor near the Cape coasts; and then, having been bound to the mainmast, in mockery they put two epaulettes on his shoulders, fastened them on by nails such as they use in naval carpentry, and covered his head with a general's hat. In this frightful condition, these savages, after having given free vent to their ferocious joy, precipitated him, with his wife and children, into the sea. Such was the destiny of this virtuous though unfortunate soldier." — *Histoire de l'Ile d'Hayti*, par Placide Justine, p. 391 — Paris, 1826.

II.

THOSE who feel interested enough in the extraordinary fortunes of Toussaint L'Ouverture to inquire concerning him from the biographical dictionaries and popular histories of the day, will find in them all the same brief and peremptory decision concerning his character. They all pronounce him to have been a man of wonderful sagacity, endowed with a native genius for both war and government; but savage in warfare, hypocritical in religion, — using piety as a political mask, and, in all his affairs, the very prince of dissemblers. It is true that this account consists neither in the facts of his life, the opinions of the people he delivered, nor the State documents of the island he governed. Yet it is easy to account for. The first notices of him were French, reported by the discomfited invaders of Saint Domingo to writers imbued with the philosophy of the days of the Revolution; and later accounts are copies of these earlier ones. From the time when my attention was first fixed on this hero, I have been struck with the inconsistencies contained in all reports of his character which ascribe to him cruelty and hypocrisy; and, after a long and careful comparison of such views with his words and deeds, with the evidence obtainable from Saint Domingo, and with the temper of his times in France, I have arrived at the conclusion that his character was, in sober truth, such as I have endeavored to represent it in the foregoing work.

I do not mean to say that I am the first who has formed an opinion that Toussaint was an honest, a religious, and a mild and merciful man. In an article in the Quarterly Review (No. XLII.) on the " Past and Present State of Hayti," so interesting an account is given of the great negro as to cause some wonder that no one has till now been moved by it to present the facts of his life in the form of an historical novel. In that article it is justly observed that the *onus* rests with those who accuse Toussaint of hypocrisy to prove their allegation by facts. I would say the same of the other charge of cruelty. Meantime, I disbelieve both charges, for these reasons among others.

The wars of Saint Domingo were conducted in a most barbarous spirit before the time of Toussaint's acquisition of power and after his abduction. During the interval, the whole weight of his influence was given to curb the ferocity of both parties. He pardoned his personal enemies (as in the instance of the mulattoes in the church), and he punished in his own followers, as the most unpardonable offence they could commit, any infringement of his rule of " No RETALIATION." When it is considered that the cruelties perpetrated in the rising of 1791, and renewed after the fall of Toussaint, were invented by the whites, and copied by the negroes (who were wont to imitate their masters in all they did), it is no small evidence of L'Ouverture's magnanimity that he conceived, illustrated, and enforced, in such times, such a principle as that of No RETALIATION.

All the accounts of him agree that, from his earliest childhood, he was distinguished by a tenderness of nature which would not let him hurt a fly. He attached to himself the cattle and horses which were under his charge when a boy, to a degree which made him famous in a region where cruelty to animals at the hands of slaves was almost universal. A man who lived till fifty, remarkable for a singular gentleness and placability, ought not to be believed sanguinary from that time forward on the strength of the unsupported charges of his disappointed enemies.

Piety was, also, his undisputed early characteristic. A slave, bringing to the subject of religion the aptitude of the negro nature, early treated with kindness by a priest, evincing the spirit of piety from his infant years, finding in it the consolations required by a life of slavery, and guided by it in a course of the strictest domestic morality while surrounded by licentiousness, may well be supposed sincere in his religion under a change of circumstances occurring after he was fifty years of age. The imputation of hypocrisy is not, however, much to be wondered at when it is considered that, at the time when the first notices of Toussaint were written in Paris, it was the fashion there to believe that no wise man could be sincerely religious.

As for the charge of general and habitual dissimulation, it can only be said, that while no proof of the assertion is offered, there is evidence in all the anecdotes preserved of him, of absolute frankness and simplicity. I rather think that it was the incredible extent of his simplicity which gave rise to the belief that it was assumed in order to hide cunning. The Quarterly Review quotes an anecdote thoroughly characteristic of the man, which is not introduced into my story because, in the abundance of my materials, I found it necessary to avoid altogether the history of the English transactions in Saint Domingo. It was only by confining my narrative to the relations between Toussaint and France that I could keep my tale within limits, and preserve the clearness of the representation. There are circumstances, however, in his intercourses with the British as honorable to Toussaint's character as any that I have related; and among them is the following, which I quote from the Quarterly Review :—

" General Maitland, previous to the disembarkation of the troops, returned the visit at Toussaint's camp ; and such was the confidence in the integrity of his character, that he proceeded through a considerable extent of country, full of armed negroes, with only three attendants. Roume, the French commissary, wrote a letter to Toussaint on this occasion, advising him to seize his guest as an act of duty to the Republic; on the route, General Maitland was secretly informed of Roume's treachery ; but, in full reliance on the honor of Toussaint, he determined to proceed. On arriving at headquarters, he was desired to wait. It was some time before Toussaint made his appearance ; at length, however, he entered the room with two open letters in his hand. ' There, General,' said he, ' before we talk together, read these. One is a letter from the French commissary, the other is my answer. I could not see you till I had written my reply, that you might be satisfied how safe you were with me, and how incapable I am of baseness.' " — *Quarterly Review*, Vol. XXI. p. 442.

The charge of personal ambition is, above all, contradicted by facts. If anything is clear in Toussaint's history, it is that his ruin was owing to his loyalty to France, his misplaced trust in Napoleon, and his want of personal ambition. He did not, as he might have done, make himself a sovereign when France was wholly occupied with European warfare. He did not, as he might have done, prepare his people to resist the power of the mother country when she should at length be at liberty to reclaim the colony. He sent away the French commissaries only when, by their ignorance and incompetency, they perilled the peace and safety of the colony. He cherished the love of the mother country in the hearts of the negroes to the very last moment, — till the armament which came to reëstablish slavery appeared on the shores, — till it was too late to offer that resistance which would have made him a king. Christophe's view of this part of his conduct is given in a manifesto, dated in the eleventh year of the Independence of Hayti : —

"Toussaint L'Ouverture, under his paternal administration, had reinstated, in full force, law, morals, religion, education, and industry. Agriculture and commerce were flourishing. He favored the white colonists, particularly the planters. Indeed, his attentions and partialities had been carried to such a length, that he was loudly blamed for entertaining more affection for them than for those of his own color. Nor was this reproach without foundation ; for, a few months before the arrival of the French, he sacrificed his own nephew, General Moyse, who had disregarded the orders he had given for the protection of the colonists. That act of the Governor, added to the great confidence he had placed in the French authorities, was the principal cause of the feeble resistance the French encountered in Hayti. Indeed, his confidence in these authorities was such that he had discharged the greater part of the regular troops, and sent them back to the tillage of the soil." — *Haytian Papers*, p. 158.

Such conduct is a sufficient answer to the allegation that Toussaint was actuated by a selfish ambition, cunning in its aims, and cruel in its use of means.

Some light is thrown upon the character of his mind by the record of the books he studied while yet a slave. Rainsford gives a list, which does not pretend to be complete, but which is valuable as far as it goes. It appears that in his years of comparative leisure he was completely engrossed by one book at a time, reading it at all spare moments, meditating its contents while in the field, and quoting it in conversation for weeks together. One of the first authors whose works thus entirely possessed him was Raynal; afterward Epictetus, in a French translation ; then others, as follows : —

Scriptores de Re Militari.
Cæsar's Commentaries. French translation by De Crisse.
Des Claison's History of Alexander and Cæsar.
D'Orleans's History of Revolutions in England and Spain.
Marshal Saxe's Military Reveries.
Guischard's Military Memoirs of the Greeks and Romans.
Herodotus.
Le Beau's Memoirs of the Academy of inscriptions and Belles Lettres.
Lloyd's Military and political Memoirs.
English Socrates, Plutarch, Cornelius Nepos, &c., &c.

Great mystery hangs over the tale of Toussaint's imprisonment and death. It appears that he was confined in the Temple as long as Napoleon had hopes of extorting from him information about the treasures, absurdly reported to have been buried by him in the Mornes,* under circumstances of atrocious cruelty. It has been suggested that torture was employed by Bonaparte's aid, Caffarelli, to procure the desired confession; but I do not know that the conjecture is founded on any evidence.

As to the precise mode of L'Ouverture's death, there is no certainty. The only point on which all authorities agree is, that he was deliberately murdered; but whether by mere confinement in a cell whose floor was covered with water and the walls with ice (a confinement necessarily fatal to a negro), or by poison, or by starvation in conjunction with disease, may perhaps never be known. The report which is, I believe, the most generally believed in France, is that which I have adopted, that the commandant, when his prisoner was extremely ill, left the fortress for two or three days, with the key of Toussaint's cell in his pocket; that, on his return, he found his prisoner dead; and that he summoned physicians from Pontarlier, who examined the body, and pronounced a serous apoplexy to be the cause of death. It so happened that I was able, in the spring of last year, to make some inquiry upon the spot, the result of which I will relate.

I was travelling in Switzerland, with a party of friends, with whom I had one day discussed the fortunes and character of Toussaint. I had then no settled purpose of writing about him, but was strongly urged to it by my companions. On the morning of the 15th of May, when we were drawing near Payerne from Freyburgh, on our way to Lausanne, I remembered and mentioned that we were not very far from the fortress of Joux, where Toussaint's bones lay. My party were all eager that I should visit it. There were difficulties in the way of the scheme, the chief of which was that our passports were not so signed as to enable us to enter France, and the nearest place where the necessary signature could be obtained was

* I believe the term " Morne" is peculiar to Saint Domingo. A morne is a valley, whose bounding hills are themselves backed by mountains.

Berne, which we had left behind us the preceding day. I had, however, very fortunately, a Secretary of State's passport besides the Prussian consul's; and this second passport, made out for myself and a *femme-de-chambre*, had been signed by the French minister in London. One of my kind companions offered to cross the frontier with me as my *femme-de-chambre*, and to help me in obtaining access to the prison of Toussaint, —an offer I was very thankful to accept. At Payerne we separated ourselves and a very small portion of luggage from our party, whom we promised to overtake at Lausanne in two or three days. We engaged for the trip a double *char-à-banc*, with two stout little horses, and a *brave homme* of a driver, as our courteous landlady at Payerne assured us. Passing through Yverdun, we reached Orbe by five in the afternoon, and took up our quarters at Guillaume Tell, full of expectation for the morrow.

On the 16th, we had breakfasted, and were beginning the ascent of the Jura before seven o'clock. The weather was fine, and we enjoyed a succession of interesting objects till we reached that which was the motive of our excursion. First, we had that view of the Alps, which, if it were possible, it would be equally useless to describe to any who have and any who have not stood on the eastern slope of the Jura on a clear day. Then we wound among the singular defiles of this mountain-range till we reached the valley which is commanded by Jougne. Here we alighted, climbing the slope to the gate of the town, while the carriage was slowly dragged up the steep, winding road. Our appearance obviously perplexed the two custom-house officers, who questioned us, and peeped into our one bag and our one book (the handbook of Switzerland) with an amusing air of suspicion. My companion told that the aim of our journey was the fortress of Joux; and that we expected to pass the frontier again in the afternoon, on our return to Orbe. Whether they believed us, or, believing, thought us very foolish, is best known to themselves; but I suspect the latter, by their compliments on our cleverness on our return. At Jougne we supplied ourselves with provisions, and then proceeded through valleys, each narrower than the last, more dismal with pines, and more checkered with snow. The air of desolation, here and there rendered more striking by the dreary settlements of the charcoal-burners, would have been impressive enough if our minds had not been full of the great negro, and therefore disposed to view everything with his eyes.

The scene was exactly what I have described in my story, except that a good road, made since Toussaint's time, now passes round and up the opposite side of the rock from that by which he mounted. The old road, narrow and steep, remains; and we descended by it.

We reached the court-yard without difficulty, passing the two drawbridges and portcullis described. The commandant was absent; and his lieutenant declared against our seeing anything more than the great wheel, and a small section of the battlements. But for great perseverance, we should have seen nothing more; but we obtained, at last, all we wanted. We passed through the vault and passages I have described, and thoroughly examined the cell. No words can convey a sense of its dreariness. I have exaggerated nothing. The dim light, the rotten floor, shining like a pond, the drip of water, the falling flakes of ice, were all there. The stove was removed; but we were shown where it stood.

There were only three persons who pretended to possess any information concerning the negro prisoner. The soldier who was our principal guide appeared never to have heard of him. A very old man in the village, to whom we were referred, could tell us nothing but one fact, which I knew before; that Toussaint was deprived of his servant some time before his death. A woman in the sutler's department of the fortress pretended to know all about him; but she had never seen him, and had no further title to authority than that her first husband had died in the Saint Domingo invasion. She did us the good service of pointing out the grave, however. The brickwork which surrounds the coffin now forms part of a new wall; but it was till lately within the church.

This woman's story was that which was probably given out on the spot to be told to inquirers, so inconsistent is it in itself, and with known facts. Her account was that Toussaint was carried off from Saint Domingo by the ship in which he was banqueted by Leclerc (the last of a line of two hundred), weighing anchor without his perceiving it, while he was at dinner. The absurdity of this beginning shows how much reliance is to be placed upon the rest of her story. She declared that the Commandant, Rubaut, had orders from the Government to treat the prisoner well; that his servant remained with him to the last; that he was well supplied with books, allowed the range of the fortress, and accustomed to pass his days in the house of the commandant, playing cards in the evenings; that on the last day of his life he excused himself from the card-table on the plea of being unwell; that he refused to have his servant with him, though urged not to pass the night alone; that he was left with fire, fauteuil, flambeaux, and a book, and found dead in his chair in the morning; and that the physicians who examined the body declared his death to have been caused by the rupture of a blood-vessel in the heart. This last particular is known to be as incorrect as the first. As for the rest, this informant differs from all others in saying that Mars Plaisir remained with his master till the last day of his life. And we may ask why Toussaint's nights were to be passed in his horrible cell, if his days were favored; and how it was that no research availed to discover to the eager curiosity of all Europe and the West Indies the retreat of L'Ouverture, if he, a negro, was daily present to the eyes of the garrison of the fortress, and of those of all the inhabitants of the village, and of all the travellers on that road, who chose to raise their eyes to the walls.

Our third informant was a boy, shrewd and communicative, who could tell us the traditions of the place, and, of course, young as he was, nothing more. It was he that showed us where the additional stove was placed when winter came on.

He pointed to a spot beside the fireplace, where he said the straw was spread on which Toussaint lay. He declared that Toussaint lived and died in solitude; and that he was found dead and cold, lying on the straw, — his wood-fire, however, not being wholly extinguished.

The dreary impression of the place saddened our minds for long after we had left it; and, glad as we were, on rejoining our party at Lausanne, to report the complete success of our enterprise, we cannot recur to it to this day, without painful feelings.

How the lot of Toussaint was regarded by the generous spirits of the time is shown in a sonnet of Wordsworth's, written during the disappearance of L'Ouverture. Every one knows this sonnet; but it may be read by others, as by me, with a fresh emotion of delight, after having dwelt on the particulars of the foregoing history.

> " Toussaint, the most unhappy man of men!
> Whether the whistling rustic tends his plough
> Within thy hearing, or thy head be now
> Pillowed in some deep dungeon's earless den;
> Oh, miserable chieftain! where and when
> Wilt thou find patience ?   Yet die not : do thou
> Wear rather in thy bonds a cheerful brow;
> Though fallen thyself, never to rise again,
> Live and take comfort.   Thou hast left behind
> Powers that will work for thee: air, earth, and skies.
> There's not a breathing of the common wind
> That will forget thee: thou hast great allies:
> Thy friends are exultations, agonies,
> And love, and man's unconquerable mind."

The family of Toussaint were first sent to Bayonne, and afterward to Agen, where one of the sons died of a decline. The two elder ones, endeavoring to escape from the surveillance under which they lived, were embarked for Belle Isle and imprisoned in the citadel, where they were seen in 1803. On the restoration of the Bourbons, not only were they released, but a pension was settled on the family. Madame L'Ouverture died, I believe, in the south of France, in 1816, in the arms of Placide and Isaac.

III.

BY JOHN BIGELOW.

THE following description of a visit to the Chateau de Joux was published two years ago in the New York *Independent*. It is from the pen of John Bigelow, Esq., the accomplished associate of William Cullen Bryant, in the editorship of the New York *Evening Post*, who is now (in 1863) a consul of the United States in Italy. It is not necessary to point out the few errors of memory that occur in it; for the reader of the preceding pages will notice them at once : —

Returning to Paris by way of Lausanne from a hurried trip to Geneva, last winter, I took the somewhat unusual route over the mountains to Pontarlier. I wanted to get a view, if possible, of Mont Blanc from the heights of the Jura; to become better acquainted with the people of this department of France, whom of all the French I most admire; and, above all, to visit the famous Chateau de Joux, where Mirabeau was confined at the time he contracted his scandalous engagements with Madame de Monnier, the "Sophie" of his Vincennes correspondence, and where Toussaint L'Ouverture died, a victim to the treachery of the French Government, and the severity of an Alpine climate. . . . . .

As the diligence passed under the Fort de Joux, — the chief object of my pilgrimage before reaching Pontarlier, — I dismounted, allowing my baggage to go on to the *bureau de poste*. The fort, now more than seven centuries old, stands upon the very summit of a solid rock about five hundred feet high, which descends very abruptly on all sides, and, by its position at a defile in the mountains, commands the approach from every direction. With three hundred men it was impregnable in former times, notwithstanding which, in consequence of its great value as a frontier fortification, it has changed hands more frequently than almost any fortress in France outside, of Paris.

I found a small garrison at the fort, consisting mostly of soldiers just returned from Italy, who were lounging about in the last stages of disgust with the monotonous perch to which they were condemned. A chatty old woman, who acted as *concierge*, promptly responded to my request to visit the castle, by running for her keys. She then led me over the portcullis, the ornaments of which showed that it was built before battle-axes and bows and arrows went out of fashion, into the court-yard where the commandant resided. The first curiosity to which she invited my attention was the well of the castle, dug through the solid rock, down to the level of the little River Orbe, which winds along the base of the hill, a depth of at least five hundred feet. My cicerone, to give me some idea of the depth of the well, threw in some stones, from which no sound or echo of any kind came up. This well was built for the use of the garrison during a siege, though in ordinary times they are supplied with water caught in cisterns. It has not been used for many centuries, if ever; the citadel, when it has changed hands, having generally been betrayed, or shared the fate of battles fought elsewhere.

The well was built, my guide told me, — and her information I have confirmed from other sources, — by the serfs and vassals of the feudal proprietor of the fort, in the ninth century. She lowered her voice when she added that multitudes who went down to work in its abysses never returned to the light of day. Indeed, the tradition is that they were told when they were sent to their work that they were not to return till it was finished. They were obliged to dig large recesses at regular and convenient distances in the sides of the pit, as their excavations progressed, and these were their homes during their frightful imprisonment, from which most were relieved only by death.

Of all the dreadful shapes which "man's inhumanity to man"

has ever taken, there are few which feed the imagination with
more fearful visions of misery and despair than were reflected
from this dark, impenetrable mirror, framed five hundred feet
deep in granite. When I considered that all the enormities of
which this structure had been the occasion and the theatre, were
perpetrated in the quest of water, in all ages and countries the
consecrated emblem of truth, I was struck for the thousandth
time with the resemblance which runs through all the forms of
human perversity.

While pondering the question whether France had gained
any more substantial advantage from her endless and sanguinary ecclesiastical wars than from the sinking of this dismal pit,
which the dews of heaven, that fall alike upon the unjust and
the just, made superfluous, my guide led me to another part of
the fort, where she showed me an opening like a closet in the
wall, about three feet deep and high, and, perhaps, four feet
long. Here, she informed me, Amaury, one of the earliest proprietors of the chateau, confined his wife, a young woman of
only seventeen years, for infidelity to him during his absence
with the Crusaders in the Holy Land in 1170. He hung her
suspected paramour upon the mountain immediately opposite,
and confined Bertha — that was her name — in this mural
sepulchre, which was too small to admit of her standing erect or
lying prostrate, or, indeed, of stretching her limbs in any direction. The only view of the outer world that she could get, was
through a little window, cut so that she could see the remains of
her lover dangling from a distant tree. After some ten years
of indescribable misery, death released her from her prison and
from her brutal jailer.

The good old woman, who related this legend tearfully, —
although I have no doubt she had told it a thousand times
before, — gave great force to her denunciation of the cruel cru-
sader by adding that, "After all, Bertha was innocent." I fear,
however, that this was a slight rhetorical embellishment, which,
as a woman and a sister, she felt at liberty to indulge me with;
for I have since seen a historical sketch of Pontarlier and its

neighborhood, made by M. Girod, the librarian of the city, and a most diligent and faithful archivist, in which Bertha's frailty is conceded. This fact, however, does not in the least diminish the horror which such a monument of cruelty and brutality inspires in our day.

Crossing the court, and passing along the gloomy corridor of stone, I was next led to a door which, as my companion proceeded to unfasten, she informed me was occupied by the "naygre." It was the dungeon of Toussaint, first called "L'Ouverture" by a French officer, because of his military prowess in opening the ranks of the English soldiers with his sword during some engagement. Though of African origin, and forty-eight years a slave, he took advantage of the revolutionary troubles in France, and subsequent hostilities between France and England, to make the blacks of St. Domingo independent, and himself President for life. Bonaparte, who approved of the lead he took in saving the colony from the English, was solicited to approve the action of the Central Assembly which made him President. Toussaint's letter bore the following somewhat memorable but not altogether conciliatory superscription, "The first of the blacks to the first of the whites." Bonaparte's answer was taken out by Leclerc, his brother-in-law, and thirty thousand of the best troops in France, who issued a proclamation apprising the islanders that the French general had been sent out as the first magistrate and Captain-General of the colony. Toussaint bade him and his master defiance, set fire to the Cape, retired to the mountains, and resisted the invaders with such success that, at the end of eight months, Napoleon's brother-in-law had but three thousand effective men out of the thirty thousand that had landed with him. Finding it impossible to conquer Toussaint, Leclerc invited him to a conference, under the usual pledges for his safety; and, when in his power, regardless of his own honor or that of his master, or of the nation so gravely compromised by his conduct, he hustled the too-confiding negro on board of a ship and sent him to France. After a brief confinement in the Temple at

Paris, Napoleon ordered him to the Fort de Joux. The room which he occupied, and to which I was now introduced, is some twenty-five or thirty feet long, by, say, twelve broad. There was a fireplace on one side near the middle, but no furniture of any kind. Its walls were all of stone, and arched with stone overhead. Near the ceiling, one end was pierced by a small window which admitted what light and air the inmates were expected to enjoy, but which seemed enough to keep the place sufficiently dry for habitation. On the mantel over the fire-place was the lower half of a skull, most of the brain-cover having been taken off, and, resting on what remained, was the following *avis*, which my guide forbade my copying, as contrary to the orders of the commandant, and for a transcript of which, as for many other gratifying attentions, I was indebted to M. Girod, to whose archeological and historical labors I have already made allusion : —

" Toussaint L'Ouverture, who effected the enfranchisement of the negroes of his country, and, in the day of his prosperity, designated himself as the Bonaparte of St. Domingo, and who wrote to Napoleon, 'The first of the blacks to the first of the whites,' terminated his career in this casement of the donjon of Fort de Joux. It is pretended that he answered an aide-de-camp of the First Consul, who came to ask him where he had concealed his treasures : ' Say to your master that I will die before he shall know anything from me.'

" The Chef de Bataillon Amiot, commandant of the Place du Fort de Joux, found him here in a corner of his fireplace struck with *apoplexie foudroyante*, the 17th Terminal, the year 11. Some days before his death he declared that he had buried 15,000,000 in the mountains by slaves whom he had destroyed."

I felt indignant at finding such a gross calumny as this upon the character of one of the bravest, and, according to his opportunities, one of the most remarkable men of his day, perpetrated by the authority of the Government ; and when I was refused permission to take a copy of it, my inference was that those who placed it there knew it was one of those lies that would not bear ventilation, and therefore kept it from the public, but left it to do what it could quietly to poison the minds of all who made the pilgrimage to his tomb. I was afterwards satisfied by M. Girod that I did the French Government injustice, at least in one respect; for he assures me that no orders to prevent copies being made of the paper on the mantel, had ever been given to the *concierge*.

It is a shame, however, for the Government to perpetuate such an absurd scandal upon the memory of Toussaint, as that he destroyed the slaves who helped him to hide his treasures; for the story not only is supported by no evidence, but it lacks the first element of plausibility. That he may have said he had treasures buried in St. Domingo, and that he may have added, for the purpose of being sent back to find them, that there were no living witnesses of their burial, is not impossible; but it is preposterous to suppose that such a man as Toussaint would have perpetrated such a gratuitous crime, or, if he did, that he would have told of it, without any apparent motive.

This story to the prejudice of " the first of the blacks" is as unfounded as another which has been current ever since Toussaint's death, and which is generally credited in Hayti now, — that he was poisoned by the orders of Napoleon, or at least upon the supposition that his speedy demise would gratify the Emperor. Even supposing there was some motive for getting Toussaint more completely out of the way than he was, which is hardly credible, the circumstances of his death are not matters of conjecture or suspicion, but of public record, and exempt the authorities of that day from any other responsibility for his sudden death than naturally attaches to his treacherous arrest and removal in mid-winter from the climate of the tropics, in which he was born, and had lived sixty years, to a bleak Alpine region more noted than any other in France for the severity of its winters.

The day after his death, two physicians of Pontarlier made an official examination of his remains, and certified that he died of apoplexy and pleuro-pneumonia. Their certificate, or *procès verbal*, as it is termed, is filed among the archives of the Hotel de Ville in Pontarlier, from whence M. Girod was kind enough to procure for me a copy duly authenticated, under the seal of the Mayoralty of Pontarlier. As this certificate has never been in print, and as it finally disposes of a very painful suspicion which is still widely credited, I give it to you entire.

Copy of the Minutes of the Post-mortem Examination of Toussaint L'Ouverture.

We, the undersigned, Doctor in Medicine and Surgeon of the city of Pontarlier, pursuant to the invitation of Citizen Amiot, Commandant of the Fort de Joux, and of Renaud, Justice of the Peace of the canton of Pontarlier, have gone to the said Fort de Joux, when, in their presence, we have proceeded to the opening and the examination of the body of the negro Toussaint L'Ouverture, prisoner, whose death yesterday we have verified.

POST-MORTEM EXAMINATION.

A little mucus mixed with blood in the mouth and on the lips, the left lateral sinus, the vessels of the *pia mater* gorged with blood, serous effusion in the lateral ventricle same side, the choroid pleurus infiltrated and strewed with hydatides, the pleura adhering almost entirely to the substance of the lungs; sanguineous engorgement of the right lung, as well as of the pleura corresponding, but of a purulent nature in this viscera ; a little fatty polypus in the right ventricle of the heart, which otherwise was in a natural state ; emaciation of the epiploon, — pathological state of this membrane such as it presents after a long sickness. The stomach, the intestines, the liver, the spleen, the veins, the bladder, exhibited no alteration.

In consequence, we declare that apoplexy, pleuro-pneumonia, are the causes of the death of Toussaint L'Ouverture.

Made and certified to be true, at the Fort de Joux, the 18th Terminal, An XI. of the French Republic.

  (Signed)   TAVERNIER, Doctor of Medicine,
         Surgeon-Major GRESSET.

Certified to conform with the original by us, the undersigned Secretary of the Mayoralty of Pontarlier.

Pontarlier, 5th December, 1859.

      (Signed)   JAQUIT, &c.

Through the kindness of M. Girod I was enabled to derive from the archives of Pontarlier some further particulars respecting Toussaint's condition and treatment during his confinement here, which seemed worthy of exhumation. They are embodied in documents, the originals of which I inspected, and of which I enclose to you copies.

The first simply acknowledges the notice sent to the Prefecture of the Department by the Sub-Prefect, that Toussaint had arrived, and informs that functionary that the arrangements for the security of the prisoner are to be under the exclusive direction of the general in command of that division.

The second notifies the Prefect that the Minister of War had given orders that Toussaint should receive healthy and suitable food, and that he should be clothed suitably for the season, with the understanding that *he must not wear a general's uniform*.

The estimation in which their prisoner was held by the French Government, and the rigor of treatment to which they deemed it necessary to subject him, are revealed in the third letter from the Prefect of the Department to the Sub-Prefect at Pontarlier. The following extract from it might have been clipped, *mutatis mutandis*, from one of Governor Wise's heroic appeals to the chivalry of Virginia against John Brown :—

"I recommend you," he writes, "not to lose sight of this important object. If any man imprisoned for the rest of his days, whatever the degree of his guilt, did not appeal to our humanity, I would say that this person, who is known only by his repeated perfidy, murders, pillage, incendiarism, and the most frightful cruelties, did not deserve any. But whatever be the opinion we ought to entertain of him, the orders of the minister are precise. Toussaint must not see any person, nor must he be permitted to leave the chamber in which he is confined, under any pretext whatever. The guard of the fort should be set with the greatest exactness, and without the relaxation of vigilance. The General of Division only can modify the rigor of these orders, and I know he will not do it without being authorized by the Minister. The commandant must sleep at the fort unless specially authorized to the contrary by his superiors. The supplies of the prisoner have been prescribed. They must not be exceeded upon any pretext. Every excess will be stricken off from the account."

The next letter, No. 4, was written immediately after receiving intelligence of Toussaint's death. In it the Prefect says, —

"You will also please, on the receipt of this letter, make an inventory, in the presence of the *Commandant d'Armes*, of all the effects used by the prisoner, and sell them at auction to the highest bidder, after the customary notices. You will prepare a report of the sale for me, and remit the proceeds of it to the Widow Benedict upon her receipt, deducting the sums due her for her supplies."

From these documents and the other enclosed, of which I will not trouble you with an analysis, it appears, if the facts are reported faithfully, —

1st. That Toussaint was guarded with unusual, if not excessive, rigor, and that the view taken of his character and career at that time by the War Department, whose agent declared that if there was an exception to the rule that pity was due to the unfortunate, Toussaint was the exception, was very different from that which is taken of him now by the world, and, indeed, by the French themselves, who, through the mouth of the most inspired of their modern poets, have said of him, " *Cet homme est une nation*," and within fifty years after his cheerless death, accepted the lesson of his life by striking the chains off every slave held under a French title.

2d. They show that he was not poisoned, but that he died, in all probability, of a disease contracted in consequence of his involuntary removal to a colder and more intemperate climate than at his age, — over sixty, — his constitution, used to the warmth of the tropics, could endure.

3d. It appears that he was abundantly supplied with fuel and artificial light, for in two months these supplies cost one hundred and fifty-six francs, which, M. Girod assures me, is a very large allowance, for wood then was much cheaper, he says, than at the present day; and now several lights and two fires could be sustained six months for ordinary necessities at an expense not exceeding two hundred francs.

4th. That he had a servant for a while after his arrival, whether a negro or a Frenchman, does not appear. From the general character of the instructions in reference to him, and in the absence of any special provision for the access to him, of one of his own color, it is to be presumed that it was a Frenchman.

5th. That he was allowed to write and have some luxuries, such as nutmegs, sugar, bath, &c. These, I presume, came out of the four francs a day allowed him from the first for board, washing, and mending.

6th. It is apparent, unfortunately, suggests M. Girod, from the moderate sum of 128fr. 70c., which the effects supplied by the Government brought after only seven months' use, that his wardrobe was not probably supplied as it should have been for such a severe climate.

7th. And, finally, it appears that a woman was provided to keep his apartment in order.

The order forbidding Toussaint to see any one not attached to the service of the garrison seems to have been unnecessarily rigorous, but it was probably aimed at Rigaud, Toussaint's ablest and most trusted aid in Saint Domingo, who was captured very soon after his chief and sent to the Fort de Joux, where he remained until after Toussaint's death, when he was released. They never saw each other, though sleeping so near together, after they separated in Saint Domingo.

Upon the walls of Toussaint's apartment I was surprised to find but one inscription from the hands of visitors; that was the name of Cataline Nau, a man whom I remember to have met at Port-au-Prince in 1854, where he discharged the functions of an Assistant Secretary of State, in the Department of Foreign Affairs, under Soulouque, and who had the credit, which I do not doubt he deserves, of having written the telling and statesmanlike despatches of the Haytian Government in reply to the agents sent out by Fillmore and the English and French Governments many years ago, to compel the Emperor to acknowledge the independence of the Spanish or eastern part of the island. M. Nau is probably the only Haytian who has ever made this pious pilgrimage to the prison and tomb of the most renowned of African statesmen. M. Nau, I understand, died within the last year, much regretted by his countrymen, whose interests he carefully watched and tended during his life.

Toussaint's remains, consigned to a grave under the chapel of the fort, were discovered by a captain of engineers in 1850. The top of his skull, which had probably been sawed off at the time of the *post mortem* examination, and replaced, he deposited in the city library of Pontarlier, where it was shown me by M. Girod, and the rest of the head stands on the mantelpiece in the room where Toussaint was confined and died.

IV.

BY JOHN GREENLEAF WHITTIER.

'TWAS night. The tranquil moonlight smile*
  With which Heaven dreams of Earth shed down
Its beauty on the Indian isle,—
  On broad green field and white-walled town;
And inland waste of rock and wood,
In searching sunshine, wild and rude,
Rose, mellowed through the silver gleam,
Soft as the landscape of a dream,
All motionless and dewy wet,
Tree, vine, and flower in shadow net:
The myrtle with its snowy bloom,
Crossing the nightshade's solemn gloom,—
The white cecropia's silver rind
Relieved by deeper green behind,—
The orange with its fruit of gold,—
The lithe paullinia's verdant fold,—
The passion-flower, with symbol holy,
Twining its tendrils long and lowly,—
The rhexias dark, and cassia tall,
And proudly rising over all,
The kingly palm's imperial stem,
Crowned with its leafy diadem,
Star-like, beneath whose sombre shade,
The fiery-winged cucullo played!
Yes,—lovelier was thine aspect, then,
  Fair island of the Western Sea!
Lavish of beauty, even when
Thy brutes were happier than thy men,
  For they, at least, were free!

Regardless of thy glorious clime,
  Unmindful of thy soil of flowers,
The wasting negro sighed, that Time
  No faster sped his hours;
For by the dewy moonlight still
He fed the weary-turning mill,
Or bent him, in the chill morass,
To pluck the long and tangled grass,
And hear above his scar-worn back
The heavy slave-whip's frequent crack;
While in his heart one evil thought
In solitary madness wrought, —
One baleful fire surviving still
  The quenching of the immortal mind, —
  One sterner passion of his kind,
Which even fetters could not kill, —
The savage hope, to deal, erelong,
A vengeance bitterer than his wrong!

Hark to that cry! — long, loud and shrill,
From field and forest, rock and hill,
Thrilling horrible it rang,
  Around, beneath, above; —
The wild beast from his cavern sprang, —
  The wild bird from her grove!
Nor fear, nor joy, nor agony
Were mingled in that midnight cry;
But, like the lion's growl of wrath,
When falls that hunter in his path,
Whose barbèd arrow, deeply set,
Is rankling in his bosom yet,
It told of hate, deep, full, and strong, —
Of vengeance kindling out of wrong;
It was as if the crimes of years, —
The unrequited toil, — the tears,

The shame, and hate, which liken well
Earth's garden to the nether hell, —
Had found in Nature's self a tongue,
On which the gathered horror hung;
As if, from cliff and stream and glen,
Burst on the startled ears of men
That voice which rises unto God,
Solemn and stern, — the cry of blood!
It ceased; and all was still once more,
Save ocean chafing on his shore,
The sighing of the wind between
The broad banana's leaves of green,
Or bough by restless plumage shook,
Or murmuring voice of mountain brook.

Brief was the silence.   Once again
  Pealed to the skies that frantic yell, —
Glowed on the heavens a fiery stain,
  And flashes rose and fell;
And, painted on the blood-red sky,
Dark, naked arms were tossed on high;
And, round the white man's lordly hall
  Trode, fierce and free, *the brute he made;*
And those who crept along the wall,
And answered to his highest call,
  With more than spaniel dread, —
The creatures of his lawless beck, —
Were trampling on his very neck!
And on the night-air, wild and clear,
Rose woman's shriek of more than fear;
For bloodied arms were round her thrown
And dark cheeks pressed against her own!
Then, injured Afric! — for the shame
Of thy own daughters, vengeance came
Full on the scornful hearts of those
Who mocked thee in thy nameless woes,

And to thy hapless children gave
One choice, — pollution, or the grave!
Where then was he whose fiery zeal
Had taught the trampled heart to feel,
Until Despair itself grew strong,
And Vengeance fed its torch from wrong?
Now, — when the thunderbolt is speeding;
Now, — when oppression's heart is bleeding;
Now, — when the latent curse of Time
   Is raining down in fire and blood, —
That curse, which, through long years of crime,
   Has gathered, drop by drop, its flood, —
Why strikes he not, the foremost one,
Where murder's sternest deeds are done?

He stood the aged palms beneath,
   That shadowed o'er his humble door,
Listening, with half-suspended breath,
To the wild sounds of fear and death, —
   Toussaint L'Ouverture!
What marvel that his heart beat high!
   The blow for freedom had been given;
And blood had answered to the cry
   That earth sent up to Heaven!
What marvel that a fierce delight
Smiled grimly o'er his brow of night,
As groan and shout and bursting flame
Told where the midnight tempest came,
With blood and fire along its van,
And death behind! — he was a man!

Yes, dark-souled chieftain! — if the light
   Of mild Religion's heavenly ray
Unveiled not to thy mental sight
   The lowlier and the purer way,
  31

In which the Holy Sufferer trod
  Meekly amidst the sons of crime, —
That calm reliance upon God
  For justice, in his own good time, —
That gentleness to which belongs
  Forgiveness for its many wrongs,
Even as the primal martyr, kneeling
For mercy on the evil-dealing, —
Let not the favored white man name
Thy stern appeal with words of blame.
Has *he* not, with the light of heaven
  Broadly around him, made the same,
Yea, on his thousand war-fields striven,
  And gloried in his ghastly shame? —
Kneeling amidst his brother's blood,
To offer mockery unto God,
  As if the High and Holy One
  Could smile on deeds of murder done! —
As if a human sacrifice
Were purer in His holy eyes,
Though offered up by Christian hands,
Than the lone rites of Pagan lands!

    .   .   .   .   .   .

Sternly, amidst his household band,
His carbine clasped within his hand,
  The white man stood, prepared and still,
Waiting the shock of maddened men,
Unchained and fierce as tigers when
  The horn winds through their caverned hill ;
And one was weeping in his sight, —
  The sweetest flower of all the isle, —
The bride who seemed but yesternight
  Love's fair embodied smile,
And, clinging to her trembling knee,
Looked up the form of infancy,

With tearful glance in either face,
The secret of its fear to trace.

"Ha,—stand or die!"   The white man's eye
    His steady musket gleamed along,
As a tall negro hastened nigh,
    With fearless step and strong.
"What, ho, Toussaint!"   A moment more,
His shadow crossed the lighted floor.
"Away," he shouted; "fly with me;
The white man's bark is on the sea;
Her sails must catch the seaward wind,
For sudden vengeance sweeps behind.
Our brethren from their graves have spoken,
The yoke is spurned, the chain is broken;
On all the hills our fires are glowing,
Through all the vales red blood is flowing!
No more the mocking White shall rest
His foot upon the Negro's breast;
No more, at morn or eve, shall drip
The warm blood from the driver's whip;
Yet, though Toussaint has vengeance sworn,
For all the wrongs his race have borne,—
Though for each drop of Negro blood
The white man's veins shall pour a flood;
Not all alone the sense of ill
Around his heart is lingering still,
Nor deeper can the white man feel
The generous warmth of grateful zeal.
Friends of the Negro! fly with me,—
The path is open to the sea;
"Away for life!"—He spoke, and pressed
The young child to his manly breast,
As, headlong, through the crackling cane,
Down swept the dark insurgent train,—

Drunken and grim, with shout and yell
Howled through the dark, like sounds from Hell!

Far out in peace the white man's sail
Swayed free before the sunrise gale.
Cloud-like that island hung afar
   Along the bright horizon's verge,
O'er which the curse of servile war
   Rolled its red torrent, surge on surge.
And he, — the Negro champion — where
   In the fierce tumult, struggled he?
Go trace him by the fiery glare
Of dwellings in the midnight air,
The yells of triumph and despair,
   The streams that crimson to the sea!

Sleep calmly in thy dungeon-tomb,
   Beneath Besançon's alien sky,
Dark Haytian! — for the time shall come,
   Yea, even now is nigh,
When everywhere thy name shall be
Redeemed from color's infamy;
And men shall learn to speak of thee,
As one of earth's great spirits born
In servitude and nursed in scorn,
Casting aside the weary weight
And fetters of its low estate,
In that strong majesty of soul
   Which knows no color, tongue, or clime,
Which still hath spurned the base control
   Of tyrants through all time!
For other hands than mine may wreathe
The laurel round thy brow of death,
And speak thy praise as one whose word
A thousand fiery spirits stirred, —

Who crushed his foeman as a worm,
Whose step in human hearts fell firm:
Be mine the better task to find
A tribute for thy lofty mind,
Amidst whose gloomy vengeance shone
Some milder virtues all thine own, —
Some gleams of feeling, pure and warm,
Like sunshine on a sky of storm, —
Proof that the Negro's heart retains
Some nobleness amidst its chains,
That kindness to the wronged is never
  Without its excellent reward, —
Holy to humankind, and ever
  Acceptable to God.

31*

V.

BY WENDELL PHILLIPS.

THE most elaborate and eloquent tribute to Toussaint L'Ouverture is the celebrated oration of Wendell Phillips, published in his "Speeches, Lectures, and Letters" (first series), which every one who has read this volume should not fail to find. We have space for the peroration only : —

I would call him Napoleon, but Napoleon made his way to empire over broken oaths and through a sea of blood. This man never broke his word. "No retaliation" was his great motto and the rule of his life ; and the last words uttered to his son in France were these : "My boy, you will one day go back to St. Domingo ; forget that France murdered your father." I would call him Cromwell, but Cromwell was only a soldier, and the state he founded went down with him into his grave. I would call him Washington, but the great Virginian held slaves. This man risked his empire rather than permit the slave-trade in the humblest village in his dominions.

You think me a fanatic to-night, for you read history, not with your eyes, but with your prejudices. But fifty years hence, when truth gets a hearing, the Muse of History will put Phocion for the Greek, and Brutus for the Roman, Hampden for England, Fayette for France, choose Washington as the bright, consummate flower of our earlier civilization, and John Brown the ripe fruit of our noon-day, — then, dipping her pen in the sunlight, will write in the clear blue, above them all, the name of the soldier, the statesman, the martyr, TOUSSAINT L'OUVERTURE. 366

THE END.

BOOKS FOR THE TIMES.

I.

SPEECHES, LECTURES, and LETTERS. By Wendell Phillips. Seventh Thousand. 1 vol., pp.
570.

Three editions of this classical work are issued.

Library Edition, "in a luxurious style of book-manufacture;"
with an illuminated title and an excellent portrait; printed on fine
tinted linen paper; bound in rich English green and maroon vellum-
cloth. Price, $2.25.

Trade Edition; printed on common paper; bound in common
cloth, with portrait. 12mo. Price, $1.50.

People's Edition, on thin paper, and in paper covers. Price, $1.00.

This work, in every edition, is printed on clear new type. It contains about one-half of the speeches of America's greatest living orator
that have been reported during the last ten years; among them his
great oration on Toussaint L'Ouverture.

> He stood upon the world's broad threshold; wide
>   The din of battle and of slaughter rose;
> He saw God stand upon the weaker side,
>   That sunk in seeming loss before its foes.
> Many there were who made great haste and sold
>   Unto the cunning enemy their swords;
> He scorned their gifts of fame and power and gold,
>   And, underneath their soft and flowery words,
> Heard the cold serpent hiss; therefore he went
>   And humbly joined him to the weaker part,
> Fanatic named, and fool, yet well content,
>   So he could be the nearer to God's heart,
> And feel its solemn pulses sending blood
> Through all the wide-spread veins of endless good.
>   James Russell Lowell.

I remember how, in the year 1837, after the killing of Lovejoy, at Alton, there was a public meeting in Fanueil Hall, called by — I was about to say — the last Puritan saint that preached in a pulpit in Boston, the eloquent saint and preacher in New England, where he made a speech, and where a certain State's Attorney, I believe he was, made a speech also, in which he cast all manner of ridicule on the martyr; and I remember how a young man took his quiet chance to spring to his feet and ascend the platform, and pour out such a flood of eloquence, that I believe the victim has never breathed largely and freely since. I remember seeing him a day or two ago, walking down Colonnade Row, where he then lived, and wondering how he had felt ever since that day. That was the first intimation of the orator of New England. All Boston was surprised, and wondered who that was. They found, however, on inquiry, that he was born well, was well-bred, well-educated, and in all respects as good as they were. Of course, that must have been a great disappointment. The difficulties must have been very much greater, of course, under these circumstances. But then, his youth was against him. From that time to this, steadily, from year to year, and almost from day to day, that eloquence has been making its way through New England and the West, and across the water, and he stands to-day the orator of America, unmatched by any preceding orator; and in this respect, that he pleads for righteousness, he pleads for the truth always, — has never been known to be on the wrong side, — always for the oppressed, never for the oppressor. So that with one exception (and I can hardly make that), in New England, in the West, and even in the National Capital itself, more persons will flock to hear that orator than any other in the country.

He stands conspicuous above others as the advocate of human rights the defender of the oppressed; Freedom's lodestar, whose lustre is leading fugitive States and statesmen fast from their bondage to the dark despotism, into this refuge of liberty here in the north of the North — New England. By happy fortune, he enjoys the privilege denied to Senators, of speaking of free and freedom-loving men everywhere, unincumbered by slave statutes or caucus.

His speeches have the highest qualities of a great orator. In range of thought, clearness of statement, keen satire, brilliant wit, personal anecdote, wholesome moral sentiments, patriotism, and Puritan spirit, they are unmatched by those of any of the great orators of the day. They have, besides, the rare merit, and one in which our public men have been painfully deficient, of straightforwardness, point, and truth to the hour. They are addressed to the conscience of the country, and were spoken in the interests of humanity. Many a soldier now in the field, many a citizen, doubtless, owes his loyalty, in large measure, to his learning of these eloquent words.

Above party, unless it be the honorable and ancient party of Mankind, they embody the temper and drift of the times. How many public men are here to survive in the pillory of his indignant invectives! The history of the last thirty years cannot be accurately written without his facts and anecdotes. There is no great interest of philanthropy in which he has not been active. His words are to be taken as those of an earnest mind intent on furthering the ends of truth and righteousness, interpreted not by their rhetoric, but consistently to principles. Why are they not collected and printed in a book for the credit of our tongue, the praise of humanity, and the good fame of their author?

Certainly the country hangs in the balance of his argument; cabinets and councils hesitating to do or undo without some regard to his words, well knowing the better constituency he better represents and speaks for, — the PEOPLE, namely, whose breath can unmake as it has made.

A. BRONSON ALCOTT.

James Redpath, 221 Washington street, publishes, in a beautifully-printed volume of 570 pages, Speeches, Lectures, and Letters, by Wendell Phillips. . . . . There are twenty-four pieces in the volume, mostly speeches, beginning with the speech on "The Murder of Lovejoy," delivered toward the close of 1837, and ending with that on "The State of the Country," delivered early in 1863. They thus cover a quarter of a century, and that quarter of a century, too, in which the struggle against the ascendency of slave-holding interest occurred. Mr. Phillips, while yet in the prime of his wonderful intellect, lives to see his views embraced by millions, most of whom used to condemn them, and to consider him a dangerous agitator. Even those who do not now agree with him must be pleased to see his great works collected; for those works are valuable as historical illustrations, and would be so even if they were, like Cicero's *Philippics*, the monuments of a ruined cause; but, as they are the everlasting lights that come from the triumph of truth, their value is immeasurably increased. Let our quarrel be settled as it may, the abolitionists, of whose opinions Mr. Phillips is "the great expounder," have made so deep an impression on the American mind that Slavery can never again become what it was in those days when it was the predominant interest of the Western World. . . . . There probably has never been published a volume in which so much powerful matter is to be found, while eloquent expressions adorn almost every page. It is a work that will live long after the quarrels of this time shall have become dull things in dull histories, and when men shall read them as we now read of the old narratives of the struggles that took place in Corcyra and Athens. — *Boston Traveller*.

II.

HOSPITAL SKETCHES.   By L. M. ALCOTT.   12mo, pp. 102.   Price, 50 cents.   (Juft publifhed.)

"Productions of uncommon merit. . . . . Fluent and sparkling in style, with touches of quiet humor and lively wit, relieving what would otherwise be a topic too sombre and sad, they are graphic in description and exhibit the healthful sentiments and sympathies of the cheerful heroism that would minister to the sick and suffering. The contrast between the comic incidents and the tragic experience of a single night, given in No. 2 of the series, is portrayed with singular power and effectiveness. 'The death of John' is a noble and touching feature." — *Boston Transcript*.

"Graphically drawn. . . . . Exceedingly well written, and the graver portions of thrilling interest. There is a quiet vein of humor, too, running all through them, so that the reader is alternately moved to laughter and tears." — *Waterbury American.*

"To say that I thank you for writing them from the bottom of my heart, would but poorly express the sentiment which dictates to me this minute; and to say that I feel humbled by the lesson which they teach me, is to pay a tribute to them which I fancy will be rather unexpected. . . . . . These papers have revealed to me much that is elevated and pure and refined in the soldier's character which I never before suspected. It is humiliating to me to think that I have been so long among them with such mental or moral obtuseness that I never discovered it for myself; and I thank you for showing me with how different eyes and ears you have striven among 'the men' from the organs which I used on the very same cases and at the same time." — *From a Hospital Surgeon.*

"It would be tedious to you to hear how much pleasure an old man like me has taken in your charming pictures of hospital service, in *The Commonwealth;* and how refreshing he found the personal revelation there incidentally made of so much that is dearest and most worshipful in woman; so I will not dwell on those particulars, but say all I have to say in this summary form, to wit: that I am so delighted with your beautiful papers, and the evidence they afford of your exquisite humanity, that I have the greatest desire to enrol myself among your friends. . . . . With the liveliest respect and affection, yours,

"NEWPORT, 10 June.   HENRY JAMES."

"The wit, the humor, the pathos, the power of brief and vivid description, which the volume evinces, will give it a wide popularity. The publisher intends to give five cents for every copy sold toward the support of orphans, made fatherless and homeless by the war." — *The Wide World.*

"Received with universal favor." — *Boston Commonwealth.*

"The writer, who is understood to describe scenes of which she was an eye-witness, is the gifted daughter of the transcendental philosopher, A. Bronson Alcott." — *Anti-Slavery Standard.*

"We hope all our readers will purchase a copy." — *Boston Saturday Evening Express.*

"These sketches are the best record we have yet seen of hospital experience; for, while the author sees and pictures the ludicrous side of every scene, she also shows, with genuine feeling, all a woman's sympathy for suffering, and all a woman's tact in relieving it. There are some passages in this little volume which will move the heart as irresistibly as the humor of others will move to laughter." — *N. England Farmer.*

"These sketches are overflowing with genius, wit, humor, pathos, and womanly compassion and tenderness. All who read them will greatly relish them." — *The Liberator.*

III.

TOUSSAINT L'OUVERTURE : A BIOGRAPHY AND AUTOBIOGRAPHY. 1 vol. 12mo. pp. 366. With a map of Colonial Hayti and a portrait of Touffaint. Price, $1.25.

This volume contains Dr. Beard's biography, revised by an American editor, and the "Mémoires de la Vie du Général Toussaint L'Ouverture, écrits par lui-même, pouvant servir à l'histoire de sa vie;" now first translated into the English language. No other one volume, in any language, contains an account of Toussaint's career, so full and so satisfactory. (Just out.)

IV.

THE BLACK MAN : his Antecedents, his Genius, and his Achievements. By WILLIAM WELLS BROWN. Third edition. 1 vol., 12mo., pp. 312. With a portrait on fteel of Prefident Geffrard, of Hayti. Price $1.00.

This work, by a colored man, gives biographical sketches of fifty-eight persons, wholly or in part, of African descent who have distinguished themselves in some profession or at some crisis.

"This work has done good service among those who are impregnated with the idea that the blacks were created for nothing but slaves." — WM. LLOYD GARRISON, in *The Liberator.*

"This book is a good one to place in the hand of any person who, through ignorance or prejudice, has been led to regard the blacks as an inferior race." — OLIVER JOHNSON, in *Anti-Slavery Standard.*

"Though Mr. Brown's book may stand alone upon its own merits, and stand strong, yet, while reading its interesting pages, — abounding in fact and argument, replete with eloquence, logic, and learning, — clothed with simple yet eloquent language, it is hard to repress the inquiry, Whence has this man this knowledge? He seems to have read and remembered nearly everything which has been written or said respecting the ability of the negro, and has condensed and arranged the whole into an admirable argument, calculated both to interest and convince." — FREDERICK DOUGLASS, in his *Monthly.*

"This is just the book for the crisis. We would that every pro-slavery man in the country would read it." — PROF. E. O. HAVEN, D.D., in *Zion's Herald.*

"I am glad that you have written such a book. It will do great good." — GERRIT SMITH.

"This is just the book for the hour; it will do more for the colored man's elevation than any work yet published." — LEWIS TAPPAN.

"An interesting work . . . . . Mr. Brown's book is an incontestible argument." — ANDREW JACKSON DAVIS, in the *Herald of Progress.*

"This is the best account of the negro ever put in print. The genius of the race is well brought out." — *Boston Transcript.*

JAMES REDPATH, PUBLISHER,

221 Washington Street, Boston.